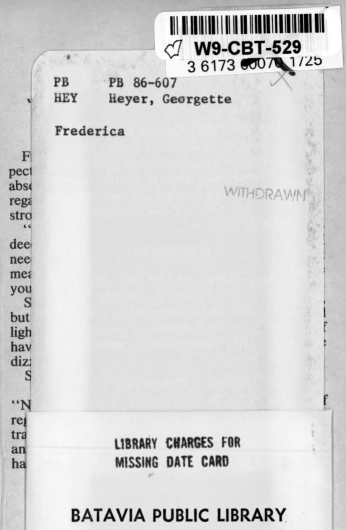

F
pect
abse
rega
stro
"
dee
nee
mea
you
S
but
ligh
hav
diz:
S

"N
reg
tra
an
ha

GEORGETTE HEYER

FREDERICA

BANTAM BOOKS

NEW YORK · TORONTO · LONDON · SYDNEY · AUCKLAND

FREDERICA

A Bantam Book / published by arrangement with
E. P. Dutton

PRINTING HISTORY

Bantam edition published December 1973
6 printings through March 1990

ISBN 0-553-24132-X

Published simultaneously in the United States and Canada

Bantam Books are published by Bantam Books, a division of Bantam
Doubleday Dell Publishing Group, Inc. Its trademark, consisting of the
words "Bantam Books" and the portrayal of a rooster, is Registered in U.S.
Patent and Trademark Office and in other countries. Marca Registrada.
Bantam Books, 666 Fifth Avenue, New York, New York 10103.

PRINTED IN THE UNITED STATES OF AMERICA

KRI   15   14   13   12   11   10   9   8   7   6

I

Not more than five days after she had despatched an urgent missive to her brother, the Most Honourable the Marquis of Alverstoke, requesting him to visit her at his earliest convenience, the widowed Lady Buxted was relieved to learn from her youngest daughter that Uncle Vernon had just driven up to the house, wearing a coat with *dozens* of capes, and looking as fine as fivepence. "In a smart new curricle, too, Mama, and *everything* prime about him!" declared Miss Kitty, flattening her nose against the window-pane in her effort to squint down into the street. "He is the most *tremendous* swell, isn't he, Mama?"

Lady Buxted responded in repressive accents, desiring her not to use expressions unbefitting a lady of quality, and dismissing her to the schoolroom.

Lady Buxted was not one of her brother's admirers; and the intelligence that he had driven himself to Grosvenor Place in his curricle did nothing to advance him in her good graces. It was a fine spring morning, but a sharp wind was blowing, and no one who knew him could suppose that the Marquis would keep his high-bred horses waiting for more than a few minutes. This did not augur well for the scheme she had in mind —not, as she had bitterly observed to her elder sister, that she cherished any but the gloomiest expectations, Alverstoke being, without exception, the most selfish, disobliging creature alive.

To this proposition, Lady Jevington, a commanding matron on the shady side of forty, lent only qualified support. She might (and did) think her only brother selfish and disobliging, but she could perceive no reason why he should be expected to do more for Louisa than for herself. As for Louisa's two sons and three daughters, Lady Jevington found herself unable to

1

blame Alverstoke for taking no interest in any of them.
It was really impossible to be interested in such commonplace children. That he was equally uninterested
in her own offspring did, however, argue a selfish
disposition. Anyone would have supposed that a bachelor who was not only of the first stare but who was
also possessed of considerable wealth would have been
only too glad to have sponsored such a promising
nephew as her beloved Gregory into the select circle
which he himself adorned, and to have exerted himself to have brought dear Anna into fashion. That Anna
had become eligibly betrothed without the least assistance from him in no way mitigated her ladyship's resentment; and although she admitted the justice of her
unfashionable lord's reminder that she disapproved of
the frippery set to which Alverstoke belonged, and had
frequently expressed the hope that Gregory would never
allow himself to be drawn into it, she still could not
forgive Alverstoke for having made no attempt to do
so. She said that she wouldn't have cared a rush if she
had not good reason to suppose that Alverstoke had not
only purchased a cornetcy in the Life Guards for his
young cousin and heir, but made him a handsome allowance into the bargain. To which Lord Jevington
replied that as he was very well able to provide for his
son, who, in any event, had no claim whatsoever upon
his uncle, he could only give Alverstoke credit for having enough good sense to refrain from making an offer
of monetary assistance which would have been deeply
resented by the Honourable Gregory Sandridge's parents. This was perfectly true; but still Lady Jevington
felt that if Alverstoke had had a grain of proper feeling
he would not have singled out for his favour a mere
cousin instead of his eldest nephew. She also felt that in
a better organized state of society his eldest sister's son,
rather than a removed cousin, would have been his heir.

Without wishing to see Gregory so unfairly elevated,
Lady Buxted was in general agreement with her sister,
both ladies being united in contempt of Mr Endymion
Dauntry, whom they stigmatized as a perfect block. But
whether their enmity towards this blameless young man
arose from their dislike of his widowed mama, or from

his handsome countenance and magnificent physique, which cast both Gregory Sandridge and young Lord Buxted into the shade, was a question no one cared to ask.

Whatever might have been the reason, his two elder sisters were convinced that no unworthier heir to Alverstoke's dignities than Endymion could have been found; and neither had spared any pains to introduce to her brother's notice all the prettiest and most eligible damsels who were fired off, year after year, into the ton.

But Alverstoke's besetting sin was a tendency to become rapidly bored. It had vanquished his sisters; for although neither of them could suppose, reviewing the numerous dazzling barques of frailty who had lived under his protection, that he was impervious to feminine charms, neither was so muttonheaded as to indulge optimism very far when he seemed to be developing a tendre for some diamond of birth, beauty, and fortune, thrust under his nose by one or other of his sisters. He was perfectly capable of making the lady the object of his gallantry for a few weeks, and then of veering off at a tangent, forgetting her very existence. When it was borne in upon his sisters that prudent parents looked askance at him, and that he was generally thought to be dangerous, they abandoned their attempts to provide him with a wife, devoting their energies instead to the easier task of deploring his indolence, condemning his selfishness, and scolding him for any of his moral aberrations which came to their ears. Only his youngest sister refrained; but as she had refused several flattering offers for her hand, and had married, to please herself, a mere country gentleman, and rarely visted the Metropolis, she was considered by her two sisters to be a negligible quantity. If they spoke of her, which they seldom did, it was as Poor Eliza; and although they knew that Alverstoke preferred her to themselves it entered neither of their heads to solicit her help in the matter of his marriage. Had it done so they would have dismissed the idea, in the well-founded belief that no one had ever, since he grew to manhood, exercised the smallest influence over him.

It was not to read him a lecture that Lady Buxted had on this occasion commanded him to visit her: indeed, she had resolved to say nothing that could set up his back. But as she awaited his entrance the hope which (despite experience) had entered her breast upon hearing of his arrival was succeeded by the reflection that it was just like him to have allowed five days to elapse before putting himself to the trouble of answering a summons, which, for anything he knew, might have been of the utmost urgency. It was with difficulty that she schooled her countenance to an expression of affectionate welcome; and with still more difficulty that she infused cordiality into her voice when he strolled, unannounced, into the room. That was just like him too: the sort of casual behaviour which her ladyship, a high stickler, much deplored, seeing no reason why he should treat her house as if it were his own.

Smothering her annoyance, she stretched out her hand, saying, "Vernon! My dear, what a delightful surprise!"

"What's surprising about it?" he enquired, lifting his black brows. "Didn't you ask me to come?"

The smile remained pinned to Lady Buxted's lips, but she replied with more than a touch of acidity: "To be sure I did, but so many days ago that I supposed you had gone out of town!"

"Oh, no!" he said, returning her smile with one of great sweetness.

Lady Buxted was not deceived, but thought it prudent to ignore what she recognized as deliberate provocation. She patted the sofa, and invited her brother to come and sit down. Instead of doing this he walked forward to the fireplace and bent to warm his hands, saying: "I can't stay for long, Louisa: what is it you want of me?"

Having made up her mind to lead up to her request by tactful degrees, she found this blunt question as infuriating as it was disconcerting. She hesitated, and he glanced up, a gleam in his rather hard grey eyes, and said: "Well?"

She was not immediately obliged to answer him, for at that moment her butler came in, with such refreshments as he considered suitable to the occasion. While he set the heavy tray down on a side-table, and informed the Marquis in the confidential voice of the privileged retainer that he had ventured to bring up the Mountain as well as the sherry, she had time in which to reassemble her ideas, and also to observe, in some dudgeon, that her brother had chosen to visit her in breeches and topboots: attire as regrettably informal as his entrance. That his boots were highly polished, his neckcloth arranged to a nicety, and his coat, which fitted him like a glove, clearly cut by a master, only served to increase her displeasure. She felt that if his general indifference had extended to his appearance she could have forgiven him for not thinking it necessary to honour her by assuming the correct dress for paying morning visits. But no one who looked as elegant as he invariably did, or whose style was copied by so many gentlemen of fashion, could possibly be indifferent to matters of mode. Indeed, she had once demanded, in a moment of exasperation, if he cared for anything but his clothing. To which he had replied, after subjecting the question to consideration, that although his clothes were naturally of paramount importance, he also cared for his horses.

He had gone across the room to the side-table; and, as the butler withdrew, he turned his head, saying: "Sherry, Louisa?"

"My dear Vernon, you should surely know by now that I never touch sherry!"

"Should I? But I have such a shockingly bad memory!"

"Not when you wish to remember anything!"

"Oh, no, not then!" he agreed. He looked across at her, and at sight of her tightened lips and rising colour, laughed suddenly. "What a chucklehead you are, dear sister! I never yet cast my line over a fish that rose more readily to the fly than you do! What is it to be? The Malaga?"

"I will take half a glass of ratafia, if you will be so good as to pour it out for me," she answered stiffly.

"It does considerable violence to my feelings, but I will be so good. What an appalling thing to drink at this hour! Or, indeed, at any hour," he added reflective-ly. He brought the glass to her, moving in his leisurely way, but with the grace of the born athlete. "Now, what is it this time? Don't beat about the bush! I don't want my horses to take cold."

"I wish you will sit down!" she said crossly.

"Very well, but do, for God's sake, cut line," he re-plied, choosing an armchair on the opposite side of the fireplace.

"It so happens, Alverstoke, that I do desire your as-sistance," she said.

"That, dear Louisa, I apprehended when I read your letter," he retorted, with horrid affability. "Of course, you *might* have summoned me to stun me with one of your rake-downs, but you couched your missive in such affectionate language that *that* suspicion was banished almost instantly from my mind, leaving me with the only alternative: that you wanted me to do something for you."

"I should be grateful, I collect, that you *remembered* that I had written to ask you to visit me!" she said, glaring at him.

"You can't think, Louisa, how strongly tempted I am to accept your gratitude with a becoming smirk!" he told her. "But never shall it be said of me that I stole another man's honours! Trevor gave me the office."

"Do you mean to tell me that Mr Trevor read my letter?" demanded Lady Buxted indignantly. "Your *secretary?*"

"I employ him to read my letters," explained his lordship.

"Not those written by your nearest and dearest!"

"Oh, no, not *them!*" he agreed.

Her bosom swelled. "You are the most abom—" She stopped, with a gasp; visibly wrought with herself; and contrived, by a heroic effort, to force the smile back to her lips, and to say, with a tolerable assumption of amusement: "Wretch! I shan't allow you to take a rise out of me! I want to talk to you about Jane!"

"Who the devil is—Oh, yes, I know! One of your girls!"

"My eldest daughter, and, let me remind you, your niece, Alverstoke!"

"Unjust, Louisa, I needed no reminder!"

"I am bringing the dear child out this season," she announced, ignoring the interpolation. "I shall present her, of course, at one of the Drawing-rooms—if the Queen holds any more, but they say her health is now so indifferent that—"

"You'll have to do something about her freckles—if she's the one I think she is," he interrupted. "Have you tried citron-water?"

"I didn't invite you to come here to discuss Jane's appearance!" she snapped.

"Well, why did you invite me?"

"To ask you to hold a ball in her honour—at Alverstoke House!" she disclosed, rushing her fence.

"To do *what?*"

"I know very well what you are going to say, but only consider, Vernon! She *is* your niece, and what place could be more suitable for her come-out ball than Alverstoke House?"

"This house!" he responded, without hesitation.

"Oh, don't be so disagreeable! I am persuaded they could not dance above thirty couples in this room, and only think of all the fuss and botheration!"

"I am thinking of it," said his lordship.

"But there can be no comparison! I mean, *here,* where I should be obliged to remove all the furniture from my drawing-room, besides using the dining-room for supper, and the parlour for the ladies' cloaks—and Alverstoke House, where there is such a splendid ball-room! And it is my own old home, too!"

"It is also *my* home," said the Marquis. "My memory is occasionally faulty, but I retain the liveliest recollection of what you so rightly term the fuss and botheration that attended the balls given there for Augusta, for yourself, and for Eliza, and my answer, dear sister is No!"

"Have you *no* proper feeling?" she said tragically.

He had drawn an enamel snuff-box from his pocket, and was critically studying the painting on its lid. "No, none at all. I wonder if I made a mistake when I purchased this? I liked it at the time, but I begin to find it a trifle insipid." He sighed, and opened the box, with a practised flick of his thumb. "And I most assuredly do *not* like this mixture," he said, inhaling an infinitesimal pinch, and dusting his fingers with an expression of distaste. "You will say, of course, that I should have known better than to have permitted Mendlesham to thrust his Sort upon me, and you are perfectly right: one should always mix one's own." He got up. "Well, if that's all, I'll take my leave of you."

"It is not all!" she uttered, her colour much heightened. "I knew how it would be, of course—oh, *I* knew!"

"I imagine you might, but why the devil you wasted my time—"

"Because I hoped that for once in your life you might show some—*some* sensibility! *some* apprehension of what is due to your family! even *some* affection for poor Jane!"

"Rainbow-chasing, Louisa! My lack of sensibility has distressed you for years; I haven't the least affection for your poor Jane, whom I should be hard put to it to recognize, if I met her unawares; and I've yet to learn that the Buxted are members of my family."

"Am *I* not a member of your family?" she demanded. "Do you forget that I am your sister?"

"No: I've never been granted the opportunity to forget it. Oh, don't fly off the hooks again—you can have no notion how bracket-faced you look when you get into one of your pelters! Console yourself with my assurance that if Buxted had left you purse-pinched I should have felt myself obliged to let you hang on my sleeve." He looked mockingly down at her. "Yes, I know you're about to tell me that you haven't sixpence to scratch with, but the plain truth is that you are very well to do in the world, my dear Louisa, but the most unconscionable pinch-penny of my acquaintance! Now, don't nauseate me by prating of affection! You've no more for me than I have for you."

Considerably disconcerted by this direct attack, she stammered: "How can you say so? When I am sure I have always been most sincerely attached to you!"

"You deceive yourself, sister: not to me, but to my purse!"

"Oh, how can you be so unjust? And as for my being well to do in the world, I daresay that you, with your reckless extravagance, would be astonished to learn that I am obliged to exercise the *strictest* economy! Why, pray, do you imagine that I removed from our beautiful house in Albemarle Street when Buxted died, and came to live in this out-of-the-way place?"

He smiled. "Since there was not the least occasion for that removal, I can only suppose that it was from your incurable love of sconcing the reckoning."

"If you mean that I was obliged to reduce my expenses—"

"No, merely that you were unable to resist the temptation to do so."

"With five children left on my hands—" She broke off, warned by the quizzical look in his eye that it would be unwise to develop this theme.

"Just so!" he said sympathetically. "I think we had better part, don't you?"

"Sometimes," said Lady Buxted, with suppressed passion, "I think you must be the most odious, unnatural creature that ever drew breath! No doubt if it had been *Endymion* who had applied to you you would have been all compliance!"

These bitter words appeared powerfully to affect the Marquis, but after a stunned moment he pulled himself together, and recommended his sister, in faint but soothing accents, to retire to bed with a paregoric draught. "For you are sadly out of curl, Louisa, believe me! Do let me assure you that if ever Endymion should ask me to give a ball in his honour I shall take steps to have him placed under restraint!"

"Oh, how destestable you are!" she exclaimed. "You know very well I didn't mean—that what I meant—that—"

"No, no, don't explain it to me!" he interrupted. "It is quite unnecessary, I promise you! I perfectly understand you—indeed, I've done so for years! You—and I rather fancy, Augusta too—have persuaded yourself that I have a strong partiality for Endymion—"

"That—that *moonling!*"

"You are too severe: merely a slow-top!"

"Yes, we all know that you think him a positive pattern-card of perfection!" she said angrily, kneading her handkerchief between her hands.

He had been idly swinging his quizzing-glass on the end of its long riband, but was moved by this interjection to rise the glass to one eye, the better to survey his sister's enflamed countenance. "What a very odd interpretation to put upon my words!" he remarked.

"Don't tell *me!*" retorted Lady Buxted, in full career. "Whatever your precious Endymion wants he may have for the asking! While your *sisters*—"

"I hesitate to interrupt you, Louisa," murmured his lordship untruthfully, "but I think that extremely doubtful. I'm not at all benevolent, you know."

"And you don't make him an allowance, I collect! Oh, no, indeed!"

"So that's what's wound you up, is it? What a very hubble-bubble creature you are! At one moment you revile me for behaving scaly to my family, and at the next you come to cuffs with me for honouring my obligations to my heir!"

"That *block!*" she ejaculated. "If *he* is to become the head of the family I shan't be able to *bear* it!"

"Well, don't put yourself into a taking on that score!" he recommended. "Very likely you won't be obliged to bear it, for the chances are that you'll predecease me. I can give you five years, you know."

Lady Buxted, unable to find words adequate to the occasion, sought refuge in a burst of tears, reproaching her brother, between sobs, for his unkindness. But if she thought to soften his heart by these tactics she was the more mistaken: amongst the many things which bored him feminine tears and recriminations ranked high. Saying, with unconvincing solicitude, that if he had guessed that she was out of sorts he would not have inflicted his presence on her, he took his leave, sped on his way by the fervently expressed hope of his sister that she would at least live to see him come by his deserts.

She stopped crying as soon as the door shut behind

the Marquis; and might have recovered some degree of equanimity had not her elder son chosen to come into the room a few minutes later, to ask her, with a sad want of tact, whether his uncle had been visting her; and, if so, what he had had to say to her proposal. Upon learning from her that Alverstoke had been as disobliging as she had always known he would be, he looked grave, but said that he could not be sorry, for, having thought the matter over carefully, he could not like the scheme.

Lady Buxted's disposition was not a loving one. She was quite as selfish as her brother, and far less honest, for she neither acknowledged, nor, indeed, recognized her shortcomings. She had long since convinced herself that her life was one long sacrifice to her fatherless children; and, by the simple expedients of prefixing the names of her two sons and three daughters by doting epithets, speaking of them (though not invariably to them) in caressing accents, and informing the world at large that she had no thought or ambition that was not centred on her offspring, she contrived to figure, in the eyes of the uncritical majority, as a devoted parent.

Of her children, Carlton, whom she rather too frequently alluded to as her First-Born, was her favourite. He had never caused her to feel a moment's anxiety. From being a stolid little boy, accepting his mama at her own valuation, he had grown into a worthy young man, with a deep sense of his responsibilities, and a serious turn of mind which not only kept him out of the scrapes into which his livelier cousin Gregory fell, but which made it quite impossible for him to understand what Gregory, or any other of his contemporaries, found to amuse them in their larks and revel-routs. His understanding was moderate, and his processes of thought as slow as they were painstaking, but he was not at all conceited, merely priding himself on his commonsense. Nor was he jealous of George, his younger brother, whose intelligence he knew to be superior to his own. He was, in fact, proud of George, thinking him a very needle-witted boy; and although his lucubrations had shown him that such ardent spirits as George's might well lead that promising youth from the path of virtue, he never divulged this apprehension to his mother, or informed her of his intention to keep a watchful eye on George, when George's schooldays came to an end. He neither confided in her, nor argued with her; and not even to his sister Jane had he ever uttered a word of criticism of her.

He was four-and-twenty years of age, but as he had as yet shown no disposition to assert himself it came as an unpleasant surprise to his mother when he said that he knew of no reason why Jane's come-out ball should be held at his uncle's house, and at his expense. He sank rapidly in her affection; and, her temper being already exacerbated, they might soon have been at dagger-drawing if he had not prudently withdrawn from the engagement.

He was grieved to discover presently that Jane partook of her mother's sentiments upon this occasion, asserting that it was detestable of Uncle Vernon to be so disobliging, and so hardfisted as to begrudge the expenditure of a few hundred pounds.

"I am persuaded, Jane," said Buxted gravely, "that you have too much propriety of taste to wish to be so much beholden to my uncle."

"Oh, fiddle-faddle!" she exclaimed angrily. "Pray, why shouldn't I be beholden to him? I'm sure it's no more than his duty, after all!"

His upper lip seemed to lengthen, as it always did when he was displeased; he said in a repressive voice: "I make every allowance for your disappointment, but I venture to think that you will find a party here, in your own home, very much more enjoyable than a vast rout at Alverstoke House, where more than half the guests, I daresay, would be quite unknown to you."

His second sister, Maria, who, with her own come-out in view, was quite as indignant as Jane, was unable to contain herself, but barely waited for him to come to the end of his measured speech before demanding why he talked such gammon. "More enjoyable to hold a nip-farthing ball here, with no more than fifty persons invited, than to make her first appearance at Alverstoke House? You must be all about in your head!" she told his lordship. "It will be the shabbiest affair, for you know what Mama is! But if my uncle were to give a ball, only think how magnificent it would be! *Hundreds* of guests, and *all* of the first consequence! Lobsters, and aspic jellies and—and Chantillies, and creams—"

"Invited to the ball?" interpolated Carlton, with ponderous humour.

"And champagne!" struck in Jane, paying no heed to him. "And I should have stood at the head of the great staircase, with Mama, and my uncle, in a white satin gown, trimmed with rosebuds, and pink gauze, and a wreath!"

This beautiful vision caused tears to well into her eyes, but failed to arouse enthusiasm in either Maria or in Carlton, Maria objecting that with her freckles and sandy hair she would look like a quiz; and Carlton saying that he wondered at it that his sisters should think so much of worldly trumpery. Neither thought it worth while to reply to this; but when he added that for his part he was glad Alverstoke had refused to give the ball, they were quite as much incensed as had been their mama, and far more vociferous. So he went away, leaving his sisters to deplore his prosiness, quarrel about rosebuds and pink gauze, and agree that while their uncle was detestable it was probably Mama's fault, for setting up his back, which neither damsel doubted for an instant that she had done.

II

When the Marquis entered his house, some time later, one of the first things that his eyes alighted on was a letter, lying on one of a pair of ebony and ormolu pier tables. Its direction was written in large and flourishing characters, and the pale blue wafer which sealed it was unbroken, Mr Charles Trevor, the Marquis's excellent secretary, having recognized at a glance that it emanated from one or other of the frail beauties temporarily engaging his lordship's erratic attention. Relinquishing his hat, his gloves, and the lavishly caped driving-coat which had excited Miss Kitty Buxted's admiration, into the hands of the footman waiting to receive them, he picked up the letter, and strolled with it into the library. As he broke the wafer, and spread open the crossed sheet, an aroma of ambergris assailed his fastidious nostrils. An expression of distaste came into his face; he held the letter at arm's length, and groped for his quizzing-glass. Through this, he scanned the missive in a cursory way, before dropping it into the fire. Fanny, he decided, was becoming an intolerable bore. A dazzling creature, but, like so many prime articles, she was never satisfied. She now wanted a pair of cream-coloured horses to draw her barouche; last week it had been a diamond necklace. He had given her that, and it would serve for a farewell gift.

The sickly scent with which she had sprinkled her letter seemed to linger on his fingers; he was carefully wiping them when Charles Trevor came into the room. He glanced up, and seeing the look of surprise on that young gentleman's face very kindly explained to him that he disliked ambergris.

Mr Trevor offered no comment, but comprehension was writ so large upon his face that Alverstoke said:

14

"Just so! I know what you are thinking, Charles, and you are perfectly right: it is time I gave the fair Fanny her *congé*." He sighed, "A nice bit of game, but as birdwitted as she's avaricious."

Again Mr Trevor offered no comment. He would have been hard put to it to have made one, for his thoughts on the delicate subject were tangled. As a moralist, he could only deplore his employer's way of life; as one deeply imbued with chivalrous ideals, he pitied the fair Fanny; but as one who was fully aware of the extent of his lordship's generosity towards the lady, he was obliged to own that she had no cause for complaint.

Charles Trevor, one of the younger members of a large family, owed his present position to the circumstance of his father's having been appointed, when newly ordained, to the post of tutor and general mentor to the present Marquis's father, accompanying him on a protracted Grand Tour. A comfortable living was not his only reward: his noble pupil remained sincerely attached to him; stood as godfather to his eldest son; and reared his own son in the vague belief that the Reverend Laurence Trevor had a claim upon his patronage.

So, when the Reverend Laurence had ventured to suggest to the present Marquis that Charles was a suitable candidate for the post of secretary, Alverstoke had accepted him with far more readiness than Charles had felt in becoming a member of his household. Charles had no desire to enter the Church, but he was a young man of serious mind and unimpeachable morals, and nothing he had heard of Alverstoke led him to expect that his appointment would prove to be anything but a mortification of the flesh. But as he had, besides commonsense, a good deal of filial affection, and knew that to a clergyman of moderate substance it was no easy task to provide for a sixth son, he kept his misgivings to himself, assured his father that he would do his best not to disappoint his expectations, and derived what consolation he could from the reflection that when he was an inmate of Alverstoke House he must surely find it easier to discover and to grasp a golden opportunity than while he kicked his heels in a country parsonage.

Since his taste ran to politics, the golden opportunity had not so far offered itself, the Marquis not sharing his ambition, and consequently making infrequent appearances in the Upper House; but he was allowed to write such brief speeches as his patron felt that it behooved him to utter, and even, now and then, to favour him with his own political convictions.

Furthermore, he had found it quite impossible to dislike Alverstoke. While he was given no reason to suppose that Alverstoke was interested in his concerns, he found him to be as unexacting as he was amiable, and never disagreeably high in the instep. Comparing notes with a college-friend, in a similar situation, whose employer appeared to regard him as a cross between a black slave and an upper servant, Charles knew himself to be fortunate. Alverstoke could give an annihilating snub to some encroaching mushroom, but if his secretary erred he raked him down in a manner which was unexceptionable, since it conveyed no suggestion of social superiority. Charles's friend had curt commands flung at him; Charles received civil requests, generally accompanied by one of his lordship's more attractive smiles. Try as Charles would, he could not resist Alverstoke's charm, any more than he could withhold admiration for his horsemanship, and his proficiency in a great many sporting activities.

"I collect," said the Marquis, faint amusement in his eyes, "from your hesitant air and sheepish demeanour, that you feel it to be your duty to put me in mind of yet another obligation. Take my advice, and don't do it! I shall take it very unkind in you, and very likely fly up into the boughs."

A grin dispelled the gravity of Mr Trevor's countenance. "You never do, sir," he said simply. "And it isn't an obligation—at least, I don't think it is! Only I thought you would like to know of it."

"Oh, did you? In my experience, whenever those words are uttered they are the prelude to something I would liefer *not* know."

"Yes," said Mr Trevor ingenuously, "but I wish you will read this letter! As a matter of fact, I promised Miss Merriville that you would!"

"And who," demanded his lordship, "is Miss Merriville?"

"She said you would know, sir."

"Really, Charles, you should know me better than to suppose that I carry in my head the names of all the—" He stopped, his brows drawing together. "Merriville," he repeated thoughtfully.

"I believe, sir, some sort of connection of yours."

"A very remote sort! What the devil does she want?"

Mr Trevor offered him a sealed letter. He took it, but said severely: "You would be very well served if I put it into the fire, and left you to explain how it was that you were not, after all, able to see to it that I read it!" He broke the seal and opened the letter. It did not take him long to master its contents. He raised his eyes when he came to the end, and directed a look of pained enquiry at Mr Trevor. "Are you a trifle out of sorts, Charles? On the toodle last night, and not feeling quite the thing today?"

"No, of course not!" said Mr Trevor, shocked.

"Well, what, in heaven's name, has made you suddenly queer in your attic?"

"I'm not! I mean—"

"You must be. Never before, in the three years of our association, have you failed to make my excuses to my more importunate relatives! As for encouraging the dirty dishes amongst them—"

"That I am persuaded they are not, sir! I fancy they may not be *affluent,* but—"

"Dirty dishes," repeated his lordship firmly. "When one considers that my sister believes herself to be living quite out of the world in Grosvenor Place, what can one think of persons owning to Upper Wimpole Street? And if—" he glanced down at the letter again—"and if this F. Merriville is the daughter of the only member of the family with whom I ever had the slightest acquaintance you may depend upon it she hasn't a souse, and hopes I may be so obliging as to remedy this."

"No, no!" Mr Trevor said. "I hope I know better than to encourage such persons as that!"

"So do I," agreed his lordship. He lifted a quizzical eyebrow. "Friends of yours, Charles?"

"I never saw them before in my life, sir," replied Mr Trevor stiffly. "I should perhaps assure your lordship that I should consider it grossly improper to try to introduce any of my friends to your notice."

"Well, don't poker up about it! I really didn't mean to insult you," said Alverstoke mildly.

"No, sir, of course not!" Mr Trevor said, mollified. "I beg pardon! The thing is—Well, I had best explain to you how it came about that I did meet Miss Merriville!"

"Do!" invited Alverstoke.

"She brought the letter herself," disclosed Mr Trevor. "The carriage drew up just as I was about to enter the house—you see, you gave me very little to do today, so I thought you wouldn't object to it if I went out to purchase some new neck-cloths for myself!"

"Now, what can have put such an idea as that into your head?"

Another grin was drawn from his staid secretary. "You did, sir. Well, the long and short of it is that Miss Merriville got down from the carriage, the letter in her hand, as I was mounting the steps. So—"

"Ah!" interpolated Alverstoke. "No footman! Probably a job-carriage."

"As to that, sir, I don't know. At all events, I asked her if I could be of service—telling her that I was your secretary—and we fell into conversation—and I said that I would give you her letter, and—well—"

"See to it that I read it," supplied Alverstoke. "Describe this charmer to me, Charles!"

"Miss Merriville?" said Mr Trevor, apparently at a loss. "Well, I didn't notice her particularly, sir! She was very civil, and unaffected, and—and certainly *not* what you call a dirty dish! I mean—" He paused, trying to conjure up a picture of Miss Merriville. "Well, I don't know much about such things, but it seemed to me that she was dressed with elegance! Quite young, I think—though not in her first season. Or even," he added reflectively, "in her second season." He drew a long breath, and uttered, in reverent accents: "It was the other one, sir!"

"Yes?" said Alverstoke encouragingly, the amusement deepening in his eyes.

Mr Trevor seemed to find it difficult to express himself; but after a pause, during which he obviously conjured up a heavenly vision, he said earnestly: "Sir, I have never before seen, or—or even *dreamed* of such a lovely girl! Her eyes! So big, and of *such* a blue! Her hair! like shining gold! The prettiest little nose, too, and her complexion quite exquisite! And when she spoke—"

"But what were her ankles like?" interrupted his lordship.

Mr Trevor blushed, and laughed. "I didn't see her ankles, sir, for she remained in the carriage. I was particularly struck by the sweetness of her expression, and her soft voice. In fact, there is something very taking about her—if you know what I mean!"

"I have a very fair notion."

"Yes, well—well, when she leaned forward, and smiled, and begged me to give the letter to you, I promised her I would do so—even though I knew you wouldn't be above half pleased!"

"You wrong me, Charles. I confess you haven't aroused the smallest desire in me to make Miss Merriville's acquaintance, but I must certainly meet her companion. Who, by the way, is she?"

"I am not perfectly sure, sir, but I fancy she might be Miss Merriville's sister, though she is not at all like her. Miss Merriville called her Charis."

"That confirms me in my dislike of Miss Merriville. Of all abominable abbreviations I think *Carrie* the most repulsive!"

"No, no!" expostulated Mr Trevor. "You misunderstood me, sir! Of course it isn't *Carrie!* Miss Merriville distinctly said Char*is!* And I thought that never was anyone more aptly named, for it means 'grace,' you know—from the Greek!"

"Thank you, Charles," said his lordship meekly. "Where should I be without you?"

"I thought you might have forgotten, sir—your memory being so bad!"

The Marquis acknowledged this demure hit by lifting one of his strong, slender hands in a fencer's gesture. "Very well, Charles—damn your impudence!"

Encouraged, Mr Trevor said: "Miss Merriville said she hoped you would call in Upper Wimpole Street, sir: *will* you?"

"I daresay—if you can assure me that I shall find the beautiful Charis there."

Mr Trevor was unable to do this, but he knew better than to urge the matter further, and withdrew, not unhopeful of the issue.

Thinking it over, later, it occurred to him that in exposing Charis to Alverstoke's destructive notice he might be doing her a vast disservice. He was not afraid that Alverstoke would try to seduce a gently-born female of tender years, however beautiful she might be: his lordship's gallantries did not include such wanton acts as that; but he did fear that he might, if Charis captured his fancy, lure her into one of his *à suivie* flirtations, bestowing a flattering degree of attention upon her and perhaps leading her to think that he had formed a lasting passion for her. Remembering Charis's melting look, and appealing smile, Mr Trevor felt that her heart could easily be broken, and his conscience smote him. Then he reflected that she could hardly be alone in the world, and decided that her protection from a notorious flirt might safely be left to her parents. Besides, very young females ranked high on the list of the things Alverstoke rated as dead bores. As for Miss Merriville, Mr Trevor felt that she was very well able to take care of herself. He had been dazzled by her beautiful companion, but he retained a vague impression of a self-possessed female, with a slightly aquiline nose, and an air of friendly assurance. He did not think that she would be easily taken-in. Further reflection convinced him that no attempt would be made to trifle with her affections: it was unlikely that so noted a connoisseur of beauty as Alverstoke would deem her worthy of a second glance. In fact, it was even

more unlikely that he would in any way bestir himself
on her behalf.

After several days, during which his lordship made
no mention of her, and certainly did not go to pay her
a morning call, it began to seem as though he had
either decided to ignore her, or had forgotten her existence. Mr Trevor knew that it was his duty to remind
him, but he refrained, feeling that the moment was
unpropitious. His lordship had been obliged to endure
three visits—two from his elder sisters, and one from his
heir's widowed mother—all of which had bored him so
much that every member of his household took great
pains not to put him out of temper. "For I assure you,
Mr Wicken," said his lordship's top-lofty valet, condescending to his lordship's butler, "that when he is
nettled his lordship can create quite a humdurgeon, as
they say."

"I am well aware of that, Mr Knapp," returned his
colleague, "being as I have been acquainted with his
lordship from his cradle. He reminds me of his
father, the *late* lord, but you, of course, didn't know
him," he added, depressing pretension.

His lordship had indeed been sorely tried. Lady
Buxted, never one to accept defeat, had come to Alverstoke House, on the flimsiest of pretexts, accompanied
by her eldest daughter, who, failing to soften her uncle's
heart by cajolery, had dissolved into tears. But as she
was not one of those few, fortunate females who could
cry without rendering themselves hideous he was as
impervious to her tears as to his sister's account of the
straitened circumstances to which she had been reduced.
Only penury, Lady Buxted declared, had compelled her
to apply to her brother for his assistance in the all-im-
portant duty of launching her dearest Jane into the ton.
But her brother, speaking with the utmost amiability,
told her that parsimony, not penury, was the correct
word; upon which her ladyship lost her temper, and
gave him what James, the first footman, who was waiting in the hall, described to his immediate subordinate
as a rare bear-garden jaw.

Mrs Dauntry was his lordship's second visitor. Like

Lady Buxted, she was a widow; and she shared her
cousin's conviction that it was Alverstoke's bounden
duty to provide for her offspring. There the resemblance between them ended. Lady Buxted was frequently designated, by the vulgar, as a hatchet; but no
one could have applied such a term to Mrs Dauntry,
who presented an appearance of extreme fragility, and
bore with noble fortitude all the trials which beset her.
As a girl she had been an accredited beauty, but a
tendency to succumb to infectious complaints had encouraged her to believe that her constitution was sickly; and it was not long after her marriage that she
began (as Lady Jevington and Lady Buxted unkindly
phrased it) to quack herself. Her husband's untimely
demise had set the seal on her ill-health: she became
the subject of nervous disorders, and embarked on a
series of cures and diets, which, since they included
such melancholy remedies as goat's whey (for an imag-
ined consumption), soon reduced her to wraith-like
proportions. By the time she was forty she had become
so much addicted to invalidism that unless some attractive entertainment was offered her she spent the
better part of her days reclining gracefully upon a sofa,
with a poor relation in attendance, and a table beside
her crowded with bottles and phials which contained
Cinnamon Water, Valerian, Asafoetida Drops, Cam-
phorated Spirits of Lavender, and any other paregoric
or restorative recommended to her by her friends or by
the maker's advertizement. Unlike Lady Buxted, she
was neither ill-tempered nor hardfisted. She had a faint,
plaintive voice which, when she was thwarted, merely
became fainter and more exhausted; and she was as
ready to squander fortunes upon her children as upon
herself. Unfortunately, her jointure (described by the
Ladies Jevington and Buxted as an easy competence)
was not large enough to enable her to live, without
management and economy, in the style to which, she
said, she was accustomed; and as she was too invalidish
to study these arts, she was for ever outrunning the
constable. She had been Alverstoke's pensioner for
years; and although heaven knew how much she

wished to be independent of his generosity she could not but feel that since her handsome son was his heir it was his duty to provide also for her two daughters.

As the elder of these, Miss Chloë Dauntry, was some weeks short of her seventeenth birthday, her presentation had not exercised Mrs Dauntry's mind until she learned, from various garbled sources, that Alverstoke was planning to give a magnificent ball in honour of Miss Jane Buxted. A weak female she might be, but in defence of her beloved children, she declared, she could become a lioness. In this guise she descended upon Alverstoke, armed with her most powerful weapon: her vinaigrette.

She made no demands, for that was not her way. When he entered the saloon, she came towards him, trailing shawls and draperies, and holding out her hands, which were exquisitely gloved in lavender kid. "Dear Alverstoke!" she uttered, raising huge, sunken eyes to his face, and bestowing one of her wistful smiles upon him. "My kind benefactor! How can I thank you?"

Wholly ignoring her left hand, he briefly clasped the other, saying: "Thank me for what?"

"So like you!" she murmured. "But although *you* may forget your generosity, I cannot! Oh, I am quite in disgrace with poor Harriet, and the girls, for venturing out-of-doors in such chilly weather, but I felt it was the least I could do! You are a great deal too good!"

"Well, that's something new, at all events," he remarked. "Sit down, Lucretia, and let me have the word with no bark on it! What have I inadvertently done to excite your gratitude?"

Nothing had ever been known to disturb the saintliness of Mrs Dauntry's voice and demeanour; she replied, as she sank gracefully into a chair: "Dissembler! I know you too well to be taken-in: you don't like to be thanked—and, indeed, if I were to thank you for all your goodness to me and mine, your never-failing support, your kindness to my loved ones, I fear I should become what you call a dead bore! Chloë, dear child, calls you our fairy godfather!"

"She must be a wet-goose!" he responded.

"Oh, she thinks no one the equal of her magnificent Cousin Alverstoke!" said Mrs Dauntry, gently laughing. "You are quite first-oars with her, I assure you!"

"No need to put yourself in a worry over that," he said. "She'll recover!"

"You are too naughty!" Mrs Dauntry said playfully. "You hope to circumvent me, but to no avail, I promise you! Well do you know that I am here to thank you—yes, and to scold you!—for coming—as I, alas, could not!—to Endymion's assistance. That beautiful horse! *Complete to a shade,* he tells me! It is a great deal too good of you."

"So that's what you came to thank me for, is it?" said his lordship, a sardonic look in his eye. "You shouldn't have ventured out on such an unnecessary errand: I said, when he joined, that I would keep him decently mounted."

"So generous!" she sighed. "He is deeply sensible of it! As for me, I wonder sometimes what must have become of me when I was bereft of my beloved husband if I had not been able to depend upon your support through every trial."

"My faith in you, dear cousin, leads me to believe that you would have lost no time in discovering some other support," he answered, in a voice as sweet as hers. He smiled slightly, watching her bite her lip, and said, as he opened his snuff-box: "And what is the trial at present besetting you?"

She opened her eyes very wide at this, saying in a bewildered tone: "My dear Alverstoke, what can you mean? Apart from my wretched health—and I never talk of that, you know—none at all! I've discharged my errand, and must take my leave of you before my poor Harriet begins to fancy I've suffered one of my stupid spasms. She is waiting for me in the carriage, for she wouldn't hear of my coming alone. Such good care as she takes of me! I am quite spoilt between you all!" She rose, drawing her shawl around her, and putting out her hand. But before he could take it she let it fall, exclaiming: "Oh, that puts me in mind of something I have been wanting to discuss with you! Advise me, Alverstoke! I am quite in a quandary!"

"You put me to shame, Lucretia," he said. "As often as I disappoint you, you never disappoint me!"

"How you do love to joke me! Now, be serious, pray! It is about Chloë."

"Oh, in that case you must hold me excused!" said his lordship. "I know nothing of schoolgirls, and my advice would be worthless, I fear."

"Ah, you too think of her as a schoolgirl! Indeed, it seems almost impossible that she should be grown-up! But so it is: she's all but seventeen; and although I had thought not to bring her out until next year, everyone tells me it would be wrong to postpone the event. They say, you know, that the dear Queen's health is now so indifferent that she may pop-off at any moment, and even if she doesn't she won't be equal to holding any Drawing-rooms next year. Which has me in a worry, because naturally I must present the sweet child—it is what poor Henry would have wished—and if the Queen were to die there can be no Drawing-rooms. As for presenting her at Carlton House, I wouldn't for the world do so! I don't know how we are to go on. Even if the Duchess of Gloucester were to take the Queen's place—which, of course, the Prince Regent might desire her to do, for she has always been his favourite sister —it wouldn't be the same thing. And who knows but what one might find that *odious* Lady Hertford in the Queen's place?"

Alverstoke, who could think of few more unlikely contingencies, replied sympathetically: "Who indeed?"

"So I feel it to be my duty to present Chloë this season, whatever the cost!" said Mrs Dauntry. "I had hoped to have been so much beforehand with the world *next* year as to have been able to do the thing handsomely, but that, alas, can scarcely be! Dear child! When I told her that I should be obliged to present her in one of my own Court dresses, because the cost of such a dress as one would wish her to wear is utterly beyond my means, she was so good and so uncomplaining that it quite went to my heart! I couldn't forbear to sigh: she is quite pretty that I positively long to rig her out to the best advantage! But if I must bring her out this season it cannot be."

"In that case, my advice to you is to wait until next year," responded Alverstoke. "Consoling yourself with the reflection that if there are no Drawing-rooms then *none* of the season's fair come-outs will enjoy and experience which is denied her."

"Ah, no! How could I be so improvident?" she countered. "Somehow I must contrive to present her this spring! A dance, too! But how to do that, situated as I am—" She broke off, apparently struck by a sudden idea. "I wonder if Louisa means to bring Jane out this season? Sadly freckled, poor child, and such a deplorable figure! However, you may depend upon it that Louisa will make a push to present her creditably, though she is such a nip-cheese that I'm persuaded she will grudge every penny she is obliged to spend on the business. Indeed," she added, softly laughing, "rumour has it that *you* are to give a ball in Jane's honour!"

"Yes?" said his lordship. "But *rumour,* as I daresay you know, *is a pipe*—er—*Blown by surmises, jealousies, conjectures*—I forget the rest, but do let me assure you, dear Lucretia, that when invitations are sent out for a ball to be held here Chloë's name will not be forgotten. And now you must allow me to escort you to your carriage: the thought of the devoted Harriet, patiently awaiting you, is beginning to prey upon my mind."

"Stay!" said Mrs Dauntry, struck by yet another idea. "How would it be if Louisa and I cast our resources into a pool-dish, as it were, and gave a ball in honour of both our daughters? I am afraid that my lovely Chloë would quite outshine poor Jane, but I daresay Louisa won't care for that, if she can but make and scrape a little." She raised her hands in a prayerful gesture, and added, in a voice of nicely blended archness and cajolery: "Would you, dearest Vernon, if Louisa liked the scheme, permit us to hold the ball here, in your splendid ballroom?"

"No, dearest Lucretia, I would not!" replied his lordship. "But don't repine! The occasion won't arise, since

Louisa wouldn't like the scheme at all, believe me! Yes, I know that I am being so abominably disobliging as to make you feel faint: shall I summon the faithful Harriet to your side?"

This was a little too much, even for Mrs Dauntry. Casting upon him a deeply reproachful glance, she departed, her mien challenging comparison with that of Mrs Siddons, as portrayed by the late Sir Joshua Reynolds as the Tragic Muse.

The Marquis's third visitor was Lady Jevington, who came, not to solicit his favour, but to adjure him not to yield to Lady Buxted's importunities. She expressed herself in measured and majestic terms, saying that while she had neither expected him to lend his aid in the launching of her Anna into the ton, nor asked him to do so, she would be unable to regard it as anything but a deliberate slight if he were to perform this office for Miss Buxted, who did not (said Lady Jevington, with awful emphasis) share with her cousin the distinction of being his goddaughter. And if, she added, his partiality were to lead him to single out That Woman's daughter Chloë, for this particular mark of favour, she would thenceforward wash her hands of him.

"Almost, Augusta, you persuade me!" said his lordship.

The words, spoken dulcetly, were accompanied by the sweetest of smiles; but Lady Jevington, arising in swelling wrath, swept out of the room without another word.

"And now," the Marquis told his secretary, "it only remains for *your* protégée to demand a ball of me!"

III

In the face of these experiences it did not seem probable
that the Marquis, who rarely felt it incumbent upon
him to please anyone but himself, would respond to
Miss Merriville's appeal; nor did Charles Trevor venture to jog his memory. But, whether from curiosity, or
because he found himself one day in the vicinity of
Upper Wimpole Street, he did pay her a visit.

He was admitted to the house by an elderly butler,
who conducted him up the narrow staircase to the
drawing-room on the first floor, at a pace eloquent of
age and infirmity, and announced him.

The Marquis, pausing on the threshold, and casting a
swift look round, felt that his suspicion was confirmed:
this unknown connection was demonstrably indigent;
for the room was furnished without elegance, and was
even a little shabby. Lacking experience, he failed to
recognize the signs which would have informed less
fortunately circumstanced persons that the house was
one of the many hired for the season, and equipped as
cheaply as possible.

It contained only one occupant: a lady, writing at a
small desk, placed at right-angles to the window. She
looked round quickly, directing at Alverstoke a gaze
that was at once surprised and appraising. He saw that
she was quite young: probably some three- or four-
and-twenty years of age: her person well-formed; and
her countenance distinguished by a pair of candid gray
eyes, a somewhat masterful little nose, and a very firm
mouth and chin. Her hair, which was of a light brown,
was becomingly braided à la Didon; and her gown,
which she wore under a striped dress-spencer, was of
fine cambric, made high to the throat, and ornamented
round the hem with double trimming. Alverstoke, no
stranger to the niceties of feminine apparel, saw at a

glance that while this toilette was in the established mode it was neither dashing nor expensive. No one would describe it as up to the nines; but, on the other hand, no one would stigmatize the lady as a dowd. She wore her simple dress with an air; and she was as neat as wax.

She was also perfectly composed: a circumstance which made Alverstoke wonder whether she was older than he had at first supposed. Since young, unmarried ladies did not commonly receive male visitors, it would have been natural for her to have been a trifle flustered by the entrance of a strange gentleman, but she seemed to be as unperturbed by this as by his cool scrutiny. So far from blushing, or lowering her eyes, she betrayed not the smallest sign of maidenly confusion, but looked him over thoughtfully, and (as he realized, with amusement) extremely critically.

He moved forward, in his graceful, unhurried way. "Have I the honour of addressing Miss Merriville?" he enquired.

She got up, and came to meet him, holding out her hand. "Yes, I'm Miss Merriville. How do you do? Pray forgive me!—I wasn't expecting this visit, you see."

"Then pray forgive *me!* I was under the impression that you desired me to visit you."

"Yes, but I had quite given up expecting you to call. Which didn't surprise me, because I daresay you thought it a tiresome imposition, besides being, perhaps, much too *coming!*"

"Not at all," he murmured, at his most languid.

"Well, I'm afraid it was. The thing is that from having lived all my life in Herefordshire I am not yet perfectly acquainted with London customs." An engaging twinkle lit her eyes; she added confidingly: "You can have no notion of how very hard it is to conform to *propriety,* when one has been—you may say—the mistress of the house for years and years!"

"On the contrary!" he responded promptly. "I've every notion of it!"

She laughed. "No, have you? Then perhaps it won't be so difficult to explain to you why I—why I solicited the favour of your visit!"

"What an admirable phrase!" he commented. "Did you commit it to memory? *I* thought that your—solicitation—was, rather, a summons!"

"Oh, *dear!*" said Miss Merriville, stricken. "And I took such pains not to appear to be a *managing* female!"

"Are you one?"

"Yes, but how could I help it? I must tell you how it comes about that—But, pray, won't you be seated?"

He bowed slightly, and moved towards a chair on one side of the fireplace. She sat down opposite him, and, after surveying him for a moment, rather doubtfully, said: "I did mean to explain it all to you in my letter, but I made such a bumble-bath of it—as my brother, Harry, would say—that in the end I thought it would be better if I could contrive to meet you, and *talk* to you! At the outset, I hadn't any intention of applying to any of Papa's relations, thinking that my Aunt Scrabster would be able to do all that I wanted. Which just shows how ignorant I was, to be so taken-in! She is the eldest of my mother's sisters, and she never wrote to us but what she prated of the modish life she led, and how much she wished she could present my sister and me into polite circles."

"Secure in the belief that she would never be called upon to make good her words?"

"Exactly so!" said Miss Merriville, bestowing a warm smile upon him. "Not that I think she could have done so, because my uncle's fortune derives from Trade. He is an East India merchant, and, although perfectly respectable, *not* tonnish. That is why, finding myself quite beside the bridge, I was obliged to overcome my scruples, and to cast about in my mind for the one of Papa's family who would best answer the purpose."

"And what was it that led your fancy to alight on me?" asked his lordship, a cynical curl to his lips.

She replied readily: "Oh, it wasn't my *fancy!* It was just commonsense! One reason was that Papa was used to say that you were the best of his relations. Though, from anything I ever heard," she added, "that wasn't praising you to the skies! I've never met any of the Merriville cousins, or my two Merriville aunts, for Papa, you must know, was cast off by his whole family when he was so disobliging as to marry my mother instead of the great heiress they had found for him. So I sincerely trust I shall never meet them. And as to applying to them for any assistance whatsoever, *no!*" She paused, considering the matter with a darkling look, before adding: "Besides, they could none of them render me the assistance I need, because they seem to be a very dull, dowdy set of people who almost never come to London, on account of not approving of modern manners. Which was another reason for choosing you."

He raised his brows. "What made you think *I* don't disapprove of modern manners?"

"Nothing. I mean, I didn't know anything about you, but *that* wasn't it! Not but what I can see for myself that you are *very* fashionable—or so it seems to me?" she said, on a note of interrogation.

"Thank you! I—er—contrive to pass myself off with credit, I hope."

"Yes, and, what is more important, you move in the first circles. That was my other reason for choosing you," she disclosed, with another of her friendly smiles.

"Was it indeed! To what end? Or can I guess?"

"Well, I should think you might, for you don't look to be at all stupid—though I own I had expected you to be older. It's a great pity that you aren't. However, it can't be helped, and I daresay you are old enough to be of use."

"I am seven-and-thirty, ma'am," said Alverstoke, somewhat acidly, "and I should perhaps inform you that I am never of use to anyone!"

She gazed at him in astonishment. *"Never?* But why not?"

He shrugged. "Pure selfishness, ma'am, coupled with a dislike of being bored."

She looked a little anxiously at him. "Would it bore you very much to present me to Lady Alverstoke? And to ask her if she would be so obliging as to lend me her aid?"

"Possibly not, but the question doesn't arise: my mother died many years ago."

"No, no, I meant your wife!"

"I am not married."

"Not?" she exclaimed. "Oh, how vexatious!"

"Disobliging of me, isn't it?" he said sympathetically.

"Well, no, not *disobliging,* precisely, because you couldn't know that I wished you had been," she said, very kindly exonerating him.

He replied sardonically: "I collect that if I had known it you would have expected me to rectify the matter?"

She coloured, fixing her eyes anxiously on his face. "Oh, *pray* don't take an affront into your head!" she begged. "I didn't mean to be *brassy,* and I daresay we can contrive well enough without your wife, if we set our minds to it."

"We?"

He spoke with quelling hauteur, but his mouth twitched in spite of himself, and under their lazy lids his eyes glinted. These signs were not lost on Miss Merriville. She heaved a sigh of relief, and said disarmingly: "Thank goodness! I thought I had put you out of temper! And I must own that I can't blame you for being provoked, for I am making a shocking mull of it. And I quite thought it would be easy to explain the circumstances to you, if only I could meet you face to face!"

"Well, what are the circumstances, ma'am?"

She was silent for a moment or two, not, as was evident from her thoughtful expression, from embarrassment, but from consideration of how best to present her case. "You may say, I suppose, that they arose from my father's death, a year ago. That isn't to say that I hadn't thought about the matter before, because I had; but while he was alive there seemed to be nothing I could do."

"I am very sorry to learn that your father is dead," he interjected, "but I must take this opportunity of informing you that my acquaintance with him was of the slightest. As for the relationship between us, I had rather have called it a connection merely. It derives from my grandmother's family, and is, as far as my memory serves me, so remote as to be almost negligible."

"But Papa was used to speak of you as his cousin!" she objected. He offered no comment; and after a short pause, she said: "Yes, and I know we meet somewhere, because I've seen your name on the family tree which is in the big Bible at home."

"Only through two marriages," he answered discouragingly.

"I see. You don't wish to recognize us, do you? Then there isn't the least occasion for me to explain our situation to you. I beg your pardon for having put you to the trouble of visiting me."

At these words, the Marquis, who had had every intention of bringing the interview to a summary end, irrationally chose to prolong it. Whether he relented because Miss Merriville amused him, or because the novelty of having one of his rebuffs accepted without demur intrigued him remained undecided, even in his own mind. But however it may have been he laughed suddenly, and said, quizzing her: "Oh, so high! No, no, don't hold up your nose at me: it don't become you! I've no objection to recognizing you, as you put it: I won't even repudiate cousinship—though I hold out no promise of lending you my aid in whatever project it is that you have in mind. What, by the way, *do* you hope I'll do for you?"

She relaxed, and smiled gratefully at him. "I am very much obliged to you! It is quite a small thing: to introduce my sister into the ton!"

"To introduce your sister into the ton?" he repeated blankly.

"Yes, if you please. And perhaps I should warn you that you might have to introduce me too, unless I can persuade my sister that I truly don't desire it. In general she is the most biddable girl alive, but in this instance she declares she won't go to parties unless I do, which is excessively tiresome of her, but comes from her having such a loving disposition that—"

He interrupted her without ceremony. "My good girl, are you seriously suggesting that you should make your come-out under *my* aegis? What you need is a matron to chaperon you, not a bachelor!"

"I know I do," she agreed. "That was why it came as a severe disappointment to me to learn that you *are* a bachelor. But I've already thought how we might overcome that difficulty! Would you object to it if we pretended that Papa had left us to your guardianship? Not all of us, of course, because Harry has just come of age, and I am four-and-twenty, but the three younger ones?"

"I should—most emphatically!"

"But why?" she argued. "You wouldn't be obliged to do any more for us than to sponsor Charis—and me, perhaps—into society! Naturally I shouldn't expect you to interest yourself in anything else concerning us! In fact, I shouldn't relish it above half if you did," she added frankly.

"You need be under no apprehension! What you don't appear to realize, ma'am, is that you wouldn't find *my* sponsorship a passport to the Polite World!"

"How is this?" she demanded. "I had thought a Marquis must always be acceptable!"

"That, Miss Merriville, depends on the Marquis!"

"Oh!" she said, digesting this, "Papa said you were a—an *out-and-out cock of the game*. Does that mean that you are an *improper* person?"

"Sunk below reproach!" he responded promptly.

She broke into a chuckle. "Oh, humbug! I don't believe it! Even poor Papa wasn't as bad as that!"

"Even poor Papa . . .!" he said. He found his quizzing-glass, and raised it to one eye, studying her through it with the air of a man who had encountered a rare specimen.

Quite impervious to this scrutiny, she said: "No, though I believe he was shockingly wild before he met Mama—and I must own that to have run off with her, as he did, was not at all the thing! It has always seemed very odd to me that Mama should have consented, for she was of the first respectability, you know, and so very—so very good! However, I believe that people who are passionately in love frequently do the oddest things—and I have sometimes thought that she was very persuadable. Not that I knew her very well, because she died soon after Felix was born, but Charis is her image, and *she* is persuadable! And, of course, they were both so young! Only fancy!—Papa came of age just a week before I was born! I can't imagine how he contrived to support a family, for his father cut him off without a groat, and I shouldn't *think* he pursued any gainful occupation. But he abandoned all his rackety ways after he married Mama; and considering that they had caused my grandparents to feel the greatest anxiety and embarrassment I must say that I think it was wickedly unjust of them not to have welcomed Mama into the family!"

The Marquis preserved a tactful silence. His recollections of the late Mr Merriville, whom he had met not so very many years previously, hardly tallied with the picture conjured up of a reformed character.

"And, for my part," continued Miss Merriville, "I think they were very well served for their unkindness when both my grandfather, *and* my Uncle James, who was the heir, were carried off by typhus within a day of each other! That was how Papa came into the property—and just in time for Harry to be born at Graynard! And after him, of course, Charis, and Jessamy, and Felix." She broke off, seeing the Marquis blink, and smiled. "I know what you are thinking, and you are perfectly right! All of us but Harry have the most ridiculous names! I assure you, they are a great trial to us. Nothing would do for Mama, when I was born, but to saddle me with *Frederica*—after Papa, you know. Then there was Harry, because Mama was Harriet. And Papa chose my sister's name, because he said she was the most *graceful* baby he had ever seen. Jessamy was named after his godfather; and Felix was a fancy of Mama's—because we were such a happy family! Which, indeed, we were—until Mama died." She paused again, but almost immediately resumed, giving her head a tiny shake, as though to cast off a bad memory, and saying, in a lighter tone: "So we had to make the best of our absurd names! And Jessamy and I exchanged vows *never* to call each other Jessie, and Freddy, and never to permit the others to do so either."

"And don't they?"

"No—well, almost never! I must own that Felix does sometimes say Jessie, but only when Jessamy is on his high ropes; and in private Harry occasionally calls me Freddy—but not to torment me! And he never calls Jessamy Jessie, no matter how much Jessamy may have

provoked him, because he is four years older, besides
being the head of the family, and he would think it
very shabby conduct to nettle Jessamy into a fight,
when he knows he could drop him in a trice. Not but
what Jessamy is full of pluck, Harry says, but—Oh,
dear, how I am running on, and without saying anything to the purpose! Where was I?"

"I rather think you had reached the point of your
mother's death."

"Oh, yes! Well—the effect of that was very dreadful. I believe—indeed, I know—that Papa was so
shattered that they feared for his reason. I was too
young to understand, but I remember that he was ill
for a long time—or so it seemed to me—and when he
recovered he wasn't the *same*. In fact, he became quite
a stranger, because he was hardly ever at home. He
couldn't bear it, without Mama. I daresay we shouldn't
have liked it at the time, but I have frequently thought
that it would have been a very good thing if he had
married again. I know it is improper in me to say so,
but he was sadly unsteady, you know."

"Well, yes," admitted Alverstoke. "I do know. But
did he leave you to fend for yourselves? I find that
hard to believe!"

"No, no, of course he didn't! My Aunt Seraphina
came to live with us—she is Mama's unmarried sister—
and she has been with us ever since Mama died!"

"And is she still with you?"

"Indeed she is! Good gracious, how could we have
come to London without her to lend us countenance?"

"You must forgive me: not having seen—or, until
this moment, heard—anything of your aunt, I had
formed the impression that you had decided to dispense with a chaperon."

"I'm not so ramshackle! Why should you suppose—
Oh! Your propriety is offended by my receiving you
without a chaperon! My Aunt Scrabster warned me
how it would be, but I'm not a girl just escaped from
the schoolroom, you know. What's more, although *we*
are quite accustomed to her ways, I cannot believe that
you would like my aunt! For one thing she's extremely
deaf; and for another, she—she is a trifle eccentric!

If she comes in, pray don't get into a quarrel with her!"

"I can safely promise you I won't!" he said. "Is she so quarrelsome?"

"No but she hates men," explained Frederica. "We fancy she must have suffered a disappointment in youth, or some such thing. I daresay she will go away immediately, if she finds you here."

"Scarcely an ideal chaperon!" he observed.

"No, and, what is worse, she is beginning not to like Harry as much as she was used to. She positively hated Papa—but that was understandable, because, besides being uncivil to her, he behaved very badly, and wasted the estate quite shockingly. Fortunately, before he had contrived to bring us all to pieces, he had a stroke."

"That *was* fortunate," he agreed, preserving his gravity.

"Yes, wasn't it? For, although he recovered, in a great measure, the use of his limbs, his brain was a little impaired. I don't mean to say that he lost his reason, but he became forgetful, and—and *different!* He wasn't wild, or resty any more, and not in the least unhappy. Indeed, I never liked him half as well before! He let me manage the estate, and all his affairs, so I was able, with a great deal of help from Mr Salcombe, who is our lawyer, to stop everything going to rack and ruin. That was five years ago, and I do think that if Harry will only hold household for a few years he will find himself quite comfortably circumstanced, and even able to provide for Jessamy and Felix, which he is determined to do, thinking it so unjust that everything should come to him, through Papa's not having made a Will."

"Good God! Then what becomes of you and your sister?"

"Oh, we are perfectly well to pass!" she assured him. "Mama's fortune was settled on her daughters, you see, so we have £5,000 each. I expect that doesn't seem to you very much, but it does make us independent, and it means that Charis won't be a *penniless* bride."

"Ah! She is engaged, then?"

"No, not yet. That is why I was determined, when Papa died, just over a year ago, to bring her to London. You see, at Graynard she had as well be buried alive! There isn't even a watering-place within our reach, so how can she form an eligible connection? She—she is quite *wasted*, Lord Alverstoke! You will understand, when you see her, why I felt it to be my duty to bring her out in London! She is the loveliest girl! She has the sweetest disposition imaginable, too, never cross or crotchety, and she *deserves* to make a splendid marriage!"

"I have it on the authority of my secretary that she is a diamond of the first water," said his lordship dryly. "But splendid marriages, Miss Merriville, in general depend on splendid dowries."

"Not always!" she countered swiftly. "Only think of the Gunning sisters! Why, one of them married two Dukes, and I know she wasn't a great heiress, because Papa told me about them, saying that Charis beat them both to flinders! Not that I expect Charis to marry a Duke—or *any* nobleman, unless, of course, one offered for her! But I do expect her to make a very good marriage, if only I can contrive to have her brought out creditably! My mind has been set on it this age, but *how* to contrive it was the question. And then, when I almost felt myself to be at a stand, Mr Salcombe came to ask me whether I would consider hiring the house furnished, for a year! The thing was that he had heard of someone who had lately retired, and wished to buy a property in Herefordshire, and not finding just what he wanted had hit upon the notion of hiring a house for a limited time in the county, so that he could look about him at his leisure, and not be obliged to post all the way from London every time he received an offer of some property which always turned out to be quite unsuitable. You may imagine how ready I was to accommodate him!"

"Oh, yes, I can imagine that—and also that your brother had nothing to say in the matter!"

"Well, he wasn't of age then, but of course I did nothing without his consent. At first, he couldn't like it: I think it wounded his pride. To own the truth, I didn't like it either—but what could be more non-sensical than to cling to one's consequence when one is living on a monkey's allowance? It is still only by practising the strictest economy that we can keep out of debt, and until Mr Porth entered into a treaty for the house it was wholly out of my power to undertake this London venture. Even if I could broach my principal, which I am not permitted to do, I don't think I should, for that would leave me dependent on poor Harry." She looked seriously across at his lordship. "That mustn't be, you know. I don't say it to him, because he is very young, and thinks that nothing could be more natural than for us all to continue at Graynard. But I shouldn't be at all surprised if he wished to be married in a year or two. Only think how much his wife would dislike having his sisters planted at Graynard, and how uncomfortable it would be for us!"

"Very true," he agreed. "If any female could be induced to marry him under such circumstances, which I strongly doubt."

Her gravity disappeared; she gave another of her chuckles. "She would be afraid that I should rule the roost, wouldn't she? Which I probably should, because I've done so for so long, and habits are very hard to overcome. No: the best thing will be for Charis to contract a suitable marriage; and for the boys, and my aunt, and me, to set up an establishment of our own as soon as Harry becomes engaged. I made up my mind to that a long time ago. But the most pressing need is to provide for Charis! It seems to me to be positively *wicked* that anyone so beautiful should dwindle into an old maid! Which is what she would do, unless she married one of the dreadfully dull young men in our neighbourhood, who have been dangling after her this age; or, worse, some wholly ineligible creature, not worth a hair! It was *that* consideration which made me regard Mr Porth's offer as a stroke of good fortune. Well, only think, sir! He hires only the house, and the Home farm, at a figure which I shouldn't have dared to suggest to him; and the rest of the property, which is beginning to pull in the pieces again, remains in Harry's possession, for, naturally, Mr Porth has no wish to be burdened with its management. And, which is of the first importance, it was of particular interest to him to hire, as well as the house, the servants, except our housekeeper, and our butler. That was another stroke of good fortune, because Mrs Hurley, and dear old Buddle, would never have consented to remain at Graynard in the employment of anyone but a Merriville. So we were able to bring them to London with us; and although they despise London, and are for ever telling me what a horrid house this is, and furnished in the most rubbishing style; and complaining that London servants are a chuck-farthing set, it is the greatest comfort to have them with us! And I must say," she added candidly, "it *is* a horrid house, and not situated, as I've discovered, in the *modish* part of town. Never having visited London, I asked my Aunt Scrabster to procure a furnished house for me. That was a mistake. She lives in Harley Street herself, and I find that this district is almost entirely inhabited by persons engaged in trade. However, I am told that the most extortionate rents are demanded for houses in Mayfair, besides fines upon entrance, so I don't repine. The worst mistake I made was believing that my aunt had either the power or the desire to introduce us to the ton!" She smiled. "My tongue runs like a fiddlestick, doesn't it? The round tale is that my aunt and uncle, being childless, have never made any attempt to live in a—in a *fashionable* way; and poor Aunt Amelia was never more dismayed than when I informed her of my decision to come to London for the season! That, sir, is why I was forced to apply to you."

He had been meditatively tapping the lid of his snuffbox, and he now flicked it open, and, frowning slightly, took a pinch, while Frederica watched him, not unhopefully. He shut the box, dusted his long fingers, and at last looked at her, still frowning. "You would be well advised to be content with something less than the first circle of society," he said bluntly.

"Are we so ineligible?" she demanded.

"By birth, no. In all other respects, yes. I don't know what your pecuniary resources may be, but—"

"Enough!"

"If you are thinking of a Court presentation for your sister you would do better to fund your money: it's an investment that would yield you no dividend."

"I know that, and I don't think of it."

"What, then?"

She clasped her hands together in her lap, and said, a little breathlessly: "Almack's!"

"You are aiming at the moon, Miss Merriville. No introduction of mine would help you to cross that hallowed threshold! Unless you number amongst your acquaintances some matron possessing the entrée, who would be willing to sponsor you—"

"I don't. If that had been the case I shouldn't have sought your assistance. But I won't cry craven! *Somehow* I shall manage—see if I don't!"

He rose politely, saying: "I hope you may. If you think my advice of value, may I suggest that you would have a better chance of success if you were to remove to one of the watering-places? Bath, or Tunbridge Wells, where you may attend the assemblies, and would no doubt meet persons of consideration."

She too rose, but before she could answer him she was interrupted by the sound of hasty footsteps on the stairs. The next instant a sturdy schoolboy burst into the room, exclaiming: "Frederica, it was nothing but a fudge! We searched all over, and I asked people, and no one knew anything about it!"

IV

Miss Merriville, unperturbed by the irruption into her drawing-room of a young gentleman who had contrived to acquire, since she had last seen him some three hours earlier, a crumpled and grubby collar and muddied nankeens, responded with quick sympathy: "Oh, no! How wretched for you! But it can't have been a fudge, Felix! It was Mr Rushbury who told you about it, and he wouldn't have hoaxed you!"

By this time Master Felix Merriville had taken cursory stock of the Marquis, but he would undoubtedly have poured forth the story of his morning's Odyssey to his sister had he not been quelled by another, and older, schoolboy, who, entering the room in his wake, severely adjured him to mind his manners. A large and shaggy dog, of indeterminate parentage, was at his heels; and just as he was apologizing to Frederica for having come in when she was entertaining a visitor, this animal advanced with the utmost affability to greet the Marquis. His disposition was friendly, as he showed by the waving of his plumed tail; and his evident intention was to jump up at the guest. But Alverstoke, wise in the ways of dogs, preserved his face from being generously licked, and his exquisitely fashioned coat of Bath Superfine from being smirched by muddy paws, by catching the animal's forearms, and holding him at bay. "Yes, good dog!" he said. "I'm much obliged to you, but I don't care to have my face licked!"

"*Down*, Lufra!" commanded Mr Jessamy Merriville, in even more severe accents. He added, with his sister's absence of shyness: "I beg pardon, sir: I would not have brought him in if I had known that my sister was entertaining a visitor."

"Not at all: I like dogs," responded his lordship, reducing Lufra to abject slavery by running his fingers along the precise spot on the spine which that grateful hound was unable to scratch for himself. *"What* did you call him?"

"Lufra, sir," said Jessamy, a dark flush rising to the roots of his hair. "At least, *I* never did so! It was a silly notion of my sisters': *I* called him Wolf, when he was a puppy! But they would persist, so, in the end, he wouldn't answer to his right name! And he is *not* a bitch!"

Perceiving that his lordship had been carried out of his depth, Frederica explained the matter to him. "It's from *The Lady of the Lake,"* she told him. "I dare say you recall the passage, when the Monarch *bade let loose a gallant stag?* And Lufra—*whom from Douglas side Nor bribe nor threat could e'er divide, The fleetest hound in all the North, Brave Lufra saw, and darted forth. She left the royal hounds midway, And dashing on the antler'd prey, Sunk her sharp muzzle in his flank—"*

"And deep the flowing life-blood drank!" interpolated Felix, with relish.

"Stow it!" growled his senior. "It wasn't a stag at all, sir—merely a young bull, which we had not thought to be dangerous! and as for drinking its life-blood—stuff!"

"No, but you can't deny that Luff saved you from being gored!" said Frederica. She looked up at Alverstoke. "Only fancy! He was hardly more than a puppy, but he rushed in, and hung on to the bull's muzzle, while Jessamy scrambled over the gate to safety! And I am very sure that not even the offer of a marrowbone could divide him from Jessamy, *could it,* dear Luff?"

Gratified by this tribute, the faithful hound flattened his ears, wagged his tail, and, after uttering a yelp of encouragement, sat panting at her feet. His master, rendered acutely uncomfortable by this passage, would have removed himself, his dog, and his brother from the drawing-room if Frederica had not detained him, saying: "No, pray don't run away! I wish to make you known to Lord Alverstoke! This is my brother Jessamy, sir, and this is Felix."

His lordship, acknowledging their bows, found that

he was being surveyed: by Jessamy, whom he judged to be about sixteen years of age, measuringly; by Felix, three or four years younger, with the unwavering yet incurious gaze of childhood. He was quite unaccustomed to being weighed up; and there was a decided twinkle in his eyes as he looked the boys over.

Jessamy, he thought, was an exaggerated copy of his sister: his hair was darker than hers, his nose more aquiline, and his mouth and chin determined to the point of obstinacy. Felix still retained the snub-nose and the chubbiness of extreme youth, but he had the same firm chin and direct gaze which characterized his seniors, and even less shyness. It was he who broke the silence, blurting out: "Sir! Do *you* know about the Catch-me-who-can?"

"Of course he doesn't! Don't be so rag-mannered!" his brother admonished him. "I beg your pardon, sir: he has windmills in his head!"

"Not windmills: railway locomotives," replied Alverstoke. He looked down at Felix. "Isn't that it? Some sort of steam-locomotive?"

"Yes, that's it!" said Felix eagerly. "Trevithick's, sir. I don't mean the Puffing Devil: that ran on the road, but it caught fire, and was burnt."

"Ay! and a very good thing too!" interjected Jessamy. "Steam-engines on the roads! Why, they would send every horse mad with terror!"

"Oh, pooh! I daresay they would soon grow used to them. Besides, I'm not talking of that one. The one I mean runs on rails—at fifteen miles an hour, and very likely more!" He turned his attention to Alverstoke again. "I *know* it was brought to London, because Mr Rushbury—my godfather—told me so, and how you could ride in it for a shilling. He said it was north of the New Road, and not far, he thought, from Montague House."

"I believe it was," said Alverstoke. "From some cause or another I never visited it, but I do seem to recall that the inventor—what did you say his name is?"

"Trevithick! The *first* locomotive he made has five wagons, and it can carry ten tons of iron and seventy men, but only at five miles an hour. It's in Wales—I forget the name of the place—but the one *here* has one carriage, and—"

"*Will* you bite your tongue, you abominable little bagpipe?" interrupted Jessamy. "Anyone would take you for a regular shabster, rattling on like that, and not allowing Lord Alverstoke to edge in a word!"

Abashed by this rebuke, Felix hastily begged his lordship's pardon; but Alverstoke, amused by him, said: "Nonsense! I can always edge in a word—when I wish to! There was such a locomotive, Felix, but I am afraid it's a thing of the past. I rather think that Trevithick hired some ground, near Fitzroy Square, fenced it in, and laid down a circular track. As I recall, it created quite a stir, but although a great many people went to *see* it, few could be persuaded to ride in it— and none at all after a rail broke, and the engine overturned! So it had to be abandoned. It must have been quite ten years ago." He smiled, seeing the look of disappointment on Felix's countenance. "I'm sorry! Are you so interested in locomotives?"

"Yes—no—in *engines!*" stammered Felix. "Steam-power—c-compressed air—! Sir, have you seen the pneumatic lift at that foundry in Soho?"

"No," said his lordship. "Have you?"

"They wouldn't let me," replied Felix sadly. A thought occurred to him; and, fixing his ardent eyes on Alverstoke's face, he asked, with pent breath: "If you wished to see it—*could* you?"

Frederica, who had resumed her seat, said: "No, no, Felix! Lord Alverstoke does *not* wish to! You mustn't plague him to take you there!"

She was right: Alverstoke had not the remotest desire to inspect a pneumatic lift, but he found himself unable to resist the pleading look in the eyes raised so hopefully to his. He sat down again, smiling a little ruefully, and replied: "I expect I could. But you must tell me more about it!"

At this, Jessamy, well-aware of what would be the outcome of such an invitation, directed an anguished glance at Frederica, but although her eyes twinkled responsively she made no attempt to silence her small brother.

It might have been a task beyond her power. It was seldom that Felix met with encouragement to expatiate on a subject which few people understood, and most thought boring. His eyes brightening, he dragged up a chair, and tried to explain the principles governing pneumatic lifts. From there it was a small step to the pattern-shop engine, which was driven by air from the blowing-machine in the same foundry; and within a very short space of time Alverstoke was being battered by oscillating cylinders, piston-rods, cross-tails, valve-gears, and blast-pipes. Since Felix's understanding of these mysteries was naturally imperfect he was somewhat incoherent; and his thirst for knowledge led him to bombard Alverstoke with questions, few of which his lordship could answer satisfactorily. However, he had just enough grasp of the subject to enable him to avoid revolting Felix by posing counter-questions betraying the abysmal ignorance which, in that young gentleman's opinion, rendered his brothers and sisters contemptible, and to promote him from the status of an irrelevant visitor to that of prime favourite. He was the most intelligent auditor Felix had encountered: a regular right one, who could even be pardoned for saying, apologetically: "You know, Felix, I know more about horses than engines!"

This confession, dimming his lustre a trifle in Felix's eyes, instantly raised him in Jessamy's esteem. Jessamy demanded to know whether the turn-out he had noticed in the street, and which he described as having a lot of *sort* about it, belonged to his lordship; and, upon learning that it did, swept his junior aside, and engaged the Marquis in a discussion of the points to be looked for in prime carriage-horses.

Had it been suggested to the Marquis that he should spend half-an-hour with two schoolboys, he would have excused himself without a moment's hesitation. It was rarely that boredom did not overcome him in any company, but he was not bored. The only son of ceremonious parents, and the youngest of their progeny, he had no experience of family-life as it was enjoyed by the Merrivilles; and since his nephews, produced, when children, in their best clothes for his inspection, and warned of retribution if they did not mind their manners, had appeared to him to be as dull-witted as they were inarticulate, he was agreeably surprised by the young Merrivilles. His sisters might not have approved of their frank, easy ways, or of the total want of diffidence which they considered proper in school-boys, but he thought them a well-mannered and refreshing pair, and encouraged them with a tolerance which would have astonished those who were best acquainted with him.

He liked them, but there was a limit to his endurance, and when Felix, elbowing Jessamy out of the conversation, sought enlightenment on tubular boilers, recoil-engines and screw-propellers, he laughed, and got up, saying: "My dear boy, if you want to know about steamboats, take a trip down the Thames—don't ask me!" He turned towards Frederica, but before he could take his leave of her the door opened, and two ladies entered the room. He looked round, and the words of farewell died on his lips.

Both ladies wore walking-dresses, but there the resemblance between them ended. One was a gaunt female, of uncertain age and forbidding aspect; the other was the most ravishing girl his lordship, for all his wide experience, had ever laid eyes on. He realized that he was looking at Miss Charis Merriville, and that his secretary had not overrated her beauty.

From her shining head of golden curls to her little arched feet, neatly shod in kid boots, she presented a picture to take any man's breath away. Her figure was elegant; her ankles well-turned; her complexion had inspired several admirers to liken it to damask roses, or to ripe peaches; her tender mouth was exquisitely curved; her nose, escaping the aquiline, was straight, with delicately carved nostrils; and her eyes, which gazed innocently upon the world, were of a heavenly blue, and held an expression of candour, and the hint of a wistful smile. She wore a modest bonnet with a curtailed poke; and her dress was concealed by an azure blue kerseymere pelisse. The Marquis's hand groped instinctively for his quizzing-glass; and Frederica, observing this with sisterly satisfaction, introduced him to her aunt.

Miss Seraphina Winsham, having had the introduction repeated to her in stentorian accents by her nephews, subjected his lordship to a hostile stare, and uttered, repulsively: "I daresay!" She than added: "Oh, go away, do!" but as this was apparently addressed to Lufra, who was frisking about her, his lordship stood his ground. The slight bow he made won no other response than a curt nod, and an even more repelling stare. Miss Winsham, informing Frederica darkly that it was just as she had expected, stalked out of the room.

"Oh, dear!" said Frederica. "She's in one of her twitty moods! What has put her all on end, Charis? Oh, forgive me!—Lord Alverstoke—my sister!"

Charis smiled at his lordship, and gave him her hand. "How do you do? It was a *very* civil young man, Frederica, in Hookham's Library, who got a book down from the shelf for me, because I couldn't quite reach it. He was most obliging, and even dusted it with his handkerchief before he gave it to me; but my aunt thought him a coxcomb. And they were unable to supply us with *Ormond,* so I brought away the *Knight of St John* instead, which I daresay we shall like quite as well."

These words were spoken in a soft, placid voice; and the Marquis, under whose critical eyes the beauties of many seasons had passed, noted with approval that this one, the most stunning he had yet beheld, used no arts to attract, but, on the contrary, seemed to be unconscious of her charms. As one who had figured for years as the most brilliant catch on the Matrimonial Market, he was accustomed to meet with every artifice designed to ensnare him; and it was with approbation that he recognized the younger Miss Merriville's unconcern. He asked her how she liked London; she replied that she liked it very well; but her attention was otherwhere, and she made no effort to pursue this opening, saying instead, in mildly reproachful accents: "Oh, Felix-love, you've torn a button from your coat!"

"Oh, botheration!" responded Felix, hunching an impatient shoulder. "It don't signify!"

"Oh, no, not a bit!" she agreed. "Frederica made the tailor supply us with another set, don't you recall? I'll sew one on for you in a trice. Only come with me! you can't go about the town looking like a shag-rag, now, can you?"

It was evident that the youngest Merriville saw no objection to presenting himself to the town in this guise; but equally evident was his acceptance of his elder sister's authority, when he received, in answer to his glance of entreaty, a decided nod. He said sulkily: "Oh, very well!" but, before suffering himself to be led away by Charis, took his leave of the Marquis, and said eagerly: "And you will take me to Soho, won't you, sir?"

"If I don't, my secretary shall," replied Alverstoke.

"Oh! Well—Well, thank you, sir! Only it would be better if you came with me *yourself!*" urged Felix.

"Better for whom?" demanded his lordship involuntarily.

"Me," replied Felix, with the utmost candour. "I daresay they would show *you* anything you wanted to see, on account of your being a—a second-best nobleman, which I know you are, because it says, in a book I found, that Marquises come directly after Dukes, so—"

But at this point his disgusted brother thrust him out of the room, pausing only, before following him, to offer Alverstoke a dignified apology for his childish want of conduct. As Lufra followed close on his heels, and Charis, bestowing a valedictory smile on Alverstoke, had already departed, the Marquis was left alone with his hostess.

She said thoughtfully: "As a matter of fact, I fancy it *would* be better if you took him to that place yourself. He is a very enterprising boy, you know, and there's never any saying what he may take it into his head to do."

"Charles will know how to keep him in order," he replied indifferently.

She looked doubtful, but said no more. It was ap-

parent to her that his lordship had fallen into a mood
of abstraction. He was staring unseeingly at the opposite wall, an odd smile playing about the corners of
his mouth. It grew, and he suddenly laughed, under
his breath, saying: "By God, I'll do it!"

"Do what?" demanded Frederica.

He had evidently forgotten her presence. Her voice
brought his eyes round to her face, but instead of answering her he asked abruptly: "What are they doing
here, those brothers of yours? They should be at
school!"

"Well, in some ways I think you may be right," she
agreed. "Papa, however, never entertained the idea of
sending any of his sons to school. He himself was
educated at home, you know. That, of course, may
not seem to you a very good reason for pursuing the
same course with the boys—and, to own the truth, it
doesn't seem so to me either—but one ought not to be
unjust, and it *would* be unjust to assume that poor
Papa thought that his—his *errors* were due to his up-
bringing. And I don't know that they were," she added
reflectively. "The Merrivilles have always had a tendency towards volatility."

"Have they indeed?" he returned, a satirical curl to
his lips. "Is a tutor employed to instruct Jessamy and
Felix, then?"

"Oh, yes, *scores* of tutors!" responded Miss Merriville. She perceived a startled look in his lordship's
eye, and hastened to reassure him. "Oh, not all at once!
One after the other, you understand! You can't think
how vexatious! The thing is that if they are old the boys
don't like it, because they can't enter into their sports;
and if they are young they only want to stay for a
month or two while they wait to take up a post in a
school, or at one of the Universities, or some such thing.
And, which is even more provoking, they always fall
desperately in love with Charis!"

"That I can readily believe."

She nodded, but sighed also. "Yes, and the mischief is
that she *cannot* bring herself to repulse them. She has a
fatally tender heart, and can't bear to give pain to anyone—particularly not to people like poor Mr Griff, who

was very awkward, and shy, and had red hair, and an Adam's apple which bobbed up and down in his throat. He was the last tutor. Just at present the boys are enjoying a holiday, but when they have seen all the sights in London, and have grown a little more accustomed, I must engage another tutor for them. But Jessamy is very good, and studies for two hours every day, because he is determined to go up to Oxford when he is eighteen, a year before Harry did."

"Is Harry at Oxford now?"

"Yes, in his second year. Which is why it seemed to me to be just the moment to come to London for a year. It will do him a great deal of good to see something of the world before he is obliged to settle down at Graynard, don't you think? Besides, he will enjoy it excessively!"

"I've no doubt he will," said Alverstoke. He looked down at her, a glint in his eyes. "Meanwhile, we have to consider *your* situation. I have the intention of giving a ball within the next few weeks, to mark the come-out of one of my nieces. You and your sister will appear at it, to be presented to the ton by *my* sister, and you will all of you doubtless receive invitations to attend a number of other such parties, to which my sister will escort you. Ah! *and* my cousin, Mrs Dauntry, who also has a daughter to bring out at my ball!"

Frederica's lips quivered; mischief danced in her eyes; she said: "I am very much obliged to you! What a fortunate circumstance it was that Charis should have come home in time to make your acquaintance!"

"Yes, wasn't it?" he retorted. "I might not otherwise have realized what a shocking thing it would be to keep such a diamond in the undistinguished shade!"

"Exactly so! And nothing could be better than for her to appear at your ball. I am *truly* very grateful to you, but there is not the least necessity to invite me as well."

"Are you proposing to go into seclusion?"

"No, but—"

"Then there is every necessity for you to appear at my ball. I am strongly of the opinion, too, that your aunt should be prevailed upon to accompany you. Since

you are not living under my sister's roof, it would
seem strangely particular if no respectable guardian
were to be seen. Her eccentricity need not trouble
you—"

"It doesn't!" interjected Frederica.

"—for eccentrics are all the rage," he continued.

"Well, it wouldn't trouble me if they were not. But I
can't help thinking that your sister may not agree to
this scheme."

The glint in his eyes became more pronounced. "She
will!" he said.

"You can't know that!" Frederica argued.

"Believe me, I do know it."

"No you don't, for you've only this instant thought
of it yourself," said Frederica bluntly. "It's all very well
to be so top-lofty, but unless your niece is also a
diamond, as you phrase it, Charis will quite outshine
her! What mother would consent to bring out her
daughter in Charis's company?"

A smile flickered on his mouth, but that was the
only sign vouchsafed her that he was attending to her.
He took a pinch of snuff, and said, as he shut his box:
"I'll accept the relationship between us—cousin!—but
it's not enough. You suggested that I should pose as
your guardian: very well! let us say that your father
commended you to my care. Now, why should he have
done so?"

"Well, he did say that you were the best of his
family," offered Frederica.

"That won't fadge! My sisters, I'll go bail, know as
well as I do how remote is the connection between us!
Some better reason must be found to satisfy their curiosity."

Entering into the spirit of this, Frederica said: "Papa
once did you a—a signal service, which you have never
till now been able to repay!"

"*What* service?" asked his lordship sceptically.

"That," returned Frederica, with aplomb, "is something you prefer not to divulge—*particularly* to your
sisters!"

"Oh, very good!" he approved, the disquieting glint
in his eyes yielding to genuine amusement. "I feel my-

self to be under an obligation to him, and for that reason have assumed the guardianship of his children." He caught the speculative gleam in her eyes, and his brows rose. "Well?"

"I was merely thinking—cousin!—that if you mean to become our guardian it will be more proper for *you* to find a suitable tutor for Jessamy and for Felix than for *me* to do so!"

"I know nothing about such matters—and my guardianship will be quite unofficial!"

"You may depend upon *that!*" said Frederica. "But I see no reason why you shouldn't be useful!"

"May I remind you that I have consented to introduce you to the ton? There my usefulness will stop!"

"No, how can it? If you mean to set it about that you think yourself in honour bound to protect us, you must do *something* besides inviting Charis and me to a ball in your house! To be sure, I am very grateful to you for that—though you wouldn't have done it if Charis hadn't bowled you out!—but—"

"Charis," he interrupted, "is a very beautiful girl— possibly the most beautiful girl I have yet encountered —but if you imagine that I shall invite her to the ball because I lost my heart to her you are wide of the mark, Cousin Frederica!"

"I must say I hope you won't do that," she replied, looking a little troubled. "You are much too old for her, you know!"

"Very true!" he retorted. "She being much too young for me!"

"Of course she is!" Frederica agreed. "So why did you decide suddenly to invite us?"

"That, cousin, I do not propose to tell you."

She considered him, a gathering frown on her brow, her unwavering gaze searching his face. She was puzzled by him. She had not, at the outset, been favourably impressed: his figure was good, his tailoring exquisite, and his countenance, though not handsome, distinguished; but she had thought that his manner held too much height, and that his eyes were cold, and unpleasantly cynical. Even his smile had seemed to be contemptuous, curling his lips, but leaving his eyes as

hard as steel. Then she had said something that had
appealed to his sense of humour, and the metallic gleam
had vanished in a smile of real amusement. Not only
did it warm his eyes, but it transformed him in a flash
from the aristocrat of haughty composure to an easy-
mannered gentleman, with a strong sense of the
ridiculous, and considerable charm of manner. Within
minutes he had pokered up again; yet there was not a
grain of starch in him when Felix had bounced into the
room; he had answered all his and Jessamy's questions
with patience and good-humour; and had looked upon
both boys with kindness. He had borne the cavalier
treatment meted out to him by Miss Winsham with indifference; and the gaze which he had fixed on Charis
had been deeply appreciative. Frederica entertained no
doubt that it was admiration for Charis that had caused
him to change his mind, but what it was that had
brought the malicious glint back into his eyes she could
not guess.

She looked doubtfully at him. His brows rose; he
said: "Well?"

"I ought to have been a widow!" she exclaimed in a
vexed tone. "Yes, and if I had a particle of sense I
would have been!"

The expression she mistrusted vanished; his eyes
held only laughter. "You will be!" he assured her.

"That's of no use!" she answered impatiently. "If I
were a widow *now*——" She broke off, quick merriment
in her face. "Well, of all the abominable things to say
—! I do have the family in charge—that's because I'm
the eldest—but I'm not *tyrannical,* or—or vixenish! At
least, I don't *think* I am!"

"No, no!" he said soothingly. "I am persuaded you
handle the reins in excellent form. I wish you will tell me
how, if you had had a particle of sense, you could have
become a widow? Or why you should wish to: have
you a husband concealed about you?"

"Of course I haven't! I meant only that I ought to
have pretended I was a widow. Then I might have
chaperoned Charis myself, and you need not have
dragged your sister into it."

"Oh, I haven't the least objection to doing that!" he said.

"Yes, but she may object very much! After all, she isn't even acquainted with us!"

"That shall be rectified." He held out his hand. "I must go now, but you shall hear from me within a day or two. Oh, pray don't pull the bell! Recollect that I've become a member of the family, and don't stand on points with me! I'll usher myself out."

This, however, he was not obliged to do, since Felix was lying in wait for him in the hall, and escorted him out to his carriage in a very civil manner which had its root in his determination to wring from him the promise of a visit to the foundry in Soho.

"Have no fear!" said his lordship. "The matter shall be attended to."

"Yes, sir—thank you! But you'll go with me yourself, won't you? Not your secretary?"

"My dear boy, why should I? I daresay Mr Trevor knows far more about these mysteries than I do."

"Yes, but—Oh, *do* come yourself, sir! It would make it first-rate!"

The Marquis believed himself to be hardened against flattery. He thought that he had experienced every variety, but he discovered that he was mistaken: the blatantly worshipful look in the eyes of a twelve-year-old, anxiously raised to his, was new to him, and it pierced his defences. He was capable of giving the coolest of set-downs to any gushing female; and the advances of toadeaters he met with the most blistering of snubs; but even as he realized how intolerably bored he would be in Soho he found himself quite unable to snub his latest and most youthful admirer. It would be like kicking a confiding puppy.

So Master Felix Merriville, presently racing up the stairs again to the drawing-room, was able to inform Frederica triumphantly that all was right: "Cousin Alverstoke" was going to take him to see the pneumatic lift *himself,* and, further, that he was a regular trump.

V

Upon the following day Mr Charles Trevor sustained a shock. Not twenty minutes after the Marquis's agent-in-chief had deposited on his desk a mass of reports and accounts which it was Mr Trevor's enviable duty to reduce to such proportions as would be tolerable to their noble employer, the Marquis strolled into his office, saying: "Good-morning, Charles. Do you know of any foundries in Soho?"

"*Foundries,* sir?" said Mr Trevor, stunned by so unprecedented an enquiry.

"Something to do with the casting of metals, I fancy," explained the Marquis, levelling his glass at the litter of papers on the desk. "Good God, Charles, why have you never told me how overworked you are? What, in the name of abomination, is all this?"

"Only quarter-day, sir!" said Charles, laughing. "Coleford has been with me—knowing that if he were to give these papers to your lordship you wouldn't read a word of them! But—*foundries?* Do you—do you wish for information about them?" An idea occurred to him; his eyes kindled, and he asked: "Is there to be some question raised? Do you mean to speak on it, sir?"

"Really, Charles, what extraordinary things you do ask me!" said his lordship. "My dear boy, *is* it likely that I should feel the smallest desire to do so?"

"No, sir," responded Mr Trevor frankly. "Indeed, I didn't know you were interested in such matter!"

The Marquis sighed, and shook his head. "Alas, I have frequently suspected that you believe me to be a very frippery fellow!"

"Yes, but—I mean, no, of course I don't, sir!" said Mr Trevor, correcting himself in a hurry.

"You lie, Charles: you do! And you are perfectly

right," said his lordship mournfully. "I have no interest in foundries. However, it is never too late to mend, and I am now about to cultivate an interest in them. Or am I? Now I come to think of it, it isn't foundries, but pneumatic lifts. Do you know anything about pneumatic lifts?"

"No, sir, I don't. But I *do* know when you are roasting me!"

"You wrong me, Charles. Somewhere in Soho there is a foundry which contains a pneumatic lift. I wish to see it. Tear yourself away from all these deplorable documents, and arrange it for me, dear boy!"

"Yes, sir—certainly!" said Mr Trevor mechanically.

"I was persuaded I might rely upon you. I own, it disappoints me a trifle to find you ignorant on the subject of pneumatic lifts, but perhaps you have instead made a study of boilers and propellers?"

Mr Trevor, eyeing him in speechless astonishment, shook his head.

"Come, come, Charles!" said his lordship reprovingly. "This must be set right! How can you expect to make your mark in the world if you make no attempt to keep abreast of the times? You shall take a trip down river on a steamboat, to learn about these things."

His much-tried secretary said roundly: "Much obliged to you, sir, but I'm not an engineer, and I don't wish to learn about boilers! And as for going on a steamboat, I'll be da—I'd as lief not!"

"Well, I'm not an engineer either," said his lordship. "And, like you, I'll be damned if I go on a steamboat. But I do hope *you* won't be, for something tells me that it will shortly be one of your duties."

Half-laughing and wholly bewildered, Charles said: "But why, sir? I know you're funning, but—"

"No such thing! When you have met my latest acquaintance—ah, a young cousin of mine!—you will perceive that this is no matter for idle joking."

"Latest—a *cousin?*" stammered Charles. "Sir, I beg pardon, but what *can* you mean?"

The Marquis, pausing in the doorway, looked back, to say, with one of his quizzical smiles: "You should know, my dear boy: it was you who edged me on to visit his sisters. So, if you find yourself accompanying my cousin Felix on a steamboat cruise, you will have come by your just deserts. But you were quite right about Charis: a pearl past price!"

The door closed behind him, and Mr Trevor was left to make what he could of this. It was not very much, for while he could readily believe that the Marquis, struck by the younger Miss Merriville's beauty, had formed the intention of making her the object of one of his fits of gallantry, he could not, by any stretch of his imagination, believe that he would go to the length of providing for her brother's entertainment merely to fix his interest with her. He seldom found it necessary to exert particular pains to attach an attractive female, since most of them, thought Charles disapprovingly, were on the scramble for him. If he did receive a rebuff he shrugged, and passed on, for he flirted for the sake of amusement, and any tendre that he might feel was neither lasting nor profound. As for putting himself out, as he now seemed to be doing, that was so very unlike him that Charles, who believed himself to be pretty well acquainted with his lordship, had to own that he was baffled to account for it. It did not occur to him that his lordship had yielded to the blandishments of a persistent urchin; and if such a notion had crossed his mind he would have dismissed it as an absurdity.

Meanwhile, the Marquis, driving himself in his curricle, was on his way to Grosvenor Place. He arrived there to find his sister's landaulet drawn up outside her house, and his sister, accompanied by her two elder daughters, on the point of stepping into it. "In the nick of time, I perceive!" he remarked. "Delay your departure for five minutes, Louisa!"

Lady Buxted, in whose breast her defeat at his hands still rankled, bade him a cold good-morning, and added that she had not the least guess what could have brought him to visit her.

His groom having run to the horses' heads, Alverstoke flung off the rug that covered his legs, and descended lightly from the curricle, saying: "How should you?" He looked her over critically. "Accept my compliments! that's a good rig, and I like your neck-ruff."

Lady Buxted might deplore her frivolous brother's à la modality, but she could not help preening herself a little. It was not often that her taste won his approbation. She touched the little ruff of goffered lawn which supported her chin, and said: "My *fraise,* do you mean? I'm indeed flattered to meet with *your* approval, Alverstoke!"

He nodded, as though he took this for granted, but addressed himself to his nieces. "You two—Jane, and —Maria, is it?—wait for your mother in the carriage! I shan't keep her many minutes."

Lady Buxted, by no means relishing this cavalier treatment of her daughters, was torn between a desire to send her brother about his business, and a rampant curiosity. Curiosity won; and she turned to go back into the house, saying, however, that five minutes were all she could spare. He vouchsafed no response, but followed her up the steps, and into the dining-room. Lady Buxted did not invite him to sit down. "Well, what is it?" she asked. "I have a great deal of shopping to do, and—"

"More, even, than you bargained for, I daresay," he interrupted. "Take that eldest girl of yours to your dressmaker, and tell her to make a ball-dress for her! And, for the lord's sake, Louisa, don't let it be white, or pale blue, or pink! She's as bran-faced as ever she was, and the only thing for it is to rig her out in amber, or jonquil, or straw!"

The unexpected hope which this command rekindled in Lady Buxted's breast made it easy for her to overlook the animad-version on Miss Buxted's freckles. Surprise almost took her breath away, but she managed to utter: "Alverstoke! Do you mean—*can* you mean—that you *will* give a ball for her?"

"Yes, that's what I mean," he replied. He added: "Upon terms, dear Louisa!"

She scarcely heeded this rider, but exclaimed: "Oh, my dear Vernon, I was positive I could depend on you! I knew you were bantering me! What a wicked, freakish wretch you are! But I shan't scold you, for I know it is just your way! Oh, Jane will be cast into transports!"

"Oblige me, then, by telling her nothing about it until I'm out of reach!" said his lordship acidly. "And do, for God's sake, abate your own ecstasies! I prefer your jobations to your raptures! Sit down, and I'll tell you what I want you to do!"

She looked for a moment as though she was on the brink of answering him in kind, but only for a moment. The prospect of bringing Jane out at a magnificent ball for which she would not be called upon to disburse as much as a halfpenny made it easy for her to ignore his lordship's incivility. She sat down, throwing open her olive-brown pelisse. "To be sure! How much we have to discuss! Now, when shall it be? I am inclined to think that it would be best to fix on a date at the beginning of the season."

"That's fortunate: it will be next month. Three weeks from now, let us say."

"April! But you cannot have considered! May is the month for the really tonnish parties!"

"No, is it indeed?" he mocked. "And does it occur to you that May is already overcrowded with balls, routs, and assemblies of every description?"

"There is that, of course," she agreed, frowning over it. "But in only three weeks the season will barely have begun!"

"It will begin, then, at Alverstoke House," he replied coolly. "And if you imagine, Louisa, that we shall find ourselves thin of company, let me reassure you!"

She was well aware that he was one of the leaders of fashion, but the top-loftiness of this remark made her long to give him a set-down. She refrained, saying instead: "I hardly know how I shall contrive! All the arrangements—"

"Don't give them a thought! They won't fall on you. Let Charles Trevor have a list of those you wish to be invited: that is all you have to do."

She said, with a touch of asperity: "Since the ball is for my daughter, I assume I shall be the hostess!"

He regarded her thoughtfully. "Why, yes! You

may be the hostess, but the ball won't be wholly for Jane's benefit. Lucretia will bring her elder girl to it, and—"

"Chloë!" she ejaculated, stiffening. "Do you dare to tell me, Alverstoke, that I owe this—this change in your sentiments to That Woman's cajolery?"

"No, you owe it to an unforeseen and damnably troublesome circumstance. Do you recall Fred Merriville?"

She stared at him. "Fred Merriville? Pray, what has he to say to anything?"

"The poor fellow has nothing to say: he's dead, alas!"

Her colour was rising ominously. "I beg you won't try to play off your tricks on me, Alverstoke! I'm sure it's nothing to me whether he's dead or alive!"

"Unfortunately it has a great deal to do with me. He consigned his family to my—er—protection. When I tell you that there are no fewer than five of them—"

"Do you mean that he made you their guardian?" she interrupted.

"No, thank God! it's not as bad as that. He commended them to my care. Two of them are of age, but—"

"For heaven's sake!" she exclaimed. "He must have been out of his senses! You, of all persons! What in the world made him do so?"

"Well," said his lordship, succumbing to the promptings of his particular devil, "he thought I was the best of my family."

"Oh, *did* he?" snapped Lady Buxted. "No doubt! It is precisely what he *would* think, for a more rackety, ramshackle, care-for-nobody I hope I may never see! *I* remember him! A handsome ne'er-do-well! What he must have cost his parents I shudder to think! And, to crown all, when they had contrived to arrange an advantageous marriage for him, what must he do but run off with the daughter of some paltry provincial! They washed their hands of him, and I don't wonder at it. Not that I was ever acquainted with them, but it was one of the on-dits of the town. I believe he came into the property later, and I don't doubt he gamed that

away too. As for leaving his family to your guardianship, it's of a piece with the rest! I strongly advise you
to repudiate them!"

"Nothing would give me greater pleasure, but I can't,
in honour, do that," he answered smoothly. "I owed
him a debt, you see, which I never found the opportunity to repay."

"*You* owed *Merriville* money? Fiddle! He never had
sixpence to bless himself with, while as for *you*—"

He interposed, and in accents of distaste. "You
should have married a merchant, Louisa. I feel sure he
would have admired you: I do not! Do you never
think of anything but money? Is it quite beyond your
power to understand that there are more important
obligations than monetary ones?"

Her eyes shifted under the contempt in his, but she
said angrily: "Yes, it's all very well for you to talk in
that imposing style, as rich as you are! If you stood in
my shoes, you would sing a different tune!"

"Don't pitch that gammon to me!" he said. "You
forget that I was one of Buxted's executors! He left
you very well to pass, my dear sister. No, don't fly
into one of your pelters! Really, I didn't come to break
a straw with you! Indeed, I'm willing—if you lend me
your aid in the matter of the Merrivilles—to grease the
wheels of Jane's come-out for you. I imagine you mean
to present her at one of the Drawing-rooms?"

These beautiful words checked Lady Buxted on the
brink of giving free expression to her wrath. They
could only mean that Alverstoke was prepared to de-
fray the shocking expense of a Court dress for his
niece. If he gave at all, he would give handsomely; and
her ladyship, doing some rapid calculations in her head,
realized that the cost of such a Court dress as she had
herself worn at her presentation could be made to
cover the additional expense of several crape and muslin dresses, suitable for a maiden to wear at Almack's,
in her first season. This reflection, though it did not
slay her resentment, made it possible for her to swallow
the unwise words hovering on her tongue, and to say,
with mere pettishness: "I can't conceive what Merriville can have done to put you in his debt!"

"That, Louisa, is something I prefer not to divulge," said the Marquis. Mindful of his instructions, and with a demon of mischief lurking in his eyes, he added: "Particularly not to my sisters!"

She was not perceptive, but it was perhaps fortunate that she was not looking at him. All she said was: "I collect he helped you out of some disgraceful scrape. So now you feel obliged to further his children's interests! It must be the first time in your life you have recognized *any* obligation! To be sure, one might have supposed that there were others, nearer to you, and with greater claims upon you, who would have excited your benevolence— *How* many children did you say he had?"

"Five. Three sons and two daughters—orphans, residing at the moment in Upper Wimpole Street, in the care of their aunt, who, I understand, assumed this charge upon the death of Merriville's wife, some ten years ago. The eldest son is of age, and at Oxford; but it is his sister who—unless I very much mistake the matter!—rules the roost! I think she is some four-and-twenty years of age, and—"

"Means to hang on to your sleeve! I wish you joy of your *obligation!* Do you mean to support *all* the family?"

"I don't mean to support *any* of the family, nor have I been asked to do so. You can't imagine, Louisa, how refreshing I find this! With the boys I have nothing to do. All that Miss Merriville requires of me is that I should render what assistance I can to introduce her, and her sister, to the ton."

She was eyeing him narrowly. "Indeed! No doubt Miss Merriville is very beautiful? But I need not ask!"

"Quite a well-looking young woman, but I should hardly describe her as beautiful," he replied indifferently. "That don't signify: she's not on the catch for a husband. Her ambition is to achieve a respectable marriage for her sister, who is the prettier of the two. Whether she can contrive to do it I think doubtful, her fortune being small, but that's not my concern: my debt will have been discharged when I—with your assistance—have launched the pair of them into society."

"Pray, what do you expect *me* to do?" she demanded.

"Oh, nothing very arduous! You will introduce them at my ball, as our cousins, escort them to Almack's, when you take Jane there, and—"

"Almack's, indeed!" she exclaimed. "I wonder that you should not have warned your protégée that she is aiming at the moon! Or do *you* mean to procure cards for her, perhaps?"

This piece of heavy sarcasm glanced off his armour. "No, I couldn't. But you can, Louisa, with two bosom-bows amongst the patronesses—as you have so frequently informed me!"

"Procure cards for Fred Merriville's daughters? You are asking a great deal too much of me! A couple of penniless girls, living in Upper Wimpole Street, who are *not* our cousins! I think it the outside of enough that you should include them in a ball to mark Jane's come-out, and as for taking them to Almack's—No, Vernon! I don't wish to be disobliging, but—"

"My dear Louisa, say no more!" he interrupted, picking up his hat. "I wouldn't, for the world, ask you to do anything you dislike! Forget the whole affair—in fact, forget that I came to see you today! I'll take my leave of you now."

She started up, temper and alarm fighting for supremacy in her. "Wait, Alverstoke!"

"No, I've stayed too long already. Think of your daughters, left to kick their heels in the carriage!"

"That doesn't signify! But you must—"

"Well, it doesn't signify to me, I must confess. What does signify is the waste of my own time. I really can't be expected to spend the whole day on this tiresome business, so, if I want to see Lucretia before she retires to her sofa, to recruit her strength after the morning's exertions, I must go immediately."

She caught his arm, digging her fingers into it. "No! Vernon, if you *dare* to appoint That Woman as your hostess—!"

"Unhand me, sister!" he said flippantly. "I do dare, and such is my amazing mettle that your threats have no power to daunt me. By the way, why should they?"

"I would never forgive you! Never!" she declared.

"Only consider for a moment! What concern of mine are these wretched girls? Why should—"

"No concern at all," he replied, removing her clutch from his arm.

"I haven't even *met* them," she urged despairingly. "Oh, how detestable you are!"

He laughed. "Yes, but not bird-witted—as you are, Louisa! Come, now, make up your mind! Will you do as I ask, or will you not?"

She stared up into his face, trying to discover some sign of relenting in it. He was smiling, but she knew that smile. She said, rather grittily, but with dignity: "Naturally I am only too ready to do what I may to oblige you. Whether I can get tickets for Almack's for two girls of whom I know nothing—though if they are presentable I will endeavour to do so—"

"That's better!" he said, still smiling, but very much more pleasantly. "Rig Jane out in the first style of elegance, and send me a Dutch reckoning: I don't want to know the particulars. I'll bring Miss Merriville to visit you. I daresay you may like her: she doesn't want for sense—or determination! Don't neglect to send Charles that list!"

On this admonition he took his departure, revolving in his mind various stratagems whereby the younger Miss Merriville could be excluded from the forthcoming visit to Grosvenor Place without opposition from her masterful sister.

In the event, the problem was solved rather sooner than he had expected, and not by him. Providence, in the guise of the dog Lufra, brought Frederica to Alverstoke House two days later, unaccompanied by Charis, and at what his lordship, no early riser, considered to be an unseasonable hour.

Since Jessamy adhered strictly to his self-imposed rule of studying every morning, his sisters had taken it upon themselves to exercise Lufra in his stead. They took him for long walks, exploring London; and if he had not tugged so hard on the end of a leash, or had behaved with more circumspection when released from it, their enjoyment of these expeditions would have been unalloyed. Country-bred, they were accustomed to much longer walks than could be achieved in London; everything was new to them; and they sallied forth whenever the weather permitted, Frederica in charge of Lufra, and Charis armed with a Pocket Guide. They viewed, from outside, the edifices, monuments, and mansions to which this invaluable book directed them, even penetrating into the City, where they attracted much attention, but were never once accosted. Not the most impudent of coxcombs cared to approach two damsels accompanied by a large and shaggy dog, straining at his leash, and exhibiting between his panting jaws a set of splendid teeth.

But two days after Alverstoke's victorious engagement in Grosvenor Place Charis awoke with a sore throat and a tickling cough; and although she came down to breakfast she was speedily hustled back to bed, Miss Winsham declaring, at her third sneeze, that she had caught one of her feverish colds, and that unless she wished to succumb to an inflammation of the lungs, she would instantly retire to her bedchamber.

This she did; and while Miss Winsham, having ordered the cook to make a bread-pudding and some water-gruel, was preparing a saline draught for the sufferer, Frederica escaped from the house, knowing that if she told her aunt that she was going for her usual walk she would be obliged to endure a scold for thinking that she could behave as freely in London as in Herefordshire. Miss Winsham would certainly try to persuade her to take one of the maid-servants with her, or Felix; but as Frederica considered herself to be past the age when a chaperon was necessary, and had already discovered that London servants were by no means partial to long, brisk walks, she thought it prudent to slip away, telling no one but Buddle where she was going. Buddle shook his head, and tut-tutted; but beyond suggesting that Master Felix should accompany her he made no attempt to deter her. And as Felix had already wheedled her into giving him half-a-crown, which was the price of admission to Merlin's Mechanical Museum (open every day from eleven until three), his sister wisely declined to issue an invitation which he would certainly have refused.

Her destination was the Green Park. Neither she nor Charis had yet visited it, the Pocket Guide not deeming it worthy of more than a glancing reference. It did, indeed, describe in enthusiastic detail the Temple of Concord, erected there as part of the pageantry of the Peace celebrations in 1814, but as this temporary structure had been demolished, Charis thought, four years later, that the Green Park was hardly worth a visit.

But Frederica, undeterred by the Guide Book's tepid praise of the park's "several pleasant promenades," decided to take Lufra there for his walk, rather than to the more fashionable Hyde Park, where the saunterers were too much inclined to ogle fair pedestrians.

Towed through the streets by her canine friend, she reached the Bath gate in a somewhat heated condition, and was glad to be able to release him from the leash to which he showed no sign of growing accustomed. He bounded ahead, and began to quest to and fro, his plebeian tail carried on high, and his nose hopefully seeking the trail of a possible rabbit. When Frederica strolled round the reservoir at the north-east corner of the park, he brought her a likely stick, and invited her to throw it into the water for him to retrieve; but when she declined to take part in this sport he went off again, and was delighted to discover that the moving objects he had dimly perceived at some little distance away were three children, playing with a brightly coloured ball. He liked children, and he liked chasing after balls: he advanced upon the group, with his tail waving, and his ears expectantly cocked. He was a large dog, and his rapid descent upon the party proved too much for the fortitude of the youngest member, a small girl, who burst into a wail of fright, and fled to the protection of a nursemaid, who was enjoying a gossip with a friend in the lee of the shrubbery surrounding the Ranger's Lodge. Lufra was puzzled, but turned his attention to the younger of the two boys, who was holding the ball, and uttered an encouraging bark. Whereupon Master John, throwing manly pride to the winds, dropped the ball, and made off after his sister as fast as his fat little legs would carry him. The elder boy stood his ground, gritting his teeth. Lufra pounced on the ball, tossed it and caught it, and finally spat it out at this stalwart's feet. Master Frank let his breath go, and shouted after his juniors: "He only wants to play with us, you—you pudding-hearts!" He then, rather cautiously, ventured to pick up the ball, and hurled it as far as he could. This was not very far, but Lufra, taking the will for the deed, dashed after it, and brought it back to him. Master Frank, much emboldened, gave him a shy pat. Lufra licked his chin, and a promising friendship was on the point of being inaugurated when the nursemaid shrieked to Master Frank not to touch that nasty, fierce dog. Master John, having tripped and fallen on his face, set up a bellow; and by the time Frederica came running up an animated and noisy scene was in full swing, the nursemaid shrilly scolding, the two younger children crying, and Master Frank rebelliously refusing to abandon his low-born playmate.

Peremptorily called to heel, Lufra came, bringing the ball with him. Frederica took it from him, and cut short the unbridled complaint of the nursemaid by saying in the voice of one who had for years ruled a large household: "That will do! You forget yourself!" She then looked at Master John, and said: "I hope you didn't hurt yourself when you fell down? Of course, *I* know you wouldn't cry because my dog tried to play with you, for I can see that you are quite a *big* boy, but do, pray, shake hands with him, to show that you didn't mean to be uncivil when you ran away from him! Sit, Luff, and give a paw!"

Obedient to the pressure of her hand, Lufra did sit, and obligingly waved one of his forelegs. Master John's loud laments ceased abruptly. He stared in astonishment at Lufra. *"Doggie* shake hands?" he demanded incredulously.

"To be sure he does!"

"With me!" said Master Frank. *"I'm* not afraid of him!"

Stung, Master John declared that Doggie did not wish to shake hands with him; and by the time this question of precedence had been settled, and both boys had solemnly clasped Lufra's paw, Miss Caroline was jealously claiming her right to share the honour. Frederica then gave the ball back to Master Frank, and parted from the family, pursued by a darkling look from their attendant, and by the children's adjurations to bring Doggie back next day.

She went on her way, unperturbed by the incident, which merely confirmed her in the belief that London-children, acquainted only with the lap-dogs cosseted by their mamas, were much to be pitied; and it was not until she had rounded the shrubbery shielding the Ranger's Lodge that it was suddenly and forcibly borne in upon her that the Pocket Guide had betrayed her: it had made no mention of a small herd of cows, with their attendant milkmaids, which (as she later discovered) were a well-known feature of the park. Not only did they provide urban eyes with a charmingly rural picture, but their attendants, all attired in the conventional garb of milkmaids, dispensed glasses of warm milk to anyone prepared to disimburse the very moderate sum demanded for the privilege of drinking milk fresh from the cow.

Too late did she realize the treachery of the Pocket Guide: Lufra, ranging ahead of her, perceived the herd before she did, and stopped for an instant in his tracks, his ears on the prick, and his bristles rising. The matron of the herd, standing within a few feet of him, lowered her head menacingly; and Lufra, either unable or unwilling to distinguish between the males and the females of the species, uttered a blood-curdling sound, midway between a bark and a growl, and launched himself into battle.

VI

A lesser woman would have fled at this stage, abandoning Lufra to his fate, for the ensuing scene was truly appalling. To the accompaniment of screams from milkmaids, nursemaids, and several elderly ladies, Lufra committed the enormous crime of stampeding a herd of milch-cows. He did not, indeed, repeat the heroic act which had earned him his name, but, finding that the cows fled before him, he scattered them, enjoying the only sport which had so far been offered him in London.

No thought of escaping so much as crossed Frederica's mind, but by the time she had managed, with the help of the head cowman and two of the Deputy-Ranger's menials, to catch and to secure the wholly unrepentant hound, she knew that her case was desperate. All about her was a scene of carnage; one of the elderly ladies had succumbed to hysterics; another was demanding that a constable should be instantly sent for; the cowman was calling down curses on her head; and the park's custodians were declaring their fixed resolve to impound Lufra, pending his certain execution. To make matters worse, the nurse with whose charges Lufra had disported himself came hurrying up, attracted by the commotion, and lost no time in deposing that he had savagely rushed upon the children, frightening the poor little dears out of their wits, stealing their ball, and causing Master John to fall flat on his face grazing his hands and soiling his nankeens.

"Fudge!" said Frederica scornfully.

Neither the cowman nor the park-keepers paid much heed to the nursemaid's testimony. The cowman was only concerned with his cattle; and the park-keepers, observing the flattened ears and waving tail with which Lufra greeted his youthful friends, did not for a moment suppose him to be savage. They recognized in him all the signs of an overgrown and outrageous mongrel, young enough to be ripe for mischief; and, in other circumstances, they would have taken a lenient view of his misdemeanour. But the rules governing London parks were strict; the hatchet-faced old griffin who was adjuring them to summon a constable, her weaker sister who was still in the throes of nervous spasms, various citizens who declared that such dangerous brutes ought never to be permitted to roam at large, and a bevy of nursemaids unanimous in demanding vengeance on the wild animal which had shattered for ever the nerves of their gently-born charges, prompted them to take an extreme view of the case. Confronted on the one hand with a number of persons bent on reporting the incident to the Deputy-Ranger, and on the other by a delinquent mongrel owned by a Young Person unattended by a footman, or a maid, they saw their duty clear before them: Lufra, the elder of the two awfully told Frederica, must be handed over to them, to be kept in custody until a magistrate should pronounce his fate.

Lufra, misliking both his tone and his purposeful advance, stopped panting, and rose, bristling, and intimating by a warning growl that any attempt to attack Frederica would be undertaken at the park-keeper's peril: a warlike display which excited the cowman to demand his summary execution, and caused the park-keeper to order Frederica to "bring that dawg along o' me!"

Amongst the assembled persons none but the cowman knew better than Frederica how unpardonable was Lufra's crime. One glance at this individual's inflamed countenance was enough to convince her that an appeal addressed to him would be waste of breath. Inwardly quaking, she said: "Take care! This dog belongs to the Marquis of Alverstoke! He is *extremely* valuable, and if anything were to happen to him his lordship would be very angry indeed!"

The younger park-keeper, who had formed his own, not inexpert, opinion of Lufra's lineage, said bluntly: "Gammon! No Markiss never bought '*im*! 'E'd be dear at a grig! 'E's a mongrel, that's what 'e is!"

"A *mongrel?*" exclaimed Frederica. "Let me tell you that he is a pure-bred Barcelona collie, brought to England at—at *enormous* expense! I am sorry that he should have chased the cows, but—but he was merely trying to *herd* them! The breed is used for that purpose in Spain, and—and he is not yet accustomed to English cows!"

"Trying to *herd* them?" gasped the cowman. "I never did, not in all my life! Why, you're as bad as he is!"

The younger park-keeper had no hesitation in endorsing this verdict. He said that Miss was coming it too strong, adding that while he knew nothing about Barcelona collies he did know a mongrel when he saw one. He also said, sticking to his original point, that, in his opinion, no Markiss never bought such a dog as Lufra.

"Indeed!" said Frederica. "And, pray, are you acquainted with my cousin, the Marquis of Alverstoke?"

"What impudence!" ejaculated the hatchet-faced lady. "Calling yourself a Marquis's cousin, and jauntering about the town alone! A likely story!"

After a good deal of argument, during which the younger park-keeper supported the hatchet-faced lady, the cowman said (several times) that Marquis or no Marquis any damage done to his cows must be paid for, and the elder park-keeper temporized, a sturdy citizen in a snuff-coloured frock-coat, proffered the suggestion that the Marquis should be applied to for corroboration of Miss's story.

"A very excellent notion!" declared Frederica warmly. "Let us go to his house immediately! It is quite close, in Berkeley Square."

Left to himself, the elder park-keeper would at this stage have abandoned the affair. If the young lady was willing to seek out the Marquis it seemed to him to prove that she really was his cousin; and although he knew that this did not affect the issue he was very unwilling to proceed further in the matter. Properly speaking, of course, the Marquis—*if* he was the dog's owner —was liable for a fine, let alone what Mr Beal's head cowman might claim from him by way of damages; but when you were dealing with lords you wanted to be careful. The younger park-keeper, who was the recipient of this confidence, became suddenly thoughtful; but the cowman grimly accepted Frederica's invitation, saying that he would have his rights even if the dog belonged to the Queen—meaning no disrespect to her; and the hatchet-faced lady, her eyes snapping, said that if the park-keepers didn't know their duty she did, and would bring the affair to the notice of the Ranger. There seemed nothing for it but to go with the young lady. The hatchet-faced lady announced that she too would go, and that if—which she doubted—a Marquis was forthcoming she would give him a piece of her mind.

The door of Alverstoke House was opened by a footman. He was a well-trained young man, but his eyes, when they perceived the cavalcade awaiting admittance, showed a tendency to start from their sockets. Frederica, carrying the situation off with a high hand, said, with a friendly smile: "Good-morning! I do trust his lordship has not yet gone out?"

The footman, his eyes starting more than ever, replied, in a bemused voice: "No, miss. That is,——"

"Thank goodness!" interrupted Frederica. "I don't wonder at it that you should be astonished to see me so—so heavily escorted! I'm surprised at it myself. Be so good as to tell his lordship that his cousin, Miss Merriville, is here, and desires to speak to him!"

She then stepped into the house, inviting her companions, over her shoulder, to follow her; and such was her assurance that the footman stood aside instinctively, offering no other opposition to the invasion of his master's house by a set of regular rum touches than the stammered information that his lordship was still in his dressing-room.

"Then tell him, if you please, that the matter is of some urgency!" said Frederica.

"Would you—would you care to see his lordship's secretary, miss?" said the footman feebly.

"Mr Trevor?" said Frederica. "No, thank you. Just convey my message to his lordship!"

The footman had never heard of Miss Merriville, his

lordship's cousin, but her mention of Mr Trevor's name relieved his mind. He thought she must be his lordship's cousin, though what she was doing in such queer company, or why she should have brought a couple of park-keepers and an obvious bumpkin to Alverstoke House he could not imagine. Nor did he know what to do with the ill-assorted visitors, for while it was clearly incumbent upon him to conduct Miss Merriville and her female companion to the saloon he could not feel that either his lordship, or the august and far more terrible Mr Wicken, would be pleased to discover that he had also ushered Miss Merriville's male attendants into this apartment.

He was rescued from this social dilemma by the dignified appearance on the scene of Mr Wicken himself. Thankful for the first time in his life to see his dread mentor, he hurriedly informed him that it was Miss Merriville—my lord's cousin—wishful to see my lord!

James the footman might not have heard of Miss Merriville, but Wicken was not so ignorant. He, with his lord's valet, his steward, his housekeeper, and his head groom knew all about the Merrivilles; and what they referred to as his lordship's latest start had been for days the main topic for discussion in the Room. Nor was Wicken ever rocked from his stately balance. He bowed to Miss Merriville, impassively surveyed her retinue, and moved across the hall to open the door into the library. "His lordship shall be informed, ma'am. If you will be pleased to take a seat in the book-room? And you, ma'am, of course," he added graciously, bestowing a suitable bow on the hatchet-faced lady, whom he had written down as a governess, or, possibly, a paid companion.

"Yes, and these men had better come in too," said Frederica.

"Certainly, ma'am—if you wish them to do so," responded Wicken. "But I venture to think that they will be quite comfortable in the hall."

With this opinion even the cowman was in the fullest agreement, but Frederica would have none of it. "No, for they too wish to speak to his lordship," she said. She then invited the hatchet-faced lady to sit down;

and Wicken, not by so much as the flicker of an eyelid betraying his emotions, held the door for the rest of the party to enter the room.

James, meanwhile, had gone up the stairs to the Marquis's dressing-room, and had tapped on the door. It was a very soft, deprecating tap, the Marquis being notoriously ill-disposed towards persons seeking admittance to his room before noon; and he was obliged to tap again, a little more loudly. He was not invited to enter, but the door was opened to him by his lordship's very superior valet, who appeared to regard his intrusion as a form of sacrilege, demanding to know, in an outraged undervoice, what he wanted.

"It's urgent, Mr Knapp!" whispered James. "Mr Wicken said I was to tell his lordship!"

These words acted, as he had felt sure they must, as a passport. Knapp allowed him to step into the room, but adjured him, still in an undervoice, not to stir from the door, or to make the least sound, until he was bid. He then trod silently back to the dressing-table, at which my lord was seated, engaged in the important task of arranging his neckcloth.

Only his sisters had ever stigmatized Alverstoke as a dandy. He adopted none of the extremes of fashion which made the younger members of this set ridiculous, and which would certainly have disgusted Mr Brummell, had that remarkable man still been the arbiter of taste in London. Mr Brummell, obliged by sordid circumstances to retire to the Continent, was living in obscurity, but the smarts of his generation had not swerved from the tenets he had laid down. Alverstoke, three years his junior, had encountered him in his flamboyant salad days, and had been swift to discard every one of his colourful waistcoats, his flashing tie-pins, and his multitude of fobs and seals. A man whose raiment attracted attention, had said Mr Brummell, was *not* a well-dressed man. Clean linen, perfectly cut coats, and the nice arrangement of his neckcloths were the hallmarks of the man of ton, and to these simple rules Alverstoke had thenceforward adhered, achieving, by patience and practice, the reputation of being one of the most elegant men on the town. Disdaining to adopt the absurdities of starched shirt-points so high that they obscured his vision and made it impossible for him to turn his head, and such intricacies as the Mathematical or the Oriental ties, he evolved his own style of neckwear: discreet, yet so exquisite as to arouse envy in the breasts of the younger generation.

James was well aware of this; and, since his secret ambition was to rise to the position of a gentleman's gentleman, Knapp's admonition was unnecessary. For no consideration would he have disturbed the Marquis at such a moment; and he saw nothing at all to provoke laughter in the Marquis's attitude: he was only sorry that he had not arrived in time to see the dexterous turn his lordship gave the foot-wide muslin cloth before it was placed round his collar. This had obviously been successful, for Knapp had laid aside the six or seven neckcloths he had been holding in readiness to hand the Marquis if his first attempts should be failures; and that gentleman was now gazing at the ceiling. Fascinated, James watched the gradual lowering of his chin, and the deft pressing into permanent shape of the creases thus created in the snowy muslin. In an expansive moment, Knapp had once told him that all his lordship did, to achieve those beautiful folds, was to drop his jaw some four or five times. It had sounded easy, and it looked easy; but his budding sartorial instinct told James that it was not easy at all. He held his breath while the operation was in progress, only letting it go when the Marquis, having critically inspected the result of his skill, laid down his hand-mirror, and said: "Yes, that will do."

He rose, as he spoke, and, as he slid his arms into the waistcoat Knapp was holding, looked across the room at James. "Well?" he asked.

"Begging your lordship's pardon, it's Miss Merriville —wishful to see your lordship, immediate!" disclosed James. "On a matter of urgency!" he added.

The Marquis looked faintly surprised, but all he said was: "Indeed? Inform Miss Merriville that I will be with her directly. My coat, Knapp!"

"Yes, my lord. In the book-room, my lord, I believe."

Having in this masterly manner disclaimed all responsibility for his superior's deviation from the normal, James withdrew circumspectly. Knapp remarked, as he shook out a handkerchief, and presented it to Alverstoke, that he wondered why Wicken should not have shown Miss Merriville into the saloon; but Alverstoke, picking up his quizzing-glass, and passing its long ribbon over his head, merely said Wicken probably had his reasons.

Several minutes later, looking precise to a pin in a dark blue coat which appeared to have been moulded to his form, very pale pantaloons, and very highly polished Hessian boots, he came down the stairs to find Wicken awaiting him. "Why my book-room, Wicken?" he enquired. "Don't you think my cousin worthy of being taken up to the saloon?"

"Certainly, my lord," responded Wicken. "But Miss Merriville is not alone."

"So I should suppose."

"I was not referring to the female accompanying her, my lord. There are three other persons, whom I thought it more proper to usher into the book-room than the saloon."

Having been acquainted with his butler from his earliest youth, Alverstoke did not fall into the error of supposing that the unknown persons came of the professorial class. Others, less familiar with Wicken, might think his countenance sphinx-like, but it was plain to Alverstoke that he profoundly disapproved of Miss Merriville's escort. "Well, who are they?" Alverstoke asked.

"As to that, my lord, I'm sure I shouldn't care to say, though two of them appear, from their raiment, to be employed in some official, but menial, capacity."

"Dear me!" said Alverstoke.

"Yes, my lord. There is also a Dog—a very large dog. I was unable to recognize the breed."

"Is there, by God! I wonder what the deuce——" he broke off. "Something tells me, Wicken, that danger awaits me in the book-room!"

"Oh, no, my lord!" said Wicken reassuringly. "It is not, I fancy, a *fierce* animal."

He opened the door into the book-room as he spoke, and held it for Alverstoke. He then suffered a slight shock, for, as Alverstoke paused on the threshold, surveying the assembled company, Lufra, who was lying at Frederica's feet, recognized in him the agreeable visitor whose magical fingers had found the precise spot on his spine which he was unable to attend to himself, and scrambled up, uttering a high-pitched bark, and launched himself forward. It was only for a moment that Wicken thought he meant to attack the Marquis; but the hatchet-faced lady, blind to the flattened ears and furiously waving tail, screamed, and called on all to witness that she had said it from the start: the creature was savage, and ought to be shot.

The Marquis, restraining Lufra's ardour, said: "Thank you! I'm much obliged to you, but that's enough! Down, Luff! *Down!*"

The park-keepers exchanged significant glances: no doubt about it: the dog belonged to the Marquis right enough. Frederica, feeling that Lufra had done much to atone for his bad behaviour, rose, and went towards Alverstoke, saying: "Oh, cousin, you can't think how glad I am to find you at home! This vexatious dog of yours has embroiled me in *such* a scrape! I declare, I'll never offer to take him out for you again!"

To her profound relief, he took this without a blink, merely saying, as he bent to pat Lufra: "You shock me, Frederica! What has he been doing?"

Three persons told him, in chorus. He interrupted them, saying: "One at a time—if I am expected to understand the matter!"

Frederica, and the cowman, were silenced; but the hatchet-faced lady was made of sterner stuff. She said that people might talk about Barcelona collies if they chose, but that she for one didn't believe a word of it, and that it was coming to something when one couldn't go for an airing in the park without being attacked by savage dogs.

The Marquis had recourse to his deadliest weapon: he raised his quizzing-glass to his eye. Strong men had been known to blench when that glass had been levelled at them. The hatchet-faced lady did not blench, but speech was withered on her tongue. The Marquis said: "You must forgive me, ma'am: I have a lamentably bad memory, but I believe I haven't the pleasure of your acquaintance? Cousin, pray introduce me!"

Frederica, who was rapidly revising her first, unfavourable opinion of him, replied promptly: "I can't, because I haven't the least notion who she may be, or why she *would* come here. Unless it was to assure herself that you are indeed my cousin, which she seemed to doubt!"

"It doesn't appear to be an entirely adequate reason," he said. "However, if, for some reason hidden from me, ma'am, you wish for reassurance on this point, you have it! Miss Merriville and I *are* cousins."

"I'm sure it's of no interest to me, my lord!" she returned, reddening. "What's more, if I hadn't thought it my duty to do so, I shouldn't have come! Or if I hadn't seen as plain as plain that the moment Miss Merriville talked about her cousin the Marquis those—those two *toadeaters* were ready to let that vicious animal attack everyone in the park!"

Faint, protesting sounds came from the park-keepers, but the Marquis ignored them. "I had no idea he was so dangerous," he remarked. "I trust you sustained no injury, ma'am?"

"I didn't say he attacked *me!* But——"

"He didn't attack anyone!" struck in Frederica.

"Oh, indeed? And I daresay he didn't knock down a poor little boy, and frighten all those sweet innocents out of their wits? Oh, no!"

Frederica laughed. "No, he didn't knock the little boy down. To be sure, the children were scared of him at first, but as soon as they understood that he only wanted to play with them they very soon recovered their wits. In fact, they begged me to bring him to the park again tomorrow!"

"It was my cows he attacked!" interposed the cowman. "And you saying as how he was herding them, miss, being as he was bred to do so, in Spain! Which he never was! I never been to Spain meself, nor I ain't wishful to do so, me not holding with furriners, but what I say, and stand to, is that cows is cows, all the world over, and not even a benighted heathen wouldn't train a dog to scatter a herd like that nasty brute done! Mr Munslow there, begging your lordship's pardon, ups and says he was a mongrel; but all *I* says is that he ain't no collie, Barcelona nor otherwise!"

The younger park-keeper was understood to say, twisting his hat between his hands and casting an imploring look at the Marquis, that no offence had been meant, but that Miss *had* said that the dog was a Barcelona collie, which he couldn't believe, not if he lived to be a hundred, no matter (drawing a resolute breath) who told him different.

"So I should hope," said the Marquis. "He is nothing of the sort, of course." He turned his head towards Frederica, and said in a voice of weary boredom: "Really, cousin, you are too shatterbrained! He is a hound, not a collie; and what I told you was not Barcelona, but Baluchistan! *Baluchistan,* Frederica!"

"Oh, dear! So you did! How—how stupid of me!" she replied unsteadily.

Neither of the park-keepers seemed to find his lordship's explanation unacceptable. The elder said wisely that that would account for it; and the younger reminded the company that he had known all along that the dog wasn't Spanish. But the cowman was plainly dissatisfied; and the hatchet-faced lady said sharply: "I don't believe there is such a place!"

"Oh, yes!" replied his lordship, walking towards the window, and giving one of the two globes which stood there a twist. "Come and see for yourself!"

Everyone obeyed this invitation; and Frederica said reproachfully: "If you had only told me it was in *Asia,* cousin!"

"Oh, *Asia!*" said the elder park-keeper, glad to be enlightened. "A kind of Indian dog, I daresay."

"Well, not precisely," said Frederica. "At least, I don't think so. It's *this* bit, you see. It's a very wild place, and the dog had to be smuggled out, because the natives are hostile. And that's why I said he was very rare. Indeed, he is the only Baluchistan dog in this country, isn't he, cousin?"

"I devoutly hope he may be," returned his lordship dryly.

"Well, all *I* have to say is that it makes it so much the worse!" declared the hatchet-faced lady. "The idea of bringing wild foreign animals into the park! Smuggled, too! I don't scruple to tell you, my lord, that I very much disapprove of such practices, and I have a very good mind to report it to the Customs!"

"I'm afraid there are none," he said apologetically, coming back in his leisurely way to the fireplace, and stretching out his hand to the bell-pull. "No postal service, either. You *could* send a messenger, I suppose, but it would be excessively costly, and the chances are that he would be murdered out of hand. It is really very difficult to know what to advise in such a case."

"I am speaking of the *English* Customs, my lord!" she said, glaring at him.

"Oh, that wouldn't be of the least use! I didn't smuggle the dog *into* the country; I merely caused him to be smuggled *out* of Baluchistan."

She said, in a voice that shook with passion: "However that may be, you have no right to let savage dogs loose in the park, and I shall report it to the proper authorities, and so I warn you, my lord!"

"My dear ma'am, what possible concern is it of mine if you choose to make a pea-goose of yourself? I may add that I am at a loss to understand what concern this unfortunate affair is of yours. You have informed me that my dog did not attack you—which I believe; you have also informed me that you came to my house because it was plain to you that, upon learning my rank, these men—whom you stigmatized as *toadeaters* —were ready to permit the dog *to attack everyone in the park*—which I do *not* believe! It appears to me that you have been indulging in a high piece of meddling. If I should be asked to give an account of this interview, I should feel myself bound to state that these men came, very properly, to inform me of my dog's misdemeanor, and to request that he should be kept under restraint; but as they were accompanied, for what reason I know not, by an officious person, wanting in both manner and sense, who took it upon herself to usurp their authority, it was all too long before they were able to lay their complaint before me." He glanced towards the open door, where Wicken stood, his countenance graven, and his brain seething with conjecture. "Be so good as to show this lady out!" he said. "And desire Mr Trevor to come to me!"

This masterly speech, listened to by Frederica with awe, and by the park-keepers with approval, cast the hatchet-faced lady into gobbling incoherence. Never, during the course of her overbearing career, had she been so much insulted, as she tried to inform his lordship. But his lordship, losing interest in her, merely helped himself to a pinch of snuff; and Wicken, interrupting her stammered utterance, said, in a voice devoid of all human passion: "If you please, madam!"

The hatchet-faced lady swept out of the room, spots of scarlet burning on her cheek-bones. No one, least of all Wicken himself, was surprised at her capitulation, the younger park-keeper going so far as to confide, later, to his senior, that he reckoned anyone would need to have uncommon good bottom to square up to that old Puffguts.

The cowman, however, while approving in general of the expulsion, was by no means mollified. He began to explain to the Marquis the enormity of Lufra's crime, the dire results that could ensue from stampeding cows in milk, and the fate that would befall him at their owner's hands if they were found to have suffered the least injury.

"Well, that isn't likely!" said Frederica. "Anyone might suppose from the way you talk that they were chased all over the town, which they were not! Though, if you choose to keep cows in a public park, I must say——"

"No, cousin, you must not!" intervened the Marquis, taking his revenge. "My instructions to you were to take Lufra to *Hyde* Park, and I hold you entirely to blame for this lamentable affair."

Frederica, seeking refuge behind her handkerchief, said in trembling accents that she feared he was right.

"Have no fear!" said the Marquis, addressing himself to the cowman. "The matter shall be suitably adjusted! Ah, come in, Charles!"

Mr Trevor, considerably astonished by the scene that met his eyes, said: "You sent for me, sir?"

"I did, yes. This Baluchistan hound of mine, which my cousin offered to exercise for me, has been getting me into trouble. I regret to say that he—er—forgot himself amongst the cows in Green Park."

Mr Trevor might have been momentarily staggered, but he was by no means slow-witted, and it did not need the warning glance directed at him from under his employer's lazy eyelids to put him on his guard. He said calmly that he was sorry to hear it; and when he looked at the Baluchistan hound, who was sniffing interestedly at his legs, only the faintest twitch at the corners of his mouth disturbed the gravity of his expression.

"Just so!" said his lordship. "I knew you would be shocked, and I'm persuaded I can leave the matter in your hands." He smiled, and added softly: "You are always to be depended on, Charles!" He then turned to the complainants, and said: "Mr Trevor will settle everything to your satisfaction, I trust, so go with him to his office! Ah!—two of the Deputy Ranger's people, Charles, and the herdsman!"

He nodded dismissal to his visitors. They departed willingly, having correctly interpreted his words to mean that suitable largesse would presently be distributed amongst them, and feeling that Mr Trevor would be an easier man to deal with than the Marquis.

Charles signed to them to precede him out of the room, and when they had filed past him, lingered for a moment, looking at Frederica. "How much damage did he do, Miss Merriville?"

Emerging from her handkerchief, Frederica showed him not a tearful but a laughing countenance. "Oh, I don't think he hurt the cows at all, because we caught him before he had time to!"

"In that case, then———"

"*No,* Charles!" interposed the Marquis. "My sole desire is to be rid of the business, and this is not the moment to be clutch-fisted!"

"Oh, I'll see to it that you're rid of it, sir!" said Charles cheerfully, and withdrew.

"Well, what an *excellent* young man!" said Frederica.

VII

"He is, isn't he?" agreed Alverstoke.

She looked up at him. "Yes, and you too! You were truly splendid, and I am *very* much obliged to you! Oh, and I do beg your pardon for having embroiled you! The thing was, you see, that they threatened to impound Luff, and only think what the consequences might have been! That was why I said he belonged to you." A gurgle of laughter rose in her throat. "L-like P-puss in Boots!"

"Like *what?*" he demanded.

"M-my cousin the M-Marquis of Alverstoke!" she explained. *"You* know!"

"No doubt I am extremely dull-witted, but I——" He broke off, as enlightenment dawned on him, and the frown left his brow. "Oh!—the Marquis of Carabas!"

"Of course! And it answered! Except with that horrid creature you gave *such* a set-down to! I never in my life heard anything so ruthlessly uncivil, but I must own that I enjoyed it!" She began to laugh again. "Oh, but you nearly overset me when you said Luff was a Baluchistan hound! And so you shall be, you bad dog!"

Gratified, Lufra reared himself on his hind legs, and licked her face. She pushed his forepaws off her knees, and got up. "You are a shameless commoner!" she informed him. She raised her eyes to Alverstoke's and held out her hand. "Thank you!" she said, smiling at him. "I must go now. You will tell me, won't you, how much Mr Trevor was obliged to pay those men?"

"Just a moment!" he said. "You haven't explained to me how it comes about that you were walking alone, cousin."

"No," she agreed. "But then, you haven't explained to me how it comes about that that is your concern, have you?"

"I am perfectly ready to do so, however. Whatever may be the accepted mode in Herefordshire, in London it won't do. Girls of your age and breeding don't go about town unaccompanied."

"Well, in general I don't do so, and, naturally, I would never permit Charis to. But I'm not a girl. I daresay you might think me one, being yourself so much older, but I promise you I ceased to be a young miss years ago! And, in any event, I am not answerable to you for my actions, Cousin Alverstoke!"

"Oh, yes, you are!" he retorted. "If you expect me to launch you into society, Frederica, you will conform to society's rules! You'll either do as I bid you, or I shall wash my hands of you. If you are determined to set the world in a bustle, find another sponsor!"

She flushed, and her lips parted. But whatever stinging reply she had been about to utter she suppressed, closing her lips firmly. After a pause, she managed to smile, and to say: "I daresay you would be very happy to wash your hands of us, after today's adventure."

"Oh, no!" he said coolly. "You may put that out of your mind!"

"That is precisely what I *can't* do, though I wish very much that I could, because it almost *slays* me to be compelled to keep my tongue between my teeth!" she told him. "I should dearly love to come to cuffs with you, my lord, but I'm not sunk quite below reproach— though I must say I think you are!" she added frankly.

"But why?" he asked, beginning to be amused.

"Because you knew very well when you pinched at me in that odious way that I was too much obliged to you to give you a set-off!"

He laughed. "Do you think you could?"

"Yes, to be sure I could! I can say *very* cutting things when I'm put into a passion."

"I'll endure them!"

She shook her head, a dimple peeping in her cheek. "No, I've come down from the boughs now. To own the truth, I think I flew into them because my aunt says exactly what you did: nothing makes one so cross as knowing one is in the wrong, does it?"

"I don't know. I've never thought about it."

She looked surprised, but decided not to pursue the matter. "Well, I'll try not to put you to the blush. The case is that Charis has one of her colds, and Jessamy, you know, works at his books every morning: that's why Charis and I take Luff out walking. He needs a great deal of exercise—more than he can get in London, poor fellow!"

"Then why not Felix, or your maid?"

"I haven't a maid—not an abigail, I mean. Only the housemaids, and they are all town-bred, and it is the greatest bore to go out walking with any of them, because they *will* dawdle, or say their shoes hurt them. I would have taken Felix, only that he was set on visiting a Mechanical Museum, and he would have been glumpish all the way if I had insisted on his bearing me company. Oh, pray don't frown! I won't do it again!"

"You need a footman," he said, still frowning.

"What, to protect me? Luff does that, I promise you!"

"To wait on you—carry your parcels—deliver your letters."

"I suspect you mean I need one to add to my consequence!"

"That too," he replied.

She looked thoughtful, and presently smiled, rather ruefully. "To present a respectable appearance, as Buddle says! He wished me to bring Peter to London, but I left him at Graynard, because, for one thing, Mr Porth was anxious to hire him; and, for another, it seemed such an unnecessary expense. However, I own I have felt the want of a footman, on Buddle's account: he's too old for these horrid London houses."

"Is the expense a bar?" he asked bluntly.

"Oh, no! I'll hire a footman, and he can take the place of the maid who at present helps Buddle."

"No, leave it to me!" he said. "Hiring footmen—London footmen—is no work for green girls."

"Thank you: you are very obliging! But there is no reason why you should be put to that trouble."

"I shan't be. Trevor will find a suitable man, and send him to see Buddle."

"Then I shall be very much obliged to him." She

held out her hand again. "Now, I'll say goodbye, cousin."

"Not yet! Unless you have some urgent business to attend to, I suggest you allow me to drive you to visit my sister. She wishes to make your acquaintance, and this seems a good opportunity to take you to see her."

Startled, she said: "Oh, but Charis——! Surely she should go too? Won't Lady Buxted think it very uncivil—when she has consented to introduce her at your ball?"

"No, how should she, when the circumstances are explained to her? She would think it far more uncivil of you to delay making this visit of ceremony."

"Yes, but Charis will be well again in a day or two!"

"I sincerely hope so. Unfortunately, I am off to Newmarket tomorrow, and shall be away for a sennight. To postpone the visit until we shall be within a fortnight of the ball would be beyond the line of being pleasing, believe me!"

She looked dismayed. "Indeed it would! Oh, dear, she would suppose us to be quite without conduct, wouldn't she? But I'm not dressed for it!"

He put up his glass, and surveyed her through it. She was wearing a hair-brown pelisse, with orange-jean half-boots, and a neat little hat trimmed with a single ostrich plume curling over its brim. He lowered his glass. "I see nothing amiss," he said.

"*You* may not, but you may depend upon it that Lady Buxted will write me down as a positive dowdy! I've worn this pelisse any time these past two years!"

"It will be quite unnecessary to tell her so."

"Yes, indeed it will!" she said warmly. "She will know it at a glance!"

"How should she, when I did not?"

"Because she's a female, of course! Of *all* the stupid questions to ask——!"

His eyes were alight with wicked laughter. "You underrate me, Frederica! I am far more conversant with feminine fashions than my sister, I promise you! Must I prove it to you? Very well, then! Your pelisse is not fashioned according to the latest mode; your boots are made of jean, not of kid; and you furbished up your hat with a feather dyed orange to match them. Am I right?"

She scanned him, gravely, but with interest. "Yes— and so, I suppose, was Aunt Scrabster."

"Oho! Did she warn you to beware of such a sad rake as I am. You've nothing to fear from me, Frederica!"

That made her give one of her chuckles. "Oh, I know *that!* I'm not nearly pretty enough!" Her clear gaze remained fixed on his face, but a crease appeared between her brows. "Charis is," she said thoughtfully. "But—but although you call me green, cousin, I'm more than seven, you know. You wouldn't!"

"How can you know that?" he asked, quizzing her.

"Well, to be sure, I'm not very familiar with rakes— in fact, I never met one before!—but I'm not such a wet-goose that I don't know you are a gentleman— however uncivil you may be, or whatever improper things you may say! I daresay that sort of carelessness comes of having been born into the first rank."

He was so much taken aback that for a moment he said nothing. Then a wry smile twisted his mouth, and he said: "I deserved that, didn't I? Accept my apologies, cousin! May I now escort you to my sister's house?"

"Well . . ." she said doubtfully. "If you think she won't—Oh, no! You are forgetting Luff! Pretty cool, to walk into Lady Buxted's drawing-room, leading a—a *country* dog! I won't do it!"

"Certainly not, if I have anything to say in the matter! One of my people can take him back to Upper Wimpole Street: I'll see to it! Sit down!—I shan't keep you waiting many minutes."

He left the room as he spoke, but although the second footman ran all the way to the stables it was rather more than twenty minutes later that Frederica was handed into his lordship's town carriage. The protesting yelps of Lufra, held in leash by James, followed her; but she resolutely ignored their frantic appeal, merely saying anxiously: "You did tell James he mustn't on any account allow him to run loose, didn't you, cousin?"

"Not only did I tell him, but so did you," Alverstoke replied, sitting down beside her. "Grosvenor Place, Roxton."

"The thing is, you see," confided Frederica, as the carriage-door was shut, "he has not yet grown accustomed to all the London traffic, and he doesn't understand that he must stay on the flagway. And, of course, when he sees a cat on the other side of the street, or another dog, perhaps, he dashes across, all amongst the chairmen and the carriages, creating the most shocking commotion, because he makes the horses shy, and puts one to the blush!"

"I can readily believe it! What the deuce made you bring him to London?"

She regarded him in astonishment. "Why, what else could we do?"

"Could you not have left him in charge of—I don't know!—your gardener—gamekeeper—bailiff?"

"Oh, no!" she cried. "How can you think we would be so heartless? When he saved Jessamy's life, just as if he knew—which Charis vows he did—that he owed his own life to Jessamy! Myself, I suspect that he doesn't remember it at all, for he isn't in the least afraid of going into water—but three of the village boys threw him into the pond with a brick round his neck, when he was a very young puppy, poor Luff! So Jessamy plunged in after him—and never did I see such a dreadful object as he was, when he came into the house, carrying Luff! Dripping wet, and blood all over his face, because his nose was bleeding, and such a black eye!"

"A fighter, is he?"

"N-no—well, only when something of that nature happens, which makes him so burningly angry that he goes in, Harry says, like a tiger. He doesn't care for boxing nearly as much as Harry does, and I believe he hasn't very good science—if you know what I mean?"

The Marquis, a distinguished exponent of the noble art, begged her to explain the term.

She wrinkled her brow. "Well, it means skill, I think. Not mere flourishing! Oh, and standing up well, and—

and showing game, and—oh, yes!—being very gay!
Though how anyone could be *gay* under such circumstances I can't conceive! I expect Harry is, because he
is naturally a gay person, but not Jessamy. No, not
Jessamy."

She fell silent, apparently brooding over Jessamy.
Idly amused, Alverstoke said, after a few moments: "Is
Jessamy the sober member of the family?"

"Sober?" She considered this, the wrinkles deepening
on her brow. "No, not sober, precisely. I can't describe him, because I don't understand him myself,
now that he is growing up. Mr Ansdell—our Vicar—
says that he has an ardent soul, and that I need not be
in a worry, because he will become far more rational
presently. He means to enter the Church, you know. I
must own that I thought this was because of his Con-
firmation, and that the fit would pass. Not that I don't
wish him to become a clergyman, but it seemed so
very unlikely that he would be. He was used to be the
most *adventurous* boy, for ever getting into dangerous
scrapes, besides being hunting-mad, and much cleverer
in the saddle than Harry—and Harry is no slow-top!
Harry told me himself that there was no need to give
Jessamy jumping powder, because he throws his heart
over any fence his horse can clear! And that was *not*
mere partiality, for the Master told a particular friend
of mine that Jessamy was the best horseman, for his
age, of any in South Herefordshire!"

Alverstoke, whose interest in Miss Merriville's
brothers was, at the best, tepid, murmured, in a voice
which would have informed those who knew him best
that he was rapidly becoming bored: "Ah? Yes, I seem
to recall that when I had the felicity of making his
acquaintance I formed the impression that he was—if
not hunting-mad, decidedly horse-mad."

"Oh, yes!" she agreed. "And every now and then he
runs wild, just as he was used to do—only *then* his
conscience never troubled him, and *now* it does!" She
sighed, but, an instant later, smiled, and said: "I beg
your pardon! I have been running on like a tattle-box."

"Not at all!" he said politely.

"I know I have—and about something which is no concern of yours. Never mind! I won't do so any more."

He was aware of feeling a twinge of remorse: it prompted him to say, in a warmer voice: "Do they worry you so much, these brothers of yours?"

"Oh, no! Sometimes—a little, because there's no one but me, and I am only their sister, besides being a female. But they are very good!"

"Have you no male relatives? I think you spoke of some guardian, or trustee—a lawyer, isn't he?"

"Oh, Mr Salcombe! Yes, indeed, he has been most helpful and kind, but he's not a guardian. Papa didn't appoint one, you see. We were in dread that the younger ones might be made Wards in Chancery, but Mr Salcombe contrived to avert *that* danger. I've heard people complain that lawyers are shockingly dilatory, but for my part I am excessively thankful for it! He kept on writing letters, and arguing about legal points, until Harry came of age, and could assume responsibility for the children. You would have supposed that he must have wished us all at Jericho, for it went on for months, but he seemed to enjoy it!"

"I don't doubt it! He appears to have your interests at heart: doesn't he keep a hand on the reins?"

"Manage the boys, do you mean? No: he is not—he is not the sort of person who understands boys. He is a bachelor, and very precise and oldfashioned. The boys call him Old Prosy, which is odiously ungrateful of them, but—well, you see?"

He smiled. "Most clearly!"

"And the only male relative we have is my Aunt Scrabster's husband. I am only slightly acquainted with him, but I know he wouldn't be of the least use. He is a very respectable man, but he's town-bred, and all his interest is in commerce."

"Unfortunate—but I daresay your brother Harry will relieve you of your care," he said lightly.

There was an infinitesimal pause before she answered: "Yes, of course."

The carriage was drawing up, and a moment later it came to a halt in front of Lady Buxted's house. He was

glad of it. He had missed neither Frederica's hesitation
nor the note of constraint in her voice, and he had
thought that it would not be long before she demanded
his advice, and even his active help, in the task of guiding her young brothers. She was quite capable of it; and
while he was just as capable of withering any such
attempt with one of his ruthless set-downs he did not
much wish to do this. He liked her. She was unusual,
and therefore diverting; she was not a beauty, but she
had a good deal of countenance, and an air of breeding
which pleased him; and her sister was a ravishing diamond whom he was perfectly willing to sponsor into
the ton. There would be flutters in more dovecots than
the one he was about to enter, and that would provide
him with some entertainment.

Lady Buxted was at home, and in the drawing-room,
her two elder daughters bearing her company. When
the visitors were announced, she rose in her stateliest
way, and rather deliberately set aside the tambour-
frame which held her embroidery before moving forward to meet Frederica. She favoured her with a hard
stare, two-fingers, and a cold how-do-you-do. Frederica
showed no signs of discomposure. She just touched the
fingers (as Alverstoke noted with approval), dropping
a slight curtsy as she did so, and saying, with her frank
smile: "How do you do, ma'am? Cousin Alverstoke
has been so obliging as to bring me to call on you,
which I have been anxious to do—to thank you for
your kindness, in being willing to lend us your countenance! My sister would have come with me, but she is
laid up with a feverish cold, and begs me to offer her
apologies."

Lady Buxted thawed a little. She had by this time
taken in every detail of Frederica's appearance; and
the harrowing suspicion that Miss Merriville would
prove to be one of those ripe and dashing beauties to
whom Alverstoke was so regrettably attracted, vanished. Having realized that Frederica was neither a
beauty nor in the first bloom of her youth, her ladyship
was able to regard her with an impartial eye, and even
to do justice to her. She would have nothing to blush
for in her protégée: the girl had pretty manners, a cer-

tain air of breeding; and she was dressed with neatness
and propriety. So it was quite graciously that her ladyship told her daughters that they must come and be
made known to their cousin; and while the three young
ladies made rather laborious conversation she drew Alverstoke a little apart, saying that Frederica seemed a
well-behaved girl, and that she would do her best for
her. "I do not, however, engage to find a husband for
her," she warned him. "With no fortune, and no extraordinary degree of beauty, she cannot expect to
make more than a respectable marriage, you know. If
she hopes to find a husband by moving in the first
circles, she is flying too high."

"Oh, I shan't ask that of you!" responded Alverstoke. "You will have enough to do finding a husband
for Jane, I daresay."

Only the reflection that the bills for Jane's finery had
already reached considerable proportions made it possible for Lady Buxted to keep her tongue between her
teeth. But however uncertain might be her temper, her
passion for funding her money was unwavering. She
certainly cast her brother an angry glance, but said
nothing, merely walking away from him to seat herself
on the sofa, where she invited Frederica to join her.

The visit lasted for only half-an-hour; and although
Lady Buxted asked Frederica a great many questions
she maintained her formal manner, offered no refreshment, and made no effort to detain her when she rose to
take her leave. Nor did she invite her to bring Charis
to Grosvenor Place; but she did say that she must try
to find time to call on Miss Winsham one day.
Frederica, who answered her questions with cool reserve, detecting in them more curiosity than kindness,
said, with a smile on her lips and a dangerous sparkle
in her eyes, that this intelligence would cast her aunt
into transports of delight; whereupon Alverstoke
chuckled, and murmured: "Served with your own
sauce, Louisa!"

He then bowed with exaggerated civility, and followed Frederica out of the room, leaving his sister and
his nieces to marvel at his interest in a commonplace
female (for girl no one could call her!) who had too

much self-consequence, and was plainly above herself.

"I shouldn't have said that," Frederica confessed, when Alverstoke took his place beside her in the carriage.

"Oh, why not? You took the wind out of her eye very prettily!"

"It wasn't pretty of me to have done it, because she *is* going to introduce Charis to society—and I'm persuaded she doesn't wish to do so!" Frederica turned her head to direct one of her disconcerting looks at him. "Did you—did you compel her, sir?"

"How should I be able to do that?" he countered.

"I don't know, but I fancy you *could*. And I don't think it was out of good-nature, or a wish to please you, because——"

"You are mistaken," he interrupted, a sardonic curl to his mouth. "She has a very earnest desire to please me."

She continued to look searchingly at him, and said, after a moment or two: "Well, I don't like it! And *she* won't like it when she sees Charis! No mother would, who had such a plain-faced daughter to present as Jane!"

"Are you going to cry off, then?"

She thought this over, saying presently, in a resolute tone: "No; if it were for myself, I would, but I'm determined Charis shall have her chance. I beg your pardon for not speaking more respectfully about your sister, but the prying questions she asked me put me all on end! I won't say any more."

"Don't refrain on my account! There's no love lost between us."

"*None?*" she asked, wide-eyed.

"Not a particle! Tell me, fair cousin: is the waltz danced in the wilds of Herefordshire?"

"In some houses it is, but not very much, and there are never any quadrilles. So I have hired a dancing-master to come to teach us the steps—that we shan't disgrace you by appearing as country cousins."

"That *does* relieve my mind!"

"It might well—except that I fancy you don't care a straw how we may appear."

"On the contrary! Think how much my credit would suffer!"

She laughed, but shook her head. "You don't care for that either. Or—or for anything, perhaps."

He was momentarily taken aback by this, but he replied without perceptible hesitation: "Not profoundly."

She frowned, turning it over in her mind. "Well, I can understand that that must be very comfortable, for if you don't care for anybody or anything you can't be cast into dejection, or become sick with apprehension, or even get into high fidgets. On the other hand, I shouldn't think you could ever be *aux anges* either. It wouldn't do for me: it would be too flat!" She turned her head to survey him again, and suddenly smiled. "I daresay that is why you are so bored!"

"I am frequently bored," he acknowledged. "Nevertheless, I—er—contrive to keep myself tolerably well amused!"

"Oh, yes, but *that's* not——" She stopped, and her colour rose. "I beg your pardon! I wish I could learn to keep my tongue!"

He ignored this, saying, with a wry smile: "You do hold me in contempt, don't you, Frederica?"

"No, no!" she said quickly. "You choose to call me a green girl, but I *have* cut my eye-teeth, you know, and I'm not wholly paper-skulled! How could you help but become bored when you have been able to command every—every agreeable luxury all your life? I expect, too," she added wisely, "that you were very much indulged, being your parents' only son."

Remembering the cold formality of his father, and, with more difficulty, the brief glimpses which had been granted to him of his fashionable mother, who had died while he was still at school, the sardonic curl to his mouth became more pronounced; but all he said was: "Very true! I came into the world hosed and shod, and was so precious to my parents that a special establishment was created for me. Until I went to Harrow, I enjoyed the undivided attention of nurses, valets, grooms, tutors, and—oh, all that money could provide!"

"Oh, *poor* little boy!" she exclaimed involuntarily.

"By no means! I don't recall that I ever expressed a wish that wasn't instantly gratified."

She checked herself on the brink of impetuous speech, and said, after a tiny pause, and in a rallying tone: "Well! I am now most truly obliged to you, cousin! You have taught me what poor Mr Ansdell never could!"

"Have I indeed? What's that?"

"Not to hanker after riches, of course! I was used to think, you know, that to be born to rank, fortune, and consequence must be so very pleasant; but I see now that it's nothing but a dead bore!" The carriage was drawing up; she held out her hand, a sparkle of mischief in her eyes. "Good-bye! Thank you for my lesson, and for introducing me to your sister! I had meant to have thanked you for coming to my rescue, but I shan't do so, because I am now persuaded that it did you a great deal of good to be obliged to exert yourself."

He took her hand, but only to place it firmly in her lap again. "Too previous, cousin! Spoilt though I am, I mean to exert myself sufficiently to escort you to your door."

"You have such distinguished manners, my lord!" she murmured demurely.

"I have, haven't I?" he retorted. "Another lesson for you—you brass-faced little gypsy!"

She burst out laughing; but when she gave him her hand again, on the doorstep, she said, looking up into his face: "Did I offend you? No, I don't think so. I *am* grateful to you for having come so splendidly to my rescue, and very sorry to have embroiled you in such a troublesome affair."

"Since it is well-known that my distinguished manners crumble at a touch, I shall make no apology for telling you that you are a baggage, Frederica!"

Her laughter bubbled up again; he smiled slightly; flicked her cheek with one careless finger; and trod down the steps to his carriage, under the disapproving stare of Buddle, who was holding open the door for his young mistress, and took it upon himself to reprove her for not keeping a proper distance. It was of no use to

point out to him that the Marquis was almost old
enough to have been her father; and worse than useless
to try and snub him; devoted retainers who (as they
never hesitate to remind one) had known one from the
cradle, were impossible to snub. "Now, that's quite
enough, Miss Frederica!" said Buddle severely. "I'm
only telling you for your own good, and I should be
failing in my duty if I didn't. Over and over again I've
told you that you can't carry on in London like you do
at home. A nice thing it would be if people was to take
you for a rackety gadabout!"

The Marquis, meanwhile, was being driven back to
Berkeley Square. It was his intention to try out his
latest acquisition, a team of high-bred grays, warranted
by their late owner to be sweet-goers, and enviously described by the gentleman who had been outbidden by
his lordship as four very tidy ones indeed. This agreeable scheme had been disturbed by the arrival of Frederica, but the day was not too far advanced for a drive
to Richmond, or to Wimbledon. Alighting from his
carriage in Berkeley Square, he gave the order for his
perch-phaeton to be brought round immediately, and
entered the house, to be greeted by joyful yelps and a
storm of mingled barks and whines. Lufra, tethered to
the lowest banister, recognized the one surviving link
with his mistress, and hailed him as his deliverer.

VIII

Since the Marquis was quite unable to make his voice heard above Lufra's, he was obliged to reassure and to quell the faithful hound before demanding an explanation from his butler. While Lufra, released from bondage, fawned at his feet, whimpering with mingled relief and entreaty, and dulling the glossy surface of his Hessians in a way that would have smitten his lordship's valet to the soul, he said, in a voice that was none the less terrible for its languor: "I thought I gave orders that this dog was to be taken to Upper Wimpole Street?"

His cold gaze rested on Wicken's face, but James, the first footman, and Walter, his subordinate, quaked in their buckled shoes. Wicken, who was made of sterner stuff, replied with majestic calm: "Yes, my lord. Every effort has been made to do so. Unfortunately, the Animal refused to leave the premises, either with Walter, or with James. I regret to inform your lordship that when pressure was brought to bear he turned quite Nasty—even with Me! I thought it best to tie him up to the banister, awaiting your lordship's return. Otherwise," he said, outdoing the Marquis in frigidity, "he would have scratched the library-door down."

"What a revolting creature you are!" said Alverstoke, addressing himself, much to the relief of his footmen, to Lufra. "No, no, down, damn you, *down!* Where is Mr Trevor?" As he spoke, his eyes alighted on his secretary, who had that instant emerged from his office at the back of the house, and was surveying the scene with something perilously like a grin on his countenance. "Oh, you're there, are you? Then, for God's sake, *do* something about this abominable mongrel!"

99

"*Mongrel,* sir?" responded Mr Trevor, in astonished accents. "I thought he was a——"

"Don't try me too far, Charles! You thought nothing of the sort! Why haven't you seen to it that he was restored to his owner?"

"Well, I did my best, sir," said Charles. "But he wouldn't go with me either."

"Now tell me that he tried to savage you, and you will have gone your length!" said Alverstoke, repulsing Lufra's adoring advances.

"Oh, no, he didn't do that! He merely squatted on his haunches!" said Charles cheerfully. "By the time I had dragged him as far as Davies Street I judged it to be time to return, no fewer than three kindly females having exclaimed at my brutality to a dumb creature. Besides, I was exhausted!"

"Why the devil didn't you bundle him into a hack?"

"We did make the attempt—all four of us—but he's not the sort of dog you *can* bundle, sir—unmuzzled! That was when Walter got bitten. I daresay we *might* have contrived to get him into the hack, but we none of us fancied a drive in his company. The thing was that his mistress left him here, and here he was determined to remain until she reclaimed him." Meeting Alverstoke's eyes with the utmost blandness, he added: "I believe these Baluchistan hounds are famous for their fidelity, sir."

"Oh, do you indeed?" said his lordship wrathfully.

"So I have always understood," said Charles. He watched Lufra paw the Marquis imperatively, and a happy thought occurred to him. "Perhaps he would consent to go with you, sir?" he suggested.

"A little more, and you will find yourself dismissed with ignominy, Charles! If you imagine that I am going to lead this misbegotten cur through the streets of London you must be out of your mind!" He turned towards his footmen, so swiftly that they had no time to wipe the appreciative grins from their faces. Having reduced both to a state of rigid imbecility by the mere power of his eye, he said: "One of you—oh, no, you are already wounded, are you not, Walter?—You, James, may betake yourself to Upper Wimpole Street!

Desire Master Jessamy Merriville to be so good as to come here to collect his dog immediately!"

But even as these words left his lips a bell was heard to clang in the nether regions, and the knocker on the front door was plied with enough violence to make his lordship wince. Walter moved to open the door, and was almost swept off his feet by the tempestuous entrance of Master Jessamy Merriville, with his brother at his heels.

"I've come for my dog—is his lordship at home? I must—Down, Luff! *Sit!*—Oh, sir, is that you? I do beg your pardon! I am *excessively* sorry, and I jumped into a hack and came the *instant* Frederica told me, because I knew what must have happened, and how she can have supposed that Luff would go off with a stranger—but females are such nodcocks! *Pray* forgive me!"

"Not at all!" said his lordship. "I am delighted to see you! In fact, I was on the point of sending one of my people to summon you, none of them being able to persuade Luff to leave the house."

"Oh, no, he wouldn't, of course! I do hope he didn't bite anyone? He isn't *savage,* but if he thought anyone was trying to steal him——"

"Ah, so that was it!" said his lordship. "He was labouring under a delusion, but I daresay that was Walter's fault, for not making the matter plain to him. My dear boy, don't look so concerned! Walter *likes* being bitten by large dogs, and so does Wicken—don't you, Wicken?"

"The Animal, my lord," replied Wicken, with dignity, "did not go so far as to bite Me."

"He will, if you keep on calling him the Animal. Well, Felix, how do you do? What brings *you* here?"

"I wanted to see you, sir—*particularly!*" replied Felix, smiling engagingly up at him.

"You terrify me!"

Jessamy, who was receiving Walter's bashful assurance that he had sustained no more than a flesh wound, turned at that, and said rather hotly: "I never meant him to plague you, sir! He *would* come, and I was afraid that if I pushed him off the step he would very likely fall under the wheels of some other vehicle, so I was obliged to pull him into the hack. And that was Frederica's fault too! If she hadn't said that you were going to Newmarket tomorrow——"

His irrepressible brother interrupted this speech without ceremony, recommending him to stop being a regular jaw-me-dead. He then raised deceptively angelic eyes to Alverstoke's face, and said: "You *promised* to take me to see the pneumatic lift, Cousin Alverstoke, and I thought p'raps you had forgotten, and I ought to remind you."

The Marquis could not remember having given any such promise; and he said so. His youthful admirer dealt summarily with this caveat, saying: "Yes, you did, sir! Well, you said *We'll see!* and that's the same thing!"

Jessamy gave him a shake. "It's nothing of the sort! If you don't hold your tongue, I promise you I'll give you pepper presently!"

"Hoo!" said Felix disrespectfully. "Try it, and see if you don't get one in the bread-basket!"

Observing the angry flush in Jessamy's cheeks, the Marquis judged it to be prudent to intervene, which he did, by saying: "Before you embark on this mill, let us repair to my book-room to partake of refreshment! Wicken, I don't know what our resources may be, but I rely on you to conjure up suitable refreshment for my guests!"

Jessamy, his flush deepening, said stiffly: "You are very good, sir, but we won't—we won't trespass upon your hospitality. I came only to fetch Luff, and—and to repay whatever sum it may have cost you to save him from being impounded! We—we need no refreshment!"

"Yes, we do!" objected Felix. He directed his seraphic gaze, strongly suggestive of a boy suffering from starvation, upon Wicken, and said politely: "If you please!"

"Felix!" exploded Jessamy.

But Wicken, not more hardened than his master against the wiles of schoolboys, visibly unbent, saying benevolently: "To be sure you do, sir! Now, you go into the book-room like a good boy, and you shall have some cakes and lemonade! But mind now!—you mustn't tease his lordship!"

"Oh, *no!*" responded Felix soulfully. "And *then* will you take me to that foundry, Cousin Alverstoke?"

A choking sound reminded the Marquis of his secretary's presence in the background. He turned his head, smiling with false sweetness, "Ah! If I was not forgetting you, dear boy!" he said, with gentle malice. "Pray come with us into the book-room! I wish to make my—er—wards known to you: Jessamy, and Felix— Mr Trevor!" He waited while the boys, mindful of their manners, executed two bows before shaking hands with Mr Trevor, and then marshalled the party into his library, saying, as soon as the door was closed: "You've put yourself in fortune's way, Felix: Mr Trevor knows far more than I do about pneumatic lifts, and is the very man to take you to the foundry."

"You are too flattering, sir!" said Charles promptly. "I am very sure I don't!"

"Well, you can't know less!" said his lordship, in an undervoice charged with asperity.

"Yes, but you said you would take me *yourself,* Cousin Alverstoke!"

Hot with embarrassment, Jessamy besought his brother to stop plaguing his lordship to do what anyone but a gudgeon could see he didn't want to do. This had the effect of causing Felix to direct a look of heart-rending reproach at the Marquis, and to say, in the voice of one mortally wounded: "I thought you *did* want to, sir. You *said*——"

"Yes, of course I do!" interrupted his lordship hastily. "But it so happens that I was about to drive to Richmond, to try the paces of my new team. How would you like to go with me there, instead of to the foundry?"

"Oh, *no!*" protested Felix.

This was too much for Jessamy. He exclaimed passionately: "You clodpole! You—you stupid little looby! Liefer visit a foundry than sit behind those bang-up grays we s-saw drive up to the house? You must have rats in your garret!"

"I like machines better than horses," said Felix simply.

In the interests of peace, the Marquis intervened yet again. "Well, there's no disputing about taste. If your heart is set on the foundry, the foundry it shall be. Do you want to inspect the grays, Jessamy? Go and talk to my groom about them! You may tell him that I shan't need them after all today."

"Oh!—Thank you, sir! I *would* like to take a look at them!" Jessamy said, his scowl vanishing.

With a passing admonition to Felix to keep Luff quiet, he hastened out of the room. By the time he returned, Felix was consuming a hearty meal of plum cake, washed down by copious draughts of lemonade; and eagerly (if sometimes a trifle thickly) holding forth on blast-pipes and safety valves. Mr Trevor, dredging from the depths of his memory such elementary knowledge of the principles governing steam-power as he had happened to acquire during the course of his career, was labouring manfully to keep pace with him; and the Marquis, lounging at his graceful ease in a wing-chair, was observing him with a smile of unholy amusement.

With the entrance of Jessamy, the conversation took an abrupt turn. Adjuring Felix not to be a dead bore, he favoured the Marquis with his enthusiastic opinion of the grays. "Complete to a shade!" he said. "Deep, broad chests, light necks, and their hocks perfectly straight! And the quarters so well let-down! I never saw such a well-matched team—and they go well together, too! Your man drove me round the Square behind them —he thought you would not object to it!—and I particularly liked their forward action! High-steppers may be all very well for barouches and landaulets, but for a phaeton, or a curricle, or even a mere gig, I prefer the forward action, don't you, sir?"

"I do," agreed Alverstoke. "Have some lemonade!"

"Oh, thank you, sir!" said Jessamy, taking the glass from Charles Trevor's hand. "No, no cake—thank you!"

"It's a *good* one!" said Felix, generously wishing his elder to share the treat.

Ignoring this interpolation, Jessamy drank his lemonade, and said: "If you please, sir, what did you give those men—the park-keepers, and the cowman?"

"Never mind that!" replied Alverstoke. "I am going to Newmarket tomorrow, and shall be away for a sennight, but when I return to London I shall try out those grays: would you like to go with me?"

The answer was plainly to be read in Jessamy's sudden flush, and kindling eyes. He gasped: *"Sir——!"* but, an instant later, his countenance hardened, and he said: "I would like it very much, sir—but—but—I *must* repay you for the sum you expended to save Luff!"

This declaration confronted Alverstoke at once with a novel situation, and a dilemma. No other member of his family had ever felt it incumbent upon him (or her) to repay the sums he had from time to time disbursed: all too many of them demanded unlimited largesse as a right; and not two hours previously he had registered a silent vow to decline to assume the smallest responsibility for Fred Merriville's sons. That was one thing. He now discovered that it was quite another to allow a stripling to hand over to him, out of what he guessed to be a small allowance, whatever sum Charles Trevor had been obliged to spend on Lufra's behalf. Fighting against fate, he said: "Believe me, it is quite unnecessary! I neither know nor care what it cost to redeem Lufra—and if you badger me on this very boring matter I shall not invite you to go with me when I try out my new team!"

There was a moment's tense silence; then Jessamy raised his eyes, no longer glowing, but uncomfortably austere. "Very well, sir," he said quietly. "Will you tell me, if you please, what I owe you?"

"No, young Stiff-rump! I will not!"

"I beg your pardon, sir, but there is no reason that I know of why you should be obliged to pay for my dog's trespass."

"Then you cannot be aware that your father—er—commended you all to my care," replied his lordship, driven into the last ditch.

"My sister told me something of the sort," said Jessamy, frowning, "but I don't see how that can have been, for I know he left no Will."

"Since the matter was between him and me, it would be astonishing if you did see how it came about. It doesn't concern you. As for Luff's misdemeanour, I wish to hear no more about it. Don't take him into the Green Park again!"

The deliberate hauteur with which he spoke had its calculated effect: Jessamy's conscience might trouble him, but it was superseded by a vague but horrid fear that he had committed a social solecism. He stammered: "N-no, sir! It—it is very kind of you! I didn't know—! Pray don't be offended! One—one doesn't like to be beholden—But if you are indeed our guardian it alters the case—I suppose!"

The Marquis smiled at him, which, as it was not given to him to read the thoughts hidden by the smile, very much relieved his mind. Had he known that the Marquis was wondering what madness had seized him, and to what tiresome lengths he might be expected to go now that he had so rashly acknowledged the Merrivilles' claim upon him, Jessamy would have suffered an agony of mortification; but as he knew nothing about his lordship's habitual reluctance to interest himself in the affairs of his relatives he was able to take his leave blithely, and to stride back to Upper Wimpole Street in the best of spirits, and with his head full of the delightful prospect of driving to Richmond with his lordship, and even, perhaps, of being allowed to handle the reins himself for a little way.

Meanwhile, the Marquis had set out for Wardour Street, his youthful companion prancing beside him, and beguiling the tedium of the way by describing to him in detail the various exhibits he had that morning seen at Merlin's Mechanical Museum. These included such attractions as a juggler, an aerial cavalcade, Merlin's Cave, and a set of Antique Whispering Busts (very ingenious); but these had not interested Felix as much as a hydraulic vase, a band of mechanical music, and a mechanical cruising frigate. If it was still in existence (but his little guide-book was rather out-of-

date), he meant next to visit an exhibition at Spring
Gardens, where Maillardet's Automaton was to be seen.
This marvel, according to the tattered guide-book he
dragged from his pocket, was a musical lady, who was
advertized, rather alarmingly, to perform most of the
functions of animal life, and to play sixteen airs upon
an organized pianoforte, by the actual pressure of the
fingers. No, he had not visited the British Museum:
except for a collection of stuffed birds, it held nothing
but fusty *old* things, which only such people as
Jessamy liked.

Several persons with whom Alverstoke was well acquainted were encountered on the way, a circumstance
which led, later, to a good deal of discussion in the
clubs. The merchant-dandy, Mr Thomas Raikes, known
to the ton as Apollo, because (said the irreverent) he
had risen in the east and was setting in the west, had
been dumbfounded to see Alverstoke with a schoolboy beside him when he had emerged from his own
house in Berkeley Square; and Mr Rufus Lloyd, meeting Alverstoke in Bond Street, and asking whither he
was bound, was later able to disclose, in bewildered
accents, that he was going to visit a foundry in Soho.
This was generally received with incredulity; but Sir
Henry Mildmay, a man of more parts than the Red
Dandy, had no hesitation in saying, with an indulgent
but odiously superior smile: "I am afraid he was
roasting you, Rufus." Lord Petersham, a lifelong friend
of Alverstoke's, came nearest to the mark when he said,
with his slight lisp: "Taking one of hith nephewth
there, I darethay."

Mr Endymion Dauntry, also meeting Alverstoke in
Bond Street, could have set Petersham right, but he was
not present at the discussion, and he had been only
mildly surprised to see the Marquis with a schoolboy in
tow. A magnificent young man, Mr Dauntry: splendidly
built, and classically featured; with a profile that commanded the admiration of a number of ladies, who declared that he might pose as a model for Greek
statuary; a pair of brown eyes; beautifully moulded
lips; and curling brown locks above a noble brow. Such
an extraordinary degree of good-looks inevitably at-

tracted attention; and if his understanding had been
more than moderate, and his conversation more entertaining, he would have been a prime favourite with the
ladies. This, unfortunately, was not the case. He was
amiable and polite, but as he was also slow-witted, and
untroubled by ideas, his conversation consisted of
laboured commonplaces, and only became animated
when he was describing the obstacles successfully
cleared in the course of a hazardous five-mile point,
the circumstances which had led to his taking a toss at
a regular rasper, or the sport he had enjoyed on some
capital scenting-day. His brother officers rated him a
very good fellow, but nicknamed him, in affectionate
derision, Noddy Dauntry, to which he raised not the
smallest objection, merely smiling sleepily, and saying
that he never had been one of the downy ones. He was
a dutiful son, and a kind brother; and although he
happily accepted an allowance from Alverstoke (as
well as his cornetcy, and his horses), he was very
grateful for these benefits, and rarely applied to him
for further monetary assistance.

When he caught sight of Alverstoke in Bond Street,
he immediately crossed the road to greet him, beaming
with honest pleasure, and saying, as he stretched out his
hand: "Cousin Vernon! Devilish good of you to invite
my sister to your ball—'pon my soul it is! Mama is
devilish obliged to you, and so am I too, of course!"

"Do you mean to grace it with your presence?" enquired Alverstoke.

"Oh, by Jupiter, yes! I should rather think I do!
What a squeeze it will be!"

"Devilish!" agreed his lordship.

"Bound to be!" said Endymion, wisely nodding.
"First ball at Alverstoke House since Cousin Eliza's
come-out—so Mama says! Bound to be a squeeze!"
Becoming aware of the presence of Master Felix Merriville, who, bored with this conversation, had given the
Marquis's sleeve an admonitory tug, he looked down
at him from his Olympian height, vaguely surprised,
and then directed a questioning look at Alverstoke.
Informed that Felix was Fred Merriville's youngest
child, he said: "No, is he? Well, by Jove! Fred Merri-

ville!" After that, he somewhat naïvely added: "Got a devilish bad memory!—Who *is* Fred Merriville?"

"He *was* a cousin of mine," coolly replied the Marquis. "Unhappily, he is now deceased; and as he was some years my senior I should doubt whether you ever knew him."

"As a matter of fact, I didn't," confessed Endymion. "But I have it now! You've become guardian to his children, cousin! Mama was telling me. Said you were giving the ball for them. She don't seem to like it above half, but I'll be dashed if I know why!" He lowered his gaze again to Felix's impatient countenance, and a frown creased his brow. "Except that—well, damn it, this nipperkin don't want to go to a ball, do you, young 'un?"

"No!" said Felix, with unnecessary emphasis. "I want to go to the *foundry!*"

"You shall, Felix, you shall!" said the Marquis reassuringly. He bent his sardonic glance upon his heir, and said: "Perhaps you would like to accompany us, Endymion?"

Mr Dauntry, though he laid no claim to being (as he phrased it) up to all the rigs, was by no means (as he also phrased it) a bag-pudding. Foundries were connected in his mind, in a rather nebulous way, with guns, and he said, knowledgeably: "Artillery, eh? No, no, beyond my touch, cousin!"

He then took leave of Alverstoke, and proceeded on his way, feeling none of the amazement or the apprehension which tortured his mother and his astute Cousin Louisa, but accepting with perfect equanimity Alverstoke's explanation of the interest he felt in the unknown Merrivilles.

Any faint hope that Alverstoke might have cherished that he would be denied admittance to the foundry perished at the outset. His estimable secretary had not failed to pave the way for him: no sooner had he presented his card than every door, metaphorically speaking, was flung wide, and the head of the foundry, attended by various senior satellites, was hastily summoned to conduct him all over the building. This extremely competent person not only declared that he was honoured by his lordship's visit, but assured him also of his readiness to explain the intricacies of whatever piece of modern machinery it was that had attracted his lordship's curiosity: a promise which convinced Felix that his instinct had not misled him when it had prompted him to reject the offer of Mr Trevor's escort. "He would have *never* have done it for Mr— Mr Thingummy!" he whispered triumphantly.

By what his lordship considered to be a rare stroke of good fortune, the manager of the foundry was not only the progenitor of a large family, but had failed to discover in any of his sons a trace of his genius. Within five minutes of making the youngest Merriville's acquaintance he recognized in him a kindred spirit; and from then on the Marquis was allowed, much to his relief, to sink into the background. He followed meekly in the wake of the enthusiasts; and the tedium of the expedition was alleviated for him by Felix, in whom he found himself taking an unexpected interest. He knew little, and cared less, about blowing-machines or pneumatic lifts, but he very soon realized that the questions Felix put to their guide showed sufficient knowledge to command that expert's respect. He began to think that there was more to Felix than he had at first supposed; and he was not surprised when, at the end of their exhaustive tour of the foundry, the manager ventured to congratulate him on that young gentleman's remarkable understanding. He was aware of a flicker of pride in his protégé, and that did surprise him.

As for Felix himself, it was evident that nothing in his experience had ever come within striking distance of the high treat he had enjoyed. Rendered almost inarticulate by the speculations engendered in his busy brain by the information he had acquired, he could only stammer out his gratitude, and express (anxiously) the hope that Cousin Alverstoke had also enjoyed himself. "J-Jessamy said you didn't w-want to come, but you *did,* sir, d-didn't you?"

"To be sure I did!" replied the Marquis, perjuring his soul without hesitation.

"And even if you didn't, you m-must have been interested!" said Felix, with a brilliant smile.

The Marquis agreed to this too. He then summoned up a hackney, and put Felix into it, directing the jarvey to drive him to Upper Wimpole Street, and at the same time bestowing a guinea upon Felix: largesse so handsome as to deprive the recipient of all power of speech until the jarvey had whipped up his horse, and to make it necessary for him to lean perilously out of the window of the hack to shout his thanks to his benefactor.

IX

While the Marquis was enjoying a hedonistic sojourn at Cheveley, attending the Second Spring Meeting at Newmarket every day, and watching his promising filly, Firebrand, win a Subscription race against strong competition, the Merriville ladies were busy with the preparations necessary for their forthcoming appearance at the Alverstoke Ball, slightly, but not (except for one incident) very seriously harassed by the exploits of the scions of the family. Finding his brother immersed in his studies, and his sisters in frills and furbelows, Felix sought amusement on his own account. He remembered that the Marquis had said that Mr Trevor should go with him to Margate on the steampacket; but when he called at Alverstoke House to remind Charles of this promise, he was disappointed to learn that Charles, having been granted leave of absence, had gone out of town. This was disappointing; but Felix thought that he might at least go down to the river to watch the packet steam away. That, as he afterwards explained, was all he had meant to do; and if the day had not been so fine, the paddle-wheels so fascinating, and the fare to Margate so moderate (if one did not object to the Common Cabin), that was all he would have done. But the combination of these circumstances, coupled with the wealth jingling in his pocket, had proved to be too much for his virtuous resolve to do nothing which Frederica might not quite like. If the guinea bestowed upon him by the Marquis was not intact, at least enough of it was left to enable him to disburse nine shillings for the privilege of spending a great many hours on a crowded boat, in the company of a set of far from fashionable persons, most of whom his more fastidious brother would have stigmatized as members of the Great Unwashed. Besides, he had made the acquaintance, on the quay, of the marine engineer, a bang-up fellow! To have missed such a chance of widening his knowledge would have been flying in the face of providence: he was sure that Frederica wouldn't have wished him to do that!

In fact, he had spent very little time in the Common Cabin: his real enthusiasm and his happy knack of making friends wherever he went stood him in good stead, and the ship's company had taken him to their hearts. That was certainly fortunate, as Frederica recognized, when she suitably recompensed the burly individual who restored him to her next day, for he would otherwise have been obliged to spend the night on the beach, the sum left in his pocket not being sufficient to pay for a lodging in Margate. So he had offered his services to the Captain (yet another bang-up fellow), and after being given a rare trimming he had been allowed to remain on board, and had been brought back to London as a stowaway: a circumstance which seemed to afford him the highest gratification.

He was very sorry, he said disarmingly, to have alarmed his family; and he was ready to accept any penalty Frederica might impose on him.

But as it was obvious that not the most severe punishment would outweigh in his mind the bliss of his stolen holiday, with the privilege of being sea-sick on the way from Margate to Ramsgate, and becoming smirched from head to foot with oil and grime, Frederica imposed no penalty, merely begging Jessamy to keep a watch on him. Unlike Charis, who had a great deal of sensibility, and had spent a sleepless night, listening for the truant's return, and conjuring up hideous visions of the accidents which might have befallen him, she had remained (in spite of some inevitable qualms) outwardly calm, adducing, when reproached by Charis, the numerous occasions when Felix, having thrown his loving sisters into agonies of apprehension, had reappeared, not a penny the worse for some hair-raising adventure. In this view she was supported by Miss Winsham, who said that the dratted boy was like a cat: you might fling him as you chose, but he would always land on his feet.

Jessamy, torn between disapproval and secret admiration of his junior's enterprise, accepted the charge laid upon him, and forbore to give Felix (much to that young gentleman's surprise) more than a mild scold. Fixed though his resolve was not to fritter away his time in London, he frequently knew an impulse to cast aside his books, and to sample at least some of the recreations offered by the Metropolis. Frederica's request furnished him with an unassailable excuse for yielding to his baser self; and although he did drag Felix up the three hundred and forty-five steps of the Monument, informing him, when, for the sum of sixpence apiece, they stood on the iron balcony at the top, that it was twenty-four feet higher than Trajan's Pillar, that was the first and last educative expedition of a memorable week. Once Felix had ascertained that the New Mint, with its powerful steam-engines, and its gas-lighting, could only be visited by special recommendation, he was perfectly ready to enjoy some less improving sights, such as the lions and tigers at Exeter 'Change; an Aquatic Representation at Sadler's Wells; a roaring melodrama at the Surrey Theatre; and a sparring-match at the Fives-Court, in St Martin's Street. But at this point Jessamy's uncomfortable conscience intervened, and he refused to take Felix either to a burletta, or to the Cock-pit Royal. Never having seen a more exciting theatrical performance than some Scenes from Shakespeare, enacted at Christmas in his godfather's house, he had been carried away by the melodrama, and had turned a deaf ear to his conscience, which had whispered to him that in taking Felix to the Surrey Theatre he had exposed his tender mind to corruption; but when he saw the company assembled in the Fives-Court there was no possibility of ignoring his conscience, which positively shouted at him that he was not only leading his young brother into haunts of vice but was himself in danger of succumbing to the wicked lures of London. Such counter-attractions as St Paul's Cathedral, the Tower, or Bullock's Museum having been unequivocally scorned by Felix,

he had the happy notion of proposing a trip from the
Paddington Basin by passage-boat on the Grand Junc-
tion Canal to Uxbridge; and Felix might have been
obliged to submit to this voyage (which, to one who
had experienced the joys of the steam-packet, could
not be anything but a dead bore), had he not discovered in his guide-book, the existence of the Peerless
Pool. This spacious bathing-place, with its covered
bath, its bowling-green, its library, and its fish-pond,
was situated in Moorfields, behind Bethlehem Hospital.
Jessamy, who was beginning to know his London,
suspected, from its location, that it might not be a
genteel resort; but when he learned that it had formerly
been known as the Perilous Pond, from the number of
persons who had been drowned while swimming in it,
his objections to visiting it naturally vanished. He readily agreed to go there, mentally resolving, however, not
to allow Felix to plunge into the Pool until he had
satisfied himself (by experiment) that it was reasonably
safe for him to do so. But as the Perilous Pond had
long since been converted into a bathing-place of perfect safety, and was, on a brisk spring day, quite deserted, the brothers tacitly decided to postpone
swimming in it until rather later in the season.

Felix naturally told the rest of the family about the
Peerless Pool, and how he and Jessamy had made up
their minds to go there again, when the weather became
warmer; but when he was alone with Jessamy he said
that he didn't mean to tell them about the visit to the
Fives-Court. "You know what females are!" he said.
"They'd very likely set up a screech—just as if there
was any harm in watching a good mill!"

These lighthearted words were the final blow to his
brother's sensitive conscience. They made Jessamy
realize that not only had he too taken care to say nothing about the visit to the Fives-Court, and the Surrey
Theatre, but that he had crowned his iniquity by teaching Felix (by his own example) to be deceitful. The
austere expression, dreaded by his family, hardened his
eyes, and thinned his lips; and he said: "No, but I
shouldn't have taken you there, and I mean to tell
Frederica about it. There was no harm in the bouts

themselves, but in the company—the betting—the—
well, never mind, but it was very wrong of me to introduce you into such a place!"

"Oh, fudge—*Jessie!*" said Felix disgustedly.

He was prepared for battle, but although Jessamy's
eyes flashed he ignored the insult, and turned away.

Frederica, when the tale was manfully disclosed to
her, took a lenient view. She did not think that a
twelve-year-old boy stood in much danger of being
corrupted by witnessing either an exciting melodrama,
or a bout of fisticuffs; and even when Jessamy told her
that there had been aspects to the melodrama which
were decidedly immoral, she said, with strong com-
mon-sense: "I don't suppose he paid the least attention to what may have been a trifle *warm:* all he cared
for was the adventure! Of course it wouldn't do to
make a practice of taking him to see such plays, but
don't tease yourself, Jessamy! You've done him no
harm at all, depend upon it! As for the boxing, I think
it perfectly horrid, but I know very well that gentlemen of the *first* consideration see nothing wrong with
it. Why even your godfather—"

"It wasn't the boxing, but the company," Jessamy
said. "I didn't know—but I might have guessed!—
that I, who mean to enter the Church, was leading my
little brother into bad ways!"

Recognizing the signs of what her brother Harry
rudely called the Early Christian Martyr, Frederica
said hastily: "Nonsense, Jessamy! You are refining too
much upon it! *You* may have noticed the company, but
all Felix cared for was the fights."

"It seems to me," said Jessamy heavily, "that ever
since we came to London you have thought of nothing
but ball-dresses for Charis, and—*worldly* things!"

"Well, if I didn't think of them, who would?" she
replied. "Someone must do so, you know, or where
should we be?" She looked quizzically at him. "Never
mind moralizing, my dear, but try for a little worldly
sense yourself, and stop encouraging our neighbour to
haunt us!"

"Haunt us!" he repeated, frowning. "If you mean
that he is friendly and obliging—"

"I don't, goose! I mean that he is dangling after Charis, and fast becoming a great nuisance."

"If you don't like him, why don't you tell Charis to keep a proper distance? Very pretty behaviour it would be for me to be giving him a set-down! Besides, why should I? He speaks to Charis with the greatest respect, I promise you. What's more, it was *I* who became acquainted with him, days before he met Charis!"

Her eyes danced, but she said gravely: "So it was!"

"And his mother came to visit you, too, which *I* thought very kind and civil! Why were you so starched up? Yes, and why did you fob her off when she invited us all to dine, and spend a snug evening in their house? Isn't she a respectable person?"

"Eminently so, I daresay, but it would not do to become intimate with that family, or with their friends. To be plain with you, Jessamy, they may be good, worthy people, but they aren't up to the rig! Mrs Nutley's patronage cannot give us consequence—in fact, it would be excessively harmful! Her manners, you know, are *not* distinguished, and, from what Buddle tells me, Mr Nutley is a very ungenteel person."

"Buddle!" he ejaculated.

She smiled. "My dear, if Buddle holds up his nose you may depend upon it he is right! Papa once told me that a good butler may be trusted to smell out a commoner in the twinkling of a bedpost! *Young* Nutley, I own, has more polish than his parents, but he's an April-squire, Jessamy!"

"If a man is good and worthy, as you've said yourself, Frederica, I care nothing for the rest!" announced Jessamy.

"Well, of all the plumpers—!" exclaimed Frederica. "You are the highest stickler of us all! Why, even the Master wasn't so severe about that poor, goodnatured man who hired the Grange two years ago! You said he was a thruster, and a City-mushroom, and—"

"Two years ago!" he interrupted, flushing. "I hope I am wiser now!"

"Yes, love, so do I!" replied his sister frankly. "For if you mean to become a parson you ought not to condemn worthy men merely because, through ignorance, they *thrust*, or *cram*, or press upon hounds!"

That retort ended the discussion. Jessamy withdrew in haughty silence; and Frederica returned to the worldly matters which had brought her to London.

In these she received indifferent support from Charis, in whom her ambition was centred, and from Miss Winsham, who despised marriage as a career for females, but who reluctantly acknowledged that it was all that such a pretty pea-goose as Charis was fitted for. Charis herself looked forward to a London season with mild pleasure. To a girl who had never gone beyond the bounds of Herefordshire, and whose amusements had been confined to summer picnics and garden-parties, and such evening entertainments as small dances, or occasional amateur theatricals, the prospect of London balls, Venetian breakfasts, routs, assemblies, visits to the theatre and to the opera, and even, perhaps, to Almack's, could not fail to be agreeable. But when she discovered that her dear Frederica meant to spend every available penny on her wardrobe, making shift for herself as best she might, she would have none of it. In general, the most docile girl imaginable, she could occasionally be obstinate; and no sooner did she realize that Frederica meant to commission Aunt Scrabster's unassuming dressmaker to make a gown for herself to wear at the Alverstoke ball than she declared, looking as mulish as such a lovely, gentle creature could, that she disliked every one of the expensive dresses offered by the fashionable modiste to whose discreetly elegant premises in Bruton Street Alverstoke had directed Frederica.

Frederica had thanked him coolly for his advice, saying that she had no doubt of his being a good judge of such matters; but when, wickedly quizzing her, he had told her just to mention his name to Madame Franchot, if she wished to command that genius's most inspired endeavours, she so far forgot herself as to respond, with a sad absence of maidenly propriety: "So I would, if I had the desire to be taken for a high flyer!"

"And what, may I ask, do you know about high

flyers, Frederica?" he enquired, controlling a quivering lip.

"Not very much but Papa told me that they are *dressy* bits of mus—"

She stopped short, but his lordship obligingly completed the phrase for her. "—muslin! Very true, but, as your guardian, I am deeply shocked, and must request you to strive in future *not* to put me to the blush—at least in public!"

"Oh, no! I wouldn't! I mean—" she met his eyes, and broke into laughter. "You are the most detestable man I ever encountered! Now tell me which milliner you think most worthy of my valuable custom!"

"Certainly: visit Miss Starke, in Conduit Street! Her taste is impeccable."

"I'm much obliged to you! I expect she is dreadfully expensive, but I shouldn't wonder at it if she lowered her prices when she learns that Charis is to make her come-out *this* season, under Lady Buxted's protection," said Frederica shrewdly.

She was quite right. Miss Starke, too often compelled to employ her art in the making of hats and bonnets which would set off a plain face to the best possible advantage, and her sensibilities too often lacerated by the determination of a client well past her prime to purchase a hat designed for a girl in her first season, recognized in the younger Miss Merriville the realization of a dream. She had designed hats for many beautiful young ladies, her unerring eye perceiving at a glance that a high crown would not be becoming to Miss A., that Miss B. must not be allowed to wear a close bonnet, or Miss C. a daring hat à la Hussar; but never before had she been invited to supply hats to a client who looked ravishing in every hat that was tenderly placed over her shining curls. It was not a question of finding the hat to set off Miss Charis Merriville to advantage: Miss Charis set off the hats, transforming even the unsuccessful Angoulême bonnet of white thread net, which had pleased no one less than its creator, into a charming confection certain to inspire four out of five fond mothers with the resolve to purchase just such a bonnet for their own daughters. As for the pride of Miss Starke's collection, with its extravagant crown, its huge, upstanding poke, and its cascade of curled plumes, when Miss Starke stood back to observe the effect of it on Charis's head, her eyes filled with tears of triumph, and although she turned them towards her chief assistant, she saw that false critic only through a haze. Miss Throckley had doubted her genius, saying that the hat was too much in advance of the mode, and too exacting for any female to wear. *Now* what had Miss Throckley to say?

Miss Throckley, as might have been expected, was expressing her rapture at the picture presented by Miss in a hat which—if she might venture to say so—very few ladies could wear. It was not for her to advise, but when she thought of seeing it on another, and unworthier head she could not—positively *could* not bear it!

This rhapsody, in which Miss Starke joined with enthusiasm, was interrupted by Frederica, who demanded to be told the price. Upon hearing it, she rose to her feet, smiling, but shaking her head. "Alas, no! I am afraid it is too costly. My sister needs several hats, you see, so we must not run mad over just one. To be sure, it's very pretty, but, then, so is the Villager hat, with the flat crown and the flowers—only that is rather too dear as well. Come, Charis! we mustn't waste any more of Miss Starke's time—or, indeed, our own! It is a great pity, but you may be sure we shall find something you will like just as well."

"Oh, yes!" agreed Charis happily, tying the ribbons of her own bonnet under her left ear. "For my part, I would as lief have the satin straw we saw in that window in Bond Street. Do let us go and look at it again!"

But during this interchange Miss Starke had been doing some rapid thinking, and as Charis began to draw on her gloves she begged her to be seated again, basely accusing Miss Throckley of having made a mistake in the price, and telling Frederica that it was her invariable custom to make substantial reductions when a lady wished to buy several hats. She added her assurance that it must be an object with her to oblige any friend of Lady Buxted.

In point of fact, she had never been called upon to supply her ladyship with so much as a lace cap, but she knew who she was, and that however dowdy she might be she moved in the first circles. Into these circles she would introduce the lovely Miss Merriville; and if the sight of that enchanting face, framed by an exquisite hat, did not bring a flock of matchmaking mamas, with their daughters in tow, to Conduit Street Miss Starke knew nothing of human nature. It was unnecessary to do anything so ungenteel as to hint to the elder Miss Merriville that an arrangement agreeable to both parties might be reached, if she let it be known that her sister's hats were made for her by Miss Starke of Conduit Street. Few of the matrons would refrain from asking Miss Charis where she had found her charming hat; and it was very unlikely that that lovely innocent would withhold the desired information. The answer must be *At Miss Starke's*, not *At Clarimonde's, in New Bond Street*.

So three delightful hats were carried down to Miss Merriville's job-carriage—now dignified by the presence on the box of Owen, the trustworthy footman chosen by Mr Trevor, and approved by Buddle.

"Well, wasn't that famous?" said Frederica, her eyes sparkling with mingled triumph and mischief. "Three hats for very little more than the price of one!"

"Frederica, they were *shockingly* expensive!"

"No more than we can afford. Oh, well, they were not precisely *dagger*-cheap, but hats are most important, you know! Don't tease yourself, love! The next thing is to decide upon a ball-dress for your come-out. Didn't you like *any* of the dresses we saw at Franchot's? Not even the one with the Russian bodice, and the in-lets of blue satin down the front?" Charis shook her head. A little disappointed, Frederica said: "I thought it would be particularly becoming to you. However, if you didn't care for it—What did you think of that very pretty one of white satin, over a pink bodice?"

"I thought *you* would look charmingly in it! Pink always becomes you."

"Charis, we are not talking about a dress for me, and, even if we were, nothing would prevail upon me to make a figure of myself in a dress designed for a girl! Besides, you know very well that Miss Chibbet is making me exactly what I want, for you were with me when I purchased that orange-blossom Italian crape, and the satin for the petticoat!"

"Yes, and I know very well what I want, too," said Charis. *"Please,* Frederica, say I may have it!"

"But, dearest—!" exclaimed Frederica. "Of course you may have anything you want! Unless you've set your heart on something quite unsuitable, and I know you haven't, because you have such good taste. Where did you see it?"

"I'll show you presently," promised Charis, giving her sister's hand a grateful squeeze.

More she refused to disclose, only shaking her head when questioned, and folding her pretty lips tightly together. But when they reached Upper Wimpole Street, she took Frederica to her own bedchamber, and laid before her the latest number of the Ladies' Magazine, opened to display a sketch of a willowy damsel elegantly attired in a three-quarter dress of white sarsnet fastened down the centre with rosettes of pearls, and worn over a white satin petticoat. "W-what do you think, Frederica?" she asked, directing an anxious look at her sister.

Critically surveying the sketch, and mentally eradicating from it such additions to the ensemble as a purple-puce shawl, a tiara, and a black lace head-veil, Frederica came to the conclusion that Charis's instinct had not betrayed her. She was a tall girl, though not (mercifully) as tall as the lady depicted, who appeared to be quite seven-foot high, and the long smooth line of the over-dress would admirably become her. "I like it!" she said decidedly. "It's simple, and yet not in the common way. You are perfectly right, Charis: it would be excessively becoming to you! Particularly those soft, graceful folds to the petticoat, without any flounces or trimming round the hem."

"I knew you would say so!" breathed Charis.

"Yes, but—" Frederica paused, a frown gathering

on her brow. She raised her eyes to the melting blue ones so pleadingly fixed on her face, and said: "You would like Franchot to copy it, I collect. But would she? I am not very sure, but I fancy that London modistes use only their own designs."

"No, no, no!" said Charis, with unusual vehemence. "I mean to make it myself!"

"No, that you shall not!" replied Frederica. "What, make your first appearance in a home-made dress? Never! Charis, if you *knew* for how long I have dreamed of presenting you with everything fine about you—!"

"You shall! I promise you shall, my darling—my *best* of sisters!" Charis declared, warmly embracing her. "Only listen to me! I know I'm not clever, or bookish, and I don't paint, or play the pianoforte, but even my aunt will own that I *can* sew! Yes, and I can cut things out, too, *and* set a sleeve! Why, don't you remember the dress I made to wear at the Squire's party, and how everyone tried to discover whether Aunt Scrabster had sent it from London, or whether we had found a dressmaker in Ross, or Herefordshire, no one else knew anything about? Even Lady Peasmore was hoaxed, for she told Marianne that there was a certain sort of something to my dress which clearly showed that it had been designed by a modiste of the first stare! And I *like* doing it, you know I do, Frederica!"

This was unanswerable, for Charis was indeed a notable needlewoman; but it was not until Miss Winsham, alone with her favourite niece, said stringently: "Let her! If she makes a botch of it—which she won't, for this I *will* say: she may be a ninnyhammer, but she has cleverer fingers than you, Frederica!—it will keep her occupied, and out of the way of that encroaching coxcomb next door!"—that Frederica agreed to the scheme.

X

Miss Winsham being only too glad to depute the duty
of chaperoning her nieces to Lady Buxted, the Misses
Merriville set out alone on the evening of the Alverstoke ball, Miss Winsham, at the last moment, flinging
up a window to demand whether they had provided
themselves with pocket-handkerchiefs, Buddle adjuring
them to take care not to allow their skirts to brush
against the step of the carriage, and Owen handing
them tenderly into this vehicle. Each of the sisters
looked forward to the party in the expectation of spending a delightful evening; neither betrayed (or, indeed,
felt) any of the nervousness common amongst young
ladies making their first appearances in society. Charis,
untroubled by ambition, and unmoved by the extravagant compliments she received, was confident that the
party would be enjoyable, because she always did enjoy
parties: people were so kind! No fears assailed her that
her hand might not be solicited for every dance, for
such a thing had never happened to her. If she had
thought about the matter at all, she would have said
that it arose from the circumstance of having so many
acquaintances in Herefordshire; and if it had been suggested to her that in London, where she was unknown
she might be obliged to sit amongst the chaperons for a
considerable part of the evening, she would have
accepted the warning perfectly placidly, and without the
smallest feeling of pique.

Frederica was not without ambition, but it was centred on her sister. Once satisfied that Charis was in
high bloom, and that the gown Charis had made for
herself would challenge comparison with Franchot's
most expensive creation, she knew no qualms: Charis's
beauty, and her unaffected manners, would ensure her
success. As for herself, being (in her own view) so far

past her prime as to have become almost an ape-leader, her only concern was to provide Charis with an impeccable background. She could see no difficulty about that. She had been the mistress of her father's household for too long to suffer agonies of shyness; the orange-blossom dress made for her by Miss Chibbet, and given a touch of à la modality by Charis's clever fingers, was just the thing for a lady who, without being precisely stricken in years, knew herself to be beyond the marriageable age; the diamond necklace, bestowed by the late Mr Merriville on his wife, gave her dignity; and the little Alexandrian cap with which, deaf to Charis's protests, she had completed her elegant toilette, clearly demonstrated that she was to be ranked amongst the dowagers.

Frederica might not be wholly conversant with the usages of ton parties, but she knew that in inviting her and Charis to dine at Alverstoke House before the ball, the Marquis was conferring a signal honour on them. The few lines he had scrawled on the back of the gilt-edged card, directed in his secretary's neat handwriting, left her in no doubt of his motive, which was to present them to his eldest sister, and several persons who might, he believed, prove useful. He underlined that word, certainly with malicious intent; and ended with a request (but it read more like a command) that they would come to his house a little before the stated hour. The brief message was rather too autocratic for Frederica's taste, but she decided to overlook this, since his lordship was clearly bent on paving the social way for her. She was not to know that he had, in fact, exerted himself most unusually on behalf of his adopted wards, arranging for their benefit a dinner-party composed, with a few exceptions, of persons whom he either avoided, or never noticed at all. Into the first category fell his eldest sister and her husband, his sister Louisa, his loving cousin Lucretia, and Lady Sefton, whose amiability did not, in his eyes, excuse the affectations which never failed to irritate him. The second category was comprised of his two nephews; his two nieces; the eligible and very dull Mr Redmure, who was betrothed to his eldest niece; his heir; his heir's sister

Chloë, and the Honourable Alfred Parracombe, who
had the doubtful felicity to be the husband of the
handsome brunette whose name had quite recently been
linked with his lordship's. It had been linked with several other gentlemen's names too, and the sight of it, on
the scribbled list which included the names of the Ladies
Jevington and Buxted, made Charles Trevor feel a
trifle giddy. He knew better than to question it, however, Mrs Parracombe being one of those who were
invited to provide leaven to what his lordship castical-
ly described as "all this dough". Further leaven was to
be supplied by Lord and Lady Jersey, and by his lordship's lifelong friend, Mr Darcy Moreton. Mr Trevor,
recovering from his astonishment at the names that met
his eyes, conned them again, and detected a fault.
"The numbers are uneven, sir," he pointed out. "There
are ten ladies, and only nine gentlemen, including yourself."

"And ten gentlemen including *your*self!" said his
lordship. "I've no doubt you'd prefer to be excused,
and I don't blame you, but if you think I am going to
preside over this atrocious party without support you
have a very odd notion of my character!"

Charles laughed, but he coloured as well, and said,
with a little stammer: "I—I shall be very happy! Thank
you, sir! Am I—do you wish me to attend the ball
too?"

"Most certainly I do! Bend your mind while I'm
away to the task of arranging the table: that should
keep you as fully occupied as even you could wish!"

"I must own," agreed Charles, glancing down the
list, "that it won't be easy to achieve an entirely successful arrangement. I mean—"

"I know exactly what you mean, my dear boy, and
have long since arrived at the conclusion that it's impossible. Do your best! Place my sister Jevington opposite to me: it will infuritate Lady Buxted, but that
can't be helped. It would be most improper to set her
above Lady Jevington—and I do feel we should consider the proprieties, don't you?"

Mr Trevor, with the name of Mrs Parracombe in
mind, replied woodenly: "Yes, sir."

The Marquis, mockery in his eyes, said approvingly: "Exactly, Charles! Having placed the matter in your competent hands, I may now leave for Cheveley with a quiet mind. No, perhaps I had better write to beg Lady Jevington to act as hostess at the dinner-party: that may mitigate her annoyance when she discovers that Lady Buxted and Mrs Dauntry are to share the honours of receiving the ball-guests. How very exhausting all these arrangements are! If anyone should come to enquire after me while I'm at Cheveley, tell him that I've gone into the country on a repairing lease. And for the rest —do as seems best to you! All I ask is that you should curb your zeal for economy, and refrain from transforming the ballroom into a tent."

"With yards of pink silk! I should rather think not, sir! If you don't dislike it, I should like to deck the room with flowers."

"By all means!" said his lordship cordially. "I perceive—not that I ever doubted it!—that you will leave me nothing to do, which, as you well know, is always my goal."

Owing to Mr Trevor's energy, his pronounced talent for organization, and the tact that won for him the willing co-operation of such jealous persons as his lordship's butler and steward, this hopeful prophesy was fulfilled. The Marquis had only one fault to find with his arrangements. When Mr Trevor laid before him a careful plan of the dinner-table, he transposed two names, as a result of which Mr Trevor found himself placed beside the younger Miss Merriville. This was an agreeable alteration, but he thought it his duty to suggest that it was just conceivable that Mr Endymion Dauntry might not wish to sit beside his cousin Jane.

"Very likely not—in fact, almost certainly not," said the Marquis. "What gave you the notion that Endymion's wishes interest me?"

That was the sort of remark, reflected Mr Trevor, which made his lordship so incalculable. He could repel and attract at one and the same time. Nothing could be more alienating than the cold indifference he showed towards the members of his family; nothing more en-

dearing than the consideration he gave to the probable
wishes of his secretary. He could, with a shocking want
of delicacy, include amongst his guests a lady who
would certainly set his sisters in a bustle of virtuous
indignation; but when he commanded his secretary's
attendance, as though it were a part of his duties, Mr
Trevor knew very well that all that was expected of
him was that he should enjoy himself, and act, in the
manner of an aide-de-camp, as a secondary host.

He had never doubted that he would enjoy the ball,
for this was a treat which seldom came in his way; and,
thanks to the Marquis's intervention, he was now able
to look forward to the dinner with pleasurable anticipa-
tion.

The first guests to arrive were the Jevingtons, bringing the eligible Mr Redmure in their train. Lady Jevington made her appearance regally attired, wearing a
magnificent and very ugly diamond tiara, and in a
mood of overpowering graciousness. This found instant expression when Alverstoke said: "I fancy I need
not introduce Charles to you, Augusta?" She replied
at once, holding out her hand to Mr Trevor, and bestowing upon him a smile of rare condescension: "Indeed, no! Well, Charles, how do you do? And how is
your worthy father? And your dear mama? Such an age
since I have seen them! you must tell me all about
them!"

He was spared this necessity by the arrival, first of
the Buxted party, and next, following hard upon their
heels, of Mrs Dauntry and Chloë, Mrs Dauntry looking
remarkably handsome in one of the clinging gowns
which she habitually wore, and which so well became
her slender figure. This one, which Lady Buxted mentally priced at fifty guineas, and Lady Jevington at
rather more, was of lilac spider-gauze over an underdress of rose satin. She too wore a diamond tiara, by
no means so imposing as the heirloom which crowned
Lady Jevington, but far more delicately made. Over it
she had cast one of her lace veils; lilac kid gloves
(French, and not a penny less than five guineas, thought
Lady Buxted indignantly) covered her arms; she carried a painted fan in one hand; and a frivolous little

reticule hung from her wrist. The other hand she extended to Alverstoke, murmuring: "Dear Vernon!" As he gratified her, and infuriated his sisters, by raising it to his lips, she turned her huge sunken eyes towards those fulminating ladies, and acknowledged them by a faint, sweet smile which held affection but not so much as a hint that she regarded either as her hostess. "Dear Vernon!" she repeated. "Am I late? How naughty of me! But I know you will forgive me! And here is quite your most constant admirer!—Chloë, my darling!"

Miss Dauntry, who had attained her seventeenth birthday three days earlier, dropped a schoolgirl's curtsy, as much surprise as alarm in her heart-shaped face. Her mama having omitted to inform her that she considered her formidable cousin in the light of a fairy godfather, she was thrown off her precarious balance, and looked anxiously at Mrs Dauntry for guidance. The Marquis, observing her dismay, said affably: "And for how long have I been—how did you phrase it, Lucretia? Ah, yes!—*first oars* with you, Chloë? Or haven't I been?"

"Oh, *no!*" she answered ingenuously. She then blushed hotly, and stammered: "I don't mean—that is, —Well, I don't know you very well, c-cousin!"

He smiled. "Good girl! It clearly behoves me to cultivate your acquaintance, doesn't it?" He then took pity on her embarrassment, and handed her over to Charles Trevor, in whose unalarming company she soon recovered her complexion. The Marquis, critically surveying her, said, in his abrupt way: "A pretty child, and may well improve. A pity she takes after her father, rather than after you, Lucretia. She'll never be a beauty, but she's a taking little thing. My compliments on her dress: your choice, I fancy!"

Mrs Dauntry was pleased by this tribute, which was indeed well-deserved. She had expended much time and thought, as well as a great deal of money, on the deceptively simple dress Chloë was wearing; and with unerring good taste, she had chosen for her a primrose muslin, which was far more becoming to her than the conventional white, or the pale blues and pinks generally considered suitable for girls. She had big brown eyes and brown hair, and a warm, creamy skin, which white or blue turned to sallow. Her figure was still immature, and she lacked height, but she would pass anywhere for a pretty girl, decided Alverstoke. Which was more than could be said for Miss Buxted, cutting a deplorable figure in an over-trimmed dress, and with a wreath of pink roses on her head. Wiser counsels had not prevailed with Jane: she had been determined on roses and pink gauze; and she had inherited her mother's shrewish disposition, and was capable of sulking for days together, Lady Buxted had allowed her to have them. The Marquis eyed her with distaste, disliking her artificial titter as much as her appearance. A plain girl, and would soon become bracket-faced: Louisa would never be able to turn her off.

Louisa and Augusta had their heads together. Augusta was making enquiries about the Merrivilles, and blandly expressing her surprise at learning that Louisa had undertaken to chaperon them. "My dear Augusta, I felt it to be my duty," said Lady Buxted. "There was Vernon, quite at a stand, as you may suppose! So like Fred Merriville to have cast the whole family on his hands! If I had not come to the rescue, I don't know what would have become of the girls, because their aunt is quite eccentric—very blue, you know!— and detests going into society."

"Indeed!" said Lady Jevington, receiving this explanation with obvious scepticism. "How grateful Alverstoke must be! And what are they like? No doubt very beautiful!"

"Oh, dear me, no! I have met only the elder: quite a good-looking girl, but I shouldn't describe her as a beauty. I believe the younger sister is the prettier of the two. Vernon, did you not tell me that Miss Charis Merriville is pretty?"

"Very likely," he responded. "*I* think her so, at all events. You must tell me how she strikes you, dear Louisa!"

At that moment, Wicken announced Miss Merriville, and Miss Charis Merriville, and there was no need for Lady Buxted to tell her brother how Charis struck her, for the answer was plainly written in her face.

Frederica entered the room a little in advance of her sister, and paused for a moment, glancing swiftly round. The impression she created was one of elegance. Not even the Alexandrian cap could make her look in the least like a dowager; but the fashion of her orange-blossom crape, with its bodice cut in the Austrian style, the shawl of Albany gauze, caught up over her elbows, the sparkle of diamonds round her throat, and, above all, her quiet assurance, clearly showed that she neither was, nor considered herself to be, a girl in her first bloom. She had more the appearance of a young matron, with several years' experience behind her.

Only for a few seconds did she come under the scrutiny of her host's relations; and it was not she who brought to an abrupt end the various conversations in progress. It was Charis, entering the room in her wake, who stunned the assembled company into silence, caused even the stolid Lord Buxted to cut a sentence off in mid-air, and made Lord Jevington wonder (as he afterwards disclosed to his austere Viscountess) if he really was attending a party at Alverstoke House, or asleep and dreaming.

Lady Jevington, a just woman, did not blame him: Miss Charis Merriville was unquestionably the embodiment of a dream. A slender snow-maiden, dressed all in white, a wreath of lilies of the valley in her shining hair, and no touch of colour about her except that which was supplied by the gold of her curls, the deep blue of her eyes, and the delicate rose of her cheeks and lips. No man could be blamed for thinking that he beheld a celestial vision. Exquisitely gowned, too! thought her ladyship, bestowing her silent approval on the slim three-quarter dress of sarsnet, fastened with pearl rosettes (procured, had she but known it, at a fascinating shop in the Pantheon Bazaar), and worn over an underdress of shimmering ivory satin. Charis's only ornament was the single row of pearls inherited from her mother: precisely the thing, further approved Lady Jevington, for a girl to wear in her first season. No more than she blamed her lord for an enthusiasm quite unbecoming to his years did she blame her volatile son, the Hon. Gregory Sandridge, for his dropped jaw,

and riveted gaze. The girl was lovely, judged by any
standards. Lady Jevington, her Anna eligibly betrothed,
was able to feel quite sorry for poor Louisa, so obviously taken-in by Alverstoke, and so foolishly betraying her fury in her glaring eyes and reddened
cheeks. Easy to see, of course, why Alverstoke had
accepted the charge laid upon him! Far too young for
him, and in every way unsuitable, but no need to worry
about that: he would become bored by her within a
month. Not very much need to worry about Gregory
either: he would fall in and out of love for some years
yet before he formed a lasting attachment; and if
Charis's charms proved stronger than his passion for
sport his mama had no doubt of her ability to detach
him from the girl. But how very well served poor Louisa
would be, if her staid Carlton succumbed to Fred Merriville's daughter! When she thought of Louisa's grasp-
ing, nip-cheese ways, her spiteful temper, and the un-
justifiable demands she made upon Alverstoke, Lady
Jevington could not even find it in her to blame her disgraceful brother for having bamboozled her so wickedly.

As Alverstoke moved forward to greet his wards,
Chloë, her rapt gaze fixed on Charis, breathed: "Oh
. . . ! How *beautiful* she is! like a fairy princess!"

Mr Trevor glanced down at her, and nodded, smiling.

"Well, my children?" said the Marquis paternally.

Frederica's eyes twinkled, but she replied calmly:
"How do you do, cousin?" and passed on immediately
to Lady Buxted. "How do you do, ma'am? May I make
my sister known to you? Charis, Lady Buxted—our
kind protectress!"

Lady Buxted pulled herself together, forcing a smile
to her lips, and giving her hand to Charis, dropping a
slight, graceful curtsy before her. "I beg your pardon,
ma'am, for not accompanying my sister when she
visited you," Charis said, in her soft voice. "I was so
sorry!"

"To be sure, you were laid up with a cold, or some
such thing, were you not? Well, now I must introduce
you to my sister, Lady Jevington," responded Lady

Buxted, rigidly cordial, and well-aware that Augusta had guessed how abominably she had been hoaxed, and was rejoicing in her discomfiture. The graciousness with which Augusta met the Misses Merriville confirmed her in this belief; and she was left to derive what consolation she might from the reflection that That Woman must be as deeply chagrined by the arrival on the scene of a transcendent beauty as she was herself.

But Mrs Dauntry, who had never been known to betray such unworthy emotions as anger or resentment, received the sisters with even more graciousness than had Lady Jevington, summoning Chloë to be introduced to her new cousins, and subsequently drawing Alverstoke's attention to the charming picture Charis and Chloë made, as they sat talking together on a small sofa at the end of the room. Well within hearing of the Ladies Jevington and Buxted, she described them as the prettiest girls in the room, which, as Frederica stood outside this category, gently paid off several old scores, the only other girls present being Miss Dandridge, and Miss Buxted. "Not," she added, with her wistful smile, "that I mean to compare them, for even to *my* partial eyes my little Chloë is a farthing to the sum of your lovely Charis. My dear Alverstoke, she will have half London at her feet!" She laughed, and looked archly up at him. "What enemies you will win to yourself amongst some of our matchmaking mamas! If my Chloë were not far too young to be thinking of marriage, I am sure I should be one myself!"

Deeply appreciative, the Marquis had just time to respond: "Admirable, dear Lucretia!" before his attention was claimed by the arrival of the Seftons.

The last of the guests to arrive was Endymion, who came in, looking like a handsome, overgrown schoolboy detected in crime, and stammering an apology for his tardiness. He begged his cousin's pardon, and—with a deprecating glance round the room—everyone's! He had been on guard-duty—Cousin Vernon would understand—But at this point he broke off, suddenly seeing Charis, and stood staring at her in undisguised admiration until somewhat acidly recalled from this trance by Lady Jevington, who said that she believed

he was already known to my Ladies Jersey and Sefton.
This made him start, flush up to the roots of his hair,
and utter some incoherent apologies, as he bowed to
their ladyships. Fortunately, both were amused rather
than offended, for although Lady Sefton was too goodnatured to take umbrage, Lady Jersey was a very high
stickler indeed. Endymion was saved from one of her
set-downs, partly because he was, in general, extremely
punctilious, as well as being just the sort of handsome
young man of breeding whom any hostess was happy
to invite to her balls and assemblies; and partly because
the Fanes and the Dauntrys had (as she phrased it)
known one another for ever. One of her closest childhood friends had been Alverstoke's youngest sister: that
Poor Eliza, who had married a mere Mr Kentmere,
and almost vanished from the London scene; and although Alverstoke, four years senior to the fascinating
Sally Fane, had never been amongst the aspirants to her
hand and fortune, she frankly owned that she had a
tendre for him, and ranked him amongst her oldest
friends. He was some ten years younger than the Earl
of Jersey, but well-acquainted with him, both being
Harrovians, and rivals on the Turf and the hunting-
field; and both residing, when in London, in Berkeley
Square: a circumstance which, according to Lady Jersey, not only made them neighbours, but posed an
insoluble problem: if invited to a dress-party at Alverstoke House, was it more proper to call out one's carriage, or to demean oneself by walking some fifty yards
to the party?

Lady Jersey was known, in certain circles, as Silence;
but anyone who supposed that her flow of light, in-
consequent chatter betokened an empty head much
mistook the matter: she had a good deal of intelligence, and very little escaped her. She had been talking
ever since she entered the room, and on an amazing
number of subjects, ranging from the spate of nuptials
imminent in the Royal Family to the escape of a grue-
some murderer from the gallows, through the discovery
of an ancient statute which allowed him to claim the
right of wager by battle; but while she rattled on she
had been taking mental notes, and very intriguing they

were. She knew already, through a fellow patroness of Almack's, the haughty Mrs Burrell, who had learnt it from the lips of Lady Buxted, that Alverstoke had assumed the guardianship of some young cousins, and was doing his languid best to introduce to the ton the two females of the family, by inviting them to the ball given in honour of his niece; and that had been quite enough to titillate her curiosity. Far better acquainted with Alverstoke than Mrs Burrell, Lady Jersey did not for a moment believe that he had ever entertained the smallest notion of giving a ball in honour of Jane, or any other of his nieces. Then he must be doing it for the sake of his unknown wards—and that was very unlike him too. When she saw Charis, the thought that Charis was Alverstoke's latest flirt entered her ladyship's head only to be instantly dismissed. The girl was lovely, but not in Alverstoke's style. Innocent buds, just unfurling their petals, had never been numbered amongst his victims; and this one, besides being his ward, lacked salt. A beautiful ninnyhammer, decided Lady Jersey, whom Alverstoke would write off as a dead bore within five minutes of making her acquaintance. As for Louise's glib explanation to her old friend, Mrs Drummond Burrell, that Alverstoke thought it his duty to take care of Fred Merriville's children, no one who knew Alverstoke could believe that. Then why—? All at once a solution of the problem occurred to her ladyship. A glance at Lady Buxted confirmed it: he had invited his beautiful ward to this ball to punish Louisa! No doubt she had been plaguing his life out to give a ball for that plain girl of hers, and this was his revenge, devil that he was! Not but what she deserved it, thought Lady Jersey, for her demands on him were ceaseless, and she didn't care a rush for him. Lucretia, too: she was wearing a sweet, wistful smile, but she must be quite as furious as Louisa, perhaps more so, for in addition to seeing her daughter cast into the shade she was obliged to watch her cherished Endymion staring at Charis like a mooncalf.

Then there were the Parracombes—or, rather, Mrs Parracombe, for it would be absurd to suppose that her rich but mutton-headed spouse was concerned with

anything beyond his dinner and his string of race-
horses. What, wondered Lady Jersey, had prompted
Alverstoke to invite them to his dinner-party? His
name had been pretty closely linked with Caroline's
during the past few months, but lately he had not
quite so often been seen in her company: in her ladyship's judgment, she had been rather too capricious,
and very much too possessive. Had Alverstoke bidden
her to this party, so obviously given in honour of his
wards, with the intention of tacitly informing her that
her reign was over? He was perfectly capable of it,
wretch that he was! Poor Caroline!—but she should
have known better than to have thought she could play
fast and loose with Alverstoke! To have attached him
was certainly a triumph; but to have supposed that she
could hold him captive while she divided her favours
between him and her other cicisbeos was a great piece
of folly: his affections had never yet been so deeply
engaged as to inspire him with the desire to outshine
his rivals. If the lady whom he chose to honour with
his (fleeting) devotion encouraged the attentions of
other admirers, he left her with no more than a shrug
of his shoulders; for, little though he might care he
would not share either. Lady Jersey suspected that
when his flirts (to put it no higher) were to be seen
squired by other men it was because he had grown
bored with them, and neglectful.

He had begun to be bored with Mrs Parracombe
some months previously. She was handsome, amusing,
and clever enough to sail close—but never too close—
to the wind. He had recognized in her a high-born lady
with the soul of a courtesan, and, as such, he had
enjoyed his discreet liaison with her, while his passion
for her had lasted. But that had not been for very
long. A luscious beauty, she had aroused his desire,
but not one spark of love in his cold heart.

She knew it; and since she too was a stranger to love
or tenderness she shrugged as carelessly as she could,
and was clever enough to let it be seen, before his
waning interest had been observed by the ton, that it
was she who had wearied of him. Not quite as clever as
Lady Jersey, she did not doubt that the beautiful Miss

Charis Merriville was Alverstoke's latest inamorata, but she bore the introduction with smiling equanimity, merely murmuring to him, at a convenient moment: "Take care, dear friend! When men of your age develop tendres for schoolgirls it is held to be a sign of senility!"

"I'll take care!" he promised, answering smile with smile.

Charles Trevor had warned the Marquis that Endymion might not relish having his cousin Jane as his dinner-partner, but he soon realized that not Endymion but Jane was the principal sufferer. He and Charis were seated immediately opposite the cousins; and Endymion, either bemused, or feeling that he owed no particular civility to Jane, spent the better part of his time gazing raptly across the table at the fair vision before him. It was not the least part of Charis's charm that she rated her beauty low; and, as she always gave her attention to whatever person happened to be conversing with her, she was generally unconscious of the admiring looks cast at her. If she did become aware that she was being stared at she was not at all gratified, but mentally condemned the admirer as a horridly rude person, and wondered if she had a spot forming, or had smudged her face. Neither of these fears crossed her mind when she looked up to find Endymion's brown eyes worshipfully upon her. She blushed, and immediately looked away, but although she wished he would not stare at her it did not occur to her that he was being horridly rude. He was the most splendid young man she had ever seen: the personification of all the heroes who (according to Aunt Seraphina) had no existence beyond the bounds of balladry, or the marbled covers of a romantic novel. If she had not known that he was watching her she would have stolen several glances at him; but she did know it, and, being a well-brought-up girl, she took care not to look at him again. Farther up the table, Frederica, with every appearance of interest, was encouraging Lord Buxted to instruct her in the details of estate management. Lady Jersey, on the other side of the table, observed both sisters from under her lashes, and said suddenly: "Very well indeed, Alverstoke! I like them. Easy, unaffected

manners, both of them; and the Beauty has a modesty
which is particularly engaging. Did you invite me here
to coax me to bestow vouchers for Almack's on them?"

This challenge, delivered with one of her ladyship's
rapier-looks, in no way disconcerted him. Satisfied that
Lady Sefton, on his left hand, was engaged in conversation with Mr Moreton, he replied coolly: "No.
Only to save me from insufferable boredom, Sally! I
rely upon Louisa to procure vouchers for them."

"She won't do it," said Lady Jersey decidedly. "She
will tell you that Mrs Burrell refused to oblige her; and
even you, unfeeling monster that you are, could scarcely expect her to apply to Emily Cowper at this moment!
The Lambs are *all* shattered by Lady Melbourne's
death, and none of them more so than Emily." She
cast another look down the table, and gave a stifled
giggle. "Oh, goodness me, look at Louisa! I'll do it!
Yes, I *will* do it! If only to bring *you* to our assemblies,
Vernon!"

"It won't do so, my loved one: I never lay myself
open to snubs! Or are your snubs reserved for Dukes?"

A ripple of appreciative laughter broke from her.
"Wellington? But he tried to violate our rules, which
you, I am persuaded, would never do!"

"Much you know about it! Ask my loving sisters!"

"No need! I know the answer. *How* they did snub
me—Augusta and Louisa, not my dearest Eliza, be
sure!—when they were young ladies, and I a scrubby
schoolgirl! Will it vex them to death if *I* sponsor your
wards? Oh, goodness me, of course it must! Maria!"

Lady Sefton, her attention thus peremptorily claimed,
turned an amiably enquiring gaze upon her friend.

"Shall we admit Alverstoke's wards to Almack's?"

"Oh, yes, I think we should do so, don't you? Such
pretty-behaved girls—don't you agree? Poor Fred Merriville's daughters, too! Oh, I think we should do what
we can for them!" agreed Lady Sefton, turning back to
Mr Moreton.

"Well, I will," said Lady Jersey. "Oh, but how provoking! Oh, goodness me, *what* a pea-goose I am! I
shall never know now whether that was why you invited me, or not!"

"Never mind!" Alverstoke replied consolingly. "Think how much you will enjoy putting my sisters all on end!"

"Very true!" She sent another glance down the table. "The Beauty will become the rage, of course. The elder has more countenance, but—What's their fortune, Alverstoke?"

"Respectable."

She wrinkled her nose. "Ah, that's a pity! However, one never knows! With *that* face the younger at least need not despair of achieving an eligible alliance. We shall see!"

XI

One part at least of Lady Jersey's prophecy was swiftly realized: Miss Charis Merriville could truly be said to have become the rage overnight. Long before the last of the guests had been received by Alverstoke and his sister Louisa, her hand had been bespoken for every dance; and young gentlemen of high fashion, arriving late, were denied the felicity of encircling her waist in the waltz, and even of leading her into a set of country dances. She would not stand up more than twice with anyone, but she allowed Endymion to escort her down to supper, yielding to his earnest assurance that their relationship made all as right as a trivet. He added, reading doubt in her face: "I'll beg your sister to join us, hey? There she is, with young Greg—m'cousin, you know! You'd like that, wouldn't you?"

"Oh, yes! How very comfortable! And do, pray, beg *your* sister to join us!"

He did not care very much for this suggestion, Chloë being squired at the moment by young Lord Wrenthorpe, who was one of the latecomers who had failed to secure a dance with Charis. One of Endymion's fellow-officers, he had not hesitated to express his opinion of sneaking rascals who stole marches on their friends; and as he was a prime favourite with the ladies, being as audacious as he was lively, Endymion was not at all anxious to include him in the supperparty. He said: "Oh—ah—yes, but she's with Wrenthorpe, y'know!"

"Wouldn't he wish to join us?" she asked innocently. "Your mama introduced him to me, and he was *so* agreeable, and so droll, too, when I was obliged to tell him I couldn't stand up with him! Your mama said that he was a friend of yours: isn't he?"

"Oh, yes! Yes, of course! Best of good fellows!"

said Endymion. "Just thought you might not like—family party, y'know! Not one of the family!"

But the matter was then taken out of his control by that best of good fellows, who descended upon them at that moment with Chloë on his arm, having been struck by the same happy notion of forming a cosy supper-party. In this he was warmly seconded by Chloë, who had conceived a youthful admiration for her wonderful new cousin, and was shyly hoping to be admitted to the ranks of her friends. It was useless for Endymion to talk about family parties; his insouciant friend retorted gaily that families always came to cuffs unless a stranger were inserted into their midst. So Endymion had nothing to do but find Frederica and his cousin Gregory, and to bid them to the feast: sped on his errand by his perfidious friend, who adjured him to: "Bustle about, Noddy, or we shan't be in time to snabble all the lobster patties!"

Lady Buxted had expressed the fear that a ball held at short notice, and before the season's various entertainments were in full feather, might be thin of company, but by the time she went down to supper she knew that not one of the forthcoming routs, balls, or assemblies would excel this one in magnificence or distinction; and she was torn between pride and resentment. Her odious brother had lifted a finger, and the ton had flocked to his house, precisely as he had foretold. That was, naturally, exactly what she had wanted, but it infuriated her nevertheless: it would have done him a great deal of good to have met with a few crushing rebuffs. He had admittedly granted her the opportunity to launch Jane into the highest and most fashionable circles, but that had not been his object: he had meant to launch the Merriville girls into those circles, and he had done it. At least half-a-dozen hostesses had begged her to bring her charming protégées to their projected parties—*her* protégées indeed!—and, to crown all, Sally Jersey had promised them vouchers for Almack's, and had had the effrontery to adjure her —*her!*—to bring them to the Assembly Rooms! "And your own—Jane, is it?—of *course!*" had said Lady Jersey, with a graciousness which had made Lady Buxted yearn to box her ears. "I'll send a voucher—yes, truly I will! And if I *don't,* remind me, Louisa! You know how shatter-brained I am!"

When Lady Buxted remembered impertinent little little Sally Fane, a wretched schoolroom-miss to whom she had administered a number of well deserved set-downs, the delicacies her brother's French cook had prepared for the refreshment of his guests turned to ashes in her mouth. At that moment, nothing would have afforded her more pleasure than to have given Sally yet another set-down. But, whatever rage might possess her soul, at no time did Lady Buxted lose sight of the main chance. No mother with a daughter to dispose of eligibly could afford to disdain the patronage of Lady Jersey, the acknowledged Queen of London's most exclusive club, known to the irreverent as the Marriage Mart. So Lady Buxted, her appetite destroyed, had felt herself obliged to accept Sally's offer with a smile as false and as sweet as the one lilting on Sally's mouth.

Only one annoyance was spared her on that night of mingled triumph and chagrin: Alverstoke invited neither of his wards to stand up with him. Other eyes than Lady Buxted's were watching curiously to see what he would do; but the owners were relieved or disappointed, according to their dispositions, to see that the only ladies he led on to the floor were those of rank or seniority. He did, indeed, pause to exchange a few words with Frederica, but there was nothing to be made of that, for he managed, in spite of his indolence, to speak to every one of his guests.

"Satisfied, Frederica?" he enquired.

She replied impulsively: "I don't know how to thank you! Indeed I am satisfied!" Her sudden smile dawned. "It's my night of triumph, don't you think? I *knew* Charis had only to be seen to be appreciated!" She added anxiously, as he said nothing: "It isn't just my partiality, is it? She *has* made a hit, hasn't she?"

"Decidedly. Do you ever spare a thought for anyone but Charis?"

"Why, of course I do!" she exclaimed, rather shocked. "I think about *all* of them, only at this present

time, you know, I do think about her more than about
the others, because she is my most *pressing* concern."

He looked curiously at her. "Have you no concern
for yourself, Frederica?"

"For myself?" she said, wrinkling her brow. "Well,
if there were any need for me to be concerned I should
be—naturally! As it is—"

"I should have said, any *thought* for yourself," he
interrupted. "You've called this your night of triumph
merely because Charis has made a hit; but it appears
to me that you have been solicited to dance quite as
often as Charis."

She laughed. "Yes—isn't it diverting? I've been positively overwhelmed: my partners hoping that if they are
very civil and attentive I may be moved to present
them to my sister!"

"You are a strange creature," he commented.

He passed on, with a nod, and a slight smile, as
Buxted came up to lead Frederica into a set of quadrilles.

She was puzzled by his lordship's last remark, but
wasted very little time in considering what its implica-
tion might be, and none at all in wondering whether the
various gentlemen who had begged her to stand up with
them a second time really did so with a view to becoming acquainted with her sister. She would have been
incredulous had she been told that amongst the many
who were demonstrably lost in admiration of Charis
there were several persons who found her the more
attractive of the two sisters.

Amongst these was Mr Moreton, who cocked a quizzical eyebrow at Alverstoke, and demanded to know
what sort of a rig he was running.

"None at all," responded Alverstoke coolly.

Mr Moreton sighed. "Dear boy, you can't think—
no, damn it, you really *can't* think to ride on *my* back!
Neither of the explanations offered me for your sponsorship of Merriville's daughters is at all acceptable to me.
On the one hand I learn that you are under an obligation to Merriville; on the other, that you have fallen a
victim to the divine Charis's beauty. Doing it rather too
brown, Ver!"

"Oh, why?" countered his lordship. "Think of the beauties to whom I've fallen a victim, Darcy!"

"I am thinking of 'em. Ripe 'uns, every one!" said Mr Moreton.

"Ah, but did you ever see such perfection of features and figure?"

"No, I've seldom met with a lovelier widgeon," replied Mr Moreton ruthlessly. "The thing is, my taste don't run to sweet simpletons—and nor, dear boy, does yours! The elder sister's the filly for my money. She don't want for sense, and she ain't just in the ordinary style. Not your style, however, so *why* have you taken the pair of 'em under your protection?"

"What else could I do, when Merriville had—er—commended them to my care?"

"Having put you under an obligation! *No,* Ver!" protested Mr Moreton. "Of all the brummish stories I ever heard—! You were never on more than common civility terms with him!"

"Perhaps," murmured his lordship, "I yielded to a compassionate impulse."

"A *what?*" gasped his best friend.

"Oh, did you think I never did so?" said his lordship, the satirical glint in his eyes extremely pronounced. "You wrong me! I do, sometimes—not frequently, of course, but every now and then!"

"Oh, no, I don't wrong you!" retorted Mr Moreton grimly. "I daresay there's very little you wouldn't do for anyone that was a friend of yours—well, good God, don't I know it? If you think I don't know that it was you who pulled poor Ashbury out of ebb-water—"

"I must suppose that you believe you know what you are talking about," interrupted Alverstoke, with considerable acerbity, "but I do not! What's more, Darcy, you're becoming a dead bore! If you must have the truth, I'm shouldering Merriville's daughters into the ton to annoy Louisa!"

"Well, that's what I thought," said Mr Moreton, unmoved. "Only it don't explain why you took a schoolboy to visit some foundry or other!"

That surprised a crack of laughter out of Alverstoke.

"Felix! Well, if ever you should meet him, Darcy, you'll know why I took him over that foundry!"

Another who had formed a very good opinion of the elder Miss Merriville was Lord Buxted: a circumstance which his mother regarded with mixed feelings. She was naturally relieved to know that he had not (like his doltish cousin) fallen instantly under the spell of Charis's beauty; but she had viewed with disfavour the unusual animation with which he had conversed with Frederica during dinner, and with definite hostility his subsequent behaviour. Not content with standing up with her for a full hour, during two country dances, he had shown a disposition to gravitate towards her between dances, which would have alarmed Lady Buxted very much, had he not later described Frederica to her as a conversable female with a good deal of commonsense. As he added that he thought her by no means a bad-looking young woman, Lady Buxted was able to allay her alarm with the reflection that such temperate praise scarcely argued any very marked degree of admiration.

She would have been less complacent had she known that he made it his business to call in Upper Wimpole Street on the following day, to see how the ladies went on after what he termed, with slightly ponderous humour, their night's raking. He was by no means their only visitor, several other gentlemen having presented themselves on the slimmest of pretexts, and Endymion Dauntry on no pretext at all; but he was generally felt to have scored a point by stressing his relationship to the Merrivilles, and by adopting towards them an air of kindness which verged on the avuncular, and would have aroused feelings of strong resentment in the breasts of the three gentlemen he found in possession had he not made it plain that it was Frederica, and not Charis, who was the object of his solicitude.

During the week after the Alverstoke ball, the Misses Merriville received a number of invitations; and Miss Winsham was honoured by a visit from Lady Jersey, who brought with her the promised vouchers for Almack's. She came partly because she was curious, partly because she wished to oblige Alverstoke, and to disoblige his sister Louisa; and by the time she was treading up the stairs in Buddle's wake she was regretting her condescension. She was capricious, but she placed herself on a high form, and had never yet been known to tolerate mushrooms, still less to lend them consequence. She thought the house shabby-genteel; and remembered that Fred Merriville was said to have married a provincial nobody. It was too late to draw back, but she entered the drawing-room with every intention of keeping Miss Winsham at a proper distance. Two minutes were enough, however, to make her abandon her high and imposing manners: Miss Winsham's dress might be old-fashioned, and she was certainly eccentric, but she was not shabby-genteel, and she set as little more by a visit from the Queen of the Ton as she had set by Lady Buxted's previous call. In one of her top-lofty moods, Lady Jersey might have got on to her high ropes; she chose instead to be diverted; and by the time Miss Winsham had favoured her with her opinion of London houses in general, and furnished ones in particular; of marriage, of coxcombs, and of the groundless self-satisfaction of the male sex, she was in a ripple of laughter, and went away to spread a report amongst her friends that Miss Winsham was the drollest creature—very blue—full of dry humour—and without an ounce of flummery about her.

Lady Jersey was not universally popular, her airs and graces leading ill-disposed persons to liken her to a Tragedy Jill, and her frequent gross incivilities to those unfortunate enough to have incurred her displeasure shocking even such haughty dames as Mrs Burrell and the Countess Lieven, but where she led few ladies refused to follow. Miss Winsham, therefore, received a number of visits which should have gratified her very much more than they did; and when (under strong protest) she escorted her nieces to Almack's, she found herself so much sought-after, and her lightest pronouncements greeted with so much appreciation, that she might have began to have thought herself a wit of the first water had she been susceptible to flattery. As it was, she was obliged to transform a twinge of rheumatism into a severe attack of sciatica, and on this score to refuse all the invitations showered upon her, delegating the task of chaperoning her nieces to Lady Buxted, or to Mrs Dauntry.

Which of these two ladies was the more reluctant to perform this office would have been hard to decide; but each was constrained by much the same considerations to do so with the appearance, at least, of goodwill, Lady Buxted having the liveliest fear that her unnatural brother would not hesitate to repudiate the steadily rising pile of bills from the modistes supplying Jane (and, indeed, herself) with gowns, shawls, hats, gloves, and all the embellishments indispensable to those wishing to make a creditable appearance in tonnish circles; and Mrs Dauntry, while not grudging one of the guineas she lavished upon her elder daughter's raiment, foreseeing that unless she could depend upon Alverstoke for rescue she would be obliged to practise a number of extremely disagreeable economies. Of the two, however, she was the more to be pitied, for whereas Lady Buxted knew that Carlton was not attracted by Charis, and believed that he had too much commonsense even to consider contracting an engagement to Frederica, Mrs Dauntry had no such consolations. Endymion, dazzled at the outset by Charis, had fallen violently in love with her, and was behaving, as even his doting parent was obliged to own, like a mooncalf, bestowing every degree of attention upon Charis, gazing adoringly at her, positively sitting in her pocket, and showing alarming signs of trying to fix his interest with her. Mrs Dauntry could only hope that his passion would wane as swiftly as it had waxed, for on his commonsense she had no dependence at all. To make matters worse, Chloë had struck up an ardent friendship with Charis: a circumstance which provided Endymion with an excellent excuse for haunting Upper Wimpole Street. Always, in his indolent way, a kind brother, he became overnight a paragon, devoting himself (as much as his not very arduous military duties allowed) to her entertainment. He squired her to parties, and even to Almack's, which he had previously avoided, thinking the select assemblies very poor sport; he promenaded with her in the park; and whenever she visited Charis she could be pretty sure of his escort. From their earliest days she and her sister, Diana, had adored and admired him, but as he was some years their senior they had regarded him more in the light of a magnificent personage who bestowed sugar-plums upon them, and occasionally took them to Astley's Royal Amphitheatre, or to the pantomime at Sadler's Wells, than as their contemporary. Chloë had not expected him to bestir himself on her behalf, even though she was no longer a schoolgirl, but a young lady launched into her first season, and she was touchingly grateful, telling her mother, in a burst of confidence, that to possess a big brother as handsome and as goodnatured as Endymion was the most charming thing in the world. "It gives me such a wonderful *feel*, Mama, when he accompanies us to parties! And you can't think how delightful it is to go out walking with him, and *not* with Diana and Miss Nunny! I'm sure no one ever had such a splendid brother!"

Only Mrs Dauntry's sincere fondness for her children enabled her to respond, after a short struggle with herself: "Very true, dearest!" To her devoted cousin Harriet, however, she later expressed herself with great freedom, bewailing Endymion's infatuation, and saying that it went to her heart to see her poor, innocent Chloë so much deluded. "Well do I know that he only escorts us to parties because he wants an excuse for dangling after that wretched Charis Merriville! Oh, my dear Harriet, she has positively bewitched him—yes, and Chloë too! Oh, what a designing creature she is!"

To these remarks, and to a great many others of the same nature, Miss Plumley responded with soothing cluckings, and a number of contradictory statements which appeared to exercise a beneficial effect on the widow. She was sure that Endymion was not bewitched; and in the same rambling sentence recalled to his mother's mind the various damsels with whom he had previously fallen madly in love. She could not think that Charis was a designing girl, but she suspected her of setting her cap at Lord Wrenthorpe, or Sir Digby Meeth. Nor could she think that Endymion—such an excellent brother!—had any ulterior motive in squiring dear

Chloë to balls; although she could not help feeling how fortunate it was that the hope of meeting Charis at them made him so willing to escort his sister to a form of entertainment to which he was not, in general, much addicted. Such a comfort it must be to dearest Lucretia, in her indifferent state of health, to be able to entrust Chloë to his care!

These amiable meanderings, if they did not entirely banish Mrs Dauntry's apprehensions, did at least alleviate them; and when Miss Plumley spoke admiringly of her truly saintly kindness to the Merrivilles, comparing it to Lady Buxted's very different behaviour, she became much less lachrymose, saying: "Harriet! Would you believe it?—That odious woman speaks of them as *poor girls,* and tells everyone that they have no fortune! All under pretence of holding them in affection, which I know very well is sham! She is afraid that Carlton will be drawn in, of course! Well, for my part I detest such Canterbury tricks, and I hope I am too good a Christian to copy them!"

Miss Plumley said that she was sure of it; and, possibly, since she was as uncritical as she was amiable, it did not occur to her that Mrs Dauntry might have said, with more truth, that she was not such a fool as to copy those Canterbury tricks.

Mrs Dauntry, in fact, was exerting herself in a most unusual way to introduce to Charis every unattached gentleman who might, in her opinion, be relied upon either to captivate her by his address, or to dazzle her by his rank. Convinced that Charis was on the catch for a title, she not only promoted the interests of Lord Wrenthorpe (well-known to have been born without a shirt), but went quite out of her way to present to Charis any scion of a noble house whom she did not at all wish to welcome as a son-in-law. To do her justice, she was not, at the moment, angling for an eligible *parti* for Chloë, who had only just emerged from the schoolroom, and was rather too young to form any serious attachment; and but for her determination not to allow Louisa Buxted to steal a march on her she would not have presented her for another year. Mrs Dauntry thought of her as a mere child, and devoted herself so

thoroughly to the task of detaching Endymion from
Charis Merriville that the growing intimacy between
Chloë and Mr Charles Trevor escaped her notice.

As for the Merrivilles, their relationship to Alverstoke, the éclat with which he launched them into the
ton, the patronage of Lady Jersey and Lady Sefton,
and their indefinable air of good breeding, brought them
a great many agreeable invitations, very few persons
lending credence to Lady Buxted's smiling hints of their
lack of fortune, and only the most jealous parents resenting Charis's beauty. It was generally agreed that she
was a very sweet, unaffected girl, and that it was just
like Louisa Buxted to try to spoil her chances, because
her own daughter was so sadly unprepossessing. If Mrs
Dauntry, also with a daughter to dispose of creditably,
dropped no such hints, it seemed safe to assume that
there was not a shred of truth in them. They had certainly hired a house in an unfashionable quarter of the
town, but that was probably due to Miss Winsham's
eccentricity. No other signs of poverty were to be dis-
cerned: they were always elegantly attired; their excellent butler had grown old in the service of the family;
and they employed a very respectable footman. Further,
it was known (on the authority of Mrs Dauntry) that
their brother's estates in Herefordshire were considerable. This made several people remember, rather vaguely, that Fred Merriville, after pursuing an expensive
course calculated to bring his parents' gray hairs down
in sorrow to the grave, had unexpectedly come into the
Merriville property. Since neither Fred's father nor his
elder brother had been at all well-known in London no
one had any very exact information about the size of
this property, even his Dauntry connections never having visited Graynard. So Mrs Dauntry was able, in the
most delicate manner possible, to convey, without fear
of contradiction, the impression that the present owner
was a young man of fortune, and his sisters handsomely dowered.

XII

It was not long before Frederica began to realize that
society had formed an exaggerated idea of her father's
inheritance. One or two casual remarks showed that if
she and Charis were not regarded as heiresses they
were at least credited with large portions; and when
Mrs Parracombe, to whom she had taken an instant dislike, asked her in what part of the country Graynard
was situated, adding that she had heard it was a most
beautiful seat, she suspected that Alverstoke must be
the originator of these rumours. She was indebted to
Miss Jane Buxted, who seemed to be unpleasantly addicted to backstairs gossip, for the information that
Mrs Parracombe was one of Alverstoke's *chères amies;*
and though she gave Jane a set-down she saw no reason
to doubt the story. His lordship's way of life was no
concern of hers; but she was vexed to find herself
thrust into what she felt to be almost an imposture, and
she determined to demand whether it was indeed he
who was responsible for it.

No opportunity to do so offered immediately, and
when it did it was under circumstances which set her at
a disadvantage and made her pose her question in a
perfectly civil way. His lordship had not forgotten his
promise to take Jessamy with him, when he drove his
new team of grays to Richmond—or, rather, it had
been recalled to his mind by Curry, his head-groom,
who had formed a very good opinion of Jessamy—
and he called in Upper Wimpole Street one morning to
pick the boy up: thus subjecting him to a severe struggle
with his conscience. He told Frederica, who had encountered Owen on his way upstairs to deliver his lordship's invitation, that having made up his mind to
devote his mornings to study he must not yield to
temptation; but Frederica very sensibly suggested that

he could resume his studies later in the day, upon which his face brightened, and he hurried away to scrub his hands, telling Owen to assure his lordship that he would be with him in a pig's whisper.

It was Frederica, however, who conveyed the message to Alverstoke, asking him, at the same time, if he would spare her a few minutes upon his return.

He looked down at her, as she stood on the flagway, his eyes, for all their laziness, curiously penetrating. "Certainly," he responded. "Something of grave importance?"

She hesitated. "It seems so to me, but perhaps you will not think so."

"You intrigue me, Frederica. Do I detect a note of censure in your voice?"

She was not obliged to answer this, for at that moment Jessamy arrived on the scene, and ran down the steps, breathlessly expressing the hope that he had not kept his lordship waiting. Bidding his sister a cursory farewell, he climbed up into the phaeton, looking so happy and excited that feelings of gratitude to Alverstoke for having granted him this treat overcame other, and less charitable, emotions in her breast.

When he returned, several hours later, it was in a mood of deep content. He ushered Alverstoke into the drawing-room, saying: "Frederica? Oh, you are here! Come in, sir! Oh, Frederica, I have had *such* a time! I haven't enjoyed anything so much since we came to London! We have been to Richmond Park—Cousin Alverstoke has tickets of admission, you know—and he let me handle the reins, and—Sir, I don't know how to thank you enough!—Sh-showing me just how to turn a corner in style, too, and how to point the leaders, and—"

"My dear boy, you have already thanked me enough —too much, in fact!" replied Alverstoke, rather amused. "If you do so any more, you'll become a bore!"

Jessamy laughed, blushed, and said, a little shyly: "I think I must have been, sir! Such—such dull work for you, teaching a mere whipster! And so *very* kind of you to let me drive those grays, when, for anything you knew, I might have been a regular spoon!"

"If I had had any such apprehension," said Alverstoke gravely, "I should *not* have let you drive them. You are not yet a top-sawyer, but you've light hands, considerable precision of eye, and you know how to stick to your leaders."

Coming from a Nonpareil, these words reduced Jessamy to stammering incoherence. He managed to thank his lordship yet again, and then effaced himself, to spend an unprofitable hour with his books open before him but his thoughts very far away from them.

"I should like to thank you, too," Frederica said, with a warm smile, "but I don't dare! *Was* it a bore?"

"Oddly enough, no. A new experience! I've never before attempted to impart my skill to another, and I've discovered that either I'm an excellent teacher, or that I had a remarkably apt pupil. But I didn't come to talk about driving. What have I done to vex you, Frederica?"

"I don't know. I mean, I *am* vexed, but I'm not perfectly sure that it was your doing," she said frankly. "The thing is that people seem to think that we are possessed of a handsome fortune. Cousin, did *you* set that rumour about?"

"Certainly not," he replied, his eyebrows slightly raised. "Why should I?"

"Well, you might have done so to be helpful, perhaps."

"I can think of few things less helpful."

"No, nor can I! Besides, it is so odiously vulgar! I detest shams! It makes it seem as though I had been cutting a wheedle, to achieve a brilliant marriage for Charis. As though such shifts could succeed!"

He smiled. "Oho! Would you employ them if they could?"

The smile was faintly reflected in her eyes, but she shook her head. "No—contemptible! Don't you think so?"

"I do, but you appear to have suspected me of selling just such a contemptible bargain."

"Yes, but I knew it must have been with the best of intentions," she assured him.

"Worse! You believe me to be a flat!"

She laughed. "Indeed I don't! I beg your pardon— but if you didn't set the story about, who can have

done so? And—and *why?* I promise you, I've never
tried to make people think we are wealthy, and nor,
I'm very sure, has Charis. In fact, when Mrs Parracombe talked of Graynard, saying how much she
would like to see it, and speaking as if it were a ducal
mansion, I told her it was no such thing."

"*Now* I know why I fell under suspicion!" he murmured provocatively.

It was so unexpected that it surprised a tiny gasp out
of her.

"I am continually shocked by the on-dits people
don't scruple to repeat to innocent maidens," pursued
his lordship, in a saddened voice.

"If it comes to that," retorted Frederica, with spirit,
"I am continually shocked by the things you don't
scruple to say to me, cousin! You are quite abominable!"

He sighed. "Alas, I know it! The reflection gives me
sleepless nights."

"Coming it rather too strong, my lord!" she said, before she could stop herself. She added hastily, as he put
up his brows in exaggerated incredulity: "As Harry
would say!"

"No doubt! But such cant expressions on the lips of
delicately nurtured females are extremely unbecoming."

Well aware of this, she was just about to apologize for
the lapse when she caught the gleam in his eye, and
said, instead: "*Odious* creature! I wish you will be serious!"

He laughed. "Very well, let us be serious! You want
to know who is responsible for the rumour that you are
very wealthy—"

"Yes, and what's to be done about it!"

"Nothing. As to who may have started the rumour, I
know no more than you do, and can perceive no reason
why you should be thrown into high fidgets over it. If
we are to be serious, let me advise you to discourage
Ollerton's advances to your sister!"

She looked quickly up at him. "Why?"

"Because, my innocent, he is what we call a man of
the town."

She nodded. "I'm glad to know that, for it's what I thought myself. Though I must own he has been very civil and obliging, and has a well-bred ease of manner —except that now and then he goes a little beyond the line of what is pleasing. However, there are others, who are even better-bred, who go a *long* way beyond it!"

"So there are!" he agreed. "Who introduced him to you?"

"Mrs Dauntry, at Lady Jersey's party. Which is why I concluded that I must have been mistaken in him."

"Did she indeed?" he said. "Well, well!" There was a gleam of amusement in his eyes, which she tried in vain to interpret. He flicked open his snuff-box, and took a meditative pinch, and suddenly laughed. Meeting her enquiring look, he said: "Who would have thought that your adoption of me would have provided me with so much entertainment?"

"You did!" responded Frederica unhesitatingly. "I didn't know it at the outset, but I am very sure now that *you* adopted *us* merely to infuriate Lady Buxted!"

"And can you blame me?"

An involuntary chuckle escaped her. "Well, perhaps not as much as I ought! But you did think it might amuse you!"

"True—and so it did! What I did not foresee was that I should find myself taking so much interest in the fortunes of the Merrivilles!" He paused, but before she could retort in kind, demanded abruptly: "Who was the rum touch I saw escorting your sister yesterday? A counter-coxcomb in a striped waistcoat?"

"Mr Nutley!" she uttered, in despairing accents.

"Who the devil is Mr Nutley?"

"Our neighbour! A very worthy young man, but *quite* ineligible, and *nutty* upon Charis! He—he languishes! Besides sending her flowers, and lying in wait for her to step out of the house with only Owen to escort her!" replied Frederica bitterly.

"Good God! Has she a tendre for him?"

"No, of course she has not! The thing is that she *cannot* bring herself to repulse him! And if you think you can convince her that it would be kinder by far to do so now than later I can only say, cousin, that you don't know her! She has a great deal of sensibility, you see, and—"

"A great deal of folly!" he interrupted impatiently.

"Yes, that too," she agreed, sighing. "I wish she wasn't such a goosecap, for I daresay anyone might impose upon her. I own it has me in a worry very often."

He nodded, but said: "It will do her no good to be seen in Ollerton's company, but he won't go beyond flirtation: I'll see to that!"

"Thank you—but he has done nothing to warrant— I mean, I don't at all wish you to say anything to him! It would be refining too much upon too little."

"Oh, it won't be necessary for me to say anything!" he replied, with one of his sardonic smiles. "In common with the rest of the world, he believes her to be under my protection. It is possible, however, that he may also believe me to be an indifferent guardian. That can be remedied. Do you go to the Crewes' assembly? I'll escort you—exercising a benevolent surveillance! I might take you both to the play, or even drive you round the park, at the hour of the Grand Strut."

"You are very obliging! We are indeed honoured!"

"Yes, I rarely drive females."

"You will find it another dead bore, I daresay!"

"Possibly, but I shall be upheld by a feeling of virtue."

"Ah, but the novelty of that will soon wear off!" she pointed out.

The sardonic expression vanished. "Very good, Frederica!" he said approvingly. "I don't think it will bore me to drive you round the park."

"Well, that's a comfort, to be sure! But there's not the least need for you to include me in your benevolence! Take Charis up beside you now and then, and I shall be excessively grateful!" She tried, unsuccessfully, to repress a mischievous chuckle, and added, with disarming candour: "You can't think how much against the pluck it goes with me to administer to your vanity, cousin, but I haven't spent all these weeks in London without realizing that your consequence is *enormous!*"

"Viper!" said his lordship appreciatively. "I will endure the company of your beautiful but bird-witted sister, but on the condition that the tedium of these sessions will be relieved occasionally by your astringent quality. By-the-by, does rumour lie, or is my equally bird-witted young cousin growing extremely particular in his attentions?"

"No—though in some ways I wish it did!" replied Frederica. "But as for *growing* extremely particular—! He seems to have conceived a violent passion for Charis the instant he laid eyes on her. I must say, I wish he were not so *very* handsome! I am afraid he is the only one of her admirers for whom Charis does cherish a tendre, and I can conceive of nothing more unsuitable! Nor, I fancy, would Mrs Dauntry welcome such an alliance."

"Certainly not. One of the tightish clever sort, my saintly Cousin Lucretia!"

"Well, you can't blame her for wishing her son to contract an advantageous marriage," said Frederica reasonably. "It is precisely what I want Charis to do, after all! I don't desire to offend you, my lord, but I cannot think Endymion an eligible *parti!* It is all very well for his mama to talk of his being your heir, but who is to say that it will ever come to that? You are not in your dotage!"

"Thank you!" said his lordship, in failing accents.

Her eyes twinkled responsively, but she said politely: "Not at all! The thing is, however, that when Endymion is Charis's escort I can be easy in my mind. He treats her with the greatest respect—almost with reverence!"

"Yes, he always was a slow-top," he commented. "Poor girl! Is Buxted also dangling after her?"

"Oh, dear me, no!" she replied, casting down her eyes, and folding her hands primly in her lap. "Lord Buxted, cousin, has a decided preference for *me!*"

He burst out laughing. "No, has he indeed? I pity you, then, but think the better of him! What do you find to talk about, I wonder?"

"Why, I am not obliged to find anything! He is never at a loss. When we have commented on the political situation, and he has been so kind as to draw my at-

tention to some article in one of the newspapers which
I might not have read, he has always plenty to tell
me about himself, and his estates, and his reflections
upon various subjects." She broke off, chuckling, but
said penitently: "But I ought not to make game of
him! He is very kind, and has a great deal of sense,
even if he *is* a trifle prosy!"

"Dull and respectable. But not, I fancy, your only
admirer. My heart positively bled for poor Aldridge
when I saw Darcy Moreton cut him out at that very
tedious soirée last Wednesday."

"Oh, fiddle!" she said. "I wish you won't be so non-
sensical! Next you will be calling Mr Moreton my *flirt*,
and nothing, I can assure you, is farther from his
thoughts, or mine!"

"Wait until the crow is hatched before you pull it
with me!"

She smiled. "I will—but pray believe that I don't
flirt, and I am not on the catch for a husband!"

"Except one for Charis. Tell me! Are you enjoying
your first London season?"

She answered impulsively: "Oh, beyond calculation!
In fact, I enjoy it all so much that I fear I must re-
semble poor Papa more than I knew!"

He was able, by the exercise of strong self-control,
to reply, with only the smallest quiver in his voice:
"What a very alarming thought! Surely you wrong yourself!"

"Well, I hope I do," she said seriously. "I don't care
much for cards, at all events. None of us do, except,
perhaps, Jessamy, and he, you know, has such deep
principles that I've no fears for him. I expect it is too
soon to know what Felix may do, but I don't *think*
he will be a gamester."

He laughed. "Good God, no! He will be far too busy
inventing a steam-shuffler, or a mechanical-dealer, to
take any interest in mere gaming! How does he go on?
Where is he? Don't tell me he has set forth on another
steamboat expedition!"

"No—though I collect he is much interested in some
project to build ocean-going steamboats! I think he
learned about it on his trip to Ramsgate, but I fancy

the inventor is an American, for which I am truly thankful! Even Felix couldn't go all that way!"

"I wouldn't risk a groat against the chance! Very likely he will sign on as cabin-boy in a sailing-vessel bound for America, and we shall next hear of him in New York!"

"For heaven's sake, don't put such a notion into his head!" she begged, between alarm and amusement. "It is precisely the sort of thing he might do! But at the moment he is upstairs, in one of the attics, which we gave him for his experiments!"

"Good God!" Alverstoke ejaculated. "We had as well sit on a keg of gunpowder! I'll take my leave of you before he blows the house up!"

"No, no, he won't do that!" she replied, gurgling with merriment. "He promised me he would remember this is not our own house!"

He regarded her with appreciation. "You'd have no objection to his blowing it up if it were your own house? Accept my compliments on the fortitude of your mind!"

"How can you be so absurd? Of course I should object to it! I meant only that at home he has a workshop, and may do as he pleases in it."

"*I* see! Does he often blow it up?"

She smiled. "He *never* blows it up! He did set fire to it once, but that was when he was trying to make a new kind of match, which would light without a tinderbox, and there was very little damage done, except that he singed his eyebrows off."

"You are a very good sister, Frederica!" he commented.

"Well, I do *try* to be," she said, colouring faintly. "My aunt, and our old nurse, were too anxious—or so it seemed to me—and for ever flying into high fidgets over the things the boys did, which didn't answer at all, because it made them fall into the sullens, and pay not the least heed to anything they said."

"It is a pity that your aunt did not save her anxiety for her nieces! I shall take leave to tell you, Frederica, that I think her a very poor chaperon!"

"Yes, but one must be just to her! She never wished

to come to London, and only consented to do so on the
understanding that she shouldn't be dragged to fashionable parties. Recollect that I am quite old enough to
chaperon Charis! Indeed, I've done so ever since she
came out!"

"That," said his lordship roundly, "is a greater absurdity than any I have uttered!"

"It isn't—but I won't argue with you on that head!
In any event, she is not to be blamed for having more
important things to think about at this present. My
Uncle Scrabster is very unwell and poor Aunt Amelia is
quite distracted with worry, and depends wholly on my
Aunt Seraphina."

He said nothing, compressing his lips, as though only
by doing so could he keep back a retort. Two deep
clefts appeared between his brows, but they vanished as
the door burst open, and Felix came eagerly into the
room, exclaiming: "You *are* here, sir! I thought it was
your phaeton I saw, when I looked out of the window!
You might have told me, Frederica, when you knew I
particularly wanted to see him! The shabbiest thing!"

"God help me!" said his lordship. "*Not* another
foundry, Felix!"

"No, no! At least, not precisely! It's the New Mint!
It has gas-lighting, and steam-engines of *vast* power, but
when I went there with Jessamy they said no one was
allowed to visit it without a—a special recommendation.
So would you *very* kindly give me one, Cousin Alverstoke? If you please!"

"But how can I?" said the Marquis. "I'm not acquainted with the Master, or even with the Controller."

"Yes, but you weren't acquainted with the manager of
the foundry either, sir!" argued Felix.

"Ah, that was a different matter! They are very particular at the Mint, you know, and wouldn't think a
recommendation from me at all 'special'."

Felix's countenance had dropped ludicrously, but at
these words it brightened, and he gave a crow of mirth.
"Yes, they would! You're trying to roast me! Of course
they would!"

"Oh, dear, what a dreadful boy you are!" said Frederica. "Stop teasing Cousin Alverstoke, I do beg of you!"

"I'm not teasing him!" replied Felix indignantly. "I only asked him to *recommend* me! I haven't asked him to go with me himself, and I won't, because if he don't care for it I daresay Mr Trevor would like it!"

"So he would!" said his lordship, much struck. "It's time he had a treat, too, poor fellow!"

"Of course, it would be *best* if you came!" said Felix tentatively.

"No, no, you mustn't spoil me!" responded his lordship, with considerable aplomb. "I've had one treat already, remember!"

"Oh, well!" said Felix, accepting this. "He isn't a Go, like you, but at least he has some sense!"

"Quite a lot of sense," agreed his lordship gravely. "He carried Honours! I daresay we shall live to see him First Lord of the Treasury, so take care to keep in his good books!"

It was plain that Felix thought poorly of this ambition, but he said innocently: "Oh, yes! But he ain't a prosy one, you know! I did think he might be, at first, but I'm pretty well-acquainted with him now, and I like him."

He then took leave of the Marquis, who cocked an eyebrow at Frederica, and said: "And how, may I ask, did your engaging brother become pretty well-acquainted with Charles?"

She answered with a little reserve: "Oh, he has visited us now and then on our Sundays when we invite a few friends to supper—nothing formal, you understand: just a family party, for people who don't care a straw for fashionable squeezes, but like to spend a cosy evening playing Jackstraws, or Bilbo-catch, or Speculation—"

"Or dangling after Charis?"

"No, you are mistaken!" she said quickly. "Mr Trevor doesn't do so!"

"I'm glad. She wouldn't do for him at all."

"If it comes to that, *he* wouldn't do for *her!*"

"Very likely not. What, then, has induced him to relax his monkish rule?"

"Ask him, my lord—not me!"

"I'm not so tactless."

"Do you object to his visiting us?"

"Not in the least. I am merely curious. Some strong inducement there must be! Charles has never lacked invitations: he is very well-liked, and comes of a good family: but until the Merrivilles came to London he has very rarely accepted any. It's my belief he has fallen in love: he forgot to remind me that I was engaged to attend a very dull dinner-party the other day. Unprecedented, I assure you! But if not with Charis—" He broke off, as a thought occurred to him. "Good God! *Chloë?*"

"I am not in his confidence, cousin. And if I were I wouldn't betray it!"

He paid no heed to this. A smile hovered about his mouth; after a moment's reflection, he said: "Life will be fraught with interest, if that's indeed so. I must cultivate Chloë's acquaintance!"

XIII

Whether the Marquis took any steps to become better acquainted with his young cousin, Frederica had no means of discovering; but he very soon redeemed his promise to demonstrate to the *ton* his interest in his supposed wards: thus confirming her gathering suspicion that the forgetfulness for which he was notorious was largely assumed. He called in Upper Wimpole Street to pick Charis up, and drove her round Hyde Park at the fashionable hour, several times reining in his grays to exchange greetings with his own friends, or to enable Charis to respond to the salutes of her many admirers. This she did very sweetly, and without a trace of coquetry. He had known many beauties, but never one as innocently unconcerned with her appearance as Charis. Nor did she seem to be at all aware of the signal honour he had conferred upon her, and the surprise and the conjectures which this gave rise to. She thanked him politely for inviting her to drive with him, but disclosed, upon enquiry, that she preferred Kensington Gardens to Hyde Park, because the flowers were so pretty, and there were several walks where one could almost fancy oneself to be in the country.

"You don't like London?" he asked.

"Oh, yes!" she replied tranquilly. "It is very pleasant, and amusing, only not so comfortable as the country."

"It is generally thought to be *more* comfortable than the country!"

"Is it?" She wrinkled her brow. "I wonder why?"

"Let us say that it has more to offer in the way of entertainment."

"Oh!" She pondered for a moment. "Yes, of course: there are theatres, and concerts, and reviews, and a great many balls. Only, London parties—though they are very splendid—aren't as enjoyable as country ones, are they?"

"Aren't they? Why not?"

"I don't know. I am very stupid at explaining things," she said apologetically. "I like best the parties where I *know* everyone—if you understand what I mean?" After further pause for cogitation, she added: "I daresay it is because I'm not accustomed to town-life, or the rude way people stare, if one is a stranger."

"Very disagreeable," he said gravely. "I perceive that I should have done better to have driven you out of town, to some sequestered spot inhabited only by yokels."

"But you would have to go a great way for that, wouldn't you?"

He began to feel bored, and replied somewhat dryly: "Very true."

She relapsed into silence. After a moment, he exerted himself to open another topic of conversation, but as she had few opinions of her own to advance, merely agreeing with all he said, his boredom rapidly increased; and, after taking one more turn about the park, he drove her back to Upper Wimpole Street, mentally apostrophizing himself for having so rashly promised to throw the mantle of his protection over her. In any ordinary circumstances he would have banished all thought of her from his mind when he set her down; but the circumstances were not ordinary: he supposed he was in honour bound to invite her to drive out with him again. He did so, asking her where she would like to go. She replied impulsively: "Oh! How very kind! I should like of all things to go to Hampton Court, sir! We have been reading about it, Frederica and I, and we wish very much to visit it. Only—" She hesitated, raising her big eyes deprecatingly to his face.

"Only?" he prompted.

"Would you—would you lend us your escort, Cousin Alverstoke? I mean *all* of us! Or—or would you liefer *not* do so? The thing is that there seems to be a famous maze there, and the boys *would* enjoy it so much!"

Thus it came about that the Marquis found himself, a few days later, conducting a family party to Hampton

Court in the barouche which, with its high-stepping horses, was so very well-known to the members of the Four-Horse Club, few of whom would have been able to believe their eyes had they seen the base use to which it was being put. His lordship was not wearing the insignia of the Club, but Jessamy, who took it in turns with Felix to sit beside him on the box, assured his sisters that anyone privileged to watch his handling of the reins would recognize him, at a glance, as one of its members.

In the opinion of the Merrivilles the expedition was quite the most most delightful they had yet experienced, even Felix considering that the joys of getting lost in the maze, and being afterwards regaled at the Star and Garter with what he described as a spanking dinner, raised it above his trip to Ramsgate. So many jam tarts did he consume that his brother, calling him a snatch-pastry, said that anyone would suppose that he was starving. To which he replied cheerfully, that as he hadn't had a bite to eat (except for a couple of ices and a few cakes, as a light nuncheon) since a breakfast of eggs, muffins, toast, and preserves, he pretty well was starving.

Owing to his forethought in having acquainted himself with the key to the maze, the Marquis spent the day far more agreeably than he had anticipated; for as soon as he had had enough of wandering about the maze he guided Frederica out of it, leaving the three younger members of the party still trying to reach the centre, all of them in high spirits, and thinking it an excellent joke every time they found themselves in a blind alley. The custodian, whose stand commanded a view of the whole labyrinth, and whose duty it was to direct exhausted persons out of it, several times offered his services, but these were unhesitatingly scorned, each of the three Merrivilles being convinced that he, or she, could discover the clue.

Frederica, strolling along the alleys beside the Marquis, was inclined to think it a lucky chance that brought them to the centre of the maze; but when he led her back to the entrance without a single mistake she looked laughingly up at him, and exclaimed: "You knew the secret! What a hoax! I was beginning to think you so clever, too!"

"Merely provident!" he replied. "The prospect of spending the better part of the afternoon between high hedges I find singularly unattractive—don't you?"

She smiled. "Well, I own I had liefer walk about the gardens and the wilderness! But the children think it famous sport: thank you for bringing them! You are very kind, for I'm persuaded it must be a great bore to you."

"By no means!" he answered. "It has the charm of novelty."

"Did you never take your nephews and nieces out with you?" she asked curiously.

"Never!"

"Not even when they were children? How odd it seems!"

"It would seem very much odder if I had, I assure you."

"Not to me."

"It should. I warned you, Frederica, that I am neither compliant nor goodnatured."

"Well, I must own that you are not at all good-natured to your sisters," she said frankly. "Not that I blame you for that—at least, not altogether! They seem positively to take delight in setting up your back! I wonder they shouldn't know that pinching at one's brothers is *fatal!* But whatever you may say you are *not* a monster of selfishness. You wouldn't be so kind to Jessamy and Felix if that were so."

"Or if they bored me," he interpolated.

"It bored you excessively to inspect that foundry," she reminded him.

"Yes, that's why Charles is going to take Felix to the New Mint," he responded coolly.

"But why didn't you send him to escort us today?" she asked, in an innocent tone at variance with the mischief in her eyes. "You cannot have supposed that such an expedition as this wouldn't bore you quite as much as the Mint!"

He glanced down at her, half-smiling, but with an

oddly arrested expression in his face. She was puzzled by it, but after a moment, she said quizzically: "Are you wondering whether you can bamboozle me into believing that you won't entrust your team to Mr Trevor?"

"No," he replied slowly, "though it would be true! I was thinking how well that bonnet becomes you."

It was certainly a charming confection, with a soft pink plume curling over its poke of gathered silk; but she broke into a gurgle of laughter, exclaiming: "Oh, cousin, you are the most complete hand! Why are you so determined to make me write you down as selfish, and altogether detestable? Are you afraid I might trade upon your goodnature? I promise you I shan't!"

"No, I'm not afraid of that."

"To be sure, you could always floor me with one of your icy set-downs, couldn't you?" she agreed, twinkling gaily.

"Unlikely! You'd come about again!" he retorted, guiding her towards a conveniently situated bench. "We will now sit down to await the children—unless you consider it too chilly?"

She shook her head, but said, as she disposed herself on the bench: "Much you would care if I did!"

"Unjust, Frederica! Almost as unjust as your previous observation! When, pray, have I attempted to give you a set-down?"

"Oh, when we first met! You were odiously starched-up!"

"Was I? Accept my most humble apologies, and acknowledge that I haven't repeated the offence!"

"No, indeed you haven't!" she said warmly. "That is, you haven't snubbed *us!* But I've twice heard you— However, that's no concern of mine! You don't like to be thanked, but pray let me tell you—just once—how truly grateful I am to you! You have done much more for us than I expected—why, you even came to Luff's rescue, and if that wasn't kind, I should like to know what is!"

"But you did expect that of me!" he pointed out.

"I didn't precisely *expect* it. I was—I was hopeful

that you would! Oh, and you have never told me what it cost you to ransom him! I had quite forgotten! Pray, will you—"

"No," he interrupted. "I neither know nor care what it cost me, and if you talk any more flummery to me, Frederica, I shall give you one of my—er—icy set-downs!"

"It's very obliging of you, but when I asked for your help I didn't mean that I wished to hang on your sleeve, cousin! What's more, I won't do it!"

"In that case I must strive to remember the exact sum I've disbursed on your behalf today," he said. "I wonder why I didn't think to keep a tally? Now, let me see! There were four tickets for the maze—oh, we paid to enter the palace, too, didn't we? Then that comes to—"

"I wish you will be serious!" she interrupted, biting a quivering lip.

"I am being very serious. Generous, too, for I don't mean to charge you carriage-hire."

"Oh, don't be absurd!" she said indignantly. "There is a great deal of difference between allowing you to discharge my debts, and paying you for our entertainment when you have invited us to drive out with you to Hampton Court!"

"Certainly, but I didn't do so," he said. "My services were bespoken by Charis."

She gave a gasp. "Why, what a—a *clanker!*" she exclaimed, most improperly. "You know she would never have thought of such a thing if you hadn't asked her where she would like to go!"

"Well, if you call that an invitation to drive out with me to Hampton Court, bringing her sister, and both her brothers—!"

"Odious, *odious* creature!" she said, trying not to laugh. "Very well, I'll say no more. Not even thank-you! Or should I beg your pardon for having foisted myself *and* my brothers upon you today?"

"On the contrary! If you had cried off, I should have recalled a pressing engagement elsewhere. Charis is a most amiable girl, but not precisely needle-witted. I find it extremely difficult to converse with her—quite exhausting, in fact! She asks me what I mean, when I venture on a mild joke."

She could not repress one of her involuntary gurgles, but she said, in swift defence of her sister: "She may not be needle-witted, but she has a great deal of commonsense, I assure you! Much more than I have, for she knows how to hold household, besides sewing exquisitely, and being able to dress a joint, and—oh, all manner of useful things!"

"Unfortunately, none of these virtues is called for when driving in the park."

"She is certainly not a *prattle-box!*" retorted Frederica.

He laughed. "No, indeed!"

"I thought gentlemen did not care for females whose tongues ran on wheels!" she said.

"True, but between gabblemongering, and casting the whole burden of maintaining conversation upon one's companion, there is a happy medium to be struck. No, no, don't rip up! I will allow Charis to be a beauty beyond compare, besides being amiable, and virtuous! But—" He paused, a crease between his brows.

"Well?" she demanded.

He raised his eyes from frowning contemplation of the gloves he held in one hand, and turned his head to look at her. He said, with unwonted gentleness: "My child, does it never occur to you that the future you have planned for her is not what she would herself choose?"

"No, how could that be? If I were scheming for what you would call a *brilliant match*—but I'm not! I promise you I'm not! I only wish to see her comfortably established: not to be obliged to make and scrape, but to be able to command the—the *elegancies* of life!" She saw his brows lift, and added: "You think such considerations don't signify, perhaps. Recollect that you have never known what it means to be purse-pinched!"

"I haven't," he admitted. "I must bow to your better knowledge of your sister, but from the little I have observed I should have said that she would find more happiness in holding household than in cutting a dash. She told me, you know, that she preferred country balls to London ones."

"Good gracious, *did* she?" Frederica exclaimed, quite astonished. "She must have been funning! Only think of her success! The bouquets that are sent her! The way our knocker is never quiet! Oh, you must be mistaken, cousin!"

He saw she was looking distressed, and replied lightly: "Very possibly. In any event, I see no reason why you should fall into dejection."

"But if she doesn't care for those things—doesn't wish to make a creditable marriage—I shall have done it all for nothing!" she pointed out.

"Nonsense! You at least are enjoying London life."

"*That* doesn't signify!" she said impatiently. "As though I should have dreamt of dragging the boys to London to gratify my own wishes!"

"I daresay Jessamy would have preferred to have remained at home, but it won't hurt him to see something of the world. As for Felix, he's as happy as a grig! I'm a little curious, however, to know what it was that made you think that Charis shares your own tastes."

She shook her head. "I didn't think that. Only that it was shameful to keep her hidden away, or to allow her to marry young Rushbury, or any of the other men of our acquaintance, before she had had a season." She hesitated, and then said rather shyly: "The thing is, you see, that she is so very persuadable! She is much inclined to agree to whatever is suggested to her, and although her principles are firm, her disposition is so yielding that I own it does sometimes sink my spirits!"

"I imagine it might—if she yields to the importunities of every callow youth who dangles after her! Does she fall in love with them?"

"I don't think she falls in love with anyone," replied Frederica candidly. "I mean, not more with one than with another! She is a most affectionate girl, and so kind-hearted that it is enough to cast anyone into high fidgets!"

"Universally benevolent, eh? Poor Frederica!"

"You may well say so! It is such a responsibility, you

see. She is bound to marry *someone*, and only think how shocking it would be if I allowed her to be snapped up by a callow youth, as you phrase it, who wouldn't know how to make her happy, or by some—some basket-scrambler!"

His lips twitched, but he replied gravely: "Shocking indeed! But—er—basket-scramblers are, in general, on the catch for heiresses."

"Well, I didn't mean that precisely," she conceded. "And perhaps I ought not to say that Charis doesn't fall in love with people. I've never done so myself, so I can't judge. It doesn't *seem* to me that she does."

He had been listening to her with idly appreciative amusement, but this startled him. "Never fallen in love?" he repeated incredulously. *"Never,* Frederica?"

"No—that is, I don't *think* so! I did once feel a tendre, but that was when I was young, and I recovered from it so quickly that I shouldn't think I was truly in love. In fact, I am much disposed to think that if I hadn't met him at a ball, when he was wearing regimentals, I shouldn't have looked twice at him." She added earnestly: "Do you know, cousin, I am strongly of the opinion that gentlemen should not be permitted to attend balls and assemblies rigged out in smart dress-uniforms? There is something about regimentals which is very deceiving. Fortunately, since I believe he was quite ineligible, I chanced to meet him the very next week, when he was not wearing regimentals, so I never had time to fall in love with him. It was the most disillusioning thing imaginable!"

"Who was this unfortunate?" he asked, his eyes warm with laughter.

"I don't recall his name: it was so long ago!"

"Ah, yes!" he said sympathetically. "Before you became so old cattish!"

"Old cattish—!" She checked herself, and then said, with a rueful smile: "Oh, dear! I suppose that *is* what I am!"

"Do you indeed? Then let me tell you, my child, that when you talk of *when you were young* you are being foolish beyond permission!"

"No, I'm not! I'm four-and-twenty, and have been on the shelf for *years!*" she retorted.

"Alas!" he mocked.

"Nothing of the sort! Pray, what do you think would have become of them all if I were *not* on the shelf?"

"I neither know nor care."

"Well, I do know, and I care very much! What's more, I find it very agreeable to be an old maid, and rid of tiresome restrictions! If I were of marriageable age, I couldn't, for instance, be sitting here at this moment, talking to you without the *vestige* of a chaperon! Everyone would suppose me to be setting my cap at you, besides being *fast!* But if the Countess Lieven, or even Mrs Burrell, were to pass by at this moment they wouldn't lift *one* of their detestably haughty eyebrows, any more than they would if I were Miss Berry!"

This comparison of herself with a lady who had some six-and-fifty years in her dish almost overset his lordship. He contrived to keep his countenance, but there was a distinct tremor in his voice when he said: "Very true! I wonder that that shouldn't have occurred to me."

"I daresay you never gave it a thought," said Frederica kindly.

"No," he acknowledged. "I didn't!"

"Why should you? Gentlemen aren't troubled with chaperons," she said, somewhat wistfully contemplating this happy state.

"I assure you, I have frequently been troubled by them! Very irksome I have found them!"

The wistful look vanished in a twinkle. "What a shocking creature you are, cousin!" she said affably.

"Yes, an ugly customer! Didn't I warn you of it?"

"Very likely, but you tell so many whiskers about yourself that I daresay I wasn't attending." She turned her head towards him, and said, with a smile in her frank eyes: "A great many people have warned me that you are excessively dangerous! You have a sad reputation, cousin! But to us you have been more than kind—in spite of not in the least wishing to befriend us! So I don't give a button for what anyone says of you."

He met her clear gaze, an expression hard to read in his own eyes. "Don't you? But that puts me on my mettle!"

"I wish you will rid your mind of the notion that I am a wet-goose!" she said severely. "Instead of talking nonsense, tell me what you know of Sir Mark Lyneham!"

"What, is he another of Charis's suitors? My dear child, he won't see thirty again!"

"No, but—something she said to me the other day made me wonder if perhaps she wouldn't be happier with an older man. Someone she could depend upon for guidance, and who would take care of her, and not come to cuffs with her if he chanced to be out of temper. From what I have seen, *young* husbands often fly into miffs, and that would never do for Charis! She has so much sensibility that even when the boys fall into a quarrel she is made miserable. And the *mildest* scold utterly sinks her spirits! Well—well, I think Sir Mark would be very gentle, don't you?"

"Since I've no more than a nodding acquaintance with him, I can't say. Judging him by myself, I should think he would murder her—or seek consolation elsewhere! I can think of few worse fates than to be married to a watering-pot."

"She is not a watering-pot! And Sir Mark would *not* seek consolation elsewhere! *His* reputation is—is spotless!"

"Ah! Well, I always did think he was a dull dog," said his lordship.

"A man need not be dull merely because he is respectable!" she retorted.

"No, he *need* not, but he too often is."

"I am informed, on good authority, that Sir Mark suffered a disappointment in his youth, and he never, until now, *looked* at another female!" said Frederica frostily.

"Oh, my God!" ejaculated his lordship, in accents of acute nausea. "No, no, don't tell me more! I haven't a strong enough stomach!"

"I shan't," said Frederica, eyeing him with hostility.

"You don't seem to me to have any sense of propriety at all!"

"I haven't."

"Well, it's nothing to be proud of!"

"Oh, I'm not proud! Tell me, Frederica, is that the kind of milkiness you admire?"

"Certainly!" she replied. "Respectability must always command admiration!"

"Humbug!" he remarked. "Trying it on rather too rare and thick, my child! I'm considerably more than seven, you know."

"Well, one *ought* to admire it, at any rate," she said defensively.

"That's better," he approved. "I was beginning to think you had a tendre for this paragon yourself, and that would never do: you wouldn't suit, believe me!"

"Readily!" she said, laughing. "So perhaps I won't, after all, try to cut Charis out! As if I could!"

"I can think of more unlikely contingencies," he said.

"Can you indeed? Then either you must be all about in your head, or a bigger humbug than I am!" she said roundly.

XIV

To the surprise of all, and the embarrassment of several, the Marquis, his wayward memory retaining a scrap of information let fall by Frederica, presented himself in Upper Wimpole Street on the following Sunday evening. Remembering also that these weekly at home days had been described to him as informal, he came in morning-dress: a blue coat of exquisite cut, a waistcoat of striped toilinette, pale buff pantaloons which appeared to have been moulded to his legs, and tasselled Hessians whose incomparable gloss was one of his valet's main pre-occupations. His nephew, Lord Buxted, was very correctly attired in the white waistcoat, the black panta-loons, and the striped stockings of ordinary evening-dress; and two very young gentlemen wore sporting ruffled shirts, highly starched collar-points projecting to their cheek-bones, neckcloths of awe-inspiring dimen-sions, and a nice array of fobs, seals, and rings. These budding dandies had expended much time and thought on their raiment, and, until the Marquis was ushered into the drawing-room, they had been satisfied with the results of their labours. But when that tall, well-made figure appeared upon the threshold horrid doubts as-sailed them. His lordship, being blessed with fine shoul-ders, had no need of buckram wadding for his coats, nor did he favour a nip-waisted style. His collar-points were moderate; his neckcloth beautifully but discreetly tied; his jewelry consisted of a single fob, and his heavy gold signet-ring; and he was unquestionably the most elegant man in the room.

He entered upon a babel of conversation, but when Buddle sonorously announced him a startled silence fell, to be broken by Felix, who bounded up, exclaiming: "Oh, famous! Cousin Alverstoke! How do you do, sir? I *am* glad you came! I am so very much obliged to you!

Mr Trevor says you have arranged it all just as I knew you would, and we are going to the New Mint this very week! Are you *sure* you don't wish to come too?"

It struck Mr Darcy Moreton, curiously watching his friend, that he had rarely seen so softened an expression in his face, as he responded to this greeting. Then Frederica went towards him, holding out her hand, and he raised his eyes from Felix's eager countenance, and smiled at her, causing Mr Moreton to suffer a shock. It was not at all the sort of smile with which his lordship beguiled his flirts, but something warmer and more intimate. *Good God!* mentally ejaculated Mr Moreton. *Sits the wind in that quarter?*

Meanwhile, Frederica, shaking hands with the unexpected guest, said politely: "How do you do?" and, in a lowered tone: "What in the world brings you here, cousin?"

"A sense of duty," he responded, quizzing her. He added, in a softly provocative tone: "In case you should be getting into the wrong company!"

She choked, but contented herself with a speaking glance before turning, and saying, with a bright smile: "I fancy, cousin, that you are acquainted with most of our guests, but I should introduce you, perhaps, to Miss Upcott, and Miss Pensby." She waited, while he bowed slightly to these damsels, and then presented the two young aspirants to fashion. He favoured them with a nod, and, as he took in their magnificence, a lifted eyebrow, and a faint, disintegrating smile, before withdrawing his attention from them, and surveying the rest of the assembled guests. Besides Darcy Moreton, and a quiet man whom he identified as Sir Mark Lyneham, there were only four other guests, all very well-known to him, and all regarding him in varying degrees of embarrassment. They were his nephew, Lord Buxted; his cousins, Endymion and Chloë Dauntry; and his secretary, Charles Trevor. Chloë might be ill-at-ease from mere nervousness of one whom she had been taught from her cradle to regard as an omnipotent being who must on no account be offended; but the three gentlemen bore the appearance of persons detected in wrongdoing. Mr Trevor offered no explanation of his presence; but Endymion, eyeing him with misgiving, said that Chloë had asked him to escort her; and Lord Buxted said that he had dropped in to enquire how the ladies did. His lordship, however, showed no signs of disapproval, but smiled upon them all with perfect amiability, before making his way into the back-drawing-room, where Miss Winsham sat, knotting a fringe, and occasionally directing a forbidding stare at the company. This, when she saw the Marquis bearing down upon her, became a glare; and she responded to his graceful salutation with unnerving brusqueness. Quite undaunted, he sat down beside her, and engaged her in a somewhat one-sided conversation, exerting himself so adroitly to please her that she afterwards admitted to Frederica that at least he had good manners, and talked like a sensible man.

His visit was not of long duration, nor did he take part in a noisy game of Speculation which was got up by the younger members, devoting himself largely to Miss Winsham. He paid little apparent heed to his relations, and none at all to the two dandies; but when he took his leave he had satisfied himself on several points. Endymion was besotted with Charis; Buxted seemed to be trying to fix his interest with Frederica; and Charles Trevor, for all his reserve, could not conceal from knowledgeable eyes the signs betokening a young man in love. Obviously his sentiments were reciprocated; equally obviously, he was afraid that his noble employer would nip his pretensions in the bud. So, too, to judge by the wary expression in his eyes, was Endymion, very much on the defensive. Buxted's uneasiness was probably due merely to a fear that Alverstoke might betray him to his mother: he was his own master, and (to give the pompous young slow-top his due) had never showed any disposition to stand in his uncle's good graces. Had they but known it, neither he nor Endymion need have been alarmed: his lordship took only a tepid interest in the future of his heir, and none at all in that of his nephew. He preferred his secretary to either of them; and, while he had no intention of thrusting a spoke into his affairs, he did disapprove of his evident desire to marry Miss Dauntry. He thought it

would be an improvident match. Charles was a young
man of parts but no fortune; his ambitions were political; and a marriage with a girl possessed of a modest
dowry and no influence would scarcely advance him in
his career. Maintaining a conversation with Miss Winsham, Alverstoke watched Chloë, under his lazy eyelids. Pretty enough, he thought dispassionately, but too
newly emerged from the schoolroom to have unfurled
her petals. Her ready blushes betrayed both her youth
and her love, but she had a thoughtful brow, and an air
of gravity which was oddly taking. His lordship began
to see what Charles, a serious young man, had found in
her to attract him. Well, if this infatuation lasted, he
supposed that he would be obliged to lend the boy his
support. Failing a rich and influential wife, he needed a
patron: someone of sufficient standing to foster his
early progress, not by monetary assistance (which
Charles would certainly refuse), but by securing employment for him in government circles, where his zeal
and his talents would win recognition and swift ad-
vancement. There would be no difficulty about that: the
difficulty would be to find a secretary whom his lordship liked as well to take his place. But the matter did
not seem to him to be pressing: he suspected that Chloë
was Charles's first serious love; he was very sure that he
was hers; and in all probability the affair would come to
nothing.

It was harder to decide whether or not Charis felt a
stronger partiality for Endymion than for any other of
her suitors. She seemed to look upon them all with kindness; and if her eyes held warm admiration when they
rested on him there was nothing to be surprised at in
that: a very handsome fellow, Endymion.

As for Frederica's paragon, his lordship, who was
impatient of melancholy romantics, thought him very
milky indeed, with no more intention of offering
for Charis's hand than if she had been a statue. He
made no attempt to engage her attention, but seemed to
be content to sit dreamily regarding her, a faint smile,
which his lordship thought singularly fatuous, lingering
about his mouth. He excused himself from joining the

party bent on Speculation, and was still sitting rapt in contemplation when Alverstoke, taking leave of Miss Winsham, strolled over to him, and said, in a drawl that held a hint of derision: "Lost in admiration of my ward, Lyneham?"

Sir Mark started, and looked up; and, seeing who had roused him from his reverie, rose to his feet, and bowed, saying simply: "Yes, my lord. She is a Botticelli, is she not? One is tempted to fancy that in another incarnation she must have sat for him when he painted his *Birth of Venus*. Alas, that one cannot set her in a frame, to be a constant refreshment to one's eyes! One would wish that countenance to remain for ever as it is today, pure and perfect!" He sighed. "It cannot be, of course. The lovely innocence we see now, as she stands at the dawn of womanhood, will vanish all too soon; age and experience will set their stamp upon her, carving furrows in her beauty; and—"

"And her chin will be doubled!" interpolated his lordship, who had no taste for whimsy.

He left Sir Mark abruptly, and went to take his leave of Frederica. She was distributing fishes and counters amongst the players seated round the card-table, but when she saw him coming towards her she gave the box into her sister's hands, and went with him to the head of the stairs. "I shan't beg you not to go away so soon," she said. "I am persuaded you were never more bored. But I do trust you are satisfied that we are not got into the wrong company?"

"Oh, yes! Quite innocuous!" he returned. "None more so than your paragon, whose only desire appears to be to set your sister in a frame, and hang her on the wall to provide his eyes with eternal refreshment."

She exclaimed incredulously: "Set her in a frame? He can never have said so!"

"Ask him!"

She looked disgusted. "Well, what a wet-goose! I never thought he could be so spiritless!"

"No, no, a romantic, with the soul of a poet, and a high appreciation of the beautiful!"

"I see nothing romantic in wishing to turn Charis

into a picture! In fact, I am much inclined to think that you were right when you told me that he was a dull dog," she said, with her usual candour.

He laughed. "Why, yes!—but deeply reverential, I assure you! He considers Charis's beauty to be pure and perfect, and wishes it might remain so."

She stared at him for a frowning moment, and then said decidedly: "That proves he hasn't the smallest tendre for her! How very vexatious! You know, he *did* seem to me to be so promising!"

His eyes gleamed, but he responded with perfect gravity: "You will be obliged to look about for another eligible *parti*. Can I be of assistance? I recall that you have come to the conclusion that a young man won't do for Charis, and it occurs to me— Tell me, would you object to a widower?"

"Yes, I should!" said Frederica. "Furthermore, cousin, I beg you won't concern yourself in our affairs! I never asked more of you than an introduction to the ton, and you gave us that—for which I am excessively grateful!—and I don't expect, or wish, you to trouble yourself further! Indeed, there is not the least need!"

"Oh, no, don't stir coals!" he protested. "Just when you've provided me with an interest, too!"

"Finding widowers for Charis!"

"That was a joke," he explained.

"Not a funny one!" she said severely.

"I beg a thousand pardons! I won't introduce my widower to your sister's notice, but you may believe me when I say that you may command my services, or my advice, at any time."

She was surprised, and for a moment suspected him of mockery. But the familiar glint was absent from his eyes; and, as she met their steady regard, he laid his hand over hers, which was resting on the banister, and clasped it strongly, saying: "Is it agreed? You don't want for sense, or force of mind, but you're not yet up to snuff, my child."

"No—no, I kn-know I'm not," she said, stammering a little. "Thank you! you are very good! Indeed, I can't think whom else I could turn to, if I needed guidance

—or got into a scrape! But I don't mean to embroil you in any *more* scrapes, I promise you!"

She would have drawn her hand away as she spoke, but he prevented her, lifting it from the banister, and lightly kissing it. She had the oddest sensation of having suffered an electric shock; she even felt a trifle dizzy; and it was several moments after he had left her before she went back into the drawing-room. It was no longer customary for gentlemen to kiss hands; and although oldfashioned persons frequently kissed the hands of married ladies, his lordship was not oldfashioned, and she was not married. She wondered what he meant by it, and was obliged to give herself a mental shake. Probably he meant nothing at all, or was trying to get up a flirtation. By all accounts that was the sort of thing he might do, for idle amusement, because she had unwisely told him she had never been in love. This was a lowering thought—not that it signified, except that she had come to look upon him as a safe friend, and it would be very uncomfortable if she could no longer do so. If he thought she was going to figure as his latest flirt he was sadly mistaken: for one thing she had no taste for flirtation; and for another no ambition to join the ranks of his discarded flirts.

However, when she met him, three days later, in Bond Street, he showed no sign of gallantry, but greeted her with a frown, and a demand to know why she was unaccompanied. "I was under the impression that I warned you that in London country ways will not do, Frederica!"

"You did!" she retorted. "And although I can't say that I paid much heed to your advice it so happens that I am accompanied today by my aunt!"

"Who adds invisibility to her other accomplishments!"

She could not help laughing, but said as coldly as she could: "She is making a purchase in that shop, and is to meet me in Hookham's Library presently. I trust you are satisfied!"

"I am not at all satisfied. Unless you wish to appear as a *fast* female, you will not show yourself unattended in any of London's fashionable lounges—least of all in

Bond Street! If that *is* your ambition, look for another sponsor! And don't nauseate me with fiddle-faddle about your advanced years! You may pass in Herefordshire for a woman of sense, but here you are merely a green—a *very* green girl, Frederica!"

These harsh words aroused conflicting emotions in her breast. Her first impulse was to give him a sharp set-down. Such arrogance certainly deserved a set-down; on the other hand, he was quite capable of withdrawing his patronage, which, if it did not ruin her plans, would be extremely inconvenient. The thought that with his friendship she would lose all her comfort she thrust to the back of her mind. She said, achieving a respectable compromise: "To be sure, I *am* very green, for until I saw you coming towards me I didn't know this *was* a fashionable lounge! I'm much obliged to you for telling me, and I can't think how I came to be so stupid! As though I had never heard of *Bond Street beaux,* which of course I have! Are you—what do you call it?—*on the strut?*"

"No, vixen, I am not on the strut!" he replied, an appreciative gleam in his eye. "Merely on my way to Jackson's Boxing Saloon!"

"How horrid!"

"That," said his lordship, "from one who lately described to me the precise significance of *good science,* is coming it very much too brown, Frederica!"

She laughed. "Well, it *is* horrid, for all that! How detestable of you to have encouraged me to make such a cake of myself, when I daresay you know much more about the sport than I do!"

"I shouldn't be surprised if I did," he agreed. "Also more about the conventions to be observed by young ladies of quality."

"That crow has been plucked already! How can you be so unhandsome as to go on scolding? Haven't I owned I was at fault?"

"If to offer me a gratuitous insult is to own yourself at fault—"

"No, no! not *gratuitous,* cousin!" she interposed.

"One of these days," said his lordship, with careful

restraint, "you will come by your just deserts, my girl! At least, so I hope!"

"Oh, how unkind!" Her eyes twinkled up at him, but she became serious almost immediately, and said contritely: "What a charge we are upon you! I beg your pardon: you have been very kind! I never meant, you know, to embroil you in our affairs, and I am determined you shan't be called upon again to rescue us from sudden dilemmas."

"From which I deduce that your brothers are not—at the moment—engaged on any hazardous enterprise," he remarked.

"Now *that*," she said indignantly, "is most unjust! *You* were not called upon to rescue Felix from the steampacket; and, as for Jessamy, he at least doesn't get into scrapes!"

He acknowledged it; but it was Jessamy who plunged him, not many days later, into the affair of the Pedestrian Curricle.

This ingenious machine was the very latest crack, and bidding fair to become the transient rage. Of simple construction, it consisted of two wheels, with a saddle hung between them, the foremost of which could be made to turn by means of a bar. It was propelled by the rider's feet on the road, and experts could achieve quite astonishing speeds, when, admirably balancing themselves, they would lift their feet from the ground and coast along at a great rate, and to the amazement of beholders. Jessamy had seen one of these experts riding his Pedestrian Curricle in the park, and had instantly become fired with the spirit of emulation. His adventurous nature, chafing as much under the loss of his horses as from his self-imposed regiment of rigorous study, flamed into revolt: here, he perceived, was the means by which he could, without involving Frederica in extra expenditure, find an outlet for his restless energy, and demonstrate to the world that his odious little brother was not the only Merriville with bottom enough to engage in hazardous exploits. He discovered that there were several schools where the new art was taught, and which were willing to hire their machines to proficient pupils. It did not take him long to become one of these, or, when he ventured to sally forth from the school on a hired machine, to learn to guide it through such traffic as he encountered in the quieter streets. Lufra was his companion on these expeditions: a circumstance which led his sisters to assume, with satisfaction, that he had relaxed his stern rule on that faithful hound's behalf. "Which makes me glad, after all, that we did bring Luff to London," said Frederica, adding, with a chuckle: "And also that he chased the cows in the Green Park, and made Jessamy think that a mere female was not to be trusted with him. Nothing else would have lured him away from his books!"

Boy enough to wish to startle his family with his unsuspected prowess, Jessamy had said nothing to them about his new hobby. Once he had perfected his balance, and could feel himself to be master of the Pedestrian Curricle, he meant to ride up to the door, and call his sisters out to watch his skill. There was sometimes a little difficulty in mounting the machine, and it would never do to make a mull of that—particularly if Felix were to be one of his audience. So he spent several hours practising this art; and then, as a final test before showing himself off to his family, boldly penetrated into the more populous part of the town. So well did he manage that he could not resist the temptation to coast down the long slope of Piccadilly, both feet daringly lifted from the flagway. This feat attracted a great deal of attention, some of it admiring, some of it scandalized; and, in the end, very much more attention than Jessamy desired.

A rough-coated retriever was to blame for the disaster. Sedately walking at his master's heels, this animal no sooner saw the strange vehicle than he took the most violent exception to it, and raced beside it, barking and snapping. Jessamy was too well accustomed to dogs who bounced out to chase any passing carriage to be discomposed by this assault, but Lufra, who had lingered a little way behind to investigate a promising smell, saw that his master was being attacked, and hurled himself to the rescue. The result was inevitable. The dogs, embarking on a fight to the death, cannoned into the Pedestrian Curricle; Jessamy, trying to recover his balance, charged into a man mending chairs, lost control of his machine, and was flung on to the cobbled highway, almost under the hooves of a high-stepping pair harnessed to a landaulet. The coachman was able to swing his horses away, and Jessamy to scramble to his feet, bruised, cut, and considerably shaken, but with no bones broken. A little dazed, and deeply humiliated, he found himself faced with a scene appalling enough to have daunted any sixteen-year-old less stiffly courageous than himself. The sudden swerve of the carriage-horses had dislocated the traffic, and the air was rent by rude, loud voices, uttering accusations and counter-accusations, embellished by threats and strange oaths; the dowager in the landaulet was indulging in a fit of mild vapours; the chair-mender, also picking himself up from the roadway, was claiming enormous damages for his personal injuries and the total wreckage of the chair; and the retriever's master was furiously shouting for help in separating the dogs. To this task Jessamy turned his attention, and once he had persuaded the irate gentleman to stop belabouring both animals, and to hold his own firmly, he speedily dragged Lufra off. He was just about to stammer an apology when the irate gentleman, stigmatizing Lufra as a savage brute, threw all the blame of the encounter upon that noble hound. That, naturally, made him bite back his apology, and point out that all the blame attached to the retriever, who had wantonly attacked him. "Would you give a *souse* for a dog that wouldn't protect his master, sir?" he demanded. "*I* would not!"

From then on the scene rose to nightmarish proportions, so many people claiming damages, or threatening lawsuits, that poor Jessamy's brain reeled. When his name and direction were demanded he had a horrid vision of a stream of injured persons descending upon Frederica, bent on extorting huge sums from her, and, of instinct, he blurted out: "Berkeley Square! My—my guardian's house—the M-Marquis of Alverstoke!"

He had no thought in his head but to protect Frederica, but it was swiftly borne in upon him that he had uttered magical words. His assurances of redress (hitherto spurned) were accepted; the irate gentleman, saying that he hoped his guardian would make him smart, resumed his progress up the street; and the dowager, recovering from the vapours, read him a severe lecture, and said she would not fail to report what she called his naughtiness to the Marquis.

Thus it came about that for the second time a Merriville arrived in Berkeley Square at an unseasonable hour, demanding instant speech with the Marquis. Unlike Frederica, however, Jessamy did not reject Charles Trevor's services; and he was impetuously, and rather incomprehensibly, pouring his story into Charles's ears when Alverstoke, wearing a long and lavishly caped driving-coat of white drab over his elegant morning-dress, strolled into the room, saying: *"Now* what? Wicken informs me—" He broke off, and raised his quizzing-glass to his eye, the better to observe Jessamy's battered appearance. He let it fall, and advanced. "Repellent boy, have you been in a mill? Why the devil haven't you patched him up, Charles?"

"I haven't yet been allowed to, sir," responded Mr Trevor.

"No, no, it's of no consequence!" Jessamy said impatiently, wiping away a trickle of blood from a cut on his forehead. "I'm not hurt! Nothing to signify! I only want—I mean I didn't come here because of *that,* but because—Oh, *pray* don't trouble yourself about it, sir!"

"Stand still!" commanded Alverstoke, taking that dogged chin in his hand, and turning Jessamy's face to the light.

"It wasn't a mill! I feel—and it serves me right!" Jessamy said bitterly, and with suppressed violence.

"No doubt, but it doesn't serve me right to have you bleeding all over my house. Charles, I wish you will be good enough to—No, I'll attend to it myself. Come along, you young cawker! You can tell me all about it while I put some sticking-plaster over this cut."

Willy-nilly, Jessamy followed him out of the room, and up the broad stairs, protesting all the way that his wounds and abrasions were of no consequence, and that he had come to his lordship's house merely to make a clean breast of his iniquity; to warn him that a number of persons of varying degree were probably following hard upon his heels, to demand compensation for the damage they had incurred at his hands; and to beg him to disburse whatever sums were required, under promise of repayment by the culprit.

Presently, having washed the dirt and the bloodstains from his face and hands, relinquished his muddy coat into Knapp's hands, submitted to having the more accessible of his many bruises anointed, and his brow adorned with a strip of plaster, and swallowed a judicious mixture of brandy and water, his jangled nerves grew quieter, and he was able to give the Marquis a fairly coherent account of his accident, speaking in a voice of rigid control, and betraying only by the clenching and unclenching of his thin hands the inward turmoil under which his spirit laboured. He ended on a harsh note, meeting Alverstoke's cool, faintly amused eyes with a fierce look in his own. "I had no right to furnish them with your name, sir, or to lead them to suppose that I live here. I know it, and I beg your pardon! I—I want to explain! I only did it because I couldn't bear to have them coming down upon Frederica! I don't know what I may have to pay: a great deal, I daresay, because the machine was smashed as well as that chair, and—But whatever it is *I* will pay, and not my sister! With all the expense of Charis's come-out—and I was determined not to add to it!"

He ended on a note of anguish, but the Marquis applied an effective damper by saying in a prosaic and slightly bored voice: "Very proper. What is it you wish me to do for you?"

Pulled up short on the verge of an emotional outburst, Jessamy flushed, biting his lip, and managed to reply with tolerable self-command: "To lend me whatever sum may be needed—if you would be so very obliging, sir! On the understanding that I pay it back to you out of my allowance. You see, I haven't very much left just—just at the moment. There were the lessons I had, and the hire of the machine, so—"

"Don't let it worry you!" advised his lordship. "I shan't dun you!"

Jessamy's flush deepened. "I know that! Pray don't

say I needn't pay you back at all, or tell me not to worry! Nothing would prevail upon me not to pay you back, and I *ought* to worry! At the first test I yielded to temptation! Vainglory! Yes, and worse! I wanted to outshine Felix! Could anything be more contemptible, or show how—how unfitted I am even to *think* of entering into Holy Orders?"

"Yes, quite a number of things," replied Alverstoke. "Stop magnifying a trivial incident into a major sin! All you have done is to get into a scrape, through no particular fault of your own, and there is no need whatsoever for any soul-searching. I am glad to know you *can* fall into scrapes: you'll be a better parson if you have understanding of human frailty than if you were to be a saint at sixteen years of age!"

Jessamy looked to be rather struck by this, but after frowning over it for a moment, he said: "Yes, but—but when one has made a resolution—not to have the strength to resist temptation shows such weakness of character—doesn't it, sir?"

"If your resolution was to behave like an ascetic, it shows that you stand in grave danger of becoming a prig!" said his lordship brutally. "Well, you've applied to me for assistance, in which you've at least shown that you don't lose your wits in an emergency! I'll settle the reckoning and you can repay me when you can do so without leaving yourself at a standstill. As for all the threats that were hurled at you, forget them! If any coachman, chair-mender, or any other such person, had the temerity to come here, demanding your blood, you may depend upon it that Mr Trevor would be fully capable of dealing with such impudence! But they won't come."

"No," Jessamy said, his brow darkening. "I didn't give your name for that reason—it didn't even occur to me!—but as soon as I said you were my guardian—" He stopped, brooding over it, and then said, raising his austere eyes to Alverstoke's face: "That's as contemptible as the rest!"

"Possibly, but you'll own it's convenient! Spare me any moralizing on the hollowness of worldly rank, and pay attention to what I am going to say to you!"

"Yes, sir," said Jessamy, bracing himself.

"You've claimed my protection as your guardian, and you must now submit to your guardian's judgment. Which is that you will henceforth moderate your studies —believe me, they are excessive!—and devote some part of every day to your physical needs. What you want, Jessamy, is not a Pedestrian Curricle, but a horse!"

Light sprang to Jessamy's sombre eyes; he exclaimed involuntarily: "Oh, if only—!" He stopped short, and shook his head. "I can't. Not in London! The expense—"

"There will be no expense. You are going to exercise one of my hacks—thereby doing me a favour!"

"R-ride your horses? You—you'd let me—*t-trust* me?" stammered Jessamy. "Oh, no! I don't deserve to be *rewarded,* sir!"

"You are not being rewarded: you are being commanded!" said Alverstoke. "A novel experience for you, young man!" The glowing eyes lifted to his, the trembling of Jessamy's lip, touched him. He smiled, and dropped a hand on the boy's shoulder, gripping it. "Pluck up, you gudgeon!" he said. "You haven't broken even one of the Ten Commandments, you know, so stop trying to turn a molehill into a mountain! If Knapp has finished furbishing up your coat, I'll drive you home now."

XV

Upon the following morning, the Marquis received a letter from Frederica, thanking him for his kind offices, and expressing her regret that he should have been put to so much trouble on Jessamy's behalf. He read it appreciatively, knowing very well that its civility hid—or was meant to hide—intense mortification. She acknowledged it, when, two days later, he met her at an assembly. She said, in answer to his quizzing accusation: "Oh, no, no, no, no, not *cross,* but so deeply mortified! After all my protestations—! I do most sincerely beg your pardon!"

"Nonsense! What had you to do with it?"

"Oh, everything!" she sighed. "I brought him to London against his wish, and I've neglected him for Charis. I ought not to leave him so much to his own devices." She thought this over, and added candidly: "Not that he would like it if I were to thrust my company on him too frequently. In fact, it would irk him past bearing. He is a—a very solitary person, you know. And that's my fault too: I expect I should have at least made a push to cure him of that."

"You would have been wasting your time. I wish you will explain to me why you are making such a heavy matter of a trivial and perfectly understandable episode? He, of course, was bound to do so, at this stage of his career, but why should you?"

"Oh, I don't!" she said quickly. "If he hadn't turned to you instead of to me I should have been excessively diverted! But it does vex me that he should have dragged you into the affair. Yes, and although he gets upon his high ropes if I question him, and says it is no concern of mine, but quite his own business, I am persuaded you must have paid for all the damage he did, and that I *cannot* bear!"

"Nor could he, so I have merely lent him the necessary sum—in return for his promise that he will abate his studies a trifle. Yes, I know you are burning to reimburse me immediately, but that, let me tell you, would be a high piece of meddling—and, if I were to allow you to do it, which I shan't—destructive of the good I rather think I may have achieved."

She looked at him, her eyes warm with gratitude. "Indeed you have! I was afraid that he would have fallen into dejection, for in general he always does so when he has kicked up a lark, but this time he is more *aux anges* than in despair. I wish you might have seen him when he rode up to our door on your horse, and called me out to admire its points! So proud and happy! I won't meddle, but at least let me thank you!"

"No, the subject has begun to bore me. Tell me, instead, who's the dashing blade with Charis?"

Her eyes travelled to her sister, who was waltzing with a lively young gentleman, obviously of the first stare of à la modality, and even more obviously bent on fixing his interest with her. "Mr Peter Navenby. We met him at Lady Jersey's party. She told me he no sooner set eyes on Charis than he begged her to present him. There's nothing unusual in that, of course, but he has become extremely particular in his attentions, and— which I think *most* significant!—he prevailed upon his mother to pay us a morning visit! I liked her so much! What's of more consequence is that *she* liked Charis. I collect, from something she said to me, that her dread is to see him snapped up by some horridly mercenary girl on the catch for a rich husband—which she instantly perceived Charis is *not!*" She looked anxiously at his lordship. "It *would* be an eligible match, wouldn't it?"

The Marquis, who was surveying Mr Navenby through his quizzing-glass, said: "Young Navenby, is he? Oh, a most eligible match! He has all the advantages of birth, and a respectable fortune—prospective, of course, but we must hope his father won't be long-lived."

"I don't hope anything of the sort!" said Frederica, flushing angrily. "An—an abominable thing to say— even for you, my lord!"

"But I thought you were determined to marry Charis
to a fortune!"

"I am not, and nor did I ever say so. I wish to see
her *comfortably* established—which is a very different
matter to scheming for titles and fortunes! What I do
not wish for her is a handsome muttonhead like your
cousin, whose fortune is as small as his brain! I shall be
very much obliged to you if you will nip that affair in
the bud!"

He looked rather amused, but merely said: "You
must have been listening to my cousin Lucretia. Let me
reassure you! Endymion was not born without a shirt.
He inherited quite an easy competence."

Conscious of having let her annoyance betray her
into a very improper speech, she said stiffly: "I
shouldn't have spoken as I did about your cousin. I beg
your pardon!"

"Oh, I've no objection!" he replied indifferently. "I
have really very little interest in Endymion, and not
the smallest intention of interfering in his concerns. So
you won't have to be obliged to me. That should at
least afford you some consolation." He glanced mockingly at her as he spoke, but she had turned her face
away, biting her lip. "Well? Doesn't it?"

"No. You made me fly into a miff, and snap your
nose off, but I didn't mean to offend you. I hope I am
not so ungrateful!"

"You haven't offended me, and I don't want your
gratitude," he said. Startled by the harsh note in his
voice, she looked up at him, doubt and a little dismay in
her face. His was inscrutable, but after a moment he
smiled, and said, in his usual languid way: "Gratitude
is another of the things which I find a dead bore."

"Then you must take care not to give me cause to
feel it," she replied.

He had transferred his attention again to Charis, and
said abruptly: "A budding Tulip, young Navenby. Am
I to understand that you have abandoned hope of her
milky suitor?"

"Yes, entirely! You were perfectly right: he's nothing
but an air-dreamer! Do but look at him now!—he
is seated beside Mrs Porthcawl, watching Charis with

the most ridiculous smile on his face! He doesn't care a rush that she should be dancing with Navenby!"

"True!" he agreed. The quizzing-glass came into play again, sweeping the room until it found its object. "So unlike my muttonheaded cousin!"

"Well, he *is* muttonheaded!" she said defiantly.

"I never denied it. I even refrained from retaliating in kind."

An irrepressible dimple peeped in her cheek, but she replied with dignity: "You mean, I collect, that my sister isn't—isn't *blue*, or—or very clever—"

"You may so phrase it, if you choose. Your sister, Frederica, is a beautiful pea-goose—and well you know it!"

Since an innate honesty forbade her to refute this charge, all she could think of to say was: "The more reason for her to marry a man of sense, and judgment!"

"You may be right. Does that description fit young Navenby? I shouldn't have thought it, but again you may be right. I know nothing about him, after all, and it never does to judge by appearances, does it?"

"Of all the detestable persons I ever met—" She stopped, gave a gasp, and said in a tone of strong resolution: "No. I won't say it! But I daresay you may guess whom I mean!" she added, her feelings overcoming her.

"No, I haven't a notion: do tell me!" he invited.

She caught her breath on a choke of laughter, and turned from him, with considerable relief, to greet Darcy Moreton, who had just come up to them. The Marquis lingered only to exchange a few words with Mr Moreton before strolling away to join a group gathered round Lady Jersey. He was apparently unaware of the interest he had aroused by singling out the elder Miss Merriville, and sitting beside her for quite twenty minutes; but he had been observed throughout by several pairs of eyes: some curious, some jealous, and some cynical; and no one had failed to notice that for a large part of this time he had been watching the younger Miss Merriville. Some thought that it would be rather too bad if he were to make that beautiful innocent his next victim; others wondered if he had at last met his fate; and a few ladies, some of whom had cherished secret hopes that their daughters might find favour in his eyes, were unequivocally disgusted. Amongst these was Lady Buxted. She had no axe to grind; she had been as anxious as her elder sister to see Alverstoke suitably married, and his presumptive heir cut out, but from the moment of setting eyes on Charis she had taken the Merrivilles in strong dislike. She was convinced that the blame for Jane's lack of success lay at Charis's door; and the compliments she received on her protégées' delightful manners and excellent style very soon made her hate Frederica as much as Charis. She had been forced to launch them into the ton, and was now able to wash her hands of them; but even this agreeable circumstance was spoilt for her by the ease and rapidity with which they had found their feet. She might tell herself that the hostesses who invited them to their parties only did so to oblige their noble guardian, but she knew very well that it was untrue. Everyone liked the Merrivilles, as the Countess Lieven, with a faint, malicious smile, informed her.

"For my part, I consider them a great deal too coming," she told her elder sister. "Charis's namby-pamby airs don't impress me; and as for Frederica, as she calls herself, I daresay you've noticed how positively *bumptious* she is!"

"No," said Lady Jevington bluntly, "I haven't. Very unaffected, pretty-behaved girls, both of them. Charis is a beautiful ninnyhammer; but I believe Frederica to be a young woman of superior understanding."

"Oh, *most* superior!" said Lady Buxted, her eyes snapping angrily. "On the catch for a husband! I wonder you should be so taken by her insinuating ways! *I* knew what her object was within a week of making her acquaintance!"

"Ah!" said Lady Jevington. "So Buxted *is* making up to her, is he? I've several times been told as much, but I never listen to *on-dits*. Make yourself easy, Louisa! Nothing will come of it!"

Her colour much heightened, Lady Buxted retorted: "No! Not if *I* have anything to say in the matter!" The condescending smile on her sister's face exacerbated her into adding: "I have no fears for Carlton: none at all!

But I wonder how you will like it, my dear Augusta, when you find yourself with your beautiful *ninnyhammer* as your sister-in-law!" She perceived that these words had produced an impression, and continued triumphantly: "How is it possible that you, who believe yourself to be so long-headed, can have failed to notice that Vernon scarcely took his eyes off that girl last night?"

Lady Jevington opened her mouth, shut it again, and, after subjecting her sister to an incredulous stare, said:

"You are a fool, Louisa!"

Meanwhile, the Misses Merriville, their thoughts far removed from matrimonial conquests, were warmly welcoming the head of the family, exclaiming joyfully at his unexpected arrival in Upper Wimpole Street, hugging him, kissing him, thrusting him into the easiest chair in the drawing-room, procuring refreshment for him, and greeting his sudden appearance with all the fond delight to be expected of two loving sisters.

Inevitably, it was Frederica who first came to earth, and who demanded to know what had brought him to London. Fortifying himself with a long drink from the tankard she had just handed him, he met her anxious gaze with an engaging grin, and said: "Oh, I've been rusticated!"

"Harry! Oh, *no!*" she cried, dismayed.

"Yes, I have—Barny too! You know: Barny Peplow, a particular friend of mine—a great gun!"

She had not so far been privileged to meet Mr Peplow, but her brother's enthusiastic praise of that young gentleman had long since inspired her with foreboding. But it was Charis who nettled Harry, by uttering in soft but stricken accents: "Oh, *dear!* What can be done?"

"Nothing is to be done! What a goose you are!" returned Harry impatiently. "You needn't look so Fridayfaced either of you! Anyone would think I'd been sent down for good! Of course I haven't been! Only for the rest of this term!"

"But why, Harry?" Frederica asked, by no means reassured.

He laughed. "Oh, nothing very much! Just a bit of bobbery! We weren't the only ones in it, either. The thing was we were rather full of frisk. It was after old George's birthday party: George Leigh, I mean, though you don't know him either, do you? A famous fellow! So there was a bit of riot and rumpus—and that's how it was! Nothing to throw you into high fidgets, I promise you!"

Her anxious mind relieved of its worst fears, she agreed to this, and asked him no further questions knowing well that these would only set up his back. Experience had also taught her that while she understood and sympathized with schoolboys' pranks, she would never be able to understand what Harry and his friends found to amuse them in their revel-routs, which seemed invariably to start with what he called a spread, or (as she gathered) a wine-party; and to end in horse-play as senseless as it was destructive.

"As a matter of fact," said Harry ingenuously, "I've been thinking for some time that I *ought* to come down, just to make sure all's right here. There's no saying but what you might have got into a scrape, and I *am* the head of the family!"

Charis giggled; but Frederica, though the ready laughter sprang to her eyes, responded, in a much-moved tone: "How *kind* of you, Harry! Of course, it was your *duty* to be rusticated!"

"Now, Freddy—!" he protested, his lips quivering in spite of himself. "I didn't say *that!*"

"I should think not indeed!" said Charis, highly diverted by this exchange. "When we have been fixed in London for more than a month, and there are only a few weeks left of the term! What a Banbury-man you are, you dearest, horridest creature!"

He laughed back at her, but said: "Well, I do think I ought to keep my eye on you all. You're neither of you up to snuff, you know, and you were never before in London."

"There, I must own, you have the advantage of us," agreed Frederica.

"Good gracious, when was Harry in London?" asked Charis, in innocent surprise.

"I don't precisely remember, but it was some years ago. Aunt Scrabster invited him, because of being his godmother, and he spent a whole week in Harley Street, and was shown *all* the sights—weren't you, Harry?"

He grimaced at her. "That's quite enough, Freddy! Lord, how my uncle did drag me about, and to the stuffiest places! But the thing is that I've learnt a great deal since I went up to Oxford, and I fancy I've a pretty fair notion of what's o'clock. And I'll tell you *one* thing I don't like, and that's this house!"

"No, nor do we, but in spite of its shabby furniture, and its unfashionable situation, we contrive to move in the first circles, I promise you!"

"I know that, and I don't like it above half. It was this fellow, Alverstoke, who brought that about, wasn't it? I never heard of him in my life until you wrote that he was a cousin of ours, but I can tell you this!—I know a great deal about him now, and I must say, Frederica, I can't understand how you came to put yourself under his protection! You ain't in general so bird-witted!"

"But, Harry, what can you mean?" exclaimed Charis. "He has been so very kind and obliging! You can have no notion!"

"Oh, can't I?" he retorted. "Well, that's where you're out, because I have! Kind and obliging! I daresay!"

"Yes, and particularly so to the boys! Are you thinking that he is very starched-up? He does *appear* to be, and I know that some people say he is odiously haughty, and cares only for his own pleasure, but it isn't so, is it, Frederica? Only think of his taking Felix all over that foundry, and arranging for him to see the New Mint, besides letting Jessamy ride that lovely horse!"

"Lord Alverstoke was under an obligation to Papa," said Frederica coolly. "It was on that account that he consented—not very willingly!—to act as our guardian."

"Guardian? He's no guardian of mine!" interrupted Harry, up in arms.

"Certainly not. Or of mine! How should he be, when we are both of age?"

"Yes, well—oh, you don't understand!"

"I assure you I do! You've been told that he's a shocking rake—"

"*Is* he?" interpolated Charis, her eyes widening. "I had thought a rake would have been very different! Well, I know they are! They try to get up flirtations, and put one to the blush by the things they say, and— oh, you know, Frederica! Cousin Alverstoke isn't at all like that. Indeed, I've often thought him dreadfully strict!"

"Yes, for ever preaching propriety, and giving one a scold for not behaving as though one had but just escaped from the school-room," said Frederica, with considerable feeling. "Make yourself easy, Harry! Whatever may be Alverstoke's reputation, he cherishes no improper designs where *we* are concerned! Nor did we come out under his aegis. It's true that he invited us to a ball which he gave in honour of his niece, but it was his sister, Lady Buxted, who fired us off, as they say."

He did not look to be perfectly satisfied; but as Jessamy came in at that moment the subject was allowed to drop. Jessamy looked grave when he learned the reason for Harry's arrival, but he only said, when warned that his senior wanted no jobations from him: "Certainly not!"

"And none of your moralizing speeches either!" said Harry, eyeing him in some suspicion.

"You needn't be afraid of that. I have no right to moralize," replied Jessamy, sighing.

"Hey, what's this?" Harry demanded. "Don't tell me *you've* been kicking up riot and rumpus, old sobersides!"

"Something very like it," Jessamy said heavily, the scene in Piccadilly vivid in his memory.

Both his sisters cried out at this; and by the time Harry had been regaled by them with the story of the Pedestrian Curricle, and had gone into shouts of laughter, Jessamy had begun to think that it had not been so very bad after all, and was even able to laugh a little himself, and to tell Harry about the adventure's glorious sequel, dwelling with such particularity on the points of Alverstoke's various hacks and carriage-horses that the ladies soon bethought themselves of tasks in some other part of the house, and withdrew.

When the subject had been thoroughly discussed, Harry acknowledged that it was certainly handsome of the Marquis to place his hacks at Jessamy's disposal, and gratified his brother by adding: "Not that he'd anything to fear. I'll say this for you, young 'un: you've as neat a seat and as light a hand as anyone I know."

"Yes, but *he* didn't know that!" said Jessamy naïvely.

Harry grinned, but refrained from comment. You never knew how Jessamy would take it, if you made game of him, and he thought it rather beneath himself to set up the boy's bristles. Besides, he wanted to know more about the Marquis. Jessamy was six years his junior, but he had a good deal of respect for his judgment, and a somewhat rueful dependence on his ability to detect weakness of moral character. If Jessamy erred, it would not be on the side of tolerance.

But Jessamy had little but good to say of the Marquis. He understood why Harry should be anxious, and owned that he had wondered, at first, if Alverstoke meant to dangle after Charis. "It's no such thing, however. He doesn't seem to me to pay much heed to her. He did take her driving in the park once, but Frederica told me he only did so as a sort of warning to some horrid rip that was making up to her; and he doesn't send her flowers, or haunt the house, like Cousin Endymion!"

"Cousin *who?*" demanded Harry.

"Endymion. Well, that's what we call him, and, according to Frederica, we are connected with him in some way or another. He's Cousin Alverstoke's heir, and in the Life Guards. Nutty on Charis, but there's no need to worry about him! He's a big, beef-witted fellow: no harm in him at all—but lord, what a clothhead! Then there's Cousin Gregory—he's one of Cousin Alverstoke's nephews; and Cousin Buxted—but *he* comes to sit in Frederica's pocket; and—"

"Here, how many more of them?" interpolated Harry, startled.

"I don't know precisely. It does seem odd suddenly

to find oneself with dozens of cousins one never knew existed, doesn't it?"

"Damned odd!"

"Yes, but they *are* cousins, or, at all events, connections of ours: they acknowledge it!"

Harry shook his head, but said: "Well, I suppose it's all right and tight. Did you say one of them was making up to *Frederica?*"

"Yes, it's the greatest joke!" replied Jessamy, fully appreciating his brother's incredulity. "And the best of it is that he's such a dead bore that—" He stopped, and frowned. "I shouldn't say that of him," he said. "He's a very respectable man. Kind, too, and thinks just as he ought. Only, somehow, he makes you want to go off and knock up a lark when he starts moralizing. I know that's wrong, but it does make me see what Cousin Alverstoke meant when he said I should make a better parson if I did fall into scrapes."

This disclosure made a stronger appeal to Harry than anything else Jessamy had said in the Marquis's favour. He declared himself anxious to make his acquaintance, even going so far as to say that he sounded as if he had a lot of rumgumption.

"Well, I daresay you will be taking the girls to balls, so you're bound to meet him."

"Taking the girls to balls?" echoed Harry, horrified. "No, by Jupiter! That I won't!"

Nothing would move him from this decision. To the persuasions of his sisters he responded that he had outgrown his evening-dress, and would be dashed if he wasted his blunt on a new rig; that he expected to be fully engaged with his friend Barny; that he rather thought he might take a bolt to Herefordshire, just to be sure all was well at Graynard; and, as a clincher, that he was such a bad dancer that he would only disgrace them if they dragged him to any of their assemblies.

They were disappointed, but not surprised. Harry, who closely resembled Charis, could never disgrace them, however badly he danced, for besides his fair, handsome face and well-made person, he had a considerable degree of lively charm; but Harry, alas, had no taste for fashionable life, and no ambition to acquire the

London touch. He was ripe for any spree (as he phrased it) with his friends; but it was easy to see that it would not be many years before he settled down very happily to the life of a sporting squire.

If anything had been needed to confirm him in his resolution it was supplied by Miss Winsham, acidly expressing the opinion that the least he could do to atone for his rustication was to make himself useful to his sisters. Ten minutes in his aunt's company were enough to set Harry, in general the most easy-going of mortals, at dagger-drawing. Frederica, seeing the spark in his blue eyes, and the mulish look about his mouth, intervened; and allowed some time to elapse before she ventured to suggest that if he wished to make Alverstoke's acquaintance he could be sure of doing so by escorting his sisters to Lady Sefton's forthcoming squeeze.

But Harry had an answer to that. Little though he might like doing the pretty amongst all the smarts and fribbles of the ton, he hoped he was not rag-mannered. Rather cool, he said, to depend on a chance meeting for the opportunity to pay his respects to the Marquis! He had given the matter some thought; and since it appeared that Alverstoke had placed them all under an obligation he felt that it behoved him to pay a formal visit in Berkeley Square not merely as a gesture of civility, but to discharge Jessamy's debt.

"Well, I own I should be glad if you could do so," said Frederica, "but I don't think he will let you! I expect you are quite right in thinking that you should pay him a morning visit, but, whatever you do, Harry, don't let it be before noon! Jessamy and I have both invaded his house before he had left his dressing-room, and for a *third* Merriville to do so would be quite dreadful!"

"What a paltry fellow!" exclaimed Harry scornfully.

But when, strictly adhering to Frederica's advice, he presented himself in Berkeley Square, one glance was enough to convince him that whatever epithet might be used to describe the Marquis, *paltry* was very fair and far off indeed.

As luck would have it, he arrived at Alverstoke's house just as Alverstoke emerged from it, exquisitely attired in a blue coat of Weston's tailoring, the palest of pantaloons, the snowiest of neckcloths, and Hessian boots so highly polished that they glinted in the sunshine. Harry, pausing with one foot on the first of the shallow steps leading up to the door, received an instant impression of tremendous elegance, but not for a moment did it occur to him that he was gazing at a veritable Tulip of the Ton. That coat of blue superfine was moulded over magnificent shoulders; and those clinging pantaloons in no way concealed the swell of muscles in his lordship's powerful thighs which unmistakeably proclaimed the athlete.

The Marquis, also pausing, but at the top of the steps, looked down at his unexpected visitor. His brows were slightly raised, but after a swift, keen scrutiny, they sank, and he smiled, saying: "Don't take the trouble to introduce yourself! Unless I am very much mistaken, you must be Harry Merriville."

Harry acknowledged it, too well-accustomed to be recognized by his resemblance to his lovely sister to feel surprise at his lordship's acumen. His lordship, correctly interpreting the look of revulsion in his face, gave him further proof of it. "There is a great family-likeness between you all," he said smoothly. "Come in, and tell me what brings you to London! Not that I need ask! For how long are you sent down?"

Since his tone held nothing but sympathetic interest, Harry saw no reason to take umbrage, and replied, with his frank, attractive smile: "Oh, only for the rest of the term, sir. It was nothing—just fun and gig! But the Bagwig was feeling out of curl, and he chose to cut up stiff. But I'm detaining you! Perhaps you have an engagement?"

"It's not of the smallest consequence," replied the Marquis, relinquishing his hat, his gloves, and his cane into his footman's hands, and leading the way into the library. "You shall drink a glass of sherry with me, and tell me in what way I can serve you."

"Good God, sir, none at all!" said Harry, shocked. "It seems to me that you have done a great deal for my family already. I came merely to thank you for your kind offices."

"How very civil of you! But pray don't!"

"Yes, that's all very well," objected Harry, "but for the life of me I can't see that we have the least claim upon you, sir!"

"You are forgetting our relationship."

"It ain't a case of forgetting, for I never knew of it," said Harry bluntly. "Frederica says you are our cousin, but I've a strong notion she's shamming it!"

"You wrong her. Our relationship is a trifle remote, perhaps, but we—er—meet somewhere on the family tree, I assure you."

"Well, that might be, I daresay," conceded Harry doubtfully. "I never took much interest in the family tree myself, but of course I know that everyone has hosts of relations one's never met in one's life."

"And some of them such very Queer Nabs!" murmured his lordship.

"Yes, by Jove, aren't they just?" exclaimed Harry, with considerable feeling. He burst out laughing at the quizzical look in the Marquis's eye. "Oh, I don't mean you, sir! How could I? But only think of my Aunt Seraphina! Not that she's an unknown relation—I only wish to God she were! I daresay you are acquainted with her?"

"I am, and you have all my sympathy."

Harry nodded, but said: "Oh, well! She don't come the ugly with the girls, and they must have *somebody* to play gooseberry, I suppose." He waited, while Wicken, who had entered the room, set a heavily embossed silver tray down at his master's elbow; but when he had accepted a glass of sherry from his host he said: "The thing is, sir, that if we are only remotely related there's no reason in the world why you should be troubled with any of us, and I don't like it at all that my sister Frederica should have jockeyed you into it! Which," he added shrewdly, "I'll go bail she did!"

"Oh, no!" replied his lordship. "I collect you were not aware that I was under an obligation to your father."

"No, I wasn't," said Harry.

"How should you be?" said his lordship, with the sweet, discomfiting smile which rarely failed to depress pretension.

Harry knew an impulse to ask in what way his erratic parent had contrived to place this unquestionable out-and-outer under an obligation, but the smile warned him that any such enquiry would be an impertinence. He refrained, therefore; but after drinking a little sherry made a recover, and said, his chin lifting a little: "How-ever that may be, sir, I must feel myself greatly in-debted to you. Not only for sponsoring my sisters, which —which is a debt I can't repay, but for coming so kindly to my young brother's rescue. That debt I can repay, and—and wish to do immediately! In fact, that forms a part of my errand to you, so will you tell me, if you please, what was the sum which you were obliged to spend on his behalf?"

"I am afraid you will have to hold me excused," replied his lordship apologetically. "For one thing, I don't know: my secretary settled the business; and, for another, I *lent* Jessamy the sum, whatever it may have been, upon certain terms."

"Yes, sir—he told me, and—and I'm very much obliged to you! Though why the silly gudgeon didn't bring his coverthack to London, instead of making a dashed martyr of himself, or even hire a horse—"

"I hardly think he would care for a job-horse. And since he is determined not to incur the expense of a horse and a groom in London, may I suggest that you leave well alone?"

Harry flushed. "I beg your pardon, but it isn't well, sir! I mean, there's no reason why Jessamy should be so much beholden to you: he should have applied to me, because *I'm* his guardian, not you!"

"Oh, I haven't the smallest intention of usurping your authority!" the Marquis assured him.

"It isn't so much that—well, as a matter of fact, it's my sister who has the younger ones in charge," con-fessed Harry. "But when it comes to letting my brother —my *ward!*—run into debt—*no!*"

"Ah, that is a matter which lies between you and him, and in no way concerns me! Give him a thunder-ing scold—if you feel it to be your duty!"

"What, when I've been sent down myself?" ex-claimed Harry. "I'm not such a mawworm! Besides," he added frankly, "I'll be damned if I give my head to Jessamy for washing!"

The Marquis smiled. "Then, I repeat, leave well alone!" Then he saw that Harry was looking far from satisfied, and the amusement deepened in his eyes. "Or you can stand surety, if you feel he won't redeem the debt," he said.

Harry stiffened; and replied in rather a gritty voice: "I have no fear of that, sir!"

"No, nor have I."

"What I do fear," said Harry, slightly mollified, "is that he'll very likely run himself aground over the business."

"In that case," replied his lordship, "it will be your duty—as his guardian—to bring him about again. I can't agree, however, that it is a likely contingency. I believe the sum involved to have been quite trifling. Meanwhile, he is happily employed every morning, exercising one or other of my hacks, instead of addling his brain with overmuch study. Really, it is I who stand in his debt: I had liefer by far entrust my horses to him than to any groom."

"Yes, indeed!" Harry said warmly. "He's got a maggot in his head over some things, but he's a clipping rider, I promise you! In the hunting-field, I mean! No need to be afraid he won't keep your hacks well in hand!"

"Then, since our minds are now relieved of care, we needn't discuss the matter further," said his lordship. "What are your own plans? Are you making a come-out too?"

Harry's mind was not quite relieved of care, but, partly from diffidence, and partly from an innate dislike of responsibility, he let the subject drop, assuring the Marquis instead that he had no desire to make a come-out. He added that he did not think it would be (under the circumstances) quite the thing. "I shall be visiting a friend, and going about with him a good deal, I daresay."

"I see. Keep away from the—er—sluiceries of Tothill Fields, and if you end up in a Watch-house, with your pockets to let, send a message here, not to Upper Wimpole Street: I'll bail you out."

"Thank you! But I don't anticipate—"

"One never does," murmured his lordship. "These things happen to one, however, and it is just as well to be prepared." He looked thoughtfully at his young guest. "I recall that your sister told me once that you are fond of boxing: if you have a fancy to attend Jackson's school—it's in Bond Street, No. 13—send this in to him! He will pay particular attention to you." He drew out his card-case as he spoke, scrawled something on one of the visiting-cards he abstracted from it, and flicked it over to Harry.

"Oh, by Jupiter!" Harry exclaimed, catching it, and eagerly deciphering the scrawled message. "That's *devilish* good of you, sir! I'm excessively obliged to you! I'm no better than a moulder, of course, but I *am* very partial to the sport! Thank you very much! Though why you should concern yourself with me, I'm damned if I know!" He coloured hotly, and added, in apologetic accents: "I mean—well, all this gammon about being under an obligation to my father—!"

"The charm of novelty," replied his lordship, bringing the interview to an end by rising from his chair. "Since I assumed the rôle of guardian—titular, of course!—of your enterprising brothers, I haven't known what might happen next. Hitherto I have always known precisely what would happen next: a dead bore, believe me!"

With this, Harry had to be content. He took a punctilious leave of the Marquis, and went off, unable to decide if he liked him, or disliked him.

The Marquis had no such doubts. Within ten minutes of making Harry's acquaintance, he had recognized in him not only his father's merits, but also his failings. A pleasing boy, with frank, well-bred manners, whom it was impossible not to like; but one who lacked strength of character, and would always be amiably ready to let another shoulder his responsibilities.

And why the devil should I shoulder them? the Marquis demanded of himself. *I must have windmills in my head!*

XVI

If Harry was doubtful of the Marquis, he found no
difficulty at all in deciding that the Marquis's cousin
and heir was a capital fellow. The young gentlemen, in
fact, took to one another on sight; and this in spite of
the slight prejudice created in Harry's mind by the
knowledge that Frederica did not look with favour upon Mr Dauntry. Endymion was not much given to
speculation, but had he thought about the matter he
would have felt sure that he would like Harry—or any
other of Charis's relations. He was some few years
older than Harry, and he had all the town-bronze which
Harry lacked; but his intellect was not strong, and,
like many other persons of slow wit to whom learning
was a painful labour, he was inclined to regard with
respect bordering upon awe anyone capable of passing
Responsions.

It might have been supposed that disparity of age
and of intelligence would have raised a barrier between
the two gentlemen. Frederica did suppose it, but she
had reckoned without one powerful factor: each was
sporting-mad. A chance word revealed to Harry that
this seeming-sapskull was a Melton man, and, from his
description of the Shires, an accomplished horseman.
Not that Endymion, a modest young man, boasted of
his prowess: the only personal anecdotes he recounted
were of having been bullfinched at a regular stitcher at
Barkby Holt, and of having once taken a toss into the
Whissendine; but you could tell, thought Harry, quick
to realize that Endymion laid the blame for these mis-
haps not upon his horse but upon himself, that however blockish he might be in a drawing-room he was a
first-rate man in the saddle. From hunting it was a
short step to almost every form of sport; and by the
time the superiority of Manton's New Patent Shot had

been discussed, the advantages of a Six or Seven over a heavier shot argued, and the fights each gentleman had had with various salmon of stupendous size, described in exhaustive detail, it would have been hard to have decided which held the other in the higher esteem.

Frederica might be exasperated by Endymion's easy conquest of her volatile brother, but Charis, listening to their exchanges with a glowing look of gratification in her beautiful eyes, was encouraged, when she found herself alone with Harry, to say imploringly: "You do like him, Harry, don't you?" Blushing, she added: "Our cousin, I mean—Mr Dauntry!"

"Oh, him!" said Harry. "Yes, a first-rate man! Bang up to the knocker, too, I should think!"

"And so very handsome, don't you think?" she suggested shyly.

Since this was not a matter which had previously excited Harry's attention, he was obliged to consider it for a moment, before replying: "Yes, I suppose he is. Too big, though: I shouldn't wonder at it if he rides as much as sixteen stone, poor fellow! Ay, and what's more he might strip well, but you may depend upon it that it would be bellows to mend with him in the ring! All the same, these big, heavy men: too slow by half!"

Slightly daunted by these strictures, Charis said: "But so very amiable—so truly the gentleman!"

He agreed to this, but added a rider. "Not much in his knowledge-box, mind you! In fact, if we hadn't got to talking about hunting I should have said he was a regular chawbacon!"

"He is not!"

"I know that. He knows the devil of a lot about horses, and—" He broke off, suddenly struck by her unusual vehemence. "You don't mean to tell me you're in love *again?*" he exclaimed.

"No! for I was never in love before! *Never!*"

"Not in love before—! Why, what about—"

"*No!*" she reiterated. "I didn't know! I didn't understand! This is different—quite, quite different!"

"Well," said Harry sceptically, "if you weren't in

love with any of the cawkers who made such dashed cakes of themselves about you, all I can say is that you're a desperate flirt! Why, you never even *hinted* them away!"

Tears sprang to her eyes; she uttered in a stricken voice: "Oh, Harry, no! Not a *flirt!* It was only that they were all such particular friends! How *could* I be unkind to anyone I've known all my life? And if you are thinking of poor Mr Griff, I promise you I didn't give him the least encouragement!"

"Or the least set-down!" said Harry.

"But, dearest, only think how—how brutal it would have been! He was so dreadfully humble, and he had so much sensibility! I *couldn't* wound him so!"

"There wasn't anything very humble about the Jack-at-warts Tom Rushbury brought home with him last year! The coxcomb who had the infernal impudence to come serenading you, and woke us all up with his damned caterwauling!"

"Oh, Harry!" she said reproachfully. "You know he had a very fine voice! Yes, and you know I didn't like him, and was only kind to him because you were so uncivil as to empty a jug of water over him, and pretend you thought he was a cat! I own, I have once or twice fancied I might be in love, but I know *now* that I quite mistook the matter. I never loved any of them as I love my dear, dear Endymion, and I never shall!"

"Yes, you will," said Harry, in a bracing tone. "Well, you know what you are, Charis! You'll have a tendre for some other fellow next week, I daresay!"

Her tears spilled over; she turned her face away, saying sadly: "I had hoped that *you* would understand!"

"For the lord's sake, don't get ticklish!" begged Harry, observing with apprehension these signs of distress. "What the deuce is there to cry about? It ain't as if Dauntry weren't nutty on you! Frederica told me he was—not that she need have done so!—any jobbernoll could see *that!*"

"Frederica doesn't like him," said Charis, on a sob.

"Well, what has that to say to anything? It's my belief she don't know you've formed a—a lasting passion for him! Why the devil don't you tell her? Good God, you surely ain't afraid of her?"

"Oh, no, no, no!" declared Charis. "But she wouldn't believe me, Harry, any more than you do! It's all so dreadful! It was on my account we came to London, because Frederica was set on establishing me c-comfortably! I *know* she doesn't think I should be comfortable with Endymion, and should f-forget him in a sennight if I didn't see him again! And she has pinched, and saved, and c-contrived all for my sake! How *could* I be so ungrateful as to—"

"Fudge!" interrupted Harry, with strong commonsense. "I'll tell you what, Charis: if you don't stop trying to do what *everybody* wants, you'll find yourself in the suds! Besides, Frederica is a dashed sight too fond of you to drive a spoke in your wheel, even if she could!"

"But she could, Harry! Oh, she would never, never do so if she didn't believe I should regret it, if I m-married my adored Endymion! But that's just what she does believe! I know she thinks that she need not care for his visiting us, because I shall grow tired of him!"

Since Harry knew this too, and was much inclined to agree with Frederica, he could find nothing better to say than: "Oh, well! No sense in getting into the hips! If—I mean, *when* she sees that you really have fixed your interest, she'll come about!"

Another sob shook Charis. "Alas, it's worse than you know! And I have the gravest fear that Endymion will be torn from me!"

"No, that's coming it much too strong!" said Harry, revolted. "I wish you wouldn't talk such balderdash! Torn from you indeed! By Frederica, I collect!"

"Oh, no, no! By Cousin Alverstoke!"

He stared. "What the devil has he to do with it?"

"Endymion is his heir," replied Charis mournfully.

"Well, what if he is?" With a stirring of his earlier suspicion, he said: "Is he dangling after you himself?"

She looked astonished. "*Alverstoke?* Good gracious, no! He likes Frederica better than me, but he isn't dangling after either of us. I expect, if he ever does marry, it will be someone of high rank and fortune, for everybody says that he is very proud, besides being of the first consequence. You may depend upon it that he means Endymion to do the same. And so does Endymion's mama. She is determined he shall make a brilliant match: Chloë told me so. She is his sister, you know, and the dearest girl! She says that Mrs Dauntry is always on the lookout for a suitable heiress. One can't wonder at it, or blame her. He is not rich, you see, and if Cousin Alverstoke ceased to make him an allowance he would be quite poor. I shouldn't care a straw for that, and he says he wouldn't either, but—oh, Harry, he has been used to live in the first circles, and to ride splendid hunters, and not to consider expense very much, and I am so afraid he would hate to be obliged to make and scrape!"

Harry was beginning to think that Frederica was wiser than he had at first supposed; but since he knew Charis would start to cry again if he said so he sought for something consoling to say instead, finally achiev-ing: "Well, I see no occasion for you to be thrown into gloom! Ten to one Alverstoke won't raise any objec-tion. After all, he *hasn't* tried to interfere, has he?"

"He doesn't know," said Charis, refusing to be com-forted. "Mrs Dauntry suspects, but Chloë says she is hoping it is only a horrid flirtation. But if Frederica was aware of my sentiments, and begged Cousin Al-verstoke to intervene—!" She shuddered, and clasped her hands tensely together. "You see, he could, Harry! He could arrange for Endymion to be sent abroad, for instance, and then I think I should die. Oh, my dear brother, there's no one to help us but you, and I count on your support!"

By this time Harry was heartily regretting that he had been rusticated. There seemed to be every prospect of finding himself embroiled in just the sort of situation he would most wish to avoid. He said uneasily: "Yes, but I don't see what *I* can do."

Charis did not appear to have any very clear idea either, for while, in one breath, she begged him not to divulge her confidence to Frederica, in the next she charged him with the office of persuading her to look with a kindly eye upon Endymion, and to forbid her to approach Alverstoke.

By no stretch of the imagination could Harry conjure up a vision of himself forbidding Frederica to do that, or anything else; but he naturally did not say so. Nor did he tell Charis that while it was not wholly impossible that Frederica would be swayed by his persuasion it was extremely unlikely that she would be. He said instead that he would do his best, and faithfully fulfilled his promise at the first opportunity that offered. He told Frederica that he wouldn't wonder at it if Endymion, whom he described as a trump, and quite up to the hub, wasn't just the man for Charis.

"A trump!" exclaimed Frederica. "Because he's a Melton man, and has an eye to a hound? Harry, how can you be so absurd? He's nothing but a handsome moonling!"

"Oh, he don't want for sense!" said Harry. "I don't say he's one of the longheaded ones, but—dash it, Freddy! there's precious little in Charis's cockloft!"

She was unable to deny this, but said: "The more reason for her to marry a man of superior sense! Surely you must perceive—Harry, I do beg of you not to encourage her in this nonsense! You must know what she is! She may have been dazzled by his appearance—I don't know, but I think it very likely, for I will allow him to be a remarkably fine young man, and she has, most unfortunately, seen him in full regimentals—but if he were to be removed from her sight she would very soon forget all about him! My dear, you cannot, in all seriousness, wish your sister to throw herself away on a personable nodcock of small fortune and no prospects worthy of a moment's consideration!"

"I don't know that," objected Harry. "He's Alverstoke's heir, isn't he?"

"Yes, at present he is. But when Alverstoke marries, and has sons, what then, pray?"

"Oh, I shouldn't think he would!" said Harry. "Well, he's quite old now, isn't he?"

"*Old?*" she ejaculated. "If you consider a man of

seven-and-thirty old, you must be a bigger greenhead than I knew! He is in the prime of life!"

Slightly taken aback, he said: "Well, past the age of falling into Parson's mousetrap, at all events! I should think he must be a confirmed bachelor, wouldn't you? Dash it, there must have been hundreds of females on the scramble for him any time these dozen years, and more!"

She replied, in a colourless voice: "Very likely!" and immediately turned the subject, asking him if he did not feel that Mr Navenby, with all the advantages of birth, fortune, and amiability, would be an ideal husband for Charis.

Unfortunately, Harry had not taken a fancy to Mr Navenby. Having himself no ambition to sport a figure in the world of fashion, he was much inclined to regard with contempt even such mild aspirants to dandyism as Mr Navenby. He exclaimed: "What, that bandbox creature? I should hope Charis would have more sense than to marry *him!* Why, Dauntry is worth a dozen of him!"

Knowing that any attempts to persuade Harry that an addiction to sport was not the most desirable quality to be looked for in a husband would be useless, Frederica said no more: a restraint which enabled him to feel that he had discharged his obligation to Charis, and might now, with a clear conscience, turn his attention to matters of more immediate importance.

Chief amongst these was the absolute necessity of presenting Alverstoke's card at No. 13 Bond Street, where John Jackson had for many years given lessons in the art of self-defence. Harry had not been born when Jackson, in the last of his three public fights, had beaten the great Mendoza in exactly ten and a half minutes, but, like every other young amateur (or indeed, professional), he could have described in detail each round of this, and Jackson's two previous encounters; and he was well aware of the unique position held, and maintained without ostentation, by the pugilist whose pleasant manners and superior intellect had earned for him the sobriquet of Gentleman. Anyone, upon payment of a fee, could get instruction at No. 13 Bond Street, but by no means everyone could hope to engage the attention of Gentleman Jackson himself, as Harry, armed with Alverstoke's card, hoped to do. If he had had any doubts of the value of this talisman, they would have been dissipated by the reverence with which his knowledgeable friend, Mr Peplow, inspected it. Alverstoke, said Mr Peplow, was a noted amateur of the Fancy: none of your moulders, but a boxer of excellent science, who was said to display a great advantage, and was always ready to take the lead in milling. A Corinthian? No: Mr Peplow, frowning over it, did not think that his lordship belonged to that, or any other, set. He was certainly a tow-sawyer, and a first-rate fiddler: might be said, in fact, to cap the globe at most forms of sport; he was extremely elegant, too: trim as a trencher, one might say; but in an unobtrusive style of his own which never included the very latest quirks of fashion. "The thing is," said Mr Peplow confidentially, "he's devilish high in the instep!" Too young to know that the Marquis had taken Mr Brummell for his model, he added: "Sets his own mode. Never follows another man's lead. Always been one of the first in consequence, you see, and holds himself very much up. Mind, I don't mean to say he's one of those stiff-rumped fellows who think themselves above their company—though he can give some pretty nasty set-downs, by all accounts!"

"Do you like him?" demanded Harry.

"Me?" exclaimed Mr Peplow, scandalized. "Good God, Harry, *I'm* not acquainted with him! Only telling you what people say!"

"Well, he didn't give me one, and my young brothers swear he's a great gun: they ain't a bit afraid of him!"

"Oh! Oh, well, you're related to him, ain't you?"

"Yes, but that has nothing to say to anything! One of his nephews is dangling after my sister Charis—some sort of a cousin of mine! Gregory—Gregory Sandford, or Sandridge: *I* don't know!—but it didn't seem to me as if he knows Alverstoke well enough to get as much as a common bow in passing from him! Which makes me wonder—" He broke off. Mr Peplow, with exquisite tact, forbore to press him; and was rewarded by a burst of confidence. "Well, I won't scruple to tell *you*, Barny, that what with his indulging Jessamy and Felix, as he does, and giving me his card, for Jackson, I can't help wondering if *he's* dangling after Charis too!"

His worldly-wise friend subjected this proposition to profound consideration, finally shaking his head, and saying: "Shouldn't think so at all. Well, stands to reason! His ward, ain't she? Wouldn't be at all the thing! Unless he wants to get riveted?"

"Well, he doesn't. Not to my sister, at all events. She says he likes my sister Frederica better than her— and neither of them above half." He grinned suddenly. "Lord, though, only to think of it! *Frederica!* Mind you, she's a capital girl—sound as a roast!—but she'll never be *married!* She hasn't had an offer in her life! She—she ain't that sort of female!"

Both he and Charis had spoken in good faith, but both were mistaken: the elder Miss Merriville had received two unexceptionable offers, from Lord Buxted, and Mr Darcy Moreton; and Lord Alverstoke liked her very much above half. She would have agreed, however, that marriage was not for her; and had indeed told Buxted so, when she declined his offer. She told him that she was born to be an aunt, at which he smiled, and said: "You mean a sister, I think!"

"Why, yes! Just at present I do, but I look forward to the day when I shall take charge of all my nephews and nieces whenever their parents are at a stand, or wish to go jauntering off to the Continent!"

His smile broadened; he said: "You will be a much beloved aunt, I daresay, for the liveliness of your spirit must make you as enchanting to children as to their seniors. But be serious for a moment, and consider whether, as a sister, a husband might not be an advantage to you? You have three brothers—for although I am aware that Harry is of age, I do not think him grown, as yet, beyond the need of guidance—and you have, with that nobility and courage which command my admiration, assumed the charge of them. But is any female, however devoted, however elevated her mind, able to succeed in such a task? I don't think it possible.

Indeed, I will venture a guess that you must frequently
have felt the want of male support."

"Oh, no!" she answered serenely. "The boys mind me
very well."

"*Very* well, when one goes off to Margate without
leave, and the other hires a dangerous machine, and—
as was to be expected!—suffers an accident!" he said,
laughing indulgently.

"I don't think it *was* a dangerous machine. In any
event I didn't forbid either of them to do these things,
so there was no question of disobedience."

"And no fear in their heads of consequences!"

"No—or of anything else! They are full of pluck, my
brothers."

"Very true. One would not wish it to be otherwise;
but boys who are—as you put it—full of pluck, stand
in need of a guiding hand, you know. It has been so
with my own young brother. You see, I don't speak
without experience! My mother has always been a firm
parent, but she has been content to leave the management of George to me, realizing that a man knows best
how and when to deliver a reproof, and is in general
better heeded."

She hardly knew how to keep her countenance. She
had not met George, but if his youngest sister were to
be believed he was a lively young gentleman, already
bidding fair to become one of those choice spirits ripe
and ready for any form of jollification, and resenting
nothing so much as what he called his brother's jobations. Nor had the result of a grave lecture addressed to
Felix been happy. Not only had it banished from
Felix's head all contrition for having alarmed his sisters,
but it had instantly transformed Jessamy into a hot
partisan. All his bristles up, Jessamy had demanded to
be told what right Cousin Buxted had to shove his oar
in; and although he had later offered Buxted a stiff
apology for this incivility he cordially agreed with Felix
that the fellow was an encroaching windsucker, a prosy
bore, and, probably, a slow-top into the bargain.

Remembering this incident, Frederica was obliged to
choke down a chuckle before she responded: "I daresay you are right, cousin, but if ever I should be mar-

ried it won't be because I wish to provide my brothers with a—with a mentor!"

"I only said that because I thought it might be—because I thought you might regard my offer more favourably!"

The humble note in his voice touched her, but she shook her head; and when he began, in rather stilted language, to enumerate and describe the various excellent qualities in her character which had excited at first his admiration, and then his ardent desire to make her his wife, she checked him even more decidedly, saying kindly, but with a little amusement: "I am very much obliged to you, cousin, but pray say no more! Only think how much your mama would dislike such an alliance!"

He looked grave, and sighed; but replied: "I hope I am not lacking in respect for my mother, but in such matters a man must decide for himself."

"Oh, no, you must not marry to disoblige her! Recollect how much she depends on you!"

"You must not think I am unmindful of my duty to her, or that I make you an offer without long and careful consideration," he said earnestly.

Her eyes danced. "No, indeed! No one could think *that!* I'm excessively flattered—I can't tell you how much!—but the long and short of it is that I'm not hanging out for a husband—in fact, I don't in the least wish to change my single state! It suits me very well: far better than I should suit you, Carlton, believe me!"

He looked disconsolate, and said nothing for several moments. But after turning the matter over in his mind, he smiled, and said: "I have been too previous, for which you must blame the natural impatience of a man in love. I fancy that your thoughts have hitherto been so wholly devoted to the interests of your family that you have had none to spare for your own future. I shall say no more on this head now, but neither shall I despair."

He then took his leave; and with real nobility Frederica forbore to regale Charis with an account of the interlude. She was not tempted to tell anyone of Mr Moreton's offer, for it was simply made; and she liked him too well to betray him. She declined it as gently as she could; but when he sighed, and said, with a faint smile: "I feared it!" her eyes twinkled irrepressibly. "And now are quite cast-down."

"Well, of course I am!"

"But also just a trifle relieved! Confess!"

"Miss Merriville! No, I swear I'm not!"

"You will be," she assured him. "You know how comfortably you go on as a bachelor, and how very much you would dislike to be tied to a wife's apron-strings."

He laughed a little ruefully, but denied it. "I shouldn't dislike being tied to your apron-strings."

"Or to play the mentor to my brothers?" she asked, quizzing him. "You would be obliged to include them in your household, you know!"

"Yes—at least, won't they live with your eldest brother?"

"Oh, no! Poor Harry! They would drive him distracted! He is too young for such a charge—too young to command either respect or obedience. Besides, he and Jessamy would be at outs within a sennight!"

"I see. Well, I know nothing about rearing boys, but I would do my best!" he said heroically.

She laughed, and held out her hand to him. "Even though your blood runs cold at the very thought of it! How kind you are, my dear friend! Thank you! What a fix you would be in if I did accept your offer! I shan't, however, so you may be easy!"

He took her hand and kissed it. "Not quite that. May I still, and always, count myself your friend?"

"Indeed, I hope you will," she replied cordially.

She could not help laughing a little, when he had gone, but kindly. There had been enough dismay in his face, swiftly though he had recovered himself, to strengthen her belief that it would not be long before he was thanking providence for his escape. The intrusion into his care-free existence of two such enterprising young gentlemen as Jessamy and Felix provided her with a vision that appealed instantly to her sense of humour. Only Buxted, she thought, could make sadder work of bridling them. Alverstoke could do it, and without rousing even the shadow of hostility, because they had decided, for inscrutable reasons, that he was a person eminently worthy of respect. But at this point her musings came to an abrupt halt. She was obliged to give herself a mental shake, renewing a resolve not to think about Alverstoke, at all. This was not easy. Whether he knew it, or not, he had developed an uncomfortable habit of intruding upon her thoughts; and to allow him to do so could only bring her to fiddlestick's end. That was certain; and she hoped she had enough commonsense to realize it. Enough pride, too, not to add to the number of his victims. He was a confirmed bachelor—far more so than Darcy Moreton, who carried a warm heart in his breast. There was no warmth in Alverstoke, and no softness. If he was kind it was for his own ends; when it pleased him to make himself agreeable he could be the most delightful of companions; but his treatment of his sisters, and of anyone who bored him, was ruthless. Hard, cold, and selfish: that was Alverstoke! And a rake into the bargain, if the on-dits were true. Probably they were, but one must be just, even to such an abandoned character: he had shown no signs of the rake in his dealings with her, or with her lovely sister. She had on one occasion suspected him of trying to get up a flirtation, but had soon decided that she was mistaken. Moreover, it was only fair to acknowledge that although he had consented to sponsor her and Charis with no other motive than a malicious wish to infuriate his sister Louisa, he had been extremely kind to Jessamy and Felix as well. Still being just to his lordship, she recalled the expedition to Hampton Court, which must surely have been intolerably boring to him; the readiness with which he had rescued Lufra from an untimely end; and the skill with which he had handled Jessamy. It was impossible to discover in these activities any base, ulterior motive: he had behaved as though he really were their guardian, so that she had come, insensibly, to regard him as one to whom she could turn in any difficulty. This vexed her, for she had not previously looked for support or advice; and she had a shrewd notion that if she were to maintain

her own strength she must not allow herself to fall into
the habit of depending upon his. For some unknown
reason it amused him, at present, to befriend the Merrivilles; but he might grow bored at any moment,
shrugging them off as easily as he had adopted them.
For what, after all, she asked herself, did she know
about him? Nothing much beyond what the gossips
recounted: not even if he liked her above the average!
Sometimes she had been encouraged to think that he
did; but at other times, when he let half the evening
slip by at some assembly before strolling over to exchange a few words with her, she had been convinced
that he regarded her with indifference. Which, when one
thought the matter over dispassionately, was in all like-
lihood the truth; for if the truly dazzling beauties who
showed themselves perfectly ready to receive his ad-
dresses bored him (as they demonstrably did), how
much more must he be bored by a country-cousin
endowed with no more than passable good-looks, and
long past the first blush of her youth? Indeed, when
she considered the handsome Mrs Parracombe, or the
dashing widow who was commonly thought to be his
latest flirt, she could only be surprised that he continued to interest himself in her affairs. Had she been
told that she was rapidly becoming an obsession with
him, she would have been incredulous.

XVII

The Marquis, in fact, was behaving with unusual circumspection, careful to give the tattle-mongers no food for gossip. Well-aware of his notoriety, of the scandalous on-dits which would instantly attend the least sign he gave of having formed a partiality for Miss Merriville, he was taking inordinate pains to shield her from envious, or merely malicious tongues. To satisfy the curiosity of those who might wonder why he was gratifying so many hostesses by appearing at their balls, drums, and assemblies, he set up the dashing Mrs Ilford as his flirt, knowing that the lively widow's charms were equalled by her shrewdness: the Marquis, man-of-the-town though he might be, had no desire to break hearts; and the objects of his gallantry had never yet included guileless innocents. In general, he had ignored the handkerchiefs thrown to him, but he had his own, remorseless way with any over-bold damsel who disgusted him by too-obviously setting her cap at him. He would indulge her with a brief, desperate flirtation, conducted under the envious or the shocked eyes of her contemporaries, and, at their next encounter, fail to remember her name, or even that he had met her before. These merciless tactics had earned for him the reputation of being dangerous, and caused prudent parents to warn their daughters against encouraging his advances. They even caused his closest friend to remonstrate with him once or twice, but Mr Moreton's accusation of cruelty was productive of nothing but a contemptuous smile, and a coldly uttered hope that the victim had learnt her lesson. From the hour of his come-out, the Marquis had been a matrimonial prize, but the years had not taught him to accept this position with equanimity, to tolerate the schemes of match-making mamas, or to be amused by the lures

cast out by their ambitious daughters. Since the day of
his discovery that his first love would have been as
ready to marry a hunchback possessed of his rank and
fortune as himself, he had grown steadily more hardened in cynicism, until, at the age of seven-and-thirty,
when Frederica thrust herself into his life, he had no
more intention of saddling himself with a wife than of
throwing himself into the Thames.

But Frederica had seriously ruffled the calm waters
of his agreeable existence. Not quite immediately, but
soon enough, he had found himself strongly attracted
to her, and in a way that was strange to him. The
only women who had previously interested him were
the well-born flirts, with whom it was amusing to dally,
and the barques of frailty with whom he enjoyed more
intimate relations. He felt no affection for any of these
ladies, and not the smallest wish to establish with any
one of them a more permanent connection. To be leg-
shackled to a female who, however lively or beautiful
she might be, would inevitably become a bore within a
very few months was a fate too hideous even to be
contemplated. He did not wish for female companionship; and still less did he wish to saddle himself with
the trials and responsibilities that attended the married
state.

Then came Frederica, upsetting his cool calculations,
thrusting responsibilities upon him, intruding more and
more into the ordered pattern of his life, and casting
him into a state of unwelcome doubt. And, try as he
would, he could discover no reason for this uncomfortable change in himself. She had more countenance
than beauty; she employed no arts to attract him; she
was heedless of convention; she was matter-of-fact, and
managing, and not at all the sort of female whom he
had ever wished to encourage. Furthermore (now he
came to think of it), she had foisted two troublesome
schoolboys on to him, which was the last thing in the
world he wanted!

Or had she? A rather rueful smile flickered at the
corners of his lordship's mouth as he considered this
point. No: she had not. He had allowed himself to
yield to the blandishments of Felix (detestable imp!);

then Jessamy had got himself into a scrape (tiresome young chub!), and had turned to him for help, which, naturally, had to be given to him; but it would really be quite unjust to blame Frederica for these happenings. She had been as cross as crabs over Jessamy's affair, top-lofty little peagoose that she was! Top-lofty, gooseish, managing, no more than passably good-looking: why the devil did he like her so much?

Unconsciously following the example Frederica had set, he began to do her justice, trying to discover what quality in her it was which had jerked him out of his idle hedonism into a state of nagging uncertainty. It was a pleasant exercise, but it brought him no nearer to solving the problem. He liked her composure, her frankness, the smile in her eyes, her ready appreciation of the ridiculous, the gay courage with which she shouldered burdens too heavy for a girl to bear, the way she caught herself up guiltily on a cant phrase culled from her brothers' vocabularies, the intent look which came into her face when she was pondering a ticklish question, the unexpected things she said, and —but what was there in all this to disrupt his present life, and to place his untrammelled future in jeopardy? Nothing, of course: she had certainly aroused in him feelings he had not known he possessed, but she could be no more than a passing fancy.

A frown gathered on his brow as he thought this over. The devil of it was that the more he saw of her the stronger grew the feeling he had for her, which was not love (an emotion which belonged to one's salad-days), nor yet mere liking. Call it affection! It caused him to think about her far too much for his peace of mind; and (really, he must be growing senile!) to be constantly aware of a wish to lift the burdens from her shoulders. As matters stood, he was powerless to render her any but the most trifling assistance, and none at all in what he guessed must be the greatest of her present anxieties. He had suspected at the outset that she had underestimated the expenses of a London season; and when his experienced eye detected, beneath velvet trimming on a drapery of Albany gauze, the evening dress which had already undergone several

transformations, he was very sure that she was beginning to feel purse-pinched. He thought, savagely, that
every available groat was squandered on Charis. He
was too well-versed in such matters not to recognize
that Charis too wore dresses which had been subtly al-
tered to present a new appearance, but he quite unjust-
ly supposed that the cunning hand at work had been
Frederica's, even going to the length of picturing her
slaving over her stitchery until the candles guttered in
their sockets. Had he been told that the drudgery, as
well as the inspiration, belonged to the younger sister
(only she did not think it drudgery), he would have
been amazed to the point of incredulity, for he had
long since decided that Charis had nothing to recommend her but her undeniable beauty. In his lordship's
prejudiced eyes, she lacked what the ton called *that
certain sort of something,* which meant, in a word,
quality, and which characterized Frederica. It was apparent, he thought, in whatever Frederica did: from
the air with which she wore her furbished-up gowns, to
the assurance with which she received visitors in the
shabby-genteel house she had hired for the season. But
he wanted to remove her from Upper Wimpole Street,
and to place her in surroundings worthier of her, fur-
nishing her at the same time with every extravagant luxury, and enough pin-money to enable her to purchase a
new gown whenever she chose to do it. And, with all his
wealth, the only assistance he had been able to render
her was the discharge of Jessamy's and Lufra's trifling
debts! There was the possibility that he might be
granted the opportunity to render further assistance of
the same kind, but even that would fall a long way
short of what he would like to do for her.

His frown deepened. That eldest brother of hers
was likely to prove an encumbrance rather than a support to her. There was no harm in the boy, but if he
was not as volatile as his father he had quite as little
sense of responsibility. He would probably settle down
happily on his Herefordshire estate in a year or two;
but at present he was clearly bent on enjoying his first
London-fling, and was perfectly willing to leave the
conduct of his household, the management of his young

brothers, and all the problems that attached to a family
living on straitened means, in Frederica's capable hands.
The Marquis had been keeping an unobtrusive eye on
him; and he believed that it would not be long before
Harry found himself in Dun territory. He seemed, mercifully, to have no taste for gaming, so that the Beau
Traps on the look out for well-breeched greenheads
from the country cast their lures in vain, and very soon
abandoned him for likelier prey. Harry could conceive
of few duller or more unprofitable ways of spending
the evening than in one of the gaming-hells against
which Mr Peplow had warned him. It would certainly
be agreeable to win a fortune, but he was shrewd
enough to guess that fortunes were not won by those
who played with a set of persons described by his
friend as Greek banditti.

Horses, however, were a different matter. If one were
a judge of horseflesh (which Harry prided himself he
was); studied the form; kept an eye on Cocker, to see
how the odds stood; carefully watched how the Tulips
of the Turf were betting their money at Tatt's and
knew when to hedge off, there was every chance that
one would come off all right. On the Monday following
his arrival in London, he had gone with Mr Peplow to
Tattersall's; and thereafter became a frequent visitor
to the subscription room. As he liked the sport more for
its own sake than for the money that could be won by
backing winners, he went to any race meeting held within reach of the city, driving himself and Barny in a
curricle which, acting on the advice of Endymion Dauntry, he had bought (really dog-cheap) in Long Acre.
The pair of sweetgoers he acquired to draw the curricle had not been quite so cheap; but, as he rather
guiltily pointed out to Frederica, it was false economy
to buy cheap prads which would inevitably turn out
to be stumblers, or limpers, or incurable millers.

She agreed to this, suppressing the impulse to protest against his extravagance. She was prompted in some
measure by the knowledge that criticism from his sister
would not be well received; and to a far greater degree
by a realization of the expenditure she was herself
incurring. Graynard had supplied the money for this

London season, and Graynard belonged not to her, but to Harry. She allowed herself to do no more than beg him, half-laughingly, not to outrun the constable. He said impatiently: "Oh, fiddle! I'm not a pauper! Do you expect me to drive job-horses, like a once-a-week beau? Why should I?"

"No, no! Only that the expense of stabling, in London—and a groom besides—"

"Gammon! The merest trifle! If you had had any rumgumption, Freddy, you would have brought our own horses to London, and John-Coachman as well! I can tell you, I don't like it above half that you should be jauntering about in a job-carriage. It don't present a good appearance—and if you thought I should have grudged the expense you're fair and far off!"

She assured him that no such thought had entered her mind, and thereafter said no more. His somewhat censorious brother, Jessamy, was not so forbearing. Not only did he refuse to take the smallest interest in Harry's neatish pair of Welsh bays, but he condemned their purchase so unequivocally, and with such a total want of the respect due to his senior, that only his sense of propriety (as he told Jessamy) restrained Harry from tipping him a settler.

Thereafter, his family saw little of Harry. His smart new set-out made it an easy matter for him to attend a good many race meetings, and several pugilistic battles, held discreetly out of town, but at such accessible places as Moulsey Hurst, or Copthall Common.

The Marquis knew all about the quarrel, and the resultant coolness between the brothers. He had once or twice invited Jessamy to ride with him in the park, and on one of these occasions they had encountered Harry, trying out the paces of his prime pair. The Marquis had said: "Two very tidy ones! Have you driven them?"

"No! And I don't mean to!" had replied Jessamy, fire in his eyes, and his upper lip lengthening ominously. "Harry knows very well what I think of this bang-up set-out of his!"

"I'm not so well-informed. What *do* you think of it?"

That was quite enough: Jessamy told him in explicit terms. He was, in general, reserved to the point of stiffness, but he had long since ceased to regard his lordship in any other light than that of a close and trusted relation; and he hoped that Cousin Alverstoke would give Harry snuff for his reckless extravagance. "Because he don't care a straw for what *I* say!" he ended bitterly.

"I don't suppose he does. It says much for his forbearance that you didn't—er—receive a chancery suit upon the nob!" had said Alverstoke, adding, with the flicker of a quizzical smile: "How would you like it if Felix raked *you* down?"

Jessamy had flushed hotly, an arrested look on his face; but after a moment or two he had replied: "Very well, sir! I shouldn't have said it! But—but it provoked me so much I don't know how I *could* have kept my tongue between my teeth! Frederica may say that he has a right to do as he pleases, but *I* think he should be considering how he can best help *her,* instead of wasting the ready on his own pleasure!"

The Marquis was much in sympathy with this sentiment, but he had not said so, preferring to cast a damper on Jessamy's wrath, and to point out to him that the purchase of a curricle and a pair of horses was hardly likely to bring the whole family to ruin.

He was sincere in this opinion; and he did not think that Frederica was much worried by Harry's slight burst of extravagance. But that something was causing her to feel anxious he was reasonably certain; and since it had become, by almost insensible degrees, a matter of importance to him that nothing should be allowed to trouble her, he set about the task of discovering what had brought just a faint look of strain to her eyes. He invited the Merriville sisters, my Lord and Lady Jevington, and Mr Peter Navenby to be his guests at the Opera one evening, mentally holding his sister Louisa and her prosy son in reserve, in case Augusta should spurn his invitation. She did not, however, which, since the Jevingtons also rented a box at the Opera House, surprised him a little, and still more her mild spouse.

Nothing, therefore, could have been more unexceptionable than his lordship's opera-party; and nothing could have been more exactly calculated to convince even the most suspicious that he was merely doing a guardian's duty than his lordship's polite but rather bored demeanour. It was a simple matter for him to engage Frederica in conversation during the interval without attracting attention: he had merely to retire with her to the back of the box, to make room for those of Charis's admirers who ventured to present themselves. He had said: "I hope you are pleased with me; I shall think myself very ill-used if I don't receive a fervent expression of your gratitude!"

Only for an instant did she look puzzled; as he watched the laughter spring to her eyes he reflected that she had never yet daunted him by asking, fatally: "What do you *mean?*" She had said instead: "Indeed, I am very much obliged to you, sir! I only wish——" She paused, sighed, and said: "Don't you think——now that you have had the opportunity to observe him more closely——that he would be the very man for her?"

He glanced at the unconscious Mr Navenby. "Perhaps: how can I tell? Is that what troubles you?"

"No, it doesn't trouble me, precisely. I am only anxious that she should be comfortably, and happily, established."

"Then what is it?" he asked.

"Why, nothing! Except that I shall be obliged to turn off the cook, which is a great bore, because she cooks well. But my housekeeper tells me that she is so much addicted to gin that she must go. Can you wonder at it if I appear a trifle harassed?——Though I hoped I did not!"

"Oh, don't be alarmed! I daresay no one who wasn't well-acquainted with you would notice the least change in you, and might even be fobbed off with this Canterbury tale about your cook."

"It isn't a Canterbury tale!" she said indignantly.

"Very well, but the cook hasn't cut up your serenity,

Frederica. Tell me, are you afraid, as Jessamy appears to be, that you will all be brought to a standstill because Harry has bought himself a stylish curricle and pair?"

"Good God, no! I own, I wish he hadn't done so, for I don't think he has the least notion of what it will cost him to maintain his own carriage in London, but I promise you it hasn't *cut up my serenity,* as you call it! Did Jessamy tell you about it? I wish you will tell him that it is not for him to lecture Harry how he should go on!"

"Oh, I've already done so!" he replied.

"Thank you!" she said, with a look of gratitude. "He pays much more heed to you than to anyone else, so I shall indulge myself with the hope that when next he sees Harry he won't look quite so disapprovingly at him!"

His brows rose. "When next he sees him? Is Harry away, then?"

"Why, yes—just for a day or two! I am not perfectly sure, but I believe—that is, I know he has gone off on an expedition with some friends," she replied lightly.

"So that's it!" he said, smiling.

"Indeed it isn't! How can you be so absurd?"

"Shall I accept that rebuke with a civil bow, or would you prefer me to reassure you?" His smile grew, as her eyes lifted involuntarily to his face in a questioning look. "You are a very good sister, and you don't in the least object to Harry's going off with his friends, but you are afraid that he may have got into bad company, are you not? Well, you may be easy on that head: I'm not personally acquainted with young Peplow, but, according to what I hear, he's not one of what we call the peep-of-day boys. I have little doubt that he and Harry will cut up a number of extremely foolish larks, but that need not concern you: such antics are to be expected of halflings." He paused, hesitating for a moment before he said: "When I first met you, Frederica, you spoke to me of your father with a frankness which makes it possible for me to tell you that I believe that you have very little need to dread that Harry may follow in his footsteps. I perceive the resemblance between them, but I can also perceive certain differences, the chief being that Harry seems to have no taste for gaming. Does that reassure you?"

She nodded, and replied in a low tone: "Yes—thank you! I own, that—that possibility has been in my mind, though I can't tell how you should have guessed it." She smiled at him, in her frank way, saying simply: "You are very good, and I'm truly grateful—in particular for your kindness to my brothers. I don't know why you should interest yourself in Harry—who can't even make a *false* claim to be your ward!—but I do thank you for it!"

He could have told her why he had made it his business to interest himself in Harry, but he had not done so, shying away from what would have come perilously near to the declaration he was determined not to make. She was a darling, but he had no intention of committing himself, and not for the world would he cause her to suffer the least twinge of mortification. Or so he had thought. It was not until later, when he searched his own mind, that he realized that there had been another reason for his abstention: he had been afraid of losing her altogether. He remembered that he had kissed her hand once, and that even that small sign of regard had made her withdraw from him a little. He had retrieved his position almost immediately; but in the resumption of cordial relations there had never been, on her side, any hint that she wanted anything but friendship from him.

This was a new experience. So many traps had been set for him, so many handkerchiefs thrown to him, that it had not previously occurred to him that his suit might not be acceptable to any lady whom he chose to honour with a proposal. But Frederica was not on the catch for him; he was very sure that she would not marry him, or any other man, for the sake of rank or wealth; he was far from sure that she liked him well enough for his own sake to accept an offer from him. Salutary! he thought, with a wry smile; and suddenly wondered whether the ease with which he had captivated Julia Parracombe, the dashing Mrs Ilford, and a score of others, had turned him into a contemptible coxcomb, who believed himself to be irresistible.

He was still, several days later, trying to discover the true state of his own mind, and Frederica's, when he returned to his house at dusk one evening to find the hall littered with portmanteaux and band-boxes, the two footmen halfway up the stairs, carrying a corded trunk, and his butler wearing an expression of fatherly benevolence.

"What the *devil*—?" he demanded.

"It's my Lady Elizabeth, my lord," explained Wicken, relieving him of his hat and gloves. "Quite like old times it seems! She arrived not twenty minutes ago."

"Oh, did she?" said his lordship, somewhat grimly.

The Lady Elizabeth—that Poor Eliza, who had married a mere Mr Kentmere—emerged from the library at this moment, still habited in her travelling-dress, and said, with great affability: "Yes, dear Vernon: she did! But you mustn't fall into raptures! It's not at all the thing. Besides, I *know* how delighted you must be!"

She strolled forward as she spoke, a tall, rather lanky woman, the nearest to the Marquis in age of his sisters, and the most like him in countenance, but with more liveliness, and less grace than he possessed. "What an elegant rig!" she remarked, laughing at him. "Everything prime about you!"

"I wish I might return the compliment!" he retorted, lightly kissing her proffered cheek. "What a quiz of a hat! You look like a dowdy, Eliza! What has brought you to London?"

"My quiz of a hat, of course. I must—I positively *must* buy a new one!" She added, in languishing accents: "If only I could afford to buy a new dress as well—my dear, dear brother!"

Since the only thing that had made the mere Mr Kentmere in any way acceptable to her parents had been his extremely handsome fortune, the Marquis was not deceived. Pushing her into the library, he said, shutting the door: "Try for a little conduct, Eliza!"

She laughed, "As though Wicken didn't know all there is to be known about us! How *is* our dear sister Louisa, by the way?"

"I've been spared the sight—and sound—of her for

over a week." He scanned her, his eyes narrowed. "Setting aside the hat, what *has* brought you to London?"

"You can't set aside hats," she objected. "I must have a new crop, too, and bring myself back into the established mode. However, the thing that really made me come was your own complaint: boredom, my dear!"

"What, tired of rural tranquillity?"

"If," she said severely, "you ever took the smallest interest in your nephews and nieces, you would not talk to me of tranquillity! We began the year with whooping-cough; three of them had that, one after the other. Hardly had the last whoop died away, than what must Caroline do—at her age, too!—than start in the chicken-pox and communicate it to Tom and Mary! And then Jack brought home some horrid infection from Eton, and they *all* succumbed to it, even John! I wish I had done so myself, for it would have been much less exhausting! I remained at the Manor, like the devoted wife and mother I am, until they had recovered, and then packed my trunks before any of them had had time to throw out a rash, complain of a sore throat, or break a limb!"

He smiled, but his steady gaze remained on her face. "And for how long do you propose to remain?" he enquired.

"Goodness, I don't know! a week or two, perhaps. Does it signify? Had you rather I went away?"

"Not at all," he replied politely.

"Well, I'm glad of that, because I mean to visit my old friends, and pick up all the threads again. Also to look about me for a suitable house to be hired for the season next year. I shall be bringing Caroline out, you know. At least, you don't, but you should. A house with a ballroom, of course—no, I haven't any desire to hold a ball under any other roof than my own, so you need not be alarmed! Vernon, what, in the name of all that's marvellous, prevailed upon you to hold one here for Jane Buxted?"

"I didn't," he responded. "I held it in order to present Fred Merriville's daughters to the ton. Can it be that you didn't know I had taken upon myself the guardianship of a very beautiful girl?"

She tried to keep her countenance, but broke into laughter under the mockery in his eyes. "No, it cannot be! What a detestable creature you are! Very well, I own I am quite consumed with curiosity. But how came it about?"

"Oh, very simply! You may call it the payment of a debt. I'm not, in fact, the Merrivilles' guardian, but they were commended to my protection. To launch the beauty into society seemed to be the least I could do—so I did it. That is to say, I persuaded Louisa to do it."

"Demon!" said his sister appreciatively. "Augusta wrote to me that she was as mad as fire when she clapped eyes on your beauty, and has been glumping ever since! And the other one? Is she a beauty too?"

"Oh, no! Not to compare with Charis!" he said indifferently. "She is the eldest of the family, and has charge of the younger ones. My guardianship, you perceive, is purely nominal: I have really very little to do with them."

At this somewhat inopportune moment, Wicken entered the room, and said demurely: "Master Felix has called, asking to see your lordship. Shall I show him in, my lord?"

"Now, what the devil does he want?" demanded the Marquis, in accents of foreboding. "Tell him I'm—no, I suppose I shall have to see him: show him in!" He glanced down at his sister, and said, with the hint of a rueful smile: "You are about to make the acquaintance of the youngest Merriville, Eliza—a devilish brat!" He turned his head, as Wicken ushered Felix into the room, and said: "Well, Felix? What's the scrape?"

"Sir!" uttered Felix, outraged. "There isn't any scrape!"

"Accept my apologies! Just a social visit! Eliza, allow me to introduce Felix to you: one of my wards! Felix, this is my sister, Lady Elizabeth Kentmere."

"Oh!—Oh, I didn't know—I beg pardon, ma'am!" said Felix, looking a trifle discomfited, but achieving a very creditable bow. He cast an anxious glance at Alverstoke. "P'raps I had better come to see you tomorrow, sir? I didn't mean to—to *intrude,* only Wicken didn't tell me—and I have something very particular to say to you!"

Lady Elizabeth, the mother of three hopeful sons, interposed, saying: "Then of course you mustn't lose a moment! Is your business of a private nature? Shall I excuse myself to my brother, and go away for a while?"

Perceiving, from the twinkle in her eyes, that she was what he termed a right one, he grinned engagingly at her, and answered: "Oh, no, ma'am—thank you! It is only a *little* private! If you won't *tell* anyone?"

"I'm true blue, and will never stain!" she replied promptly.

"Cut line, Felix!" commanded Alverstoke. "If it isn't a scrape, *what* is it?"

"Well—well, it's a balloon, Cousin Alverstoke!" disclosed Felix, taking his fence in a rush.

Lady Elizabeth was betrayed into laughter, which she hastily turned into a fit of coughing; but his lordship merely said, in the voice of one inured to misfortune: "Is it indeed? And what have I—or you, for that matter!—to do with balloons?"

"But, sir—!" said Felix, deeply shocked. "You *must* know that there is to be an ascension from Hyde Park, on Thursday!"

"I didn't, however. And let me tell you, here and now, that I have no interest in balloons! So, if you are going to ask me to take you to see this ascension, my answer is NO! You can very well go to Hyde Park without my escort."

"Yes, but the thing is, I *can't!*" said Felix. Suddenly assuming the demeanour of an orphan cast penniless upon the world, he raised melting blue eyes to his lordship's face, and said beseechingly: "Oh, Cousin Alverstoke, do, pray, go with me! You *must!* It's—it's obligary!" he produced urgently.

"Why is it obligatory?" asked his lordship, preserving his iron calm, but directing a quelling glance at his sorely afflicted sister.

"Well—well, you're my guardian, and—and I told Cousin Buxted you had invited me to go with you!" said Felix, with disarming frankness. He smiled blindingly at the Marquis, and added: "I *know* you'll un-

derstand when I explain it to you, Cousin Alverstoke!
You don't like Cousin Buxted either!"

"When have I ever said so?" demanded his lordship.

"Oh, you don't *say* it, but a pretty good lobcock I
should be if I didn't know it!" replied Felix scornfully.
"Besides, when I told you about the bear-garden jaw he
gave me when I went on the steam-boat, you said—"

In some haste, the Marquis interrupted, saying: "Yes,
well, never mind that! In what way is Buxted concerned with this balloon of yours?"

"He has invited us all to drive with him to the park,
to watch the ascension—well, not Harry, but the rest of
us!" said Felix, in the voice of one relating a catastrophe.
"And don't *you* say that it is very kind and obliging of
him, sir, like Jessamy, because if you don't like a person, you don't *wish* to be obliged to him!"

"That is very true!" remarked Lady Elizabeth, much
struck. "In fact, one would prefer him *not* to be kind
and obliging!"

"Yes, one *would!*" agreed Felix, bestowing a look of
warm approval upon her. "Besides, I know just how it
would be, and I had almost liefer not go at all! Because,
you may depend upon it, Jessamy will sit on the box,
with the coachman, and I should have to sit beside
Cousin Buxted and listen to him prosing on and on,
and very likely gibble-gabbling to the girls about aeronautics, just as if he *knew,* which he doesn't, and then
explaining it to me, in a very *kind* way, and—Oh, *you*
know, sir! I—I *couldn't!*" He saw the corners of
Alverstoke's mouth quiver, and said triumphantly: "I
knew you would understand! So when I came into the
room—not knowing he was there—and Frederica told
me that he had invited us, I said I couldn't go with
him, because you had invited me to go with you, sir!
And if Jessamy tells you I was rag-mannered it is not
true! I thanked him very civilly, I promise you! Yes,
and naturally I see that I can't go at all, if you don't
take me, because that *would* be uncivil."

"And you said you weren't in a scrape! Did you
bamboozle your family into believing your mendacious
story?"

"Oh, no! Frederica and Jessamy knew it wasn't true,

of course. In fact, Frederica said, afterwards, that she utterly forbade me to *plague* you to take me. But I am not plaguing you: I am just *asking* you, sir! She says you don't wish to see a balloon ascension, but I think it would be a *treat* for you!"

"Oh, do you?" said the Marquis. "Then let me tell you, you repellent and unscrupulous whelp—"

He was interrupted. "So it would be!" said Lady Elizabeth. "A high treat! For my part, I should enjoy it excessively, because it so happens that I have never watched a balloon ascension. Dear Vernon, you have been wondering how you may best entertain me, haven't you? And now you know! You shall drive Felix and me to Hyde Park, to see the balloon go up!"

"Wretch!" said the Marquis. "Very well!"

"I *knew* you would!" cried Felix. "I *told* Jessamy you would!" He paused, before adding tentatively: "In your phaeton, sir?"

"Now, what do you care for phaetons, or horses?" asked Alverstoke. "What you would like me to do would be to drive you to Hyde Park in a Catch-me-who-can!"

"Yes, by Jupiter, wouldn't I just!" exclaimed Felix, his eyes kindling. "Only you couldn't, you know, because it ran on lines. The thing is that Jessamy is getting to be so top-lofty, because you let him drive your team, besides riding with him, that there's no bearing it! So it would be *splendid,* if you took me instead of him!" A doubt shook him; he cast a look at Lady Elizabeth, and said politely: "If you wouldn't object to it, ma'am!"

"Certainly not! I shouldn't dream of watching a balloon ascension from anything so stuffy as a barouche," she said promptly. "Besides, how else could we take the shine out of Cousin Buxted?"

This very proper speech confirmed him in his impression that she was a right one, and earned for her his fervent gratitude. A caveat, entered by Alverstoke, that phaetons were not designed to accommodate three people, was summarily disposed of, and he then took himself off, leaving Lady Elizabeth to the enjoyment of the mirth that had been consuming her.

XVIII

As a result of Felix's visit, Lady Elizabeth went to visit
Lady Jevington on the following morning. It was surprising, but understandable, that Alverstoke should take
an interest in so engaging a young gentleman; but it
appeared, from Felix's artless conversation, that his
interest extended to Jessamy—whom he permitted to
drive his cherished horses; and that was by no means
so understandable, unless this unprecedented behaviour sprang from a wish to gratify the Beauty of the
family. Eliza had learnt all about the divine Charis
from one of her oldest friend's rare letters, but she had
not set much store by Sally Jersey's prophecy that
Alverstoke would marry a girl who had not yet attained her twentieth birthday. Sally might say that it
was always so with hardened bachelors, but she fancied
she knew her brother rather better than Sally did, and
she had dismissed the prophecy as a mere on-dit.

Dining tête-a-tête with him, she was careful to evince
little curiosity about the Misses Merriville, merely saying: "I hope you mean to introduce them to me. If
they are as delightful as Felix, I don't wonder at it that
you consented to befriend them! How do they go on?
Did you contrive to fire them off successfully?"

"Yes, and without the smallest exertion. I had merely
to present them to the ton. I wish you might have
seen Louisa's face when they came into the room! She
had met Frederica already, and was agreeably surprised,
I fancy, to discover that she is neither in the first blush
of youth, nor a beauty, but a passably goodlooking
young woman, with a great deal of commonsense, and
a somewhat masterful disposition. Louisa was therefore
unprepared for Charis." A reminiscent smile curled his
lips. "I suppose I must have seen the Beauties of close
on twenty seasons, but I must own I have never seen

one comparable to Charis Merriville." He raised his
wineglass, and drank a little. "Face and figure are perfection, and her expression most winning. Impossible
to find a fault! Even her carriage is graceful; and it is
universally agreed that her manners are particularly
pleasing."

Startled, and considerably dismayed, Eliza said:
"Good gracious! I must certainly meet this paragon!"

"You may do so tomorrow, if you choose. She will
be at the assembly the Seftons are holding, I imagine.
You had better accompany me to it—if only to spare
me the gush of reproaches Maria Sefton would swamp
me with for not having brought you. I shall be
astonished if Charis doesn't take your breath away."

Unlike her sisters, Eliza had never tried to provide
her only brother with an eligible wife. Relations
between them had always been amicable, even mildly
affectionate, but no strong ties bound any member of
the Dauntry family to another. Happily married to her
John Kentmere, absorbed in her progeny, and rarely
visiting London, she had little interest in Alverstoke's
future, and had once infuriated Louisa by saying that
his marriage was no concern of hers. But installed once
more in Alverstoke House, picking up the threads of her
old life, she did feel some concern, for it seemed to
her that he was on the verge of contracting an alliance
which could only end in disaster. However beautiful
she might be, this school-room-miss of his would become a dead bore to him within a year of their marriage—probably even sooner! She had set no great store
by Lady Jersey's disclosures, and even less by an im-
passioned letter from Louisa, recommending her to try
what her supposed influence over Alverstoke would do
to save him (and the Family) from a shocking *mésal-
liance;* but the dithyramb Alverstoke had sung in praise
of Charis Merriville had the effect of sending her off
next day to visit Augusta. With all her faults, Augusta
did not want for sense or judgment.

Lady Jevington received her with temperate pleasure,
enquired, with meticulous civility, after the health of
her family, and expressed the hope that she would
replenish her wardrobe while she was in London. "For

I should be failing in my duty as your eldest sister, Eliza, if I did not tell you that that outmoded gown you are wearing gives you a very off appearance," she said. "No doubt you have come to London for that purpose."

"Well, I haven't," replied Eliza. "I've come to discover if it's true that Vernon had fallen head over ears in love with some highly finished piece of nature not yet out of her teens."

"Not to my knowledge," replied Lady Jevington, with majestic calm. She favoured her sister with a thin smile, in which tolerance and contempt were nicely mixed. "I collect that Louisa has been writing to you. Louisa is a fool."

"Yes, but Sally is no fool, and she too wrote to me that Vernon stands within an ace of committing what I can't but feel would be the greatest imprudence of his life!"

"I have never," stated Lady Jevington, "rated Sarah Fane's understanding above the average."

"Augusta, he described the girl to me last night in such terms as I have never heard him use before!"

"He was hoaxing you," said Lady Jevington.

Eliza frowned in perplexity. "Do you mean to say that she is not so excessively lovely? But, if that's so, why should he—"

"I do not think I have ever seen a more beautiful girl than Charis Merriville—and rarely one who is more prettily behaved," pronounced her ladyship judicially. "She made an instant hit when she appeared at Vernon's ball, which was not wonderful, and now has more than half the eligible bachelors languishing at her feet. Gregory," she added, with unruffled composure, "is one of them. But nothing will come of that, and I am happy to know that his first fancy should have alighted on a modest girl of excellent principles. I daresay it will do him a great deal of good."

Eliza said impatiently: "Yes, but Vernon? If he is not in love with the girl, what in the world prevailed upon him to bestir himself, not only on her behalf, but on her brothers' as well? It is not at all like him!"

"I do not pretend to be in his confidence, but I am

tolerably well-acquainted with him, and I believe he
presented the Merriville girls merely to spite Louisa,
and Lucretia. That Woman," said Augusta, with awful
restraint, "was not behindhand in badgering him to
hold a ball at Alverstoke House, to mark Chloë's come-
out, as well as Jane's. One may guess the means he used
to compel Louisa to chaperon the girls! He is at liberty
to indulge his freakish whims as he pleases, but I
consider that his conduct was most reprehensible. Indeed, I strongly advised him not to yield to Louisa's
and Lucretia's importunities."

Restraining the impulse to remind her that Alverstoke had never been known to listen to sisterly advice,
Eliza said: "I dare say he might have invited the Merrivilles to his ball to punish Louisa, but that doesn't
account for the rest of it. One of his so-called wards—
Felix: the most delightful urchin!—invaded the house
yesterday, and it was perfectly plain that he looks upon
Vernon as a certain source of indulgences. He doesn't
stand in the least awe of him either, which tells its own
tale. Now, why, pray, should Vernon, who is utterly
indifferent to *our* children, interest himself in the
Merrivilles, if not because he wishes to make himself
acceptable to their sister?"

"That, no doubt, is the reason. But unless I am much
mistaken it is the elder and not the younger sister for
whom he has conceived a decided tendre."

Eliza stared at her. "Good God, how is this? He told
me she was passably goodlooking, not in her first youth,
full of commonsense, and masterful!"

"Very true," agreed Lady Jevington. "I believe her
to be some four-and-twenty years of age, but from the
circumstances of her mother's early demise, which left
her the virtual mistress of the household, one would
suppose her to be older. I think her a young woman of
character, and I have come to the conclusion that she
will suit Alverstoke very well."

"Augusta!" Eliza gasped. "A woman who is no more
than *passably goodlooking* for Alverstoke? You must be
all about in your head! When, pray, has he had a
tendre for any but regular out-and-outers?"

"And when, my dear Eliza, have any of these out-

and-outers, as you call them, failed to bore him within a few months?" retorted Augusta. "Frederica cannot, I own, hold a candle to Charis, in respect of beauty; but she has a great deal of countenance, and a liveliness of mind which Charis lacks. They are both agreeable, well-bred girls, but Charis is a lovely ninnyhammer, while Frederica, in my judgment, is a woman of superior sense."

A trifle stunned by this measured pronouncement, Eliza said: "Augusta, am *I* all about in my head? Do you seriously mean to tell me that you think one of Fred Merriville's daughters an eligible match for Alverstoke?"

"It is not, perhaps, the match I should have chosen for him," admitted her ladyship. "Upon reflection, however, I believe it will do very well. Unless you are prepared to face with equanimity the prospect of seeing that Block, Endymion, step into Alverstoke's shoes, you will agree that it is of the highest importance that Alverstoke should marry, and set up his nursery, before he becomes wholly abandoned to the single state. I think I may say that I have spared no pains to introduce to his notice every eligible female of my acquaintance. I shall not attempt to deny that my exertions were useless—as were Louisa's! But that was to be expected!" she said, momentarily descending from her Olympian heights. "If I were to tell you, Eliza, of Louisa's folly—!" She checked herself, resuming her dignity, and said: "But that is of no moment. Suffice it to say that neither her nor my efforts were attended by success." She paused again, but continued after a moment, with austere resolution, and fixing her sister with a quelling eye. "My natural partiality," she stated, "has never blinded me to the faults in Alverstoke's character, but much as I deprecate them, I feel bound to say, in common justice, that they are not to be laid wholly at his own door. Setting aside the indulgence that was granted him from the hour of his birth, he has been so much courted, flattered, and positively *hunted,* that much as one may deplore the cynicism with which he regards females one cannot wonder at it. I assure you, Eliza, I have frequently *blushed* for my sex!

And that, I fancy, is why he seems bent on fixing his interest with Frederica. You may depend upon it that I have closely observed her. But if you were to ask me whether she is aware of his interest in her, or would welcome an offer from him, I should be obliged to reply that I do not know. All I can say is that I have never seen her throw out the smallest lure to him, or betray by the least sign that she cherishes for him any warmer feeling than a cousinly friendship."

Digesting this, Eliza said slowly: "I see. You think that intrigues him, and you may well be right. But it seems very odd to me that both Louisa and Sally believe him to be in love with the other sister!"

"He is being extremely cautious," said Augusta.

"It must be for the first time!"

"Exactly so! I am of the opinion that he does not yet know his own mind. But I consider it significant that he is taking pains—also, I daresay, for the first time!—to do nothing that might make Frederica the subject of malicious on-dits. Even Louisa has failed to perceive that there is a very different expression in his eyes when he talks to Frederica than the quizzing look he gives Charis."

"Well!" said Eliza. "I had no notion of this, or that matters had become so serious! To be sure, it did occur to me, when we sat cosing together last night, and when Felix set out to cajole him, that he was not as—as *inhuman* as he was used to be! If that is Frederica's influence at work—Oh, but Augusta, you can't have considered! Only think of her encumbrances! He told me himself that Felix and his brother are in her charge; can you conceive of his being willing to undertake any part of that responsibility?"

"By what I hear," responded Augusta dryly, "he has already begun to do so. I am heartily glad of it: it has given him something to think of besides his own pleasure. I have never made any secret of my conviction that idleness has been his ruin. His wealth has made it possible for him to indulge his every extravagant whim without even troubling himself to count the cost; he has never been obliged to consider anyone but himself; and what is the result? He was bored before he was thirty!"

"So you advocate the guardianship of two schoolboys as a remedy?" Eliza gave a chuckle, as she passed her own sons under mental review. "Well, he certainly wouldn't be *bored!*" she said. She began to draw on her gloves. "I hope to make the acquaintance of the Misses Merriville this evening, and am now doubly anxious to do so. It will be hard to convince me, however, that such a female as you have described would make Alverstoke a suitable wife."

But when she drove away from the Seftons' house that night, she was much inclined to think that Augusta might be right. She felt strongly drawn to Frederica, liking her frank, natural manners, her air of quiet elegance, and the laughter in her eyes. That must have been what had attracted Alverstoke, she decided—if he was attracted. It was impossible to make up her mind on that question, for while, on the one hand, he plainly stood on terms of friendly intimacy with her, on the other, he did not linger beside her for many minutes, but strolled away to engage Mrs Ilford in a light flirtation. Lady Elizabeth noted, with approval, that Frederica's eyes neither followed him, nor afterwards searched for him in the crowded room. Augusta was right, she thought: the girl has quality. But to describe her as *passable* merely was to do her a gross injustice: she was certainly dimmed by her sister's brilliance, but in any other company she would rank as a very pretty girl. She possessed, moreover, the indefinable gift of charm, which, unlike Charis's fragile beauty, would remain with her to the end.

She said smilingly: "I must tell you that I have quite lost my heart to your brother Felix! You are aware, I daresay, that I made his acquaintance yesterday. A most engaging child!"

Frederica laughed, but shook her head. "Yes, but he is very naughty, and is quite in my black books—if he would but care for that! I strictly forbade him to plague Lord Alverstoke, who has been much too kind to him—indeed, to all of us!—already."

"Oh, but he didn't plague him! He told us that you had forbidden him to do so, and assured my brother that he was only *asking* him—!"

"Oh, dear, what a dreadful boy he is! I do beg your pardon: he told me that you said you wished to watch this ascension, and I'm very sure you don't, ma'am!"

"On the contrary! I shall enjoy it excessively—and in particular the spectacle of my brother being brought round a small and probably grubby thumb!"

"Certainly grubby!" said Frederica ruefully. "Isn't it odd that you may send a little boy out as neat as wax, and within half-an-hour he will be a perfect shag-rag?"

"Yes, and in that respect they are all exactly alike. I have three sons, you know, Miss Merri—Oh, no, why should we peel eggs? Frederica! We are cousins, are we not?"

"Well, I *think* we are," said Frederica. "Only—only rather remote, I'm afraid!" She hesitated, and then said candidly: "It must seem very odd to you that I should have asked Lord Alverstoke to befriend us. The thing was he was the only relation whose name I knew. My father had several times spoken of him, so—so I was so bold-faced as to apply to him. I was very anxious, you see, that my sister should have a London season."

"I can readily understand that," Eliza said, looking towards Charis, who made one of a group of young people on the opposite side of the room. "I see she has Endymion Dauntry on a string: if he were not so handsome one would take him for a mooncalf! Is that his sister, Chloë, talking to young Wrenthorpe? How monstrous that he should be so much the better-looking!" She withdrew her gaze, and smiled at Frederica: "Alverstoke tells me that you are under the chaperonage of an aunt, but that she is not here tonight: I should like to make her acquaintance, so I shall pay her a morning visit, if you think she would not dislike it?"

"She could not do so, but I fear you would not be very likely to find her at home," said Frederica. Her brow was creased, and she sighed. "It is a most unfortunate circumstance—well, a very *sad* circumstance! —that my uncle, who lives in Harley Street, is dangerously ill, not expected to recover, which, indeed, one would not wish him to do, for he has been a sufferer from a painful and incurable disease for a long time. My Aunt Seraphina feels it to be her duty to support her sister, and spends almost the whole of every day in Harley Street. My Aunt Amelia is in great affliction, which seems to suspend her every faculty. She is—er —all sensibility, and the least thing overpowers her." She added hastily: "Not that I mean to say this is a little thing!"

"I know just what you mean," interposed Eliza. "Poor soul! I sincerely pity her, but I shall spare you any flowery commonplaces. I fancy we are alike in preferring the word with the bark on it: it is in the highest degree unfortunate that this should have happened just now! You must be most awkwardly placed, without your chaperon. Well, I mean to stay in London for a few weeks, so perhaps I may be able to come to your rescue."

"Oh no, no! It is most kind of you, but *that* doesn't signify! My aunt dislikes ton-parties, and rarely accompanies us to them. Indeed, she only consented to come to Upper Wimpole Street on the understanding that she need not do so. I thought that perhaps it would present a—a more correct appearance if she were known to be with us. But, in point of fact, *I've* always been Charis's chaperon. You see, by the time she was seventeen I was quite beyond the age of needing a chaperon myself—whatever Cousin Alverstoke may say!"

"What *does* he say?" enquired Eliza.

"Everything that is disagreeable!" replied Frederica, laughing. "He thinks me sunk beneath reproach—positively a hurly-burly woman!—because I don't take my maid with me when I go out! It is too absurd! As though I were a green girl, which anyone can see I am not!"

"No: but not, if I may say so, at your last prayers!"

Frederica smiled. "I daresay no female ever reaches her last prayers. But that doesn't signify: the thing is that if my uncle were to die *now* it would be most improper, wouldn't it? for Charis to attend any such parties as this." The laughter sprang into her eyes again; she said comically: "Oh, dear! How odious that sounds! But when one has schemed and contrived, as I have, to bring a very beautiful and very dear sister to London for at least *one* season—it—it does seem hard to be

obliged to forgo it all because an uncle, whom we
scarcely know, and who is not a blood-relation—though
a kind, worthy man!—should die at such an ill-chosen
moment!"

A responsible twinkle came into Lady Elizabeth's
eyes, but she replied quite seriously: "Yes, I see. Awkward! But if he is only related to you by marriage I am
much inclined to think that you need do no more than
go into black gloves."

"But not *dance* in black gloves!" objected Frederica.

Lady Elizabeth thought this over. "Perhaps not. I am
not perfectly sure about dancing, but I do know that we
were in black gloves for one of my great-aunts when
my mother presented Louisa, and I seem to remember
that she went to parties every night. I don't care a rush
for proper modes myself, and should have supposed
that you do not either."

"I'm obliged to care, for my sister's sake. What might
be thought eccentricity in Lady Elizabeth Dauntry
would be condemned in Miss Merriville as very unbecoming conduct," said Frederica dryly.

Eliza wrinkled up her nose distastefully. "I suppose
that's true. How detestable! Well, the only thing to be
done is to—"

But at that moment she was interrupted by Lady
Jersey, who came up to her with her hands outstretched,
exclaiming: "*Eliza!* Oh, goodness me, I hadn't the least
notion—My dearest wretch, how dared you come to
London without one word to me?"

So Frederica, moving away, did not learn what, in
her ladyship's opinion, was the best thing to be done.
She could only hope that Mr Navenby, who had puncti-
iously asked her leave to address himself to Charis,
might succeed in winning that soft heart. Since Charis
showed a tendency to burst into tears whenever his
name was mentioned, the hope was not strong; but
when Frederica compared him to Endymion she found
it hard to believe that Charis, ninnyhammer though she
was, could really prefer a handsome block to so admirable a young man. Indeed, she had been so much
exasperated by the sight of Charis gazing worshipfully

up into Endymion's face, at Almack's, two days previously, that she had quite tartly requested her not to make such a figure of herself at the Seftons' party.

"You cast just such sheep's eyes at young Fraddon, when you fancied yourself in love with him," she reminded her wilting sister. "But then you were only seventeen. You are past nineteen now, and indeed, my dear, it is time that you showed a little commonsense! Instead, you show less! Will Fraddon had more than his handsome face to recommend him, and, had your tendre for him endured, neither I nor his parents would have raised any objection to the match. It didn't, however, and *now* you choose to make a goose of yourself over another, and far less eligible, handsome face! Charis, surely you must know that I am not more opposed to such a match than is Mrs Dauntry—or, I don't doubt, Lord Alverstoke? No, no, don't cry! I don't mean to be unkind, and I promise you I perfectly understand how you came to be dazzled by so magnificent a—a clodpole! Only try to give your thoughts a more rational direction! How *could* you be happy with a man whom his own relations think a block?"

The effect of this practical homily was to cast Charis into a fever of apprehension, which she communicated to Endymion at the first opportunity that offered. No sooner had he succeeded, at the Seftons' assembly, in drawing her apart from the throng of her suitors than the story was poured into his ears, and his beloved was entreating him not to come near her for the rest of the evening. "I have the most dreadful *feel* that Frederica has divulged the secret of our attachment to Alverstoke!" she said tragically. "You cannot have failed to notice the way he watched us, when you first came up to me! I declare, I was ready to sink, when I looked up, and found his piercing gaze upon me!"

Endymion had not, in fact, noticed this unnerving circumstance, but he agreed that it was sinister. After painful cogitation, he said: "There's only one thing for it: I must sell out!"

"Oh, no, no!" Charis breathed. "Never would I let you do so for my miserable sake!"

"Well, to own the truth, I've never cared for military life above half," confided Endymion. "But the thing is that Cousin Alverstoke will very likely cut off my allowance, if I sell out, and then, you know, we should find ourselves obliged to bite on the bridle. Should you object to being a trifle cucumberish? Though I daresay if I took up farming, or breeding horses, or something of that nature, we should soon find ourselves full of juice."

"*I?* she exclaimed. "Oh, no, indeed! Why, I've been *cucumberish,* as you call it, all my life! But for you it is a different matter! You must not ruin yourself for my sake."

"It won't be as bad as that," he assured her. "My fortune ain't handsome, but I wasn't born without a shirt. And if I was to sell out my cousin *couldn't* have me sent abroad."

"But could he do so now?" she asked anxiously. "Harry says the Life Guards never go abroad, except in time of war."

"No, but he might contrive to get me sent off on a mission."

Her eyes widened. "What sort of a mission, dear love?"

"Well, I don't know precisely, but we're always sending missions somewhere or other, and very often they have a military man attached to them. Diplomatic stuff," explained Endymion vaguely. "Like Lord Amherst going to China, a couple of years back, and staying there above a twelvemonth. Something to do with mandarins," he added, in further elucidation of the mystery. "Wouldn't suit me at all, but there's no saying what might happen if I don't sell out. Got a devilish lot of influence, Alverstoke."

Since it never entered her head that nothing short of Royal influence could avail to obtain a place for Endymion on any diplomatic mission, Charis was instantly assailed by a hideous vision of death and disaster. If the ship which bore so precious a burden escaped wreck, he would either perish at the hands of unknown, but probably murderous mandarins, or succumb to one of the deadly fevers peculiar to Eastern countries. Her face perfectly white, she said, in a low, passionate voice, that to avert such a fate she would be prepared to renounce him. Endymion was much moved, but, not having visualized any of the disasters which had sprung so immediately to her mind, he did not feel that the situation, even at its worst, called for so great a sacrifice. But when Charis suddenly begged him to leave her, because Lady Elizabeth was looking at them, he did feel, and forcibly, that they could not go on, he said, in this devilish havey-cavey way.

"Oh no! It is the greatest misery to me!" Charis agreed.

"Ay, and so it is to me, seeing you by scraps and not getting on in the least," said Endymion gloomily. "I'll tell you what, Charis: we must talk about it—decide what's to be done, you know. Dashed if I won't bring Chloë and Diana to see the balloon tomorrow! Ay, that's the barber! You can tell your sister you wish to speak to Chloë: no harm in that! I'll play least-in-sight, and while everyone's watching the balloon we'll slip off together. Shouldn't think it will be difficult: bound to be a devilish crowd in the park."

"No, no!" she said distressfully. "If you bring your sisters to see the ascent, you must promise not to come *near* me! Felix has persuaded Lord Alverstoke to take him there, and you may depend upon it that he will bring his carriage as close to ours as he may!"

"Alverstoke going to watch a balloon go up?" exclaimed Endymion incredulously. "You're bamming!"

"No, indeed I'm not! He is taking Lady Elizabeth too, so you see—!"

"He must be getting queer in his attic! Well, I mean to say—! *Alverstoke!* Why the deuce must he take it into his head to come and play boots with everything? What a dam—what a dashed thing! Seems to me the end of it will be that we shall have to take a bolt to the Border!"

"*Endymion!*" she uttered, in shocked dismay. "You *couldn't* ask me to do anything so dreadful! You're joking me! It would be beyond everything!"

"Yes, I know it would. My Colonel wouldn't like it, either. But we can't stand on points for ever, love! Got to bring ourselves about somehow!"

"We will—oh, I know we shall succeed in the end! Hush, here comes Lord Wrenthorpe!"

XIX

When Knapp drew back the blinds in his master's bedroom upon the following morning, the Marquis was first revolted by the sight of brilliant sunshine, and then by his valet's announcement that it was a beautiful day. He had hoped for rain, gales, or even snow: anything, in fact, which would make a balloon ascension impossible. But a cloudless sky met his gaze; and when, hope dying hard, he asked Knapp if it was not very still and windless, Knapp replied, with all the air of one bearing good tidings: "Just a nice, light breeze, my lord: what you might call a perfect June day!"

"You are mistaken!" responded his lordship. "At what time does this damned balloon make its ascension?"

"At two o'clock, my lord—according to what Master Felix told Wicken," said Knapp demurely.

"And you may depend upon it," said his lordship, "that that brat will be upon the doorstep on the stroke of noon!"

But when he himself emerged from his dressing-room at noon he found that young Mr Merriville had arrived some little time earlier, and was discussing a hearty luncheon under the aegis of Lady Elizabeth. Owing to the exertions of his sisters, he was impeccably attired in spotless nankeens, his best jacket, and a freshly laundered shirt; with his nails scrubbed, and his curly locks brushed till they glowed. Between mouthfuls of mutton-pie, he was initiating his hostess into the mysteries of aeronautics. He greeted Alverstoke with acclaim, explaining that he had come to the house perhaps a little early because he knew that he and Cousin Elizabeth wouldn't wish to reach the park too late to obtain a good place for the phaeton. Upon receiving a somewhat embittered rejoinder, he at once subjugated his lordship

251

by saying anxiously: "You do *wish* to go, don't you, sir?"

"Yes—but you are a vile and an abominable young thatchgallows!" said his lordship.

Accepting this as a compliment, Felix bestowed a seraphic smile upon him, and applied himself again to the pie.

"Also," said his lordship, levelling his glass at the loaded plate, and slightly shuddering, "a bacon-picker!"

"I know. Sir, do you know how they were *used* to fill balloons, and how they *now* do it?"

"No," said Alverstoke. "I've no doubt, however, that I soon shall."

He was right. From then on Felix, who had acquired a tattered copy of the *History and Practice of Aerostation,* maintained a flow of conversation, largely informative, but interspersed with eager questions. He sat wedged between Alverstoke and Eliza in the phaeton; but since he addressed himself exclusively to Alverstoke, Eliza was able to sit back at her ease, listening with amusement and some surprise to her brother's very creditable answers to the posers set him by his youthful admirer. Felix, though much indebted to Cavallo's *History,* had discovered that it was deplorably out-of-date, which, as he ingenuously told Alverstoke, was disappointing, since he felt that there was a great deal he did not yet know about aeronautics. And what was the peculiar virtue of silk, which made it a better covering for balloons than linen?

From the properties of silk to the intricacies of valves was a short step, but it was one which seemed to Eliza to sweep her companions into a foreign language. Abandoning all attempt to grasp the subject, she withdrew her attention, until it was reclaimed by Felix, who startled her by expressing a wistful desire to float through the air attached to a parachute. She exclaimed: "What an appalling thought! I should be frightened out of my life!"

"No, why, ma'am?" he said. "Only fancy what it must be like! Cousin Alverstoke says he once saw a man giving displays: I wish *I* had!"

They had by this time entered the park; and when

they reached the site of the ascension Felix was delighted to see that, although the balloon was already tethered, the casks of hydrogen, from which the bag would presently be inflated by means of a hosepipe, were still being assembled within the roped-off enclosure. He drew a deep breath of gratification, demanded of Alverstoke if he wasn't *now* glad they had started early, jumped down from the phaeton, and made all haste towards the scene of activity.

"I do hope he won't meet with a repulse!" remarked Eliza. "It would quite ruin his day!"

"From what I know of him he is more likely to meet with quite unnecessary encouragement," replied Alverstoke. "They took him to their bosoms at the foundry, to which it was my fate to escort him; and he appears to have had a similar success on the steam-boat he once boarded. He has a thirst for information on all forms of mechanical invention, and, for his age, a remarkable grasp of the subject."

"You too seem to know more about such things than I had suspected!"

"No more than any other man of moderate understanding. I am now going to withdraw into the shade of the trees—no matter how anxious you may be to remain as close as possible to the enclosure!"

She laughed. "I shall be thankful—though I fear Felix will think it very poor-spirited of us!"

Early though it was, they had not been the first of the spectators to arrive. A number of persons had gathered round the enclosure already; and several carriages had taken up positions under the shade of the trees. Amongst these was Lady Buxted's landaulet: a circumstance which made Eliza ejaculate: "Good God, isn't that Louisa's carriage? I wonder how she was induced to lend it? She detests the Merrivilles, you know."

"I should suppose that she had little choice in the matter. I find Carlton intolerably boring, but I'll say this for him: he's not afraid of Louisa's tongue, and he doesn't knuckle down to her. Or so I collect, from the complaints she has from time to time poured into my unwilling ears."

"I had not credited him with so much spirit. Do

draw up beside the carriage! I should like to pursue my
acquaintance with Frederica."

He complied with this request, backing the phaeton
into place on the right of the landaulet, so that although
the high perch of the phaeton made it impossible for
his sister to shake hands with Frederica she was able to
exchange greetings with her, and might have maintained a conversation had she not decided that to be
obliged to talk to anyone sitting so far above her would
soon give Frederica a stiff neck. Jessamy had descended
from the landaulet, and, with an awkward gallantry,
helped her to climb down from her seat, when she expressed her intention to enjoy a comfortable cose with
his sisters. She smiled upon him, saying: "Thank you!
You, I believe, are Jessamy—the one who handles the
reins in form! How do you do?"

He flushed, and, as he bowed over her extended
hand, stammered a disclaimer. Her ladyship was very
good, but quite mistook the matter! He was the
merest whipster, as Cousin Alverstoke would tell her!

"Oh, no! He says you have a—a bit of the drag
about you! How do you do, Carlton? I am delighted to
see you, but you had liefer go to watch what they are
doing to the balloon than talk to an aunt, so you shall
give me your place for a while."

There seemed to be no reason why her ladyship
should not have occupied Jessamy's place, but Lord
Buxted, taking his smiling dismissal in good part, forbore to point this out to her. He handed her into the
carriage, and turned to look up at his uncle, saying
humorously: "I can guess what—or perhaps I should
say *who!*—has brought you here in such excellent time,
sir!"

"Yes, an irresistible force. But what the devil
brought *you* here so early?"

"Oh, much the same cause!" said Carlton, glancing
towards Jessamy, who was paying no heed to him, his
attention being divided between his lordship's horses,
and his lordship's groom. He continued, lowering his
voice: "I knew that our young cousin there would want
to see everything, from the start, and would think him-

self very hardly used if we had arrived only in time to watch the actual ascension!"

A deadly, and all too familiar boredom crept over the Marquis; an acrid rejoinder hovered on his lips, but remained unspoken. As his derisive eyes scanned his nephew's countenance he realized that the pompous young slow-top was sincere: he believed in all honesty that he was giving Jessamy a high treat; and, as his next words proved, he had taken pains to render it as instructive as it was exciting.

"Knowing that I should be expected to answer all manner of questions, I took the precaution of consulting my *Encyclopaedia* yesterday," Buxted said. "I must own that I became quite absorbed in the subject! The information was not quite up-to-date, but the adventures of the first ballooners held me positively spellbound! I have been entertaining my companions with an account of Professor Charles's experiments. I daresay Jessamy will be able to tell you the height to which he rose on one occasion, eh, Jessamy?" he added, raising his voice.

He was obliged to repeat the question before he could divert Jessamy's attention from the leader to whom he was addressing soft blandishments, and even then it was Alverstoke who supplied him with the answer.

"Two thousand feet," he said, coming to Jessamy's rescue. "Not for nothing have I endured your brother's company this day, Jessamy! So don't attempt to tell me that Lunardi filled his balloon with gas procured from zinc; or that Tyler ascended half-a-mile, at Edinburgh; or even that Blanchard once came to rest in an oak-tree, because I am already fully informed on these and a great many other matters!"

"Ah, Felix has an enquiring mind!" said Buxted, smiling indulgently. "Where is the little rascal?"

"Probably taking an active part in the excessively tedious preparations within the enclosure."

"I hardly think he will have contrived to gain admittance, but perhaps we should go to see that he isn't in mischief, Jessamy. I daresay you too will like to watch the bag being filled," said Buxted kindly.

He turned away, to suggest that the ladies might care to go with them; and Jessamy, looking up at the Marquis, said: "I wish I were in Felix's shoes! Your grays too! Did he ask you to drive him behind a team, sir? I told him you would not, so now he's got a point the best of me. Little ape!—Yes, Cousin Buxted, I'm coming!"

The ladies having declined the offered treat, Buxted and Jessamy went off together; but it was not many minutes before Jessamy returned. Alverstoke, who had alighted from the phaeton, and was standing talking to Frederica, turned his head. "Murdered him?" he enquired.

Jessamy was betrayed into a laugh, which he instantly checked, saying: "No, no! But there was no bearing it, so I made an excuse to come away. It was bad enough when he *would* prose on for ever about these intolerable aeronautics—just as though I hadn't heard enough of them from Felix!—but when he got to reading Felix a lecture, and begging those men's pardons for having permitted him to plague them, I knew I should be at dagger-drawing with him, if I stayed! So I didn't."

"*Is* Felix plaguing them?" asked Frederica. "Ought I to fetch him away?"

"He wouldn't come—particularly now that Cousin Buxted has told him to do so! Saying that people engaged on important matters didn't want 'little boys' under their feet. That set up Felix's bristles in a trice, I can tell you! Well, can you wonder at it?"

"A very ill-judged remark," agreed Alverstoke gravely.

"Well, *you* wouldn't call him a *little boy* to his face, now would you?"

"Of course he wouldn't!" said Eliza, her eyes dancing. "I distinctly recollect that he called him, this very day, an abominable young thatchgallows!"

"Exactly so, ma'am!" said Jessamy. "He wouldn't care a straw for that, any more than he cared for my telling him that he was a disgusting little scrub! But to call him a *little boy*—! Why, *I* wouldn't do so, no matter how angry I might be!"

"I collect," said Frederica, in a resigned voice, "that the pains Charis and I took to send him out in good trim were wasted."

"He looks like one of the scaff and raff," said Jessamy candidly. "But as for getting under those men's feet—! They *like* him, Frederica! And even if they didn't it's no concern of Buxted's! What right has he to behave as if he were our guardian? Pinching at one in that—that *kind* way which gets up one's back till—" He stopped, clipping his lips together, and after a moment's struggle said: "I shouldn't say so. He is a very respectable man, and—and he bore me no malice when I was shockingly uncivil to him. I am determined not to let him provoke me again. So I came away."

"Very proper," said Alverstoke. "Did you learn when the balloon is going to make its ascension?"

"No, sir. That is, I heard someone say that there is very little wind, and I believe they were discussing whether to make the flight, or to postpone it. But I wasn't really attending."

"Then I wish you had been!" said Alverstoke. "I find this affair quite as tedious as you do, and should be delighted to withdraw from it. O my God!—if it is postponed Felix will expect me to repeat this performance!"

Frederica laughed. "Don't be alarmed! I won't let him tease you to bring him here again."

"An empty promise! He will assure you—and me too!—that he has no intention of teasing me, and—"

"He will just *ask* you!" interpolated Eliza.

"Yes—or offer it to me as a high treat, and look like an orphan without means of support if I decline it," said his lordship bitterly.

"Playing off his tricks!" said Jessamy. "Of course he will do so, when he knows he can bamboozle you, sir! Why don't you give him a set-down?"

"Instead of encouraging him to think he can depend on you for every indulgence!" agreed Frederica. "Jessamy, do you think you should perhaps bring him away? I daresay they must be wishing him at Jericho!"

Jessamy shook his head, saying with a reluctant smile: "No, they ain't. One of them told Cousin Buxted that he was making himself useful! As a matter of fact, he's getting as much encouragement as he gets from Cousin Alverstoke—and, lord, won't he be intolerable for weeks to come!"

"It would be a waste of breath, I imagine, to say that I have never offered him encouragement, nor, I might add, perceived the smallest need to do so!" said Alverstoke. He saw that his nephew was approaching, and greeted him with a demand to know how much longer they were to be kept waiting.

"Oh, not for long now, I fancy!" responded Buxted. "I have been talking to the chief aeronaut, a very agreeable man! There are two of them, you know. This one —Oulton, I believe his name is—has been telling me a number of interesting facts concerning the difficulties and dangers of ballooning: the unexpected currents of air at high altitudes, the delicacy of the valve, the hazards of descending in a strong wind when the grapnels have frequently been known to tear away whole bushes, so that the balloon swiftly reascends—to name only a few! One needs to be intrepid indeed to venture into the sky: I don't scruple to say I would not do so for the world!"

"No, indeed!" said Charis, shuddering.

"The speed to which they attain, too!" he continued. "Conceive of travelling at fifty miles an hour! But that, it seems, cannot be seen today, for there is too little wind. I fear that nothing more than a short flight will be attempted, unless, of course, a stronger current is encountered as the balloon rises. I wonder, Charis, if you know to what enormous—one might say *incredible*— heights they have been known to rise?"

"Felix told me, half-a-mile. Oh, I hope they will not do so today! It terrifies me only to think of it!"

The Marquis, interpreting with fiendish accuracy the expression on his nephew's countenance, said: "Come, come, Carlton! Surely you can't be such a clunch as to have hoped to astonish Felix's sister? If she has been attending, for the past week, to his instructive discourse, she must be very well able to recite all the statistics to you!" He glanced at Charis, with a smile that drew a soft laugh from her. "But I do beg you won't, Charis!"

"Oh, no, how could I? I am too stupid to understand such things!"

"Or perhaps your little brother didn't perfectly understand all that he tried to tell you!" said Buxted. "It is not the *height* which constitutes the danger, but the delicacy of the *valve,* which controls the height. Owing to the atmospheric pressure the cord attached to it has to be operated with great caution. If the valve cannot be sufficiently opened the place of descent may be missed. If, on the other hand, it is opened, and cannot be closed again, the gas escapes with such violence that the balloon collapses so rapidly that it falls to the earth with fatal velocity!"

Fortunately, since Charis had turned pale at the thought that she might be going to witness so terrible a disaster, Jessamy created a diversion by exclaiming: "Look! they have begun to fill it!"

And, indeed, the silken bag, which had previously been spread on the ground, could now be seen, rising above the heads of the crowd. As it swelled and mounted it drew gasps of admiration from the spectators, for although those who had had the curiosity to observe it at close quarters knew that its classically-shaped boat was painted in blue and red, with a scroll-work of gold, it was not until the bag began to fill that the huddle of colours on the ground resolved themselves into vertical stripes of red and white, with a blue band, like a sash, running across them.

"Your ordeal is nearly over, cousin!" said Frederica.

Before he could reply they were both startled by a hoarse shriek from Charis. Frederica turned quickly, just in time to see her pointing hand drop, and to catch her as she sank into a swoon. She looked round in alarm, and saw that the balloon, released from its moorings, was swiftly soaring upwards, with a small figure cling-ing, monkey-like, halfway up one of the dangling ropes which had tethered it to the ground. She sat rigid, so paralysed with dread that she could neither speak nor move. Her eyes, drenched with horror, remained fixed on Felix's diminishing form; and she was unaware

either of the noise made by the crowd of startled on-
lookers, or of the shocked silence which had fallen upon
her companions.

That silence was broken by Jessamy. As white as
Charis, he croaked suddenly: "They are pulling him
up! Don't try to climb, you little fool! *Don't*—*!* O God!
he'll never keep his hold!"

He buried his face in his hands, but raised it again,
as Alverstoke said coolly: "Yes, he will. Steady, my
child! They are hauling him up fast."

His gaze, like Frederica's, never wavered from Felix,
already a tiny, indistinguishable figure against the sky.
The suspense lasted for seconds that seemed hours.
Buxted said: "I can't see! I can't make out . . .!"

"Yes, yes!" cried Jessamy, his lips trembling.
"They're pulling him into the boat! Oh, well done,
you little brute, you little devil! Just *wait* till I get my
hands on you! Just *wait!*" He then sat down abruptly on
the grass, and ducked his head between his knees.

Alverstoke, mounting the step of the landaulet,
grasped Frederica's wrist. "Come!" he said authori-
tatively. "*You* are not going to faint! He's quite safe
now."

Buxted, also suffering, like Jessamy, from reaction,
ejaculated: "*Safe?* Upon my word, sir, if you think it
safe to be—"

"Be quiet, cloth-head!" interrupted Alverstoke, with
so much menace in the glance he cast upon his nephew
that that well-meaning young man almost quailed.

Frederica pulled herself together. She said, out of a
dry throat but with a calmness to match Alverstoke's:
"No, I never faint." Becoming aware of Charis, limp
against her shoulder, she said: "Charis! My—my wits
must have gone begging! I forgot—!"

"Take this!" said Eliza, producing a vinaigrette from
her reticule. "No, never mind! lay her back against
the squabs! I'll attend to her! For heaven's sake, Vernon, what's to be done?"

"Revive Charis!" he recommended.

"That's not what I meant!" she snapped, untying the
ribbons of Charis's bonnet, and casting his modish con-

fection aside. "Frederica, change places with me, or let
Vernon hand you out of the carriage!"

Still dazed by shock, Frederica yielded to the com-
pulsion of Alverstoke's hand, and climbed down from
the landaulet. Her knees were shaking so much that she
was glad to cling to his arm. She tried to smile, and said:
"I beg your pardon: I am being very stupid! I don't
seem to be able to think, but you will know what I
should do! *Tell* me, cousin!"

"There is nothing you can do," he replied.

She stared rather blindly at him for a moment, but
then said: "Nothing! You are right, of course. *Nothing!*
I don't even know—Cousin, where are they going? It's
an object with aeronauts, isn't it, to discover how far
they can travel?"

"So I believe, but you need not let that alarm you!
They will be quite as anxious to set Felix down as you
are to recover him! I can't tell you where that will be,
but from the direction of what little wind there is I
should suppose they will descend somewhere in the region of Watford."

"Watford! Is not that a considerable distance?"

"No, less than twenty miles. They will hardly dare to
risk a landing until they are clear of the metropolis, and
all the environs, you know. It is one thing to make an
ascent from Hyde Park, but quite another to bring their
infernal balloon down in an area dotted all over with
towns and villages."

"Yes. Yes, I see. I had not realized. . . . And they are
bound to take every care—don't you think?"

"Undoubtedly."

She managed to summon up a smile. "I am not afraid
of accident—not *much* afraid of it! But Lord Buxted
has been telling us that the cold becomes intense at
high altitudes, and I do fear that! You see, although he
is perfectly stout, Felix does catch cold more easily than
most, and it goes to his chest. He is *not* of a con-
sumptive habit: our doctor at home calls it bronchitis,
and says he will very likely grow out of it, but I—I can't
forget how ill he was, two years ago, when he suffered a
very bad attack. And he has gone up there in that thin

jacket—!" She stopped, and again forced herself to smile. "I am being foolish. There is nothing anyone can do."

"There is nothing we can do, but you may depend upon it that the balloonists will wrap him up."

He spoke in his habitual tone of cool unconcern, and it had its effect: she was insensibly reassured. On Buxted it also had its effect, but a different one. He said angrily: "Good God, sir, is that all you can find to say in this dreadful situation?"

Alverstoke looked at him, his brows lifting. "That's all," he replied. He saw Buxted's hands clench themselves into fists, and smiled faintly. "I shouldn't," he advised him.

For a moment it seemed as if Buxted would yield to impulse; but he mastered himself. His face was still much flushed, and he said with suppressed passion: "Are you ignorant of the dangers that boy is exposed to, or insensate?"

"Neither," said Alverstoke. "I'm glad to see you have some red blood in you, but if you don't keep your tongue between your teeth I shall be strongly tempted to let some of it!"

"Oh, be quiet, both of you!" exclaimed Eliza. "Charis listen to me!—Felix is *safe!* There is nothing to cry for—do you hear me? Come, now!"

But Charis, recovering consciousness, had broken into hysterical sobs, and seemed to be unable either to check them, or to understand what Eliza was saying to her.

"Vapours!" said Alverstoke. "It needed only that! Now we shall have a mob gathered round us!"

Frederica, stepping quickly up into the carriage, said: "Let me come there, cousin, if you please! Soothing will only make her worse."

As she spoke, she pulled Charis out of Eliza's arms, and dealt her one deliberate slap across her cheek, which startled the rest of the company almost as much as its recipient. Charis caught her breath between a sob and a whimper, and stared up out of frightened, tear-drenched eyes into her sister's purposeful countenance. "Felix!" she uttered. "Oh, Felix, Felix! Oh, Frederica!"

"Stop!" Frederica commanded. "Not another word until you are able to control yourself."

Eliza, who had got down from the carriage, remarked, in an undervoice to her brother: "Well, that seems to have done the thing, but it was rather drastic! After all, the poor child has had a dreadful shock, and one can see that she has a great deal of nervous sensibility."

"Too much!" he returned.

Jessamy, overcoming by sheer force of will his sudden nausea, had got to his feet again. He was very pale, and he was breathing short and fast, as though he had been running. He fixed his stern eyes on Alverstoke's face, and jerked out: "Lend me your phaeton, sir! I—I *beg* of you! I won't drive it—Curry can do so! You have my word I won't! Sir, you *must* let me have it!"

"Are you proposing to chase the balloon?" asked Alverstoke, regarding him in a little amusement.

"For heaven's sake, Jessamy, don't be so shatter-brained!" exclaimed Buxted. "As though things were not bad enough already! Really, I wonder at you! This is not the moment to indulge in theatrical airdreaming!"

"On the contrary!" said Alverstoke. "It appears to be exactly the moment!"

"Nor is it the moment for frivolous jests!" retorted Buxted, his colour mounting again.

"Sir!" Jessamy begged. "Will you? will you?"

Alverstoke shook his head. "I'm sorry, Jessamy. The balloon is already some miles distant. Yes, I know it can still be seen, but that's deceptive, believe me. Matters are not as desperate as Buxted would have you think, either: accidents are the exception rather than the rule."

"But they do occur!" Jessamy said. "And even if all goes well Felix will be nearly dead with cold, and hasn't any money, or—Sir, you said they would descend as soon as they can do so safely, and if only I can keep it in sight—"

"Moonshine!" snapped Buxted.

"Could that be done?" demanded Eliza, of her brother.

"I daresay, but to what avail? It will come to earth

long before we could be within reach of it, and however strongly they might be tempted to do so the men won't abandon Felix. By the time we had found the place of descent—if we ever did, which I think doubtful—Felix would probably be on the way back to London in a hired chaise."

"You said yourself they would come down in open country, sir! They may be miles from any town! And if —if they don't land safely—I *must* go! I tell you I *must!* Oh, why isn't Harry here?" Jessamy said, anguish in his voice.

Frederica said: "Cousin. . . !"

He met her eyes, reading the unspoken question in them. He smiled crookedly, shrugged, and said: "Very well!"

The anxious expression melted into one of brimming gratitude. "Thank you! I've no right to ask it of you, but I should be so grateful—so *very* grateful!"

"To think that I came here in the expectation of being bored!" he said. "Eliza, I regret that I must now leave you: accept my apologies!"

"Don't give me a thought!" she returned. "I shall take our cousins home, and Carlton may then drive me back to Alverstoke House."

He nodded, and turned to Jessamy. "Up with you!"

His face transformed, Jessamy cried: "You'll go with me yourself? Oh, *thank* you! *Now* we shall do!"

XX

The mood of exaltation was not of long duration. By the time the Stanhope Gate had been reached the various disasters which might threaten Felix had been recollected, and Jessamy became silent, his eyes, an instant earlier full of fiery light, sombre and frowning. As the phaeton approached the gate a smart tilbury came through it, driven by a very ugly man, dressed in the height of fashion, who no sooner clapped eyes on Alverstoke's grays than he reined in the showy chestnut between the shafts of his own carriage, and called out: "Alverstoke! The very man I want!"

The Marquis had checked his team, but he shook his head. "No use, Kangaroo! I haven't an instant to spare!"

"But I only want—Where the devil are you off to?" shouted Cooke, slewing round in his seat as the phaeton passed him.

"Chasing a balloon!" Alverstoke threw over his shoulder.

"Why did you say that?" demanded Jessamy. "He will think you've run mad!"

"Very likely! And it will be no more than the truth!"

There was a moment's silence; then Jessamy said, in a voice of resolute calm: "Do you mean, sir, that this is a wild goose chase?"

"Oh, no!" said Alverstoke, catching the note of anxiety, and relenting. "We may be behind the fair, but I've never yet been out-jockeyed!"

Silence reigned for another half-mile. Jessamy broke it, saying violently: "He deserves to be *flayed!* And if we find him safe I will, too!"

"Not if I have anything to say in the matter!" replied the Marquis. "The thought of flaying him has been sustaining me for the past hour, and not even Harry shall rob me of that pleasure."

That drew a laugh from Jessamy, but he said, after a moment: "You had better flay me. It was my fault—all my fault!"

"I was wondering how long it would be before you contrived to convince yourself that you were to blame," said Alverstoke caustically. "I haven't the slightest wish to know how you arrived at such an addlebrained conclusion, so don't put yourself to the trouble of telling me! If blame rests on any shoulders but Felix's, it rests on mine! He was in my charge, not yours, I would remind you."

Jessamy shook his head. "I ought never to have left him in the enclosure. I *know* what he is, sir!"

"Oh? You suspected, in fact, that he would risk his life in an attempt to take part in this flight?"

"No. Good God, no! I never dreamed—But I did think I ought to keep an eye on him, perhaps, and—and if I hadn't let Cousin Buxted hackle me I—I think I should have done so," Jessamy confessed, staring rigidly ahead. "My curst temper! Jealousy, self-importance, getting up in the boughs, only because my cousin took it upon himself to tell Felix to come away! And he was *right!*" He buried his face in his hands, and said in a stifled voice: "I shall never be fit, never!"

"Not, I agree, until you have got the better of your tendency to fall into distempered freaks," said Alverstoke unemotionally. He allowed Jessamy a moment or two to digest this blighting remark, before adding, with far more encouragement: "I've no doubt that you'll succeed. I won't insult you by calling you a little boy, but you are not very old yet, you know!"

Dropping his hands, Jessamy managed to smile. "Yes, sir. I—I know. One should have fortitude of mind—not allow oneself to be overpowered, or to—to magnify even one's own sins, because that's a form of self-indulgence—don't you think?"

"Possibly. It is not one in which I've so far indulged," replied his lordship dryly.

"Frederica doesn't either. *Or* read curtain lectures! And she is the best person I know!" He added, with unexpected naïveté: "I daresay that seems an odd thing

to say of one's sister, but it's true, and I'm not ashamed
to say so! She may not be a *beauty,* like Charis, but
she's—she's—"

"Worth a dozen of Charis!" supplied his lordship.

"Yes, by Jupiter, she is!" said Jessamy, his eyes kindling.

He relapsed after that into silence, which he broke
only to return monosyllabic answers to such remarks as
Alverstoke addressed to him; to ask him, once, at what
speed he judged the balloon to be travelling; and once
to say, in a burst of confidence: "It was wrong of him—
very wrong, but you can't deny he's pluck to the backbone, sir!"

"Oh, yes! Full of foolhardiness and ignorance."

"Yes, I suppose—But I couldn't have done it!"

"Thank God for that!"

"I shouldn't have had enough spunk," said Jessamy,
making a clean breast of it.

"It's to be hoped that you have more sense!" said
Alverstoke, with asperity. "If, at your age, you did anything only *half* as hare-brained, the only place for you
would be Bedlam!"

"Yes—if I did it! The thing is that one can't help feeling mortified when one's young brother does something
one knows one wouldn't have the spunk to do oneself!"

This betrayal of boyishness made Alverstoke laugh,
but he would not tell Jessamy why, recommending him
instead to keep his eyes on the balloon, which, except
for brief periods when houses or woods obstructed their
view, had all the time remained within their sight. It
had risen to a considerable altitude, but it did not seem
to be travelling fast, its distance from the phaeton, so
far as Alverstoke could judge, being some eight or ten
miles, and only slowly increasing. From the start it had
sailed to the west of the road: a circumstance which
several times, when it seemed to be drawing farther
westward, cast Jessamy into such a fret that it was as
much as he could do to bottle up his impatience. He
managed to do so, however, for although he wanted to
urge Alverstoke to leave the post-road, following the
balloon along some lane which appeared to run directly

in its wake, the saner part of his brain knew that this would be folly. Country lanes pursued erratic courses, and too often ended at some farm or hamlet. He controlled his nervous irritation, telling himself that the balloon was travelling steadily north-westward, and that when it appeared to be drawing away this was merely due to the divergences of the road from the straight; but whenever they were obliged to pull up at a toll-gate, or a pike-keeper was slow in responding to the imperative summons blown by Curry on his yard of tin, he could have screamed with exasperation. Even Alverstoke's unruffled calm exacerbated him; and whenever Alverstoke eased his horses he had to dig his nails into the palms of his hands to keep from bursting into hot and unwise speech. It seemed as though Alverstoke wasn't even trying to catch up with the balloon! But then, as he stole a glance at that impassive profile, he saw that Alverstoke had turned his head a little, and was looking with narrowed, measuring eyes at the balloon, and he felt better, and was able to believe that Alverstoke knew exactly what he was doing.

Just beyond Stanmore, Alverstoke said over his shoulder: "Where, after Watford, can I get a change, Curry?"

"I been thinking of that myself, my lord. I reckon it'll be Berkhamsted."

"Then, if that curst balloon doesn't come down soon I must change at Watford. I imagine it must be close above Berkhamsted now, and I'll be damned if I kill my grays! You'll stay with them, of course."

"How far away is Berkhamsted, sir?" asked Jessamy.

"About ten or twelve miles."

Dismayed, Jessamy exclaimed: "We are an hour behind, then!"

"Rather more—probably very much more!"

"Hold on, sir!" interrupted Curry. "Seems to me it *is* coming down!"

Jessamy stared at the balloon until his eyes watered. He brushed his hand across them, saying angrily: "Oh, curse this sunshine! It isn't coming down! It's as high as—No, by Jove, it is, it *is! Look,* sir!"

Alverstoke cast a fleeting glance at it. "It is undoubtedly coming down. How gratifying! I said the descent would be in the region of Watford."

This way of receiving the glad tidings struck Jessamy, soaring into optimism, as exquisitely humorous. He gave a crack of laughter, exclaiming: "What a hand you are! Oh, I shouldn't have said that! I beg your pardon, sir!"

"So I should hope!"

"As though you cared a button! You can't hoax me, sir, because I know very well—" He broke off; and after a tense moment said uneasily: "Why is it veering like that? It was coming down almost straight a moment ago!"

"You may be seeing it from a different angle."

"No, I'm not! I mean, that wouldn't account for the way it's travelling now!"

In another minute, a spinney shut the balloon from his view; and by the time the phaeton had passed the last of the trees it had dropped altogether out of sight. Jessamy began to pose unanswerable questions to the Marquis: what had caused the balloon to swerve? did he know if it could be steered in any way? did he think there might be something amiss with the valve?

"I should think it more likely that when they dropped nearer to earth they found there was more wind than they had expected," said Alverstoke.

Jessamy's eyes widened. "Wind! Do you remember what Cousin Buxted told us, about the grapnels tearing away whole bushes, not anchoring the balloon at all, so that they had to shut the valve, which made them shoot up again, and—"

"I have some faint recollection of his pitching various tales to your sisters, but as I have yet to hear him say anything worth listening to I fear I didn't attend to him. I daresay there may have been such mischances, but as this particular balloon has *not* shot up into the air again it seems safe to assume that that fate has not befallen it."

"Yes, that's so! I hadn't thought—ah, but—"

"Jessamy," interrupted his lordship wearily, "your reflections on the subject are as valueless as Buxted's. Neither of you knows anything about it. Nor, I may add, do I, so that it is quite useless to bombard me with questions. It is even more useless to harrow your-self by imagining disasters, which really, my dear boy, you have very little reason to expect."

"You must forgive me, sir!" said Jessamy stiffly. "I had no intention of boring you!"

"No, that's why I ventured to give you a hint," said his lordship apologetically.

Jessamy was obliged to bite his lip at this description of a masterly set-down, and to turn his face away, so that Alverstoke should not see how near to laughter he was. He was still on his dignity when, at last, they reached Watford; but the news that met them at the Essex Arms drove all other thoughts from his mind.

Oh, yes, said the landlord, they had seen the balloon as plain as print! Such an uproar as it had caused his lordship wouldn't hardly credit, with everyone rushing out-of-doors to get a sight of it, and then rushing in again because it was so low they thought it was going to come down right in the middle of the town. "Which of course it didn't, as any but a set of jobbernolls would have known it wouldn't, my lord. By what I hear it came down between here and King's Langley. And if there's a boy in the place, barring my own lads, it's more than I'd bargain for! They was all off, and others old enough to know better than to take part in such foolishness, for they might have known they wouldn't see the balloon land, and where's the sense of running miles to look at it on the ground?"

"How long ago was it when it came down?" Jessamy asked eagerly.

"Well, I can't rightly say, sir," replied the landlord, smiling indulgently at him. "It was an hour ago when it came by the town—maybe an hour-and-a-half."

Jessamy's shining eyes lifted to Alverstoke's; a smile wavered on his lips; he said simply: "The *relief* of it! How far is that place—King's Langley?"

"Just a matter of five miles, sir. But I don't believe all I hear, and there's no saying that the balloon did come down there. All *I* say is that none of those cod's heads that went chasing after it has come back yet, so if they ain't still gawking at it where it lays they're maybe following it into the next county!"

"I see," said Alverstoke. "You can draw me a tankard of your home-brewed. Order what you like, Jessamy: I'm going to have a word with Curry."

He strode out of the inn as he spoke, to find Curry and the head ostler leading the grays towards the stables. He ran his experienced eye over his horses. They were sweating, but not distressed. Curry said, with pride: "Prime 'uns, my lord! Didn't I say to your lordship they'd go well upon wind?"

Alverstoke nodded, but Curry saw that he was slightly frowning, and looked an enquiry. "They've taken no hurt, my lord. I'll give 'em some warm gruel, and—"

"Yes, see that done, and give the ostler exact instructions. I'm taking you on with me."

"Very good, my lord. Nothing wrong, I do hope?"

"I'm not sure. No need to say anything to Mr Jessamy, but there's no question that when we last saw the balloon it was being borne off its course. Well, if the wind took it, the country is fairly open, and it may have made a safe landing."

"No reason why it shouldn't have, my lord."

"None, but it appears that none of the people who ran off to see it have yet returned. If there was nothing more to look at than the boat, and the empty bag, what should be keeping them so long?"

"Well, your lordship knows what boys are!" suggested Curry.

"I do indeed! But they were not all boys. I may have become infected by Mr Jessamy's alarms, but I've a feeling I may need you. Fifteen minutes!"

He went back into the inn, to find Jessamy refreshing himself from a large tankard. He lowered it, with a sigh of satisfaction, and handed a similar one to the Marquis, saying: "Lord, I was thirsty! Here's yours, sir: the ale-draper says it's a regular knock-me-down!"

"In that case, you will shortly be top-heavy, and I shall abandon you, so that you may sleep it off at your leisure."

"Well, I thought I might be a trifle overtaken, so I ordered a half-and-half for myself."

"Thank God for that!"

Jessamy laughed, but said, a littly shyly: "I expect

I've plagued you enough already, with my—my distempered freaks, sir."

"Now, what can I have said to make you think so?" demanded Alverstoke, in astonished accents.

"You may choose to poke bogey at me, but you know very well, sir! *Such* a set-down—! I—I am afraid I took snuff, and I shouldn't have done so!"

"Handsomely said!" approved Alverstoke. "But if you took *that* for one of my set-downs—!"

"Well, if it wasn't I hope you'll never give me one," said Jessamy frankly. "Sir, when do we set forward again? I have been thinking, and I shouldn't wonder at it if we met them on their way back to London. Except that—what becomes of the balloon?"

"I haven't the least idea. It's a nice point, I admit."

"It occurred to me a minute ago. They can't carry it, and they can't fill the bag again, because where would they get the hydrogen? And all those casks couldn't be brought on the wagon—at least, they could, but it would take them all day to get here, even if they knew where the thing meant to make its descent, which they never do."

"Very true. One can only assume that they must have it conveyed by farm-cart, or some such thing, to a place of safety—leaving it there to be recovered later."

"Well, if that's how they manage, doesn't it *prove* what a crackbrained thing it is?" said Jessamy scornfully. "A fine way to go on a journey! Getting set down in a field, very likely miles from where you wish to be, and then being obliged to pack the boat, and the bag, and the anchors, and all the rest of the gear, on to a cart, before you trudge off to find some sort of a carriage!"

"A sobering thought," agreed Alverstoke. "I fancy, however, that balloons are not intended for mere travel. Are you ready to set forward again?"

Jessamy jumped up at once, and went out into the yard. He was critically inspecting the new team when Alverstoke joined him, exchanging with Curry various disparaging remarks about job-horses. He was surprised when Curry sprang up behind, but beyond saying that he had thought Alverstoke had meant to leave him in charge of the grays, he made no comment. His mind was preoccupied; and he only nodded when, a mile out of Watford, Alverstoke acidly animadverted on leaders which had acquired the habit of hanging off.

No other vehicles than the Mail, and a private chaise, both southward bound and travelling fast, were encountered; and the only pedestrian was a venerable gentleman in a smock, who disclaimed all knowledge of balloons, adding that he didn't hold with them, or with any other nasty, newfangled inventions; but at the end of the second mile Alverstoke saw a cluster of people ahead, and drew up alongside them. They were mostly of immature age, and they had emerged on to the post-road through a farm-gate opening on to undulating pastures. They were talking animatedly amongst themselves; and (said the Marquis sardonically) bore all the appearance of persons capable of running two miles to marvel at a deflated balloon.

So, indeed, it proved; and they had been richly rewarded. Not that any of them had been in time to *see* anything; but there were them as had, and (as several voices assured his lordship) a rare bumble-broth it must have been, such as hadn't happened in these parts, not since anyone could remember. Dicked in the nob they were, surely, for what must they do, with a good three acres of clear ground under them, but bear down on a clump of trees, and get all tangled up in the branches. Oh, it was a terrible accident! for although one of the gentlemen climbed down safe enough, the other, which was trying to help the nipperkin they had with them, made a right mull of it, by all accounts, and broke his arm; while, as for the nipperkin, he came crashing through the branches, with blood all over him, and was taken up for dead. "Which," a senior member of the gathering told the Marquis, "wasn't so laughable, nor anything like."

"Where?" Jessamy demanded hoarsely. *"Where?"*

"Oh, you won't see nothing *now,* sir! They was all gone off to Monk's Farm above an hour ago, with the nipperkin stretched out on a hurdle. Well, all of us which came from Watford was too late to get a sight of aught but the balloon, with its ropes caught up in the elm-tree, and there's no saying when they'll start in to get it down, which don't hardly seem worth waiting for. So we come away."

"I seen the doctor drive up in his gig!" piped up an urchin.

"Ay, so you did, and got a clout from Miss Judbrook for your pains, poke-nose!"

"Where is the farm?" asked Alverstoke, interrupting the goodnatured mirth caused by this last remark.

He was told that it was at Clipperfield: a statement immediately qualified by the ominous words, *as you might say;* but when he asked for more precise information all that he was able to gather from the conflicting, and generally incomprehensible, directions offered by half-a-dozen persons was that the lane leading to the village joined the post-road at King's Langley.

Cutting short the efforts of a helpful youth to describe the exact situation of Monk's Farm, he drove on, saying: "We shall more easily discover the whereabouts of the farm when we reach Clipperfield." He glanced briefly at Jessamy, and added: "Pluck up! There's a doctor with him, remember!"

Jessamy, ashen-pale, trying desperately to overcome the long shudders that shook his thin frame, managed to speak. "They said—they said—"

"I heard them!" interrupted Alverstoke. "He was taken up for dead, and he was covered with blood. Good God, boy, have you lived all your life in the country without discovering that illiterates always invest the most trifling accident with the ingredients of melodrama? *Taken up for dead* may be translated into *was stunned by his fall;* and as for *covered in blood*—! What the devil should make him bleed but scratching his face, when he missed his hold, and tumbled down through the branches?"

Achieving a gallant smile, Jessamy said: "Yes—of course! Or—or a nose-bleed!"

"Very likely!"

"Yes. But—" He stopped, unable for a moment to command his voice, and then said jerkily: "Not—a *trifling*—accident!"

"No, I am afraid he may have broken a bone or two," replied Alverstoke coolly. "Let us hope that it will be a lesson to him! Now, my young friend, I am going to do what you have been wishing me to do from the start of this expedition: spring 'em!"

As he spoke, the team broke into a canter, quickly lengthening their strides to a gallop. At any other time, Jessamy's attention would have been riveted by the consummate skill displayed by a top-sawyer driving strange horses at a splitting pace along a winding road, too narrow for safety, and by no means unfrequented; but, in the event, a dreadful anxiety absorbed him, and his only impulse, when Alverstoke faultlessly took a hill in time, or checked slightly at a sudden bend, was to urge him to a faster speed. It was not he, but Curry, grimly hanging on, who shut his eyes when Alverstoke feather-edged a blind corner, leaving an inch to spare between the phaeton and an oncoming coach; and it was Curry, who, when the first straggling cottages of King's Langley came into sight, gasped: "For God's sake, my lord—!"

But even as these words were jerked out of him, he regretted them, for the Marquis was already checking his horses. As the team entered the little town at a brisk trot, he said, over his shoulder: "Yes, Curry? What is it?"

"Nothing, my lord! Except that I thought you was downright obfuscated, for which I'm sure I beg your lordship's pardon!" responded his henchman, availing himself of the licence accorded to an old and trusted retainer.

"You should! I'm not even bright in the eye."

"Look! There's a signpost!" Jessamy said suddenly, leaning forward in his seat.

"Clipperfield and Sarratt!" read Curry.

His lordship turned the corner in style, but was forced immediately to rein the team in to a sober pace. The lane was winding and narrow, bordered by unkempt hedges, and so deeply rutted, so full of holes, that Curry remarked, with dour humour, that they might think themselves lucky the month was June, and not February, when the lane would have been a regular hasty-pudding. At the end of two difficult miles, which stretched Jessamy's nerves to snapping-point, he said: "Cross-road ahead, my lord, and I can see a couple of chimneys off to the left. This'll be it!"

Whatever excitement had been aroused in Clipperfield by the recent accident had apparently died away. There was only one person to be seen: a stout woman, engaged in cutting a cabbage in the patch of garden in front of her cottage. Having, as she informed him, far too much to do without troubling herself with balloons, she was unable to give Jessamy any news of Felix; but she told Alverstoke that Monk's Farm lay about a mile down the road, towards Buckshill. She pointed with her knife to the south, and said that he couldn't miss it: a statement which he mistrusted, but which turned out to be true.

It was set a hundred yards back from the lane, a large, rambling house of considerable antiquity, with its barns, its pigstyes, and its cattle-byre clustered round it. Before its open door stood the doctor's gig, in charge of his man. Alverstoke turned in through the big white gate, and drove up to the farm.

Before the phaeton had stopped, Jessamy sprang down from it, and almost ran into the house. A shrill voice was heard demanding to know who he might be, and what his business was. "Ah!" said the Marquis. "The lady who clouted young—er—poke-nose, I fancy!"

stretched Jessamy's nerves to snapping-point. He said:
"Cross-road ahead, my lord, and I caught a couple of
chimneys off to the left. This'll be in Chipp——

XXI

The door of the farmhouse opened on to an unevenly
flagged passage, at the end of which a flight of worn
oak stairs rose to the upper floor. Jessamy, hesitating
after his impetuous entrance, found himself confronted
by an angular woman, whose sharp-featured countenance wore all the signs of chronic ill-temper. In answer to her angry enquiry, he stammered: "I beg pardon! It's my brother! The——the boy who was carried in
here!"

This reply, far from mollifying her, had much the
same effect as a match applied to a train of gunpowder.
Her eyes snapped, her colour rose, and she said: "Oh,
he is, is he? Then I'm mightily glad to see you, young
sir, and I trust you've come to take him away! This
house isn't a hospital, nor a public inn neither, and I've
got too much to do already without looking after sick
boys, let me tell you! What's more, I'm not a nurse, and
I won't take the responsibility, say what you like!"

At this point, in what threatened to be a lengthy
diatribe, she stopped, and her jaw dropped. Alverstoke
was standing on the threshold. At all times an imposing
figure, he was, on this occasion, a startling one, for
although he wore a long driving-coat of white drab,
with a number of shoulder-capes, it was unbuttoned,
and revealed the exquisite attire he habitually wore in
London, which included an extremely elegant waistcoat, the palest of pantaloons, and highly polished Hessian boots. In Bond Street he would have been complete to a shade; in a country village he looked quite
out of place; but Miss Judbrook was almost as much
impressed as she was astonished.

He said, pleasantly, but with a faint touch of hauteur:
"Why should you, indeed? I fancy you must be Miss

277

Judbrook: I am Lord Alverstoke. I should like to see
the doctor, if you please."

Miss Judbrook was so much overcome that she
dropped a slight curtsy, and said: "Yes, my lord!" However, she was a redoubtable woman, and she made a
swift recovery. "I hope I'm not an unfeeling woman,
my lord, nor one as doesn't know her duty, but it's
none of my business to be nursing boys which fall out
of balloons, and I can't and I won't undertake it, as
Judbrook should have known, instead of having him
brought here without a word to me, let alone calling
Betty out of the dairy to sit with him! *I'm* not going
to do her work, so he needn't think it! I'm sure I'm very
sorry for the young gentleman, but as for having him
laid up here, as bad as he is, and having to be sat with,
and waited on hand and foot, I haven't the time nor
the patience to do it, which I told Dr Elcot to his head.
And if Mrs Hucknall sets foot inside this house I leave
it, and that's flat!"

"Yes, well, all these matters can no doubt be arranged—when I have had word with the doctor!" said
Alverstoke.

Miss Judbrook sniffed resentfully, but his evident
boredom disconcerted her. She said, rather more mildly:
"I'm sure I hope so, my lord! The doctor's in my
parlour—mussing it up with his splints and his ban-
dages, and bowls of water, and I don't know what more
beside! This way!"

She opened a door on the left of the passage, saying:
"This is my Lord Alverstoke, wanting to see you, doctor,
and the little boy's brother. And I'll be obliged to you
not to slop any more water on to my new carpet!"

"Oh, go away, woman, go away!" said the doctor
testily.

Contrary to Jessamy's eager expectation, the doctor
and the second of the two aeronauts were the only people in the room. The aeronaut, his brow adorned with
sticking-plaster, was sitting in a chair by the table, while
the doctor was bandaging his splinted forearm.

"Felix?" Jessamy blurted out. "My brother?"

The doctor paused in his task to direct a penetrating
glance at him from under his bushy brows. "His broth-

er, are you? Well, there's no need for you to be in a stew: he hasn't managed to kill himself!" He transferred his gaze to Alverstoke, and favoured him with a nod. "Good-day to you, my lord. Are you related to the boy?"

"Cousin, and—er—guardian!" said Alverstoke.

The doctor, continuing his work, said: "Then you'll give me leave to tell you, my lord, that you're a mighty careless guardian!"

"So, indeed, it would appear," agreed Alverstoke. "How badly is the boy hurt?"

"Early days to tell you that. He suffered a severe concussion, cut his face open, and sprained a wrist, but there are no bones broken, barring a couple of ribs. Badly bruised, of course. He came round half-an-hour ago. Complained of headache. Which might mean—"

"That would be the altitude!" said his present patient. "Many people suffer from acute headache when—"

"I'm not an ignoramus!" growled the doctor. "Keep still!"

"Is he—has he—injured his brain?" asked Jessamy, as though he dreaded to hear the answer.

The doctor shot another of his piercing looks at him. "No reason to think so. He wasn't himself—couldn't expect him to be—but he knew what had happened to him, I think. Sang out that he *couldn't,* and some gabble about falling."

Again the aeronaut intervened, addressing himself to Alverstoke. "I thought he was safe, my lord! Everything was going well till we started the descent! That was when we veered. You see, when you drop down close to the earth—"

"Yes, I understand that you frequently meet winds that were not encountered at higher altitudes," interrupted Alverstoke. "Also that you were blown amongst trees. Never mind why! just tell me, if you please, what happened when you became entangled with—an elm tree, wasn't it?"

"Yes—that is, it may have been an elm, my lord! I don't know anything about trees. When Mr Oulton saw that we weren't going to clear it, which we should have done, if the valve hadn't stuck, when he tried to close

it, he shouted to me to grab hold of a branch, and
climb out of the boat on to it. 'You first, Beenish, and
lend the boy a hand!' he told me. Which I did, and it
was easy enough, and there wasn't much danger either,
as long as the weight was taken out of the boat, so that
it wouldn't break through the branches, and crash down
on to the ground. The valve being open, and the gas
escaping pretty fast, there was no fear the balloon would
rise again, you understand. And the little chap wasn't
a scrap afraid! That I'll swear to! Cool as a cucumber,
he was, and thinking of nothing but ways of controlling
balloons! 'Don't be in a worry about me!' he said. 'I
shall do!' Which I never doubted, my lord! There was
Mr Oulton, helping him to climb out of the boat, and I
was just thinking he wouldn't want me to lend him a
hand when he suddenly seemed to lose his head. At
least—I don't know, but I can't think what else it could
have been, for it looked to me as if he had hold of the
branch all right and tight, though it all happened so
quickly, of course, that I can't be sure of that. All I do
know is that he cried out: 'I can't!' and—and fell! My
lord, I swear I did my best! I tried to grab hold of
him, but I lost my balance, and the next thing was that
I fell out of the tree!"

Jessamy, who had been listening to him in gathering
incredulity, exclaimed: *"Felix?* Why, he climbs like a
cat!"

"Young man," said the doctor, "if you don't know
why your brother couldn't grasp the branch I can tell
you! His hands were numb with cold, that's why!"

"O my God!" uttered Beenish. "He never said—"

"Don't suppose he knew it. Knew they were frozen.
Didn't know he couldn't use 'em. Only a boy—excited
too!"

Beenish, looking at the Marquis, was plainly torn between a feeling of guilt and a desire to exculpate himself
from blame. He said: "My lord, it wasn't our fault!
Maybe I should have sent him about his business, but
he wasn't doing any harm, and as Mr Oulton said himself, he's such an intelligent little fellow—not like most
of his age, only wanting to see the balloon go up for the

marvel of it, and not caring for what makes it rise, or—"

"Pray don't think I blame you!" said the Marquis. "If anyone is to blame it is I, for he was in my charge."

"Not your blame! Mine—mine!" Jessamy said, in a stifled voice.

"The thing was, my lord, we never suspected what he meant to do! But I can't deny I did say we should be happy to take him up with us, never dreaming—He begged us to, you see, and Mr Oulton answered him a bit sharply, telling him he was much too young, and—well, he looked so *hurt*—if your lordship knows what I mean?—"

"I know exactly what you mean," said the Marquis grimly.

"Well, that's how it was, my lord! I told him we couldn't take him without his father's consent—and Mr Oulton bore me out! Yes, and it was him which said if we took up a boy which was under age, without his Pa's consent, we should be clapped into jail, not me!" A reminiscent grin stole over Mr Beenish's face. "And damme if the little rogue didn't throw it up at him, when we'd hauled him into the boat! 'It's all hollow!' he told Mr Oulton, game as a pebble! 'You won't be clapped into jail,' he said, 'because I haven't *got* a father!' " A chuckle escaped him. "Pluck to the backbone!" he said. *"His* nerves won't ever lose their steel! When I saw him clinging to that rope, and the balloon rising fast, as they do, my lord, I thought he was bound to take fright, and do something silly, and much good it was for us to shout to him to hold tight! But he did, and we got him in, like you saw. Ay, and he enjoyed every minute of the flight, even though the teeth were chattering in his head!" A groan from Jessamy made him turn his head. "We did the best we could, sir, but there wasn't much we *could* do."

"No, I know. And you saved him. I—I am very grateful. Sir, where is he? Can I see him?"

"Oh, yes, you can see him!" replied the doctor. "He's upstairs, snugly tucked into bed: first door to the right of the stairs. You go and sit with him, and tell the girl I left there that she can go back to the dairy. He's sound asleep, and don't you dare try to rouse him! And don't fall into despair because his head's bound up! I've had to put a couple of stitches in his face!"

"No," said Jessamy humbly. "If he wakes shall I call you?"

"He won't wake: I've drugged him, for I want him to sleep for as long as possible. Off with you!" He watched Jessamy hurry out of the room, grimaced at Alverstoke, and adjusted the sling he had knotted round Beenish's neck. "I've done with you now," he said. "Let it be a lesson to you! If the Almighty had meant men to fly He'd have provided us with wings! You'd best sit still for a while."

"Oh, this is nothing!" Beenish said cheerfully. "I'm in a capital way, doctor—thanking you for what you've done! I only wish the little fellow hadn't had the worst of it. I'll be off now to see if they've rescued the balloon."

"More guts than brains!" said the doctor, as the door shut behind Beenish. "Balloons—! What next, pray?"

"Felix might furnish you with the answer: I can't," replied Alverstoke, stripping off his driving-coat, and casting it over a chair. "Now, doctor, if you please! How seriously is that boy hurt?"

The doctor, packing the instruments of his trade into his bag, said gruffly: "Ask me tomorrow, my lord. I wasn't shamming it when I told you it was early days yet. Not but what I would have done so, while that brother of his was here! I know his kind, and I don't want him on my hands as well. More nerves than flesh! Well, the other one—what do you call him? Felix?—ay, well, he's broken no bones but what I told you, and you've no need to trouble yourself over a couple of ribs. He's suffered a severe shock, however—which is why I've given him pretty well as much laudanum as he can hold! In general, I don't do so—don't believe in it!—but in such cases as this it's of the first importance to keep the patient quiet. I don't set much store by the headpains, but there's no knowing yet, and if you're thinking of removing him from here, my lord, you'll do it against my advice!"

"Rest assured, doctor, that I have no such intention!"

"Good! But, unless I'm much mistaken, the boy will need careful nursing, and there's the rub. Judbrook is a decent fellow, but that sister of his can't be depended on, and the devil of it is I can't send in a nurse. There's only one hereabouts, and she has a cross-birth on her hands—"

"If," interrupted his lordship, "you are referring to a Mrs Hucknall, we need not waste our time in discussing her merits! Miss Judbrook has already informed me that when Mrs Hucknall enters the house, *she* will leave it. Let me reassure you on one point at least! Tomorrow, either Felix's aunt, or, more probably, his sister, Miss Merriville, will come here to nurse him. Now tell me, without roundaboutation, what it is that you fear!"

Dr Elcot, strapping his bag, did not answer for a moment. He was frowning heavily, and at last said: "That boy, my lord, was cold to the marrow!"

"My guardianship is of very recent date, but I have it, on the authority of Miss Merriville, that Felix is subject to some chest-complaint, which she called bronchitis."

The doctor snorted. "Oh, yes! A new word for an old complaint! If nothing worse than that befalls him, he may think himself fortunate! I'm saying no more until I know more, my lord. We shall see! Polly Judbrook is a cross-grained spinster, but at least she had enough sense to wrap the boy up in blankets, and to put a hot brick to his feet. He's a stout-looking lad, too—an excellent constitution, I should suppose!" He added brusquely: "Send for one of your London practitioners, if you choose, my lord: I've no objection! He can tell you no more, at this present, than I can, and he wouldn't give you any other directions. Keep the boy warm, and quiet, let him drink as much barley-water as he likes—I've told Polly to make some, and she'll do it, never fear!—and, if he should be feverish, give him a saline draught! I'll make one up, and send my man over with it. No hot wine, mind, or any other old woman's remedy!" He paused, and eyed the Marquis doubtfully. "I take it your lordship means to remain with him?"

"Naturally! But as I have little or no experience of illness, and have never before attempted to nurse a sick person, I shall be obliged to you, doctor, if you will tell me exactly what I am to expect, and to do; and where, in case of need, you are to be found."

"Anyone here could tell you that; and if there were to be any alarming change in the boy's condition Judbrook would send one of his lads to fetch me. I might come, too," he said, with a flash of mordant humour, "for you look to me like a rational man, my lord: not one to fly into a great fuss because a sick boy might become a trifle delirious when the drug wears off. His case isn't desperate. I'll visit him in the morning."

When the doctor had gone away, the Marquis spent several minutes considering his situation. It was certainly unusual; and while he was prepared to deal with it without losing either his head or his sangfroid, he could have wished, glancing at the few scribbled reminders the doctor had given him, that these instructions had been rather more extensive. He looked a little ruefully at the paper, before folding it, and slipping it into his pocketbook, and going out to find Curry.

"Properly in the briars we are, my lord!" said Curry. "They tell me—Betty, and the old griffin—that Master Felix is going to cut his stick, but I hope and trust that ain't so?"

"No, I think not. Curry, I'm going to send you back to London."

"You are, my lord?" Curry said, staring at him.

"Yes, and as soon as possible," said Alverstoke, drawing out his watch. "You should be there well before midnight: change horses as often as you think desirable! You are going to take Mr Jessamy with you: he can do no good here, and Miss Merriville might well believe that matters are far more serious than they are if neither he nor I returned to London tonight. He may even be of assistance to her, and can at all events bear her company tomorrow, when I am very sure she will come to nurse Master Felix."

"If he don't throw her into gloom," said Curry. "He was fretting like a fly in a tar-box all the way here, my lord!"

"He was indeed! But, unless I am much mistaken in him, he won't do so when he feels himself to be re-

sponsible for her. You'll drive back to Watford in the
phaeton, and leave it there. The rest of the journey by
post: you can take this!"

Accepting the roll of bills, Curry demurred a little.
"You might need 'em, my lord!"

"Not immediately. You will bring me a fresh supply
tomorrow: Mr Trevor will attend to that. When you
reach Upper Wimpole Street, try for a word with Miss
Merriville! Inform her that my travelling-carriage will
take her up tomorrow at whatever hour she may appoint, but don't allow her to set out tonight! I think she
has too much sense to do so. When you have arranged
matters with her, go on to Alverstoke House, and give
Mr Trevor the letter I am about to write to him. He'll
do the rest. You will escort Miss Merriville here—or
possibly Miss Winsham—tomorrow, as far as to Watford, where you may pick up the grays, and my
phaeton, and bring them to me here. And understand
this, Curry! I am putting you in command of this
journey, and if Miss Merriville should talk of hiring a
postchaise, or some such thing, you will tell her that *my*
orders are that she is to travel in my carriage—which
will certainly be needed when it becomes possible to
remove Master Felix from this place. Now try if you
can procure a pen, some ink, and some writing-paper
from that extremely disobliging woman, and bring
them to me in the parlour! It might be as well to puff
off my consequence, perhaps!"

"Oh, I've done that, my lord!" returned Curry, grin-
ning at him. "A regular brimstone, *she* is! But I said to
her: 'What his lordship wants,' I said, 'he'll pay for—
handsome!' which made her change her note, my lord!"

"I'm happy to hear it. Tell her to hire a woman from
the village—as many women as she wants—and hang
it up to me! Where's her brother? Have you seen him?"

"Not yet, I haven't, my lord. He went off with some
of his lads to help get that balloon packed up, and
loaded on to his wagon—which is another thing Miss
Brimstone don't like!"

"You astonish me!" said his lordship.

The writing-materials which Curry presently brought
to him in the parlour left much to be desired, the ink

being muddy, the pen in urgent need of repair, and the
paper both dog-eared and a trifle grimy. His lordship
made the best of them, but revolted against a selection
of coloured wafers, merely folding the note he had
written to Charles Trevor. He might be forced to write
with a spluttering pen on dirty paper, but for no consideration would he seal his letter with a wafer of
virulent pink, green, or blue.

Handing his missive to Curry, he was about to go
upstairs when he was delayed by the arrival on the
scene of Mr Oulton, accompanied by the farmer. He
was obliged to listen to Oulton's explanations, accusations, and excuses with what patience he could muster;
but he found Judbrook to be a man of few words and
simple goodwill. Judbrook said: "You've only to tell me
what you want, my lord, and I'll see you get it. My
sister has her crotchets, but it's me as is master here,
never you fear!"

Felix had been carried up to a large, low-pitched
room, and was lying in a four-poster bed, hung with
crimson curtains, and covered with a patchwork quilt.
He was heavily asleep, breathing stertorously, his head
bandaged, and looking so small and broken that Alverstoke's anger melted, and he was aware only of pity.
He stood watching Felix for a moment, and then turned
his head to find that Jessamy's eyes were fixed on his
face, a painful question in them. As he met them, he
realized suddenly that there was more than a question
in them: there was trust as well. This queer boy, who
was sometimes so much older than his years, not only
trusted him, but was depending on him too, confident
that he, who had all his life evaded irksome responsibilities, had seldom exerted himself on another's behalf,
and knew nothing about sickrooms, was competent to
take charge of Felix, himself, the doctor, and even the
hostile Miss Judbrook. It was the height of absurdity,
but his lordship was not much amused: he thought Jessamy's faith in him rendered him almost as pathetic a
figure as his brother. If the boy only knew how little
he wanted to accept the charge laid upon him, and how
uneasily aware of his unfitness for it he was—! As well
that he didn't know it, perhaps!

He smiled at Jessamy, and said, in a lowered voice: "We might have guessed he would come off with nothing worse than a couple of broken ribs, and a cut face, might we not? Little devil!"

There was a lightening of anxiety, but Jessamy said: "The doctor said it was too early to be sure. He looks dreadfully bad—and the way he's breathing. . . ."

"Merely because he's heavily drugged," said Alverstoke.

"Oh! Are you sure, sir?"

"Yes," Alverstoke replied, salving his conscience with the reflection that truth was of less importance than the need to allay Jessamy's fears. "As for what the doctor said, he shares your own apprehension. It would be marvellous indeed, you know, if Felix didn't contract a very severe cold after having been exposed as he was. Therefore, my child, the most immediate need is to fetch his sister. She will know just what to do for him."

"Yes—oh, yes! I have been wishing that she was here! She always knows! But how—"

"I am going to send you back to London to bring her here tomorrow," Alverstoke said.

Jessamy recoiled. "Oh, no! No, no, I won't leave him! How could you think—"

"I am thinking of Frederica, not of you, Jessamy."

"Yes, yes, but—cannot you go, sir, and leave me to take care of Felix? It ought to be me!"

"You are mistaken: he was in my charge, and mine must be the responsibility of taking care of him." He saw that Jessamy was looking stubborn, and added quizzically: "Do you think you could do that better than I could—and shall?"

"No! I didn't mean that! You'll know just what to do, if he wakes, and grows restless, and—and he'll mind you better. But—Oh, couldn't Curry go, sir?"

"Curry is going. He is putting the horses to now. You will dine at Watford, and go on post from there."

"Dine! I couldn't swallow a mouthful! And why must I go as well as Curry?"

"Hush! not so loud! You are going to be of help to Frederica, and to reassure her. Don't fly into one of your ways! Consider instead how uneasy she must be if neither you nor I returned to London tonight! Curry could never convince her that Fe'ix's case was not desperate. She won't think it extraordinary that I have stayed with Felix, I assure you; but if you stay too she will imagine him to be at death's door—as well she might! As for not dining, you have eaten nothing since breakfast, and it would not be very helpful of you to arrive in Upper Wimpole Street in a fainting condition. And, really, my dear boy, to starve yourself because Felix has knocked himself up would be just a trifle melodramatic, don't you think?"

A burning flush rose in Jessamy's thin cheeks; he hung his head, muttering: "I'm sorry! I didn't mean to fall into a—a distempered freak! If you think it's my duty to go, I will."

"Well, I do think it. She may need you. There will be arrangements to be made, I daresay a score of things to be done. She may even wish you to remain in London, to be with Charis, for she certainly won't care to leave her alone, and as far as I can discover, your aunt spends her whole time in Harley Street."

"And Harry has gone off with his bacon-brained friend to Wells, for the races!" said Jessamy bitterly. "Just when he is most needed!"

"He can scarcely be blamed for not having foreseen that he would be needed. You mustn't think I don't value Harry, but I can't but feel that if I stood in Frederica's shoes I should look to you for support rather than to him."

The flush rose again, but this time from gratification. "Th-thank you!" Jessamy stammered. "I don't think— But I'll do my best! And if Frederica does wish me to stay with Charis I—I will!" He drew a breath, and said heroically: "In fact, I'll *offer* to!" Doubt shook him, and his anxious look returned. "Only—Sir, will you, if you please, tell me exactly what I must do? I mean, about postchaises, and hiring the boys, and how much it will cost? And—and I'm afraid I haven't enough blunt for *my* journey!"

"Curry will take care of that, and there will be no need for you to hire a chaise for Frederica: she will come here in my travelling-carriage, which will remain here until Felix can be taken home. It will be far more comfortable for him, you know, than a chaise."

"Yes, *indeed* it will be!" Jessamy said, raising eyes brimming with gratitude to his face. "Thank you! You —you think of *everything,* sir! I'm so *very* much obliged to you! I'll do *exactly* what you tell me to!"

Alverstoke's smile was a little twisted, but he only said: "Curry will tell you what my orders are. Go down to him now: it's time you were gone."

Jessamy nodded, but lingered for a moment, looking down at Felix. He turned away, biting his lips. "Yes, sir. I—I *know* he'll be safe with you, of course! It's only that—You won't leave him, will you? Oh, no! I beg pardon! I know you won't!"

"You may be very sure I won't," Alverstoke replied, gently pushing him towards the door. "Though I may be strongly tempted to do so when he wakes up, and tries to tell me how one might propel a balloon by the use of steam!"

Jessamy laughed rather shakily, gripped his hand for an instant, and went quickly away.

The Marquis shut the door, and, after glancing at Felix, walked over to the leaded casement. Curry had brought the phaeton up to the house; and in another minute Jessamy emerged, climbed into it, and Curry gave the horses the office. The Marquis watched until the phaeton was out of sight; then turned, and went back to the four-poster, looking down at Felix.

It was hardly surprising, he thought, that the boy's appearance should have dismayed his brother. It was not the bandage round his head which was alarming, or his stertorous breathing, but his immobility, and the position in which he lay, which was on his back, perfectly straight, and with the bedclothes drawn up under his chin. No doubt the doctor had settled him in this position; perhaps the broken ribs made it uncomfortable for him to lie on his side; but it made him look almost as if he had been laid out for burial. The Marquis saw this, but his mind was neither fanciful nor ill-regulated, and he was easily able to maintain his calm. He had formed a good opinion of Dr Elcot, and was content to abide by his pronouncements. Elcot plainly felt uneasy about possible developments, but he did not expect any great change to take place immediately; and he certainly did not consider Felix to be in danger. The Marquis felt that what lay before him was not anxiety but tedium. Hours of it, too! he thought, consulting his watch. And with nothing whatsoever to do, if Felix continued to sleep soundly, but to try to keep awake. Probably the armchair would help him to do that: it looked to be hard and unaccommodating. He remembered that he was engaged to join a convivial party at the Castle Inn that evening. He smiled crookedly, contrasting that engagement with his present situation. It was to be hoped that Charles Trevor would recall this, and make his excuses for him. He would, of course: he never forgot things like that. He would be waiting up for news, too, for Eliza would have told him what had happened, and he would guess that his services might be needed. A most reliable secretary, Charles: he would miss him damnably, but he would have to let him go. Which reminded him that he must bring him to the notice of one of the coming men of affairs.

So his lordship sat down in the armchair, to occupy his mind with consideration of this question.

XXII

It was not long before the Marquis's meditations were interrupted by a gentle scratching on the door. He opened it, to admit Judbrook, who came in, bearing a tray, which he set down stealthily on the table, whispering that, besides the barley water, his sister had sent up a bowl of vinegar and water, in case the poor young gentleman should have the headache. He seemed to be very much concerned, and shook his own head sadly when he looked at Felix. "Eh, he's bad!" he muttered.

"Not, I hope, as bad as he looks. Do you think your sister could send me up some cold meat, or something of that nature?"

"Indeed, my lord, she'll do no such thing, nor wouldn't think of it! She bid me tell you your dinner will be laid out for you in the parlour in half-an-hour, and begs you will excuse it not being what your lordship's used to, her having had no time to dress a joint, or a chicken. We have our own dinner midday," he explained apologetically, "but Polly knows fine how to manage for gentlemen, being as she was housekeeper to a gentleman in London for fifteen years. Which I sometimes wish she was still, because she don't like living in the country, and never did, which is what makes her so maggoty! Still, she thought it was her duty, when my missis died, and she's right enough at heart, my lord, for all her crotchets. It was me bringing the young gentleman in without a word to her which set her on end, her being one as likes to act contrary. Though how I was to ask her leave, when I was in my Three-acre field, which was where it happened, my lord, and all of a quarter-of-a-mile from here, I *don't* know, nor she neither! But, there!" A slow smile crept over his face, and he said, with more truth than he knew: "Your lordship knows what females are!"

"None better," agreed his lordship. "I trust I shall be able to come to terms with Miss Judbrook, however—which is a matter I wish to discuss with you. As for my dinner, pray tell her not to put herself to any trouble over it! Cold meat and cheese will do very well. But bring it to me here, if you please!"

"I was thinking that I could stay with the young gentleman while your lordship was in the parlour?"

Alverstoke shook his head. "No. Very obliging of you, but if the boy were to wake, and see only a strange face, it might alarm him," he said tactfully.

"Just as you say, my lord. There's just one other thing, which—Well, I'm fairly put about to know what to offer your lordship to drink!" Judbrook disclosed. "Barring the cowslip-wine Polly makes—and she says it ain't fitting—we don't have any wine in the house. I could send one of my lads down to the alehouse, but I doubt—"

"On no account! Unless you have no beer in the house either? That's all I want—and I *do* want that!"

"Oh, if that's so, my lord—!" said Judbrook, his mind relieved of care. "I'll bring you up a mug straight!"

He also brought up a second tray, loaded with the mute witnesses to his sister's mettle; and by the time the Marquis had disposed of a meal which began with a bowl of excellent soup, and included a dish of hasty mutton, and two pigeons roasted on a spit, the long summer's day had begun to close in, and he had had the satisfaction of seeing his charge stir a little, slightly altering his position, and turning his head on the pillow. He then entered into lengthy negotiations with the farmer, whose reluctance to accept any payment for his hospitality would, under different circumstances, have bored him intolerably; and sent for Miss Judbrook, to compliment her on her culinary skill, in the hope that a little flattery now would, later, benefit Frederica. She gave him no reason to congratulate himself on this manoeuvre, for although she was civil, her countenance remained forbidding, and never more so than when he told her that she would shortly be relieved of all responsibility by the arrival of Miss Merriville at Monk's

Farm. Judbrook then showed him where his own bed-chamber was situated, adjured him to rouse him at need, supplied him with a number of candles, and left him to while away the night-hours as best he might, only reappearing (in his bedgown, for which he blushfully begged pardon) to give his lordship a bottle containing the saline draught brought by the doctor's man.

The Marquis resigned himself to hours of tedium; but he had not many of them to endure. Long before even the earliest farm-worker was awake, he would readily have compounded with fate for a week of tedium in exchange for the anxiety which beset him as soon as the effects of laudanum began to wear off.

At first only restless, muttering unintelligibly, but sinking back into a slumber, Felix grew steadily harder to quieten, passing from a state of semi-consciousness to a confused realization of his aches and pains, and of his strange surroundings. He uttered his sister's name, from a parched throat, and struggled to free his arms from the blankets, hurting his sprained wrist, and giving a sharp cry; but when Alverstoke took his other hand in a firm clasp, and spoke to him, he seemed to recognize him. His fingers clung like claws; he stared up into Alverstoke's face, and panted: "Don't let me fall! don't let me fall!"

"No, I won't," Alverstoke said, stretching out his hand for Dr Elcot's saline draught, which he had poured out at the first sign of agitation. "You are perfectly safe now." He disengaged himself, and raised Felix, setting the glass to his lips, and saying: "Here's a drink for you! Open your mouth!"

"I want Frederica!" Felix said, fretfully turning his head away.

He responded, however, to the note of command in Alverstoke's voice when he said again: "Open your mouth, Felix! Come! do as you're bid!" and Alverstoke, whose small experience of medicines included none that were not extremely nasty, gave him no chance to recoil from the dose, but tilted it ruthlessly down his throat.

Felix choked over it, but after his first slightly tear-

ful indignation, he seemed to grow more rational. Alverstoke lowered him on to his pillow, and withdrew his
arm. "That's better!" he said.

"I want Frederica!" reiterated Felix.

"You shall have her directly," promised Alverstoke.

"I want her *now!*" stated Felix. "*Tell* her!"

"Yes, I will."

A short silence fell. Alverstoke hoped that Felix was
sliding back into sleep, but just as he was about to
move away from the bed he found that Felix was looking at him, as though trying to bring his face into
focus. Apparently he succeeded, for he murmured, with
a sigh of relief: "Oh, it's you! Don't leave me!"

"No."

"I'm so thirsty!"

Alverstoke raised him again, and he gulped down
the barley-water thankfully; and, this time, when lowered on to his pillow, dropped asleep.

It was an uneasy sleep, however, and of short duration. He woke with a start, and a jumble of words on
his lips. He was evidently in the grip of a nightmare,
and it was not for several moments that Alverstoke's
voice penetrated it. He said then, vaguely: "Cousin Alverstoke," but an instant later moaned that he was cold.
The Marquis began to look a little grim, for the hand
which clutched his was hot and dry. He spoke soothingly, and with good effect: Felix lay quiet for a while, but
he did not shut his blurred eyes. Suddenly he said, in
a troubled voice: "*This* isn't my room! Why am I in this
room? I don't like it! I don't know where I am!"

The Marquis answered matter-of-factly: "You are
with me, Felix."

He spoke instinctively, uttering the first words that
came into his head, and thinking, an instant later, that
they were singularly foolish. But, after blinking at him,
Felix smiled, and said: "Oh, yes! I forgot! You won't
go away, will you?"

"Of course not. Shut your eyes! You are quite safe, I
promise."

"Yes, of course, as long as you're *here,* because then
I shan't fall," murmured Felix hazily. "I know *that!*"

Alverstoke said nothing, and presently had the satisfaction of knowing that Felix was asleep. Carefully withdrawing his hand from the slackened hold on it, he moved away, to alter the position of the candle, so that its flickering light should not fall on Felix's face. It seemed to him that the boy had dropped into a more natural sleep; but his hope that this would endure was speedily dashed, and he did not again indulge it. For the rest of the night Felix, even to his inexperienced eyes, grew steadily worse, his face more flushed, and his pulse alarmingly rapid. There were intervals when he dozed, but they were never of long duration; and when he woke it was always in a state of feverish excitement bordering on delirium. He seemed to be suffering considerable pain; in one of his lucid moments he complained that he "ached all over," but when Alverstoke bathed as much of his brow as was not covered by the bandage, he was relieved to have his hand struck away. "It's not my *head!*" Felix said angrily.

A second dose of the saline mixture produced an alleviation, but Alverstoke hovered a dozen times on the brink of summoning Judbrook, and telling him to send for Dr Elcot. Only the doctor's last words, which had been a warning that Felix might become feverish, and the knowledge that he could still recall the boy's wandering wits, restrained him.

With the dawn, the fever abated a little, but not the pains. Felix wept softly, and moaned: "Frederica, Frederica!" At five o'clock, the Marquis heard the creak of a door being cautiously opened, and went swiftly out of the room to intercept Judbrook, who was tiptoeing along the passage, with his boots in his hand.

Judbrook was very much shocked to learn that Felix, far from going on prosperously, was extremely ill. He promised to send one of his lads to the doctor's house in Hemel Hempstead immediately, saying that it was only a matter of four miles, and the lad could ride there on the cob. He took a look at Felix, and upon hearing that more barley-water was needed, ventered to suggest that a cup of tea might do good. The Marquis felt doubtful, but Felix, whom he had thought to be asleep, said, in the thread of a voice: "I should like that," so he nodded to Judbrook.

"You shall have it in an ant's foot, sir!" said Jud-brook, adding, under his breath: "At all events, it won't do him any harm, my lord!"

The Marquis felt still more doubtful when the tray was brought to him. He was not, like his friend Lord Petersham, a connoisseur, but he profoundly mistrusted the mahogany brew which issued from the pot, and fully expected Felix to reject it. Felix did not, however, and it seemed to refresh him; and when, an hour later, Dr Elcot arrived, he merely said: "As long as you didn't give him hot wine, I've no objection. Now, my lord, before I go in to him, what's amiss? You're look-ing a trifle out of frame yourself: had you a bad night with the boy?"

"A very bad night," replied Alverstoke, somewhat acidly. "As for what's amiss, I trust *you* will supply the answer! He has been extremely feverish, sometimes de-lirious, and he complains all the time of pain—he says it is all over him, but it doesn't appear to be in his head, thank God!"

"Dutch comfort!" growled the doctor.

He stayed for some time in the sickroom; and, at the end of a long and careful examination, said cheerfully, as he drew the bedclothes over Felix again: "Well, young man, I don't doubt you're feeling pretty down pin, but you'll hold for a long trig! Now I'm going to give you something to make you comfortable."

Felix was not delirious, but he was not by any means himself. He had objected violently to the doctor's exami-nation, saying that it hurt him to be touched; and had only submitted when the Marquis had commanded him to do so. He now revolted against the evil-looking potion Dr Elcot had measured into a small glass, and the Marquis, prompted by a significant glance from the doctor, again intervened, taking the glass from Elcot, and administering the dose himself, saying, when Felix jerked his head away: "You are becoming a dead bore, Felix. I dislike bores; so, if you wish me to remain with you, you will do as I bid you—and at once!"

Cowed by this threat, Felix swallowed the potion. He said anxiously, as Alverstoke lowered him, and withdrew his supporting arm: "You won't leave me, will you?"

"No."

Felix seemed to be satisfied; and after a few minutes the lids sank over his eyes. Dr Elcot touched the Marquis on the shoulder, and led the way out of the room. "Children of your own, my lord?" he said, as he closed the door.

"Not to my knowledge."

"Oh! Thought you must have: seem to know how to handle 'em. Well, it's what I expected: rheumatic fever. No use asking me how serious it may be, for I can't tell you yet. What I can tell you is that he needs to be carefully nursed. You told me his sister would be coming to do that: is she to be depended on? You'll pardon me if I'm speaking too freely: it's a matter of the first importance."

"You may repose complete confidence in Miss Merriville," replied Alverstoke. "She is a woman of excellent sense; and she has stood to Felix in the relationship of a mother ever since his childhood. Now, I know nothing of illness, so I must request you to enlighten me. I collect that this rheumatic fever is more serious than I had supposed?"

"It might have serious consequences," replied Elcot. "However, the boy's a fine little fellow, and I should rather think he has an excellent constitution, so we won't alarm his sister. When does she arrive?"

"I can't tell that, but from what I know of her I'm confident she will come as soon as may be possible. She will wish to see you, of course."

"Ay, and I wish to see her! The boy will do well enough for a while: I've given him a paregoric draught, and I expect him to sleep for the better part of the morning. You'd be wise to do the same, my lord!"

"I had liefer shave!" said his lordship.

"Do both!" the doctor recommended.

The Marquis contented himself with the shave. He regarded with considerable misgiving the oldfashioned razor which Judbrook lent him, but although it felt clumsy in his hand its blade was well-honed, and he

managed to shave himself without mishap. Miss Judbrook, meanwhile, restored his creased muslin neckcloth to something approaching respectability; and although he would not entrust his coat to her for pressing
he was able to meet Frederica in tolerably good order.
But he avoided his valet's eye.

She arrived shortly after ten o'clock, in his own well-
sprung and lightly-built travelling-carriage, and she
was unaccompanied. The Marquis lifted her down from
it, and held her for a moment between his strong
hands, saying: "Good girl! I knew you wouldn't delay."

"I didn't leave London as early as I had wished,
but your postilions brought me here like the wind." She
looked up at him, in the frank way he had grown to
love, and said, with a smile in her eyes: "I have been
obliged to thank you so many times, cousin, that there
seem to be no words left."

"You can't think how glad I am to know that!" he
retorted.

"Oh, yes! You think it a dead bore to be thanked—
but I hope you know what is in my heart!"

"No—but I wish I did!"

The smile touched her lips. "Now you are joking
me! I forgive you only because I know you wouldn't
do so, if—if matters were desperate! Tell me! How is
he?"

"Still sleeping. The doctor gave him some sort of a
paregoric medicine, when I sent for him this morning.
He means to visit him again at noon, or thereabouts. I
told him that you would wish to see him, and he replied
that *he* wished to see *you!* He had the impudence to ask
me if you were to be depended on, too! Will you come
in? A bedchamber has been prepared for you, and the
parlour is set aside for your use."

"If you will be pleased to come with me, ma'am, I
will show you the parlour," said Miss Judbrook, who
was standing in the doorway.

She spoke in frigid accents, but thawed a little
when Frederica said, holding out her hand: "Thank
you! I am so very much obliged to you for all you
have done. I am afraid it must have meant a shocking
upset for you, too."

"Oh, well, as to that, ma'am, I was never one to grudge trouble!" responded Miss Judbrook, taking the hand, and dropping a reluctant curtsy. "I'm sure, if Judbrook had asked me, I should have told him to bring the young gentleman in straight, but nursing him I cannot undertake!"

"No, indeed!" agreed Frederica. "You must have enough to do without that!" Following her forbidding hostess to the parlour, she paused on the threshold, cast a swift look round the room, and exclaimed: "Oh, what a handsome carpet!"

The Marquis, who thought the carpet quite hideous, blinked; but realized, an instant later, that his Frederica had said exactly the right thing. Miss Judbrook, bridling with pleasure, said that it had been laid down not a month ago; and almost cordially invited Frederica to step upstairs with her.

The Marquis, prudently remaining below, went out to confer with his henchman. He found Curry, who had driven up to the farm behind the carriage in the phaeton, assisting one of Judbrook's farmhands to remove from the carriage a quantity of baggage; and his valet, having survived a journey on the box-seat without loss of dignity, directing these operations. The Marquis instructed his postilions to take the carriage on to the Sun, at Hemel Hempstead, which hostelry had been recommended to him by Dr Elcot; told Knapp to procure accommodation there; and Curry to wait with the phaeton until he himself should be ready to leave the farm; and went back into the house.

It was not long before Frederica joined him in the parlour. She declined the armchair, and sat down at the table, laying her clasped hands upon it. "He is still sleeping, but not restfully. I think I should go back as soon as I may, but before I do so will you tell me, if you please, cousin, what the doctor has said? I can tell that Felix is very feverish, and can guess how anxious a night you must have passed." She read hesitation in his face; and added quietly: "Don't be afraid to open the budget! I'm not a fool, and I'm not easily overpowered." She smiled faintly. "Nor is this the first time one of my brothers has been ill, or has done his best to kill himself. So tell me!"

"Elcot speaks of rheumatic fever," he said bluntly.

She nodded. "I was afraid it might be that. My mother had it once. She was never quite well after it: it affected her heart. I was only a child at the time, but I recall how very ill she was—worse, I think, than Felix is. But our doctor wasn't skilful, and she wasn't carefully nursed. I can remember that she dragged herself out of bed, because she heard the baby crying —that was Felix, of course. Well! Felix won't do so! He is more robust than my mother ever was, and medical science is more advanced. I don't mean to fall into despair, I promise you, so you needn't look at me as if you feared you might at any moment be obliged to recover me from a swoon!"

"I certainly don't fear that: you have too much force of mind! If I look grave, it's because I am afraid you have an anxious, as well as an exhausting, time ahead. I only hope you may not be quite worn down."

"Thank you! I'm not such a poor creature! I shall have Jessamy to help me, too—perhaps as soon as to-morrow, if Harry returns to London this evening, as we believe he will. Dear Jessamy! he wanted so much to come with me today, but he never said so. He understood at once how improper it would be to leave poor Charis with only the servants to bear her company, and said he should stay in Upper Wimpole Street until Harry arrived to relieve him of that duty. He means to travel to Watford on the stage, and I own I shall be glad to have him with me. I can trust him to watch over Felix when he sleeps, so that I may lie down on my bed for a while. You see how rational I am, cousin!"

"I never doubted that. May I ask what part Miss Winsham plays in this?"

"A very small one," she confessed. "My uncle died last night, you see."

"Accept my condolences! I should have supposed that this must have released Miss Winsham from what she conceived to be her most pressing duty, but I collect that I'm mistaken."

"Yes, because my Aunt Amelia is now prostrate, and falls into hysterics as soon as Aunt Seraphina leaves her side. She has spasms, vapours, and——Oh, dear, I ought not to talk so! I have so little sensibility myself that I find it very hard to sympathize with people like Aunt Seraphina. *I* should be much inclined to——*No!*"

"I know exactly what you would be much inclined to do," he said, smiling. "I saw how you dealt with Charis, in a similar situation!"

"It was not at all similar!" she replied. "Poor Charis had suffered a severe shock! There was every excuse for her! My uncle's death has been expected for weeks—and, in any event, I should *not* slap my aunt's face!"

"However much you might wish to," he agreed.

"Certainly not!" she said, with a severity belied by the laughter in her eyes. "You are quite—that is to say, if I were not so deeply indebted to you, I should say—"

"That I was quite the most detestable man alive?"

"*Abominable* was the word I had in mind!" she returned instantly. Then her eyes softened. "No, I shouldn't! To us you have been all kindness, however abominable you may be! Now, do be serious, sir! The case is not as bad as you think! My aunt has promised to keep a watch over Charis, but she feels that her sister has the greater claim on her. Well—well, I expect I should feel that too, so I can scarcely blame her! She thinks that, since it would be most improper for Charis to attend any parties at this moment, and will have Harry to accompany her out walking, or driving, besides Mrs Hurley to take good care of her, *her* presence cannot be deemed necessary. I must tell you also that your sister—Cousin Elizabeth, I mean,—has been as kind as you are! She sent Charis a note this morning, inviting her to stay at your house, while I was away, and offering to escort her to Lady Castlereagh's assembly tonight. Charis declined it, of course—indeed, nothing would prevail upon her to go junketing abroad under these circumstances!—and—and I know I can depend on Harry! He is very much attracted to Charis, you know, and won't let her fall into dejection." She rose. "I must go. Would you, when you reach London, tell

Charis just how the matter stands here, and assure her that there is no need for undue misgiving? I should be so much obliged to you!"

"Willingly, but I am not returning to London yet awhile. Did you think that I meant to play nip-shot? I'm not as abominable as that, I hope! You goose! why did you suppose that I had sent for my valet?"

"I didn't! I mean,—oh, was he your valet? I thought he must be some sort of a courier, and wondered that you should think it necessary to provide me with him!"

"As well you might! Foolish beyond permission, Frederica!"

"No! How should I know what freakish thing you might take it into your head to do?" she countered. "I never met anyone as extravagant as you are! But you must not stay here on my account! Indeed, there is no need!"

"You are quite mistaken. After the anxieties and exertions of the past twenty-four hours I am wholly exhausted, and must ruralize for a few days. I shall be putting up at the Sun, in Hemel Hempstead—and pray don't argue with me! Few things are more boring than fruitless arguments!" He took her hand, and pressed it. "I'm off now, but I shall come back presently—to assure myself that you are taking good care of my ward!"

XXIII

The Marquis did not return to Monk's Farm until shortly before six o'clock, by which time he had been re-
freshed by a long sleep, a complete change of raiment,
and a tolerable dinner. After a brief conversation with
both the Judbrooks, he went upstairs to the room in
which Felix lay, and entered it softly. The curtains had
been drawn across the window, shutting out the west-
ering sun, but he was immediately aware of a change.
The room was redolent, not of the mustiness of disuse,
but of lavender; and, as his eyes grew accustomed to
the dimness, he saw that a truckle-bed had been set
up, the heavy patchwork quilt removed from the four-
poster, and a screen placed to shield from Felix the
light that would later be cast by the oil-lamp which
now stood upon the table. Felix was uneasily asleep,
moaning a little, and muttering; and Frederica was sitting in the armchair, which she had drawn up to the
window. She rose when she saw who had entered the
room, and came towards his lordship like a ghost,
breathing: "Don't wake him!"

She passed before him out of the room, and he drew
the door to behind them both. He saw that she was
looking pale, and very tired, and said: "He's no better?
I can see you've been having the devil of a time!"

She shook her head. "No. We can't expect him to be
better yet, you know. And at this hour a feverish person is always at his worst. But Dr Elcot has told me
just what to do."

"Are you satisfied with Elcot? If you would wish to
have another doctor's opinion, tell me! I'll set out for
London immediately, and bring Knighton here—or any
other you choose to name!"

"Thank you—but no: I think Dr Elcot knows just
what he is about."

"Very well, then go down to the parlour now, to
your dinner! You will offend Miss Judbrook if you
don't: she appears to have exerted herself to prepare an
elegant repast for you, which is ready, and—so she tells
me—rapidly spoiling. And let me inform you, my dear,
that if you mean to say that you dare not leave Felix in
my care you will offend me too!"

"I shan't say that, at least! Dr Elcot told me how
well you managed Felix, and how good you have
been to him. The truth is that I am not at all hungry—
but I know how stupid it would be to refuse my
dinner, so I will go downstairs. If Felix should wake,
and complain that he is thirsty, there is lemonade in
the blue jug on the table."

"Now, why the devil didn't I think of lemonade,
when he was so thirsty last night?" he exclaimed.

She smiled. "How should you? In any event, I don't
think Miss Judbrook has any lemons. I brought some
from London—which reminds me that I shall need
some more. Will you procure some for me in Hemel
Hempstead tomorrow, cousin?"

"Yes, and anything else you need, but go down now!"

She went obediently, returning half-an-hour later to
find him supporting Felix with one arm, and trying,
not very successfully, to turn the pillow with his other
hand. She went at once to the rescue; and he said
apologetically: "I fear I'm not yet very deedy! He has
been turning his head continually, trying, I think, to
find a cool spot. Frederica, are you sure you don't wish
another doctor to see him? I won't disguise from you
that he seems to me more feverish now than he was last
night."

She began to bathe Felix's face and hands with a
handkerchief soaked with lavender-water. "Dr Elcot
warned me that he expected him to be worse before he
is better. It will soon be time for his medicine again,
and that will make him easier: you'll see! At least—do
you mean to go back to the Sun immediately, or would
you wait for just twenty minutes? To hold him for me,
while I give him the dose? When he is like this, quite
out of his senses, it is very difficult for me to manage
him without assistance."

"I am entirely at your disposal, Frederica. Did you eat your dinner?"

"Yes, and drank the glass of wine you provided for me, cousin. Miss Judbrook told me that you brought over a bottle from the Sun. Thank you! it has made me feel as fresh as a nosegay!"

"I'm happy to hear it," he said dryly. He moved away, but after watching her struggles to control Felix, and to keep his body covered, he came back again, saying: "Let me try what I can do! No, leave him to me! I succeeded last night, and may yet be able to do so."

She yielded her place to him, and he sat down, possessing himself of Felix's burning hand, and speaking to him in the compelling voice which he had previously used to such good effect. It did not this time recall Felix to his senses; but it seemed to Frederica that although there was no recognition in the fevered eyes the implacable voice at last penetrated the mists. Felix grew quieter, moaning, but no longer trying to fling himself about. He fought against the medicine, but Alverstoke held him clamped against his shoulder, and Frederica was quick to tilt the mixture down his throat when he opened his mouth to utter a wild, incoherent protest. He choked, coughed, and burst into spasmodic sobs, but gradually these ceased, and he sighed wearily. Alverstoke laid him down again, and said softly over his shoulder: "Go to bed, Frederica!"

She blinked, and whispered: "I shall lie down presently on the truckle-bed. Pray don't—"

"You will go to bed in your own room. I'll wake you at midnight—before, if I should see any need! Oblige me by sending for Curry, and telling him to put the horses to then."

"You cannot drive back to Hemel Hempstead at that hour!"

"I shall do precisely that—and by the light of a full moon! Don't stand there raising bird-witted objections! Of what use will you be tomorrow if you are three parts dead of fatigue?"

She was obliged to acknowledge the truth of this. Anxiety had made it impossible for her to sleep on the previous night; she had been up almost at dawn, with packing to do, and arrangements to make; she had travelled for some twenty-five miles; and had been in attendance on her patient for eight hours; and she was indeed exhausted. She smiled waveringly upon his lordship, said simply: "Thank you!" and went out of the room.

When she came back, rather before midnight, she was looking very much better, but conscience-stricken. She said: "The most shocking thing! I must have been more tired than I knew: I forgot about the medicine! He should have had another dose at eleven, cousin!"

He smiled. "He did have it. Fortunately, you left Elcot's instructions on the table, and I read them. Have you slept well?"

"Oh, so well! Four hours, and I don't think I even stirred! How has Felix been?"

"Much the same. I'll leave you now, and be with you again later in the morning. No need to tell you to stand buff! Good-night, my child!"

She nodded gratefully, uttering no protest, either then, or when he returned, after breakfast, and informed her that henceforward they would strictly divide the watches. Her commonsense told her that while Felix was critically ill it was beyond her power to bear the whole burden of nursing him; and while she was aware, in the recesses of her brain, that neither she nor Felix had the smallest claim upon the Marquis, it had begun to seem so natural to rely on his support that the thought only occurred to be dismissed. He was able to manage Felix as well as she could and sometimes better; and Felix was perfectly content to be left in his care. No other considerations mattered to her; if Alverstoke had announced his intention of returning to London she would have strained every nerve to induce him to remain. He did not do so, and she accepted his services almost as a matter of course.

The Marquis, well-aware that she had no thought for anyone but her abominable little brother, was wryly amused. He liked Felix, but it would have been idle to suppose that he liked the task of nursing him; and, if he had not fallen deeply and reluctantly in love with Felix's sister, it would never have entered his head to have undertaken so arduous a duty. But it was not from a wish to advance himself in Frederica's esteem that he remained in Hertfordshire, exerting himself so unusually: the only conscious thought in his mind was that she was in dire trouble, from which it was his privilege to extricate her. He had told Charles Trevor to cancel all his immediate engagements, if not without a certain amount of regret, at least without hesitation. For the first time in many years his fellow-members of the Jockey Club would look in vain for him at Ascot Races: it was a pity, but it couldn't be helped. He had a horse running, too, but much pleasure would he have derived from watching it win, as he thought it well might, when he knew that Frederica was in trouble, and needed his support.

So the Marquis, who rarely put himself out for anyone, and whose whole life had been spent in opulent and leisured ease, entered upon the most strenuous and uncomfortable period of his career. He was obliged to put up at a modest and oldfashioned inn; he spent nearly all his waking hours attending to a sick schoolboy; and since his arrival at the farm was the signal for Frederica to retire to bed, the only conversations he held with her were brief, and were concerned only with their patient. In after years he was wont to say that he could not recall his sufferings without a shudder, but not one word of complaint did he utter at the time, and not for an instant did he lose his air of calm self-possession.

Jessamy arrived on the second day. His intention had been to have walked from Watford, across the fields, but the Marquis had sent Curry to meet the stage-coach, with the phaeton, so that he was not obliged to do this, which was perhaps just as well, since he had brought with him, in addition to a modest portmanteau, a large valise, crammed with books. He explained to Alverstoke, who was on duty at the time, that they included, besides those necessary for his studies, a number of books which he thought Felix would like to have read to him. "For that is something I *can* do," he said. "He likes to be read to when he's ill, you know. So I brought all his old favourites, and also *Waverley*. Harry put me in mind of that: I'd forgotten that when Frederica read it aloud to the rest of us, in the evenings, Felix was always in bed and asleep, being much too young to enjoy it. He will now, though, don't you think, sir?"

"I've no doubt he will, but not just at present, I fear."

Jessamy's face clouded. "No. Curry has been telling me. Oh, thank you for sending him to meet me, cousin! Curry said that it is rheumatic fever, and that he's very ill, and in great pain. Sir, he—isn't going to *die*, is he?"

"No, certainly not, but he's in a bad way, and may be worse before he begins to mend. He's sleeping at the moment, but he seldom sleeps for long at a time, so I must go back to his room. You may come with me, if you choose: you won't disturb him if you talk quietly."

"Yes, please," Jessamy said. "I—would like to see him."

"Of course you would. But you mustn't be surprised if he doesn't know you when he wakes: he is not always himself, you see."

Fortunately, since Jessamy was so much shocked by Felix's appearance that he was quite unable to command his voice, and withdrew to a chair by the window to master his emotions, Felix did know him when he woke. He said fretfully: "I'm so hot! I'm so thirsty! Frederica!"

"Well, that shall soon be mended," said Alverstoke, sliding an arm under his shoulders, and raising him. "Here's your lemonade, and while you're drinking it Jessamy will shake up your pillows, so that you may be comfortable again. You didn't know Jessamy had come to see you, did you?"

"Jessamy," said Felix vaguely.

But when he was laid down again, he looked round, and seeing his brother, managed to smile, and to say again, with definite pleasure: "Jessamy!"

Taking his hand, Jessamy said awkwardly: "That's the barber, old chap!"

"I wish I hadn't done it!" Felix said unhappily. "I didn't know it would hurt so much. Are you very angry?"

"No, no, I promise you I'm not!"

Felix sighed, and, as Alverstoke began to bathe his face, closed his eyes again.

Jessamy was so much relieved that Felix should have wakened in full possession of his senses that he began to feel more cheerful, and was able, when Felix dropped off again, to give Alverstoke an account of what had been happening in Upper Wimpole Street.

On the whole, the news seemed to be good; for although Charis cried whenever she thought of poor Felix, and Miss Winsham, always put out of temper by adversity, regarded the accident as a piece of mischievous spite designed by Felix expressly to add to the cares besetting her, and said, amongst a great many other things, that she had no patience with him, or with Frederica, whose fault it was, because she had spoilt him to death, Harry had returned from Wells on the previous evening, and had at once assumed control of the household. Jessamy thought his arrival an unmixed blessing, but as his first act had apparently been to quarrel with his aunt, to such purpose that she then and there packed her trunk, and removed to Harley Street, Alverstoke doubted whether Frederica would think so. But Jessamy said confidently: "Yes, she will, sir, for she knows that my aunt and Harry always rub against each other, and I shan't scruple to tell her that Charis will go on better without her! She—she said such things—such *uncharitable* things!—as wholly overset Charis! You know, sir, Charis's spirits require *support!* And Harry *does* support them! Why, she plucked up the moment he came into the room! And if he is to remain with her—which, I promise you, he means to do!—there can be no need for my aunt to be there."

In answer to a dry enquiry, Jessamy said that however much at outs he might frequently be with his senior he had never doubted Harry's devotion to his family. He adduced, in proof of this statement, that Harry, to his own certain knowledge, had told his friend, Peplow, that he must exclude him from all their engagements: even from the Ascot Races! Harry's first impulse had been to post off to Hertfordshire immediately, but he had been persuaded to remain in Lon-

don. "And I'm bound to own, sir," said Jessamy handsomely, "that it does him credit! For I quite thought he
would take a huff when I reminded him that he was
never of the least use when any of us have been ill!"

Not only had Harry accepted this stricture meekly: he
had furnished Jessamy with the money to pay for his
journey; charged him with a reassuring message for
Frederica; joked Charis out of the dismals; and had
even promised to take care of Lufra. "And he didn't call
Luff *that misbegotten mongrel*, either!" said Jessamy.

"That was indeed kind of him," responded Alverstoke gravely.

"Yes. Well, he *is* kind! I mean, he never tries to
bullock one, or comes the ugly if one provokes him,
which I daresay most elder brothers would." He sighed,
and added wistfully: "I wish I might have brought Luff
here, but they wouldn't have permitted me to do so, on
the stage, would they?"

The Marquis, mentally rendering thanks to Providence for having refrained from adding the task of preserving Farmer Judbrook's herd from Lufra's onslaughts
to his other duties, said, with as much sympathy as he
could infuse into his voice: "No, I am afraid they
wouldn't. But you have the comfort of knowing that he
will be well cared for while you are away."

"Oh, yes!" said Jessamy naïvely. "Owen has promised
me that he will feed him, and exercise him."

If Frederica was not wholly pleased to know that
her aunt had washed her hands of her young relations,
she received the news philosophically, telling Alverstoke
that perhaps it was just as well that she had retired to
Harley Street. "For it is not at all helpful to be scolding
all the time, just as if any of this were poor Charis's
fault! She doesn't mean everything she says, and I don't
doubt she will keep her eyes on things, even if she has
taken up residence with my Aunt Amelia. Charis will
be much happier with Harry, and I know he will take
good care of her. The only thing is—"

She broke off, a worried frown in her eyes; and,
after a moment, Alverstoke said: "What is the only
thing, Frederica? My blockish young cousin?"

A tiny smile acknowledged that he had scored a hit, but she replied: "Whatever it is there's nothing I can do about it, so it would be stupid to tease myself."

He said no more, knowing that her thoughts were concentrated on Felix. Charis's future was a matter of indifference to him, except as it affected her sister, so he was content to let the matter drop. He was much inclined to think that Endymion was indulging a fit of gallantry that would be as fleeting as it was violent; if the affair proved to be more serious than he supposed, and Frederica was troubled by it, he would intervene, and without compunction. His lordship, in fact, previously ruthless on his own behalf, was now prepared to sacrifice the entire human race to spare his Frederica one moment's pain. Except, perhaps, the two youngest members of the family she loved so much: Jessamy, concealing his chagrin at being allowed so little share of the nursing, and humbly holding himself in readiness to fetch, carry, run errands, or to perform any task which was required of him; and Felix—little devil that he was! —who was depending on his strength, and could be quietened by his voice. No: he wasn't prepared to sacrifice Jessamy or Felix: he had become attached to the infernal brats—though he was damned if he knew why.

During the next two days he had no leisure, much less inclination, to consider this problem. Fulfilling the doctor's prophecy, Felix's fever mounted; and although Alverstoke maintained his imperturbable demeanour he entertained the gravest fears. That Frederica shared them he knew, though she never spoke of them, or showed a sign of agitation. She was invincibly cheerful, and apparently tireless; but when he saw how strained her eyes were, and how drawn her face, he wondered how long it would be before she collapsed.

But in the early hours of the third day, when he entered the sickroom, he found it strangely quiet. So critical did he feel Felix's condition to be that he had not left the farm that evening. He checked now upon the threshold, filled with foreboding. Felix was lying still, neither muttering, nor twitching; and Frederica was standing by the bed. She turned her head at the sound of the opening door; and Alverstoke, seeing that tears were rolling down her face, went quickly forward, saying involuntarily: "Oh, my poor girl—!"

Then he saw that she was smiling through her tears. She said simply: "He is asleep. The fever broke. Suddenly I saw that he was sweating, and I *knew!* Cousin, we've *done* the thing!"

XXIV

With Felix out of danger, and slowly winning back to strength, life at Monk's Farm underwent several changes. It was no longer necessary to keep a constant watch over him; and although Frederica, sleeping on the truckle-bed in his room, might be obliged to get up three or four times during the night to attend to him, she no longer needed either relief or assistance; nor, during the day, was it imperative for her to remain always within call. He slept a great deal, and was docile when awake, too weak to display any of his customary recalcitrance: a circumstance which made Jessamy, permitted at last to share the task of nursing him, so uneasy that he sought counsel of the Marquis. "For I don't wish to alarm Frederica, sir," he explained. "Only it does seem to me very unlike him! I don't mean because he does what you or Frederica bid him, because he would, of course. But he does what *I* say he must, and doesn't even argue! You don't think, do you sir, that his brain is affected?"

Preserving his countenance, the Marquis reassured him; but he was not wholly satisfied until the day when Felix had to be coaxed to swallow his medicine, and apostrophized him as the greatest beast in nature. "So now I *know* all's right!" he told the Marquis radiantly. "I daresay he will soon be throwing the glass at me!"

"Well, if it will afford you pleasure I hope he may," said his lordship. "Warn him not to throw it at me!"

Another change was provided by Knapp. After a struggle with his pride, he allowed the boredom he was suffering at the Sun, and his jealousy of Curry, who spent his days at the farm, in attendance on the Marquis, to overcome his reluctance to demean himself, and offered his services.

So Felix, quite unimpressed, was waited on by a valet

313

of rare quality; the kitchen quarters were dignified by
the presence of a refined personage of great condescension, in whom Miss Judbrook recognized a gentleman's
gentleman of the first stare; and Frederica, as she told
the Marquis, found herself with nothing to do.

It might have been expected that his lordship would
now have returned to London, but this was a change
which had not taken place. He continued to put up
at the Sun, under conditions to which he was in no
way accustomed, and to spend his days at Monk's
Farm. As soon as Frederica felt it safe to leave Felix
in his brother's charge for an hour or two, he persuaded
her to take the air in his phaeton; and, later, when she
had recovered from her exhaustion, to go with him for
strolling walks. She was very ready to do so; she talked
to him with the ease of long-standing friendship; she
consulted him on any problem that arose; but her entire lack of consciousness showed him that it had not
entered her head to regard him in the light of a suitor.
He could not help wondering if she treated him as she
might an elder brother, or even (a lowering thought!)
an uncle.

His own doubts were at an end. The more he saw of
her the more he loved her, and as he had never loved
any woman before. Not the most beautiful of his mis-
tresses had inspired him with a desire to shield her
from every adverse wind; he had never pictured the
most amusing of his well-born flirts presiding over his
several establishments; and far less had he contemplated a permanent relationship with any of these ladies. But after knowing her for little more than two
months Frederica had so seriously disturbed the pattern
of his life that he had been cast into a state of in-
decision: a novel experience which had not been at all
agreeable. When he was pitchforked into her little
brother's fantastic adventure he had still been in a state
of uncertainty; since then he had spent more than a
week in close companionship with her, and under conditions as unromantic as they were uncomfortable, and
all his doubts were resolved: he wished to spend the
rest of his life with her, because she was the perfect
woman he had never expected to encounter.

His lordship, in fact, had fallen deeply in love. He was also undergoing yet another new experience: Frederica showed no sign of returning his regard. He knew that she liked him; once or twice he had dared to hope that the feeling she had for him was becoming more than mere fondness, but he could never be sure of this, or forget that on the only occasion when he had given her the faintest reason to suspect him of gallantry she had instantly set him at a distance. It seemed a long time ago; she might have changed her mind; but since he had then, and for the succeeding weeks, been unable to make up his own mind, he had never made any attempt to fix his interest with her. In the situation in which they had found themselves, when she joined him at Monk's Farm, it would have been both stupid and improper to have embarked on courtship. On the one hand, no moment could be more ill-chosen; on the other, it must (if she repulsed him) have created embarrassment between them, while his assistance in the task of nursing Felix had been so indispensable.

But Felix had survived and was on the mend, making it unnecessary for himself to remain in Hertfordshire. The Marquis, yielding to impulse, resolved to put his fate to the touch.

He had accompanied Frederica on a rambling walk, and they had paused by a stile before retracing their steps. Leaning on the topmost bar, she stared ahead, a troubled look on her face.

"Frederica!" said his lordship, recklessly taking the plunge.

She paid no heed; but when he repeated her name she turned her head, and said: "I beg your pardon! I wasn't attending! Did you say something to me, cousin?"

"Not yet!" he replied. "I was merely trying to recall your attention! What were you thinking about so deeply?"

"I was trying to remember the name of an excellent jelly which Mrs Ansdell—our Vicar's wife, you know—recommended to me when Jessamy and Felix were so pulled by the measles," she said seriously. "It did them a great deal of good, and I think it would be just the thing for Felix now, if only I could—Oh, I have it!

Dr Ratcliffe's Restorative Pork Jelly! How could I be so stupid? Now, what have I said to make you go into whoops?"

"Nothing in the world!" responded the Marquis, still laughing.

"Well, what did you wish to say to me?" she demanded, her brow puckered in a puzzled frown.

"Nothing in the world, Frederica!" he said again. "How fortunate that you should have remembered the name of this jelly! Shall I go at once to Hemel Hempstead to procure it for you?"

"No, very likely you wouldn't be able to. If Dr Elcot approves, I shall write to Harry, and ask him to bring me some."

"Oh, is Harry to visit us?" he asked.

"Yes—didn't I tell you? Curry brought me a letter from the receiving-office this morning. He writes that he can come post, and be in London again in time to dine with Charis. He would have come immediately, you know, if Jessamy had not dissuaded him, which was very right. It could only have overset him to have seen Felix then, and there was nothing he could have done, because he is very rarely ill himself, and hasn't a notion of what to do for sick persons. But naturally he is anxious to come now, and I shall tell him he may do so, but must *not* allow Charis to accompany him. I am sorry for it, and should dearly love to see her, but we *cannot* have her sick on our hands as well!"

"Certainly not!" Alverstoke said, startled. "Er—should we?"

"Well, quite out of sorts for a day or two, at all events. On account of the post-chaise," she explained. "You know what those yellow bounders are! She would be queasy before ever they reached Edgware."

His lordship, recognizing that it was still not the moment to make a declaration, very wisely refrained, and, as they wended their way back to the farm, talked to her on indifferent subjects.

Harry, who arrived in due course, bringing with him a supply of Dr Ratcliffe's Restorative Pork Jelly, was quite unmanned at the sight of Felix, so thin and white, and so lanquid; and it needed the united endeavours

of Frederica and Alverstoke to convince him that the
boy was not lying at death's door. He was inclined to
think that Frederica took too lighthearted a view of the
case, and was so insistent that a London practitioner
should be sent for—even saying that he, and not she,
was the poor little fellow's guardian—that Alverstoke
was impelled to come to her rescue, drawing him apart,
and explaining to him, with wonderful patience, why it
would be both unnecessary and inadvisable to call in
another doctor at this stage. Harry did not look to be
perfectly satisfied, but he brightened when Alverstoke
suggested that if Felix did not pluck up as fast as he
should, when he was carried home, Harry should certainly consult a London physician.

To see Felix had not been Harry's only reason for
posting down to Monk's Farm: he wished to discharge
his debt to the Marquis. "You have been put to a great
deal of expense, sir, and I am much obliged to you for
acting on my behalf," he said punctiliously. "I should
like, if it is convenient to you, to give you a draft
on my bank."

There was a mulish look about his mouth, and the
hint of a challenge in his eyes, but the Marquis, who
had foreseen the demand, took the wind out of his sails
by responding affably: "Oh, perfectly! I'll hand you the
reckoning when I return to London. Do you want it in
detail, or will a Dutch one suffice?"

"No, no, of course I don't want it in detail, sir!"
Harry exclaimed, ludicrously disconcerted. "I only
meant—that is to say, you won't forget, will you?"

"If I do, you must remind me," said the Marquis.

With this Harry had to be content; but he took care
to tell Frederica that she must instruct Dr Elcot not to
present his bill to Alverstoke. "I've brought you a roll
of flimsies," he said, "and if you should need any more
of the ready, mind you write to me for it, for I won't
have Alverstoke standing the nonsense! A pretty fellow
I should be not to look after my own brothers and
sisters!"

She agreed, but said: "I wish you had not been
obliged to—and you ought not!"

"Gammon!"

"No, it's the truth. I should be more beforehand with the world. I thought, you know, that Graynard would have paid for everything, but living in London, and going to so many ton-parties, has cost much more than I was prepared for."

"Oh, pooh! Who cares?"

"I do—indeed, I am dreadfully mortified! I never meant to be a charge on you, Harry! I shall pay it back to you, but I fear I may be forced to draw on you."

"Freddy, *will* you stop talking such flummery? Anyone would suppose I was on the rocks!"

"No, I know it's not as bad as that, but I'm very sure it isn't high tide with you. I daresay you may have debts, too."

"Nothing to signify!" he said, with a betraying flush. "You needn't worry your head over that! As for your expenses, I can always raise the wind, you know: Salcombe will manage it for me."

"Do you mean, sell you out of the Funds? No, that he shan't!"

"Oh, you may depend upon it Salcombe will know of some other way! What's the figure?"

"My dear, I'm not yet on the rocks either! I was looking ahead—merely warning you that I might be obliged to demand your assistance! The thing is that I must not keep Felix in London, and I hired the house there for six months. I thought we might have stayed there during the summer, living very economically, which we could well do, when the season is over. But I have been talking to Dr Elcot, and he advises me to take Felix out of town until he is perfectly recovered. The racket and all the excitements of London won't do for him: I shall have to take the greatest care of him, you see, not letting him tax his strength. He is going on very prosperously, but rheumatic fever, as we know, can sometimes leave certain weaknesses behind it."

"Mama!" he exclaimed. "Good God, Freddy, he must and shall be seen by a London doctor! One who is bang up to the hub!"

"Yes, that's what I feel, too. Indeed, Dr Elcot has himself recommended me to do so, before I leave Lon-

don. So we will ask Sir William Knighton to call in
Upper Wimpole Street as soon as Felix is well enough
to travel, which won't, I hope, be long now—particularly in Alverstoke's carriage, which is the most luxurious
one I ever was in! And then, if Sir William approves
the scheme, I mean to remove to some quiet, unfashionable place—perhaps by the sea? Only I must
take Charis and Jessamy as well, of course, and I am
afraid it may cost a good deal, even if we can find a
cheap lodging. Harry, will you discover which of the
seaside resorts would be the best, and go there to find
a eligible lodging-house for us? Or hire a furnished
house, if you think none of the lodgings suitable?"

But this Harry did not feel himself competent to do.
He thought it would be better for Frederica to choose
the lodgings herself, handsomely offering to escort her
on this exploratory trip.

She did not press the matter, reflecting that it might
indeed be unwise, not to say foolhardy, to leave the
choice of lodgings to his uninstructed judgment. She
asked him instead for news of Charis. He said she was
not to tease herself, for Charis was going on tolerably
well; but he admitted that her spirits were not high. She
was wearing black gloves, of course, and had excused
herself from attending any of the parties to which she
and Frederica had been invited. No: he did not think
she was moped precisely; and as for being lonely, much
cause there was for that! Lord, the knocker was never
still! Which reminded him that he had meant to ask her
who the devil was the queer touch who was for ever on
the doorstep, enquiring after Felix, handing Buddle
flowers and billets for Charis, and in general making a
curst cake of himself? A regular counter-coxcomb: Nutley, or some such name.

"Oh, dear! Our neighbour," said Frederica despairingly. "A very respectable young man, but—but encroaching! Not that I altogether blame him, because I
know very well that Charis—not in the least meaning
to do so, but because she is such a soft-hearted goose
—did encourage him! I have tried to hint him away—"

"Well, I've done more than that!" interrupted Harry
callously. "What a jackstraw to be making up to a sister

of mine! When it came to his saying that he wished
to serve her in *this time of affliction*—such impudence!
—I told him to his head that she needed no services
from him, or from anyone other than myself! Which
put him in the bag, I'm happy to say!"

"Poor Mr Nutley! and Mr Navenby? Has he
called?"

"Oh, yes! Brought his mother with him. *She* was
much inclined to laugh at the affair, but he wasn't! He
didn't seem able to believe it at first, and then he sat
staring. It was all in the papers, you know—not very
much, thank the lord, but enough!"

"I suppose it must have been," she sighed. "Has it
shocked everyone?"

"I shouldn't think so. Well, Lady Elizabeth wasn't
shocked, was she? And I can tell you of two others who
aren't: Barny, and Dauntry! They think Felix is as
game as a pebble—but I've told 'em not to put that
notion into his head!"

"So I should hope! Harry, I do hope Endymion
Dauntry isn't haunting the house?"

"No such thing! Haunting it, indeed! But why you
should prefer that fribble, Navenby, to Endymion I'm
dashed if I know! If I were you, Freddy, I'd give him
my blessing! I don't say it's a brilliant match, but it's
perfectly eligible. And if Charis don't care for his being
a nodcock why should you? At least he's a right
one, and not a man-milliner!"

"And if he were removed from her sight she would
forget him within the month," Frederica answered.
"Don't let us fall into a dispute! We shall never agree
on *that* subject. Tell me instead what Charis is doing
today! Is she with Lady Elizabeth?"

"No, but she's not alone. Chloë Dauntry is spending
the day with her, and they were going to walk in the
park this morning. I daresay they have been pittle-
pattling all the afternoon!"

"And I wish your idiotish cousin may not have been
their escort!" Frederica said, later, when recounting this
to Alverstoke.

He was amused. "I imagine that their escort—if they
had one—may quite as well have been my far from

idiotish secretary. Is that affair likely to prove lasting?"

She glanced quickly up at him. "Are you opposed to it?"

"My dear girl, what possible concern is it of mine? I own I think Charles might do much better for himself, and I am very sure that he will meet with formidable opposition from Chloë's fond momma. I am even of the opinion that he would be well-advised not to rivet himself before his feet are firmly set on his particular ladder; but I haven't the remotest intention of meddling."

"I'm glad. I agree with you, too—and Chloë is too young to be thinking of marriage—except, of course, that she *is* thinking of it! Too young for a formal engagement. But I fancy that their attachment *will* prove to be lasting. As for Mrs Dauntry, I know exactly how she may be brought to consent to the marriage. In fact, I have an excellent scheme in my head!"

The Marquis eyed her with foreboding. "If your scheme involves me, Frederica,—"

"Well, it does, but only a very little! How long is it since you saw Diana?"

"I should think it must be a very long time, for I can't immediately recall anyone of that name," he confessed. "But you know how wretched my memory is! Who—er—*is* Diana, and in what way is she concerned in the business?"

"Alverstoke!" she exclaimed. "She is Chloë's sister, of course! How *can* you have forgotten that?"

"Oh, easily!" he assured her, adding, with an air of mild triumph: "But now that you've put me in mind of it I do remember that there were three of them!"

Her eyes danced, but she said severely: "You know, sir, you *are* an abominable person!"

"Yes, indeed I do! You have frequently told me so, and I have complete faith in your judgment."

She choked on one of her involuntary chuckles. "Moonshine! Do, pray, be serious for a minute!"

"I am utterly serious."

"And I cut my eye-teeth years ago!" she retorted. "Stop joking me, and pay attention! Unless I very much mistake the matter, Diana will become the rage when she makes her come-out. My dear sir, she is the most

promising girl! She and Endymion favour Mrs Dauntry, and if you mean to tell me that Mrs Dauntry was
not a diamond of the first water when she was young,
you may spare your breath! Furthermore, it is of no
consequence at all when a *female* is bird-witted—"

"Is she?" he interrupted.

"Oh, yes! a lovely widgeon!" She paused, and said
carefully: "That is to say, her understanding is no more
than—than moderate! It doesn't signify: she will take
just as Charis has, and will very likely achieve a splendid alliance—with just a very little help from you! You
will naturally give a ball for her—"

"I *beg* your pardon? Did you say *naturally?*"

"Certainly I did! You gave one for Chloë, remember!"

"I remember nothing of the kind. I gave a ball for
you and Charis."

"Yes, and with the most ignoble motive! However, I
am too much obliged to you to say more on that
head. The thing is that you were thought to have given
it for Jane Buxted, and for Chloë Dauntry, so *naturally*
you will do the same for Diana!"

"And shall I naturally do it for Jane's sisters?" he enquired.

She wrinkled her brow, considering this. "I must
own," she acknowledged candidly, "that that is a very
daunting thought! But recollect that *they* have a brother
who is well able to provide for them, and—to do him
justice!—would much prefer to do so. What I wish
you will do, cousin, when the time comes—and assuming that Chloë is still of her present mind—is to suggest
to Mrs Dauntry that it is of the first importance to dispose of her, before she fires Diana off! Which it will be,
if Chloë has formed no other attachment at the end of
her second season. So do bear it in mind, I beg of you!"

He looked down at her, with his glinting smile. "I
can't. You must remind me, Frederica. But why do you
care?"

"Do you mean that it's no concern of mine? It isn't,
of course, but I like them both so much—and one can't
but care for what becomes of persons one holds in affection, and try to help them."

She seemed to take it for granted that he shared her sentiments. He said nothing, but when he thought the matter over he could only suppose that there were very few people whom he held in affection—no one, in fact, for whom he was prepared to put himself out. He had more than once come to a friend's financial rescue, but there was little virtue in that: such assistance had entailed no sacrifice on his part. Charles? Yes, he was fond of Charles, and he meant to foster his career, but there was little virtue in that either: it would be an easy thing to do. The only person on whose behalf he had really exerted himself was Felix, and he had done that because he loved Frederica. Or had he? If Frederica had not been in question, would he have handed Felix over to the unknown Mrs Hucknall, an ignorant woman, skilled in nothing but midwifery? No, he would not! He had no real responsibility for either of the Merriville boys, but he had grown to be fond of them: perhaps because they interested him, perhaps because they had such a touching faith in his ability to solve all problems, and never doubted his willingness to do so. None of his sisters had desired, or needed, his help in rearing her offspring; but, little though she might think it, Frederica did need it. If he had his way, Felix should go to school, and he would find a suitable tutor for Jessamy, not some needy usher ready to undertake the education of two boys of widely differing ages and abilities.

While these plans were revolving in his lordship's head, another of Frederica's suitors, equally convinced that her lawless brothers stood in urgent need of guidance, was on his way to Monk's Farm, and arrived there two days after Harry's visit.

He entered the parlour to find Jessamy seated at the table, with his books spread about him, and Alverstoke frowning over the obscure passage on which he had been consulted. He exclaimed: "*You*, sir? *Still?* I had thought you must have been at Ascot!"

The Marquis, looking up, said, in repelling accents: "Then you were mistaken! What the devil brings you here, Buxted?"

"I have come to see how my little cousin goes on, of

course—and to offer my services to his poor sister. A shocking business! I blame myself for not having asserted my authority, and insisted on his leaving that enclosure, and coming back with me to the carriage."

The Marquis had been leaning one hand on the back of Jessamy's chair, but he transferred it to Jessamy's shoulder. Obedient to its pressure, Jessamy remained silent. "You blame yourself quite unnecessarily, Carlton," said his lordship. "You had no authority, and the responsibility was—and still is—mine. That is why you find me here. For the rest, Felix is going on as well as could be expected; and no doubt Frederica will be obliged to you for your offer of service—which, if I had been so entirely lost to all sense of propriety as to have abandoned my ward in these circumstances, would have been most opportune."

Lord Buxted was neither dependent upon his uncle nor afraid of him, but whenever he found himself in his company he was invariably made to feel much more like a callow youth than the head of his house, and the wise guide of his brother and sisters which he knew himself to be. Colouring, he said: "Oh, if I had known that you were here, sir—! Not but what—Well, I am excessively glad to hear that the poor little boy is on the mend! It must be a lesson to him, though no one would have wished him to suffer so severe a punishment. I wonder, Jessamy, if you would conduct me to his room? I have brought him a book to read, and a diverting puzzle."

"Oh, no!" Jessamy said involuntarily. "I mean, it is most kind of you, sir—he will be very grateful—but —" He stopped, as Alverstoke's long fingers gripped his shoulder.

"I am afraid I can't permit you to see him," said Alverstoke. "The doctor's orders are that he is to have no visitors yet—not to be excited in any way!"

"Oh, certainly, but I assure you I don't mean to excite him! He and I are quite old friends, you know!"

"Hardly such old friends as he and Harry," said Alverstoke dryly. "We did allow Harry to see him, but regretted it, since it led to a set-back. Jessamy, go upstairs, and tell Frederica that Buxted is here!"

Left alone with his uncle, Buxted looked frowningly at him, and said: "I must say, sir, it seems very surprising to me that you should have remained here all this time! I should have thought—since I collect that Miss Winsham remains in London—"

"Oh, are you worrying about the proprieties?" said Alverstoke. "Let me reassure you! I am putting up at the Sun, in Hemel Hempstead—and damnably uncomfortable it is! However, I hope to be able to return to London within a very few days now: as soon, in fact, as Felix can dispense with my valet's services."

Buxton almost goggled at him *"Your valet,* sir? Waiting on *Felix?* Well, I am astonished that you could spare him!"

"I can't," said Alverstoke. "That's why I'm tied by the heels." He turned, as Frederica came into the room, and smiled at her, a satirical gleam in his eyes. "Ah, Frederica! I knew you would wish to see Buxted, who has come all this way to enquire after Felix!"

"Yes, indeed!" she responded promptly. "How very kind it is of you, cousin!"

He grasped her hand, and held it, saying: "I could not stay away!"

The Marquis, having observed this through his quizzing-glass, and with unruffled calm, recommended Frederica to furnish him with the whole history of Felix's illness, and withdrew.

For this desertion he was taken roundly to task as soon as Buxted had departed. "How *could* you have left me alone with him?" demanded Frederica indignantly. "The—the shabbiest thing!"

"But you have told me a score of times that you are long past the age of needing a chaperon!"

"Chaperon! Of course I am! I didn't mean that, and you know it! But to abandon me in that heartless way—"

"Not at all! I take great credit to myself for *not* being heartless enough to deny him the solace of the tête-à-tête he so plainly desired. Poor fellow, he deserved some reward for his devotion! Did he renew his offer for your hand?"

"Yes, he did! Nothing could have been more horrid,

for he put me in a flame, talking about Felix as he did, but I had to keep my tongue between my teeth, because I know he meant only to be kind, and helpful— besides bringing Felix a book, and a puzzle which would make him feverish again (if it didn't drive him out of his mind), if I were such a ninnyhammer as to give it to him, which, of course, I shan't, and saying how happy he would be to take my *burdens* on his own shoulders—as though the boys could ever be burdens to me! It was all I could do to refuse his offer civilly! And now I wish I hadn't been civil, because he says he shall not despair! He is as stupid as Endymion!"

"No, no!" said Alverstoke soothingly. "Nobody could be as stupid as Endymion!"

"Well, if you can think of anything stupider than to make me an offer of marriage at such a time as this—!" she exclaimed. "Would *you* do such an idiotish thing? Of course you would not! I don't believe even Endymion would!"

He looked at her for a moment, an oddly twisted smile on his lips. Then he said: "I can't answer for Endymion, but for myself—no, Frederica, I would not!"

XXV

The Marquis left Hertfordshire three days later. When he announced his decision to Frederica, he thought, for an instant, that there was a flicker of dismay in her eyes; but she answered almost at once, and with composure: "Yes, indeed, sir! My conscience had begun to trouble me, for there is no longer the least need for you to kick your heels here, and however much *we* may enjoy your company, *you* must be bored to death!"

"Do you know, Frederica, the odd thing is that I am not in the least bored," he told her.

She laughed. "To be sure, you have no time to be bored, have you? If you are not taking me for a walk or a drive, or entertaining Felix, you are being coaxed —if not bludgeoned!—into helping Jessamy with his classical studies!"

"That, I admit, is a severe trial, but I console myself with the reflection that it is doing me a great deal of good. I have become shockingly rusty! Nor, I fear, did I ever apply myself, as Jessamy does."

"Well, I can believe *that,* at all events!" she said, twinkling. "You would naturally be enchanted to be granted the opportunity to rub up your scholarship! But don't attempt to gammon me into thinking that you are equally enchanted to be obliged to emerge from your bedchamber long, *long* before noon!"

"Oh, I never keep town-hours in the country!" he returned.

"How detestable it is that you always have an answer!" she observed. "Now, do, pray, let us be serious for a moment! I can never hope to express to you my deep obligation for—"

"You have now had your moment!" he said. "And as it is apparent to me that you have nothing of the smallest importance to say, I don't scruple to interrupt

you. What *I* have to say is very much more to the
point! I have had some conversation with Elcot, and I
learn from him—*not,* to my chagrin, from you—that
you have the intention of carrying Felix off to some seaside resort. It won't do, Frederica! At this season you
would have the greatest difficulty to obtain a suitable
lodging at even the most unfashionable place; and if
you did obtain it you would find yourself jostled by
shabby-genteels, mushrooms, and April-squires!"

"But surely there must be quiet resorts!"

"No doubt, but I don't know of them, and nor do
you! By the time we had discovered one, the summer
would be half-over. If you are thinking of Worthing,
put it out of your mind! It is expensive, and all the
dowdies and dowagers of the ton engage accommodation there from year to year. I have a far more eligible
scheme to propose to you, which is that you should remove, with your family, to Alver, and remain there for
as long as you choose."

"To Alver?" she repeated, startled. "But—but do you
mean Alver Park—which the guide books describe as
your principal seat?"

"Yes, of course I do. I have had it in mind to send
Felix there ever since I realized that it would be necessary to take him out of London. It is situated within
twelve miles of Bath, so that he could, at need, go there
to drink the waters, or to take the hot bath, or whatever is recommended. It is very much quieter than any
watering-place, but will offer both him and Jessamy
much more entertainment. I'll tell my people to look
after that. They will find several hacks which they may
ride, and if they like to fish the trout stream they have
my permission to do so."

"Oh, how much Jessamy would love it!" she exclaimed. "Thank you, thank you! How good you are!
But of course I must not accept such an offer! Don't
tempt me!"

"Why must you not accept it? Is it your custom to refuse all invitations?"

"No, no, but—but this is different! We are already
too much beholden to you, and to—"

"Don't be commonplace, Frederica! it doesn't be-

come you! Do you feel that there should be a hostess at
Alver? Nothing could be easier than to provide one for
you! If Miss Winsham doesn't mean to leave her sister,
I have one widowed aunt, two elderly spinster ones,
and a collection of cousins, any one of whom would
be delighted to take up residence at Alver! Most of
them have been trying to do so for years."

She was obliged to laugh. "And then you would
never be rid of them!"

"You underrate me! Failing Miss Winsham, I'm inclined to think I will instal one of my aunts—or, perhaps, invite her to stay, if I should wish to visit Alver
myself. Not that I think it at all necessary: my housekeeper there, who knew the place before I was born,
will take excellent care of you and Charis, and cosset
the boys to death. You may remain for as long or as
short a time as you please—and pray don't imagine that
I am conferring a favour on you! the boot is on the
other leg: I shall be glad to have the house occupied.
So let us consider that settled!"

"But—"

He sighed wearily: "If you are wondering what people may say, let me assure you the likeliest comment
will be that it is just like me to rid myself of my
troublesome wards by packing them all off to Alver at
the earliest opportunity."

"You always contrive to leave me without a word to
say. I don't feel I ought to yield, but I shall, because
it would be just the thing for Felix, and for Jessamy,
too. It is high time I made them my chief concern. I've
neglected them for Charis, and it was very wrong of
me. Quite—quite useless, as well. I hoped so much that
she would have contracted an eligible alliance!"

"Don't despair! She may yet do so."

She agreed, but she knew that she would be unable
to give Charis another London season, and her voice
lacked conviction.

"There is one other matter which I wish you will
consider," Alverstoke said. "I don't know what your
thoughts may be on the subject, but I am of the opinion
that it is time the boys were provided with another
tutor—particularly Jessamy. That he should be grateful

for such help as so indifferent a scholar as I am can give
him tells its own tale. As for Felix, if Harry means to
send him to school in the autumn, he should be prepared—and, in any event, he has run wild for long
enough. Oh, don't look so harassed, my dear! It is for
you to decide: I am merely offering you my advice—
thereby rendering myself even more abominable!"

She shook her head. "No, that you are not! You are
very right, and it is a further proof of my neglect that I
shouldn't have attended to the matter weeks ago. Tell
me what will be best for me to do! If we were to be
fixed in London, I imagine it would be an easy matter,
but—"

"The best thing for you to do is nothing, but to leave
it to me to find a tutor scholarly enough to satisfy
Jessamy, yet not so steeped in scholarship that he cannot enter into Jessamy's other interests; too old to fall
in love with Charis, but not so old as to be a dead bore
to the boys—"

"Stop, stop!" she cried, throwing up her hands in
mock dismay. "An impossible task! And even if it were
not I shouldn't ask it of you, cousin!"

"But how is this?" he enquired, raising his brows.
"You did ask it of me!"

"*I?* Asked you to undertake to engage a tutor for my
brothers? That would be the outside of enough! I never
did so!"

"When I first made your acquaintance, Frederica,
you told me that if I became the boys' guardian it
would be proper for me to do so. You added that there
was no reason why I shouldn't be useful. Remember?"

"No. If I said it I could only have been funning. And
my memory is reasonably good—unlike yours, dear
sir!"

"Mine is erratic," he said imperturbably. "I remember only what interests me. I shan't presume to engage
a tutor, but if I can discover an eligible candidate I
shall send him to wait on you when you return to London."

"Thank you," she said meekly. "I only wish you
may not find it a most wearisome task!"

He was quite sure that he would, but events proved

him to be wrong. On the day after his arrival in Berkeley Square, when he was going through some papers with his secretary, he said casually: "By-the-by, Charles, I suppose you don't number amongst your acquaintance anyone willing to undertake the education of Jessamy and Felix? Quite a temporary arrangement—let us say, for three months."

"Well, no, sir, unless—"

He paused, and Alverstoke, lifting his eyes from the document in his hand, saw that he was looking embarrassed. "Unless what?" he asked. "You don't mean to tell me that you do know of such a man?"

"N-no, sir. That is, it did occur to me that Septimus might be the very person. But I hardly like to put him forward, and I beg you won't hesitate to—"

"Septimus?"

"My brother, sir. He is working for a Fellowship, but I know he meant to seek a post as crammer during the Long Vacation, and I should think he would prefer this one to any other—particularly as you mean to establish the Merrivilles at Alver. He could ride over every day, and continue to live at home, which would please my father."

"Charles, you are a prince of secretaries!" said Alverstoke. "Write to him immediately! That is, if you think he won't flinch from the task of coping with two such —er—enterprising pupils?"

Charles laughed: "Lord, no, sir! He'll like 'em— and I'm pretty confident that they'll like him. He's the best of good fellows—no muffin, I promise you! He plays all manner of games, and is fond of field-sports too." He caught himself up, flushing. "You must judge for yourself, sir! Don't take my word for it!"

"My dear boy, when have you ever misled me? Invite him to come up on a visit next week! I fancy Felix will be well enough to travel by then, so that he will be able to make Miss Merriville's acquaintance. Which reminds me that I must call in Upper Wimpole Street tomorrow, to give Charis the latest news of Felix. Don't let me forget!"

Charis, meanwhile, had been passing through a variety of emotions. Her first agitation had been soothed by Harry's bracing treatment; but it had been succeeded by alternating fits of hope and despair, not on Felix's account, but on her own; and by rapid transitions from bliss to dejection. When Endymion was with her (which he frequently was), her troubles were forgotten: he loved her, and he was a rock of strength. To a dispassionate observer his strength might seem to lie partly in his magnificent physique, and partly in his optimistic pronouncements, but Charis was not a dispassionate observer. When Endymion said that she was not to get into the hips, because everything would be all right and tight; or nobly, if rather vaguely, that she must leave it all to him, she was comforted, never doubting the wisdom or the resolution of so God-like a creature. Doubt assailed her when he was not present, not of his perfection, but of the possibility that they would succeed in their aim. Alverstoke assumed the proportions of a malignant magician, who could cause Endymion to be carried out of reach by the waving of a wand; and Frederica was transformed from her beloved sister into her implacable enemy. Fortunately, perhaps, Frederica's absence, coupled with his own light duties, made it possible for Endymion to visit her often enough to save her senses from becoming wholly disordered. When he presented himself in Upper Wimpole Street it was on the pretext of visiting Harry, or as escort to Chloë, and however suspicious Buddle might be he could scarcely refuse to admit him. Harry, having decided that he was a right one, connived at these manoeuvres, but behaved with what he considered to be the greatest propriety, never absenting himself from the drawing-room for more than half-an-hour when Endymion was in the house. As for Chloë, deeply sympathetic, and attached almost as fondly to Charis as to her brother, she was ready at all times to provide Endymion with an excuse for presenting himself in Upper Wimpole Street. In this, providence came to her aid, in the guise of influenza. Mrs Dauntry, laid low by this malady, suffered an attack compared with which all other persons' attacks were as nothing. Assured of the attendance of her maid and of her devoted cousin, she excluded her daughters from her bedchamber, consigning

them to the care of Miss Plumley and of Diana's governess. But as Chloë had emerged from the schoolroom,
and Miss Plumley was fully occupied in the sickroom,
neither of these ladies placed any bar in the way of her
friendship with Charis, or her expeditions under her
brother's aegis.

It was otherwise with Miss Winsham, who, learning
from Mrs Harley how often Endymion was to be found
in Upper Wimpole Street, instantly took Charis to task,
scolding her so severely that Charis burst into tears, and
completing the work of disintegration by warning her
that she would be wise to put Endymion out of her
head, since Frederica would never consent to such a
marriage.

The news, brought by Harry, that Frederica was bent
on removing her family from London, struck dismay
into both the star-crossed lovers' hearts. Endymion, the
first to recover, said stoutly that he could very well
contrive to post down to Ramsgate, or any such seaside resort, to steal (little though he liked such shuffling
behaviour) clandestine meetings with Charis; but
Charis was filled with tragic forebodings.

It was at this stage that Alverstoke returned to London. Calling in Upper Wimpole Street upon the following day, he was ushered into the drawing-room, to find
it occupied only by Charis and Endymion.

The discomfiture of the young couple was patent, and
in no way lessened by the raising of his lordship's
quizzing-glass. Endymion, red to the roots of his hair,
stammered: "I ca-came to enquire after—after Felix,
sir! And to have a word with Harry!"

"Only Harry has just stepped out," said Charis,
courageously supporting him. "But only for a moment,
so I begged C-cousin Endymion to wait for his return!"

His lordship, suppressing a desire to laugh, responded
with an amiability the stricken pair thought sinister in
the extreme: "How fortunate, then, that I should have
arrived in time to relieve you of suspense, Endymion! I
am glad to be able to tell you that Felix is on the mend,
and will, I trust, shortly be well enough to return to
London. So now you need not wait any longer! If your
errand to Harry is important, may I suggest that you

charge Buddle with a message for him? No doubt he
will be happy to call at your lodging!"

In the face of this annihilating speech, there was
nothing else for Endymion to do than to retire, in the
best order possible. A wild idea of disclosing the truth
to Alverstoke entered his mind only to be dismissed.
For one thing, the message conveyed to him by Charis's
eyes was unmistakeable; for another, he had been taken
at a disadvantage, and had had no time in which to prepare his announcement, or to assemble the arguments
in favour of a marriage which he knew, on his mother's
authority, would be unacceptable to the Marquis.

When the door shut behind him, the Marquis let his
eye-glass fall, and advanced into the room, saying: "In
the absence of both your sister and your aunt, Charis, it
behoves me to tell you that it is not at all the thing for
you to be entertaining young men without even the
chaperonage of your brother. In fact, it is quite improper!"

She blushed, trembled, and could only master her
voice sufficiently to stammer: "A cousin! Surely—when
he is Harry's friend—and wanted only to know how Felix goes on—!"

"You are a mighty poor liar, my child," he commented. "That may stand to your credit, but you must
learn to be more skilful before you play off your tricks
on such an old hand as I am! Oh, no, pray don't dissolve
into tears! I have the greatest dislike of weeping females. I'll give you a piece of good advice: never treat
your flirtations *au sérieux,* and always conduct them
with discretion!"

She tried to smile, but it was a wan effort. The familiar and paralysing sense of boredom began to creep
over him; he repressed it, and said with a faint smile:
"Blue-devilled? I have every sympathy with you, and
will present you with another leaf from my book: these
little affairs can be delightful, or they can be painful,
but they don't last, believe me! You won't, of course,
but you should: I speak from a vast experience. Yes,
isn't it shocking? Don't tell your aunt!"

She gave a hysterical laugh, but said: "It isn't like
that!"

"Of course not: it never is!" he replied.

"You don't understand!" she exclaimed bitterly.

"That," said his lordship, with a touch of acidity, "is a foolish accusation which lacks even the saving grace of originality! Every generation, my child, has said, or thought, that the preceding one was devoid of understanding or experience. Let us turn to another subject! When I left Hertfordshire Felix was sitting out of bed for the first time, playing cards with Jessamy. As he was also expressing a strong desire for a mutton-chop I fancy that it won't be many days before he is restored to you."

She attempted another smile, but it conveyed little gladness; and it was almost listlessly that she murmured: "Oh! Dear Felix! Such a relief!"

Alverstoke found her so exasperating that he was obliged to bite back a caustic rejoinder. It would certainly make her start to cry again, and lachrymose females ranked high on the list of his pet abominations. He thought it prudent to take his leave without disclosing the Alver-scheme to her. It was obvious that the silly girl had fallen violently in love with his equally silly cousin, and would probably revolt him with an attack of the vapours if she learned that she was shortly to be removed from Endymion's ambit.

He was inclined to think that no very serious thought of matrimony had entered Endymion's head, for as he had no idea that he was supposed to wish his heir to make an advantageous marriage he could not imagine why (if Endymion did want to marry Charis) the silly cawker had not applied to him for support. Endymion invariably laid all his problems before him, and he must know that his cousin's influence would be of paramount importance. Probably he was passing through one of his fits of gallantry, and would soon recover from it. However, since Charis seemed to be developing a lasting passion, and was just the sort of girl to go into a decline if her hopes were blighted, the sooner the affair was nipped in the bud the better it would be: he would drop a word of warning in Endymion's ear.

Since he had never done such a thing before this deviation from the normal operated powerfully on Endymion, but scarcely in accordance with his lordship's intention. Endymion carried the news of the intervention to Charis, who turned as white as her shift, and exclaimed: "I knew it! He means to separate us! Oh, what are we to do?"

"Well, what if he does?" said Harry, on whom the lovers' troubles and indecisions were beginning to pall. "You're not dependent on him, are you, Endymion?"

"No—that is, he makes me a devilish handsome allowance, y'know. I've about £2000 a year of my own—and the expectancy, of course, but to tell you the truth I never set much store by that. Well, what I mean is, who's to say he won't get buckled himself?"

"Oh, I shouldn't think he would! Not at his age!" said Harry. "And if he doesn't he can't disinherit you, can he? Any more than he can have you sent off in a crack to foreign parts! I'm dashed if I can see why you should be in such a quake!"

"It ain't that," growled Endymion. "I mean, I'm not afraid of Cousin Vernon! It's—it's his sisters, and my mother, and Frederica! I daresay you don't know."

This inarticulate appeal for understanding touched a chord of sympathy. Harry had had no personal experience of the trials which Endymion so obviously feared, but he had the instinctive male dread of feminine storms. He said, in an awed voice: "Jupiter! I hadn't thought of that! Lord, what a dust they would kick up!"

Endymion cast him a look of gratitude. "Ay, that's it. Not my mother," he added scrupulously. "Never kicks up a dust, precisely."

"Well, if *that's* so—"

"Takes to her bed," said Endymion simply. "Spasms! Got a weak heart. If I was to tell her I was going to marry Charis, she'd go into strong convulsions: always does when any of us puts her in a stew! Then Cousin Harriet would send for that devilish doctor of hers, Halford, and I should have the pair of them ringing a peal over me as if I was a dashed murderer! Devilish unpleasant, y'know! Mustn't drive one's mother to pop off the hooks: shocking thing to do! Besides, I don't want to: fond of her!"

"Oh, no, no!" Charis said quickly. "I wouldn't have you do so for the world! Poor Mrs Dauntry, how can she help but feel as she does? Oh, how sorry I am for her!"

Deeply moved, Endymion seized her hand, and kissed it fervently, informing her that she was an angel. Her brother, less enthusiastic, recommended her not to be mawkish; and told Endymion, bristling in defence of his adored, that he would sing a different tune when she began to be sorry for him too. "Which is what she will do, you mark my words!" he said. "*You* may call it angelic to be for ever trying to please everyone, and being sorry for those she *can't* please, but I don't! Addle-brained is what *I* call it!"

"Oh, no!" uttered Charis imploringly.

"Oh, yes!" he retorted. "Told you so before! If you don't take care, Charis, you'll end by being sorry for yourself! All for the want of a little resolution! What if Mrs Dauntry and Frederica don't like it? They'll come round! And you needn't look at me as ugly as bull-beef, Endymion, because I'll say what I choose to my own sister!"

At this point, a diversion was created by Charis, who took the strongest exception to his unflattering description of her beloved Endymion's noble demeanour, and rose to his defence with unaccustomed vigour. During the interchange which followed, Endymion, conceding to Harry his brotherly rights, became plunged in profound thought, from which he emerged presently, to startle the combatants by saying: "Ay, so they would!" Perceiving that the two Merrivilles were staring at him with a sad want of comprehension, he added: "What you said, Harry! My mother, and Frederica! Come round! What's more, if we could do the thing—get the knot tied!—without either of 'em knowing it, we should have it blocked at both ends! Well, what I mean is—no sense in kicking up a dust! no sense in having spasms! Come to think of it, no sense in getting me transferred, or sent on a curst mission, or some such devilish thing! Stands to reason!"

Charis's soft eyes glowed with admiration of this powerful ratiocination, but Harry was unimpressed.

"No, and there's no sense in airmongering either! How the deuce could you get the knot tied without everyone's knowing all about it? If you've got a notion of eloping with Charis, I'll tell you to your head it won't fadge! And if you think I'll help my sister to sink herself below reproach, a mighty pretty notion you must have of me!"

"Never, never would I do such a thing!" declared Charis.

"No!" said Endymion, flushing darkly. "And a mighty pretty notion *you* must have of *me*, Harry, if you think I would either! Talk of loose screws—! I wonder at it that you should allow Charis even to exchange the time of day with me!"

"Oh, take a damper!" said Harry. "Of course I don't think it! But if you haven't got elopement in mind, what *have* you got? I'm dashed if I can see any other way of doing the thing secretly!"

"No," agreed Endymion gloomily.

"Well, for God's sake—!"

"Haven't got anything in mind," explained Endymion. "Just thinking it would be a devilish good thing if it *could* be done."

Luckily, since Harry, striving to recover his breath, showed alarming signs of allowing his feelings to overcome him, the symposium was brought to an end by the clock on the mantel-shelf, which, inexorably striking the hour, recalled Endymion to the realization of his military duties. Taking hurried leave, he fled.

"If ever I met such a knock-in-the-cradle!" exploded Harry. " 'Just thinking it would be a devilish good thing if it *could* be done—!' Yes, and another devilish good thing would be if either of you had as much rumgumption as a couple of sparrows! Only you haven't, and it's my belief you never will have!"

Charis burst into tears.

XXVI

Except that Harry, repenting of his harsh words, became reconciled with his sister, matters were in the same unsatisfactory state when the Hertfordshire party returned to London three days later.

Before her feet had touched the flagway, Frederica saw that Charis was looking pale and fagged; but in the bustle of arrival there was no opportunity for any private talk. Not until the baggage had been carried in, the servants greeted, Felix's medicine unpacked, and Felix himself persuaded, not without difficulty, to retire to bed, to recover from the journey, was Frederica able to turn her attention to her sister. She then invited her to come to her own bedchamber, to help her to unpack her portmanteau, saying: "It seems as if I hadn't seen you for months! I hope to heaven we never have to live through another such period!"

"Oh, no!" said Charis, shuddering. "It must have been so dreadful for you!"

"Well, it was," admitted Frederica. "Indeed, if it hadn't been for Alverstoke I don't know how I should have managed. I can never be sufficiently grateful to him. So firm and patient with Felix! Such an unfailing support to me, particularly during those two days when I feared—But don't let us talk of it! My dear, have you been ill? You are looking positively whey-faced!"

"Oh, no! I am perfectly well! It's the hot weather."

"Very likely. I have been feeling it very much myself, even in the country: horridly languid, and a sort of lowness and oppression. It must have been far worse here. Indeed, when we got between the houses Jessamy said it was like driving into an oven. Never mind! I hope we shall be many miles from London within a few days. Did Alverstoke tell you of the delightful scheme he has made for us?"

"No," Charis answered, staring at her apprehensively.

"We are to go down to Alver, and to stay there for as long as we choose!" said Frederica, beginning to unpack her portmanteau. "I daresay I ought to have declined the offer, but it was too tempting! so exactly what the boys will like! It is in Somerset, you know, and quite near Bath, which is an advantage. —Oh, dear, just look at this muslin! I shall coax you to do my packing when we set out for Alver!" Receiving no reply, she looked round, to find that Charis had sunk into a chair, and had buried her face in her hands. "Charis! Dearest, what's the matter?"

"I am so very unhappy!"

"Good God, why?"

"I don't want to go to Alver!"

Curbing her exasperation, Frederica said calmly: "Do you mean that you had liefer go to the seaside?"

"Oh, no! I don't wish to go anywhere!"

"Charis, I don't think you perfectly understand the case," said Frederica. "It is necessary for Felix's health to take him out of London. And if this is what London is like during the summer months, so intolerably stuffy and dusty, I am very sure it is necessary for all our healths! Are you thinking that it will be dull? Perhaps you may find it so, after our rakings, but you were not used to think the country dull. I believe Alver is a most beautiful place, too: do you remember what the guide-book said about its park, and its pleasure gardens, and its lake, with all the rare shrubs planted round it? We shall never be tired of sketching there! Alverstoke says that the boys may fish the trout-stream, too —I wish you might have seen Jessamy, when he learned of the scheme! You wouldn't want to deny him such a treat! After all, love, neither he nor Felix grudged us ours, did they?"

"Oh, no, no! I didn't mean—Of course they must go! If only I might remain here! I thought perhaps I could stay in Harley Street. If Aunt Seraphina goes with you, poor Aunt Amelia will be glad to have me, I daresay."

"Aunt Seraphina will not go with us, for I don't mean to ask her. I see no need for any chaperon, and if I did

I shouldn't call upon her services, for I'm quite out of charity with her! As for leaving you with Aunt Amelia, you may put that notion out of your head!"

"Oh, Frederica—!"

"If you don't want to drive me into a pelter, stop *moaning!*" snapped Frederica. "You may stop shamming it, too! Upon my word, Charis, I wonder at you! What you wish to do is to remain in London, making a cake of yourself over Endymion Dauntry, and well I know it! I should suppose that that is what you have been doing while I was away! I wish you may not have set people in a bustle!"

"I *love* Endymion!" declared Charis, rearing up her head. "And he loves me!"

"Then I see no occasion for all these die-away airs," responded Frederica prosaically.

Charis started up, eagerness in her face. "Do you mean—can you mean that you consent to our marriage?"

"There's no saying what I might do, if your attachment proved to be more lasting than any of your previous ones," replied Frederica lightly.

"You don't mean to let me marry him—ever!" said Charis, in throbbing accents. "You mean to separate us!"

"What, by spending a few months at Alver? If your mutual passion won't survive—"

"Always! Always!" Charis interrupted. "You will contrive to keep us apart, hoping that I shall forget him! But I shan't, Frederica, I shan't!"

"Well, don't fall into a lethargy! Remember that in two years you will be able (if I haven't relented) to do precisely what you choose!"

"Oh, you don't know what it is to be in love!" Charis said passionately.

"No, and I must own that I'm thankful I don't—if it means fretting, and fuming, and falling into this sort of extravagant folly! You may be thankful too, let me tell you! Excessively uncomfortable you would have found it! Do, pray, draw bridle, my dear! This isn't the moment to be making such a piece of work about nothing. You shall see how you feel when you have had time to reflect. There, don't let us rub against one another! I don't mean to be unkind, but I've suffered too much anxiety to be able to enter into what seems to me to be such a very—"

She stopped, but Charis finished the sentence for her. "Unimportant matter!" she flashed, and ran out of the room.

Frederica made no attempt to follow her. She had managed to keep her temper, but she had never been nearer to losing it with her sister. It seemed to her monstrous that, after all she had undergone, she should have been greeted on her homecoming by such a scene, and when she herself was suffering from lowness of spirits. Perhaps Charis did not realize that when one had passed through a time of terrible anxiety relief did not immediately restore the tone of one's mind. To be sure, she herself had not expected that after the first raptures she would find herself subject to fits of dejection, and much inclined to be crotchety; but still Charis should have known better than to have enacted a tragical scene within an hour of her arrival.

The truth was, she told herself, that she was still very worndown, and perhaps allowed herself to be too easily provoked. The last week at Monk's Farm had tired her, when Alverstoke was no longer there to arrange everything for her. She had grown so much accustomed to turning to him for help or advice that naturally she had felt quite lost without him. She had missed his companionship, too; and rather thought that if he had remained at Monk's Farm she would not have fallen into such low spirits. That also was quite natural: however much one loved one's young brothers one couldn't talk to them as one could to Alverstoke—or, of course, to any other adult person.

This reflection led her into reverie; and while she hung her dresses in the wardrobe, and transferred her chemises and her petticoats from the portmaneau to the chest of drawers, she recalled the drives and the walks she had enjoyed in Alverstoke's company, pondering some of the things he had said to her, smiling reminiscently at others.

These pleasurable, if nostalgic, thoughts were interrupted by a perfunctory knock on the door, followed immediately by the entrance of Harry, who demanded impetuously: "What is this I hear, Freddy? Charis says you mean to spend the summer at Alverstoke's place in Somerset! Upon my word, I wonder that you should wish to be so much beholden to him, and I'll tell you to your head that I do *not!* I am very well able to take care of my family myself, and so you may tell him! What's more, I should like to know what sort of a rig he's running! *You* may not know what his reputation is, but I do, and—and *damme,* I won't have it!"

"Won't you, Harry?" said Frederica, in a voice of dangerous quiet. "Then *start* to take care of your family! You haven't yet made the least push to do so! You wouldn't even find me a lodging, when I asked you! You have permitted—oh, no! you have *encouraged* Endymion Dauntry to sit in Charis's pocket, without caring a straw for the consequences! You have never made the smallest attempt to—to accept your responsibilities! You have been content to leave everything to me! And now—*now,* when I am almost at my wits' end, and my cousin—not my brother!—comes to my aid, you have the effrontery to say that you *won't have it,* and that you don't choose to be beholden to him! You wonder that I should wish to be! Well, I don't wish it, but I shall be, because there is no one else on whom I can depend! You wonder at me! Not as much as I wonder at you, believe me!"

Her voice broke; she turned away, as aghast as Harry. She had kept her temper with Charis; she had not dreamt that she would lose it with Harry; she had not meant to utter such reproaches to him; and was now horrified that she had done so. What had come over her she could not imagine; but suddenly she had found herself trembling, and with such rage possessing her as she had never before experienced. It left her weak, bewildered, and struggling to hold back a rush of tears. She said, in a stifled voice: "I'm sorry! I didn't mean it —I'm out of frame—tired! Forget it—pray! And go away, if you please!"

"Oh, certainly!" replied Harry. "I am very willing to do so!"

With that, he stalked out of the room, seething with mortification, and a burning sense of injustice. There was just enough truth in Frederica's intemperate accusations to touch his conscience, and this made him much angrier than if there had been none. Whose fault was it that he hadn't accepted his responsibilities? Frederica's, of course! a rare dust there would have been, if he had tried to interfere in her management of the family! When had she asked him for aid? Never! At all events, never until she had begged him to devote himself to Charis during her own absence from London. Had he done it? Yes, he had, and without a word of complaint, although he had been obliged to forgo all the entertainments to which he had been looking forward! Was it to please himself that he had remained in London during the past few weeks? No, by God it was not! He had done so at her request. Left to himself, he would have posted down to Monk's Farm immediately.

He continued in this way for some time, posing questions to himself, and finding answers to them which were irrefutable, and yet afforded him little satisfaction. His sense of ill-usage increased; and when Charis sought him out presently to implore him to help her he was in exactly the right mood to lend himself to any enterprise likely to vex Frederica.

In view of her enforced, and possibly imminent, incarceration at Alver, Charis considered it to be of vital importance to consult Endymion: would her dearest Harry convey a message to him? and could he think of any *respectable* rendezvous?

Certainly he could! He would visit Endymion that very evening; as for a respectable rendezvous, nothing could be easier! They would meet in Kensington Gardens, and he himself would escort Charis there.

"Oh, Harry, I knew I might depend on you!" breathed Charis.

This was balm to his injured feelings. At least *one* of his sisters appreciated him! It was a pity, in a way (but not in other ways), that Frederica wasn't present to hear this declaration of faith; but at all events she would very soon be made to realize that he was not the contemptible fribble she seemed to think him, but a force to be reckoned with.

But when she came into the drawing-room, just before dinner, much of his rancour faded. He was alone, and she went straight up to him, and put her arms round his neck, kissing his cheek, and saying: "Oh, Harry! Such an archwife as you have for a sister! Forgive me!"

The sense of injury was still strong in him. It was melting fast, but it prompted him to say: "Well, I must own, Freddy, I think it was pretty unjust of you!"

He was prepared to prove to her, point by point, just as he had proved it to himself, that she had grossly misjudged him; and had she allowed him to do it he would very soon have talked himself into goodhumour. But she did not. She had already endured two agitating scenes; she was tired; her head ached; she wanted, more than anything, to go to bed; and less than anything to become engaged in any further argument. So she said: "Yes, dear, I know it was. Let us talk of something else!"

"That's all very well, but it was you who brought up the subject of Endymion and Charis, and—"

"For heaven's sake, Harry, no!" she exclaimed. "I can't and I won't enter into argument with you!"

He read into this an elder sister's contempt for his opinion, and instantly stiffened, saying with freezing civility: "As you wish!" She knew that she had wounded his sensibilities, and that she ought to reassure him, but she also knew that it would require tact and patience, both of which virtues had deserted her; so she merely smiled wearily at him, excusing herself with the reflection that Harry's miffs never lasted for long.

Charis came down to dinner, rather red-eyed, but quite composed; and when she and Frederica retired to the drawing-room, she took up her stitchery, responding to Frederica's attempt at conversation, but inaugurating none herself.

They went early to bed; and Frederica's heart was lightened by the clinging embrace she received, in answer to her good-night kiss.

She fell asleep almost at once, but Charis lay awake,

listening for Harry's step on the stairs. When it came, she sat up expectantly, for he had promised to let her know the result of his mission. She called "Come in!" in a hushed voice, when he tapped softly on her door, and scarcely waited for him to shut it before demanding: "Oh, Harry, did you see him?"

"Yes, of course I did. Don't speak so loud!" he replied, with a significant glance at the wall which separated her room from Frederica's.

"What did he say?" she asked, obediently lowering her voice. "What does he think we should do?"

"He said he must have time to consider the matter," he answered, unable to repress a grin.

"It naturally came as a great shock to him," said Charis, with dignity.

"Lord, yes! Knocked him bandy! Didn't seem able to say anything at first but 'What a devilish thing!' However, we're to meet him tomorrow, so you may be easy! By-the-by, we had better decide on some errand, in case Frederica wants to know where we are off to—which you may lay your life she will!"

"Oh, no, Harry, must we? I can't bear to deceive her!" Charis said wretchedly.

"Well, if that's the case you had better not meet Endymion!"

"But I *must!*"

"Then stop being a goose! Isn't there anything you wish to purchase?"

After prolonged thought, Charis said that if she were forced to go to Alver she would need some drawing-paper—not that she would have the heart to use it; so this subterfuge was agreed upon, and Harry went off to bed, recommending her not to get into one of her worries.

She was terribly nervous next day, but fortune favoured her. When it was time to set out for Kensington Gardens, and she went to take leave of Frederica, she found that she was entertaining a morning visitor, in the person of Lord Buxted.

Her entrance created a welcome interruption. His evil genius had prompted his lordship, as soon as he had shaken hands with Felix, who was lying on the sofa,

to express the hope that he would never again
cause his sister to suffer so much anxiety. Frederica intervened, but to no avail. Lord Buxted had decided
long since that she was by far too indulgent, and he said,
with a smile which instantly set up the hackles of all
three Merrivilles: "You have a very forgiving sister, Felix! I am afraid I think you deserved all that happened
to you! I'll say no more, but—"

"I wouldn't listen to you, whatever you said!" Felix
burst out, his cheeks scarlet, and his blue eyes flaming.
"You've no right! *You* aren't my guardian!"

"Felix, hold your tongue!" Jessamy said sharply,
pressing him back against the cushions. He glanced at
Buxted, and said, carefully choosing his words: "It is
quite unnecessary to scold my brother, sir, I assure
you."

"It isn't his *business* to scold me!" declared Felix
furiously. "It's Cousin Alverstoke's business, and he
did! And it wasn't a—bear-garden jaw, because he's a
right one, and he knew I was as sorry as I could be,
and if he chooses to make me regret I was ever born if
I do it again he *may!*"

Since it was obvious that Felix was fast working himself into a state of undesirable excitement, and even
more obvious that an attempt to wring an apology from
him would be violently rebuffed, Frederica greeted her
sister's entrance with heartfelt relief.

She did not for a moment believe that Harry was
going to escort Charis on a shopping expedition, but she
accepted the story, merely saying: "Are you taking
Lufra? I shouldn't, if I were you!"

"Oh, no!" Charis said, releasing her hold on Lufra's
collar. "Only he knows we are going out, and he's
bound to try to get out the instant the door is opened,
so I brought him to you, Jessamy."

He nodded, and snapped his fingers at Lufra, who
was sniffing at Buxted's well-polished boots; and Charis
went away, thankful to have escaped questioning.

Buxted's presence must have precluded suspicious
enquiries, but Frederica would not, in any event, have
made any. She was not a gaoler, nor did she wish Charis
to feel that she was being kept under surveillance. There

was little doubt that she had an assignation with Endymion, and deplorable though this was it would be needlessly unkind to prevent what would probably be their last meeting for some months. And at least she was taking Harry with her.

She dismissed the matter from her thoughts, and set herself to divert Lord Buxted, who was annoying Jessamy by commenting humorously on the astonishment visitors must feel to find such a monster as Lufra in Frederica's drawing-room.

But none of the three visitors who were presently ushered into the room evinced any astonishment. The first was Darcy Moreton, whom Buxted eyed with hostility; and within a few minutes Lady Elizabeth Kentmere and Lord Alverstoke were announced.

The effect of this was electric, and was observed by Mr Moreton rather ruefully. There was no misreading the smile in Frederica's eyes, and no doubt whatsoever that Alverstoke was on the best of terms with his wards. Felix shouted joyfully: "Cousin Alverstoke!" and struggled to his feet; and Jessamy, pausing only to bow to Lady Elizabeth, began instantly to tell him of something that had happened at Monk's Farm after his departure. As Felix also had something to tell him, and Lufra, catching the spirit of these demonstrations, uttered some yelping barks, pandemonium reigned for several minutes. Lady Elizabeth was laughing, and said, as she shook hands with Frederica: "I knew that they liked him, but not that his arrival would cause a riot!"

"No, and I apologize for them!" said Frederica, smiling. "You would suppose them to have been reared in a back-slum!"

"Hardly that!" said Buxted. "But surely it cannot be good for Felix to be so much excited? Would it not be as well if Jessamy took him into another room?"

"Oh, no!" replied Frederica. "Alverstoke knows exactly how to handle him."

This was soon seen to be true. His lordship quelled the riot without the smallest difficulty, ordering Felix back to the sofa, requesting Jessamy to call off the Baluchistan hound, and adding that when he felt a desire to be deafened by a couple of gabblemongers he would inform them of it. These trenchant words were received with the utmost good-humour: a circumstance which Buxted observed with some surprise, and considerable disfavour. Nor was he better pleased when Alverstoke went over to sit beside Frederica, and engaged her in what appeared to be an intimate discussion. Since Eliza, who was talking to Mr Moreton, good-naturedly drew her nephew into the conversation, he was obliged to give his attention to her, instead of trying jealously to hear what Alverstoke was saying, in a lowered voice, to Frederica.

It could scarcely have been more innocuous. "A marked improvement!" Alverstoke said.

"I think so. He was a little tired after the journey, and this hot weather seems to bring back some aches and pains."

"The sooner you can get him to Alver the better. Have you written to Knighton?"

"This morning. I mentioned your name, as you bade me, and enclosed the letter Dr Elcot gave me for him."

He nodded. "I shall hope to see you off before the end of the week. By-the-by, in the matter of a tutor I fear I have exceeded your instructions."

"You don't mean to tell me you've discovered one?" she exclaimed.

"No, Charles did. He offered me his brother, Septimus, and I engaged him. He is staying in Berkeley Square now: a pleasing young man, and one whom the boys will like. I only trust you may!"

"Oh, there can be no doubt! A brother of Mr Trevor's must be acceptable to me! Pray tell Mr Trevor how grateful I am!"

"Certainly, but the arrangement will be as much to Septimus's advantage as yours. He was already seeking a post as coach during the Long Vacation, and this one —if you will be content to remain at Alver for the summer—will enable him to continue living at home. The Rectory is only a few miles from Alver. Tell me when it will be convenient for him to call to see you, and I'll send him round!"

"At any time: I don't go out at present, or only for a few minutes." She paused, as a thought occurred to her.

"I wonder if I should ask Harry to conduct the interview? I think he might wish to do so."

"Are you? I am tolerably certain that he wouldn't! He would be extremely embarrassed—if he could be persuaded to undertake the task of enquiring into Septimus's scholarship, which I strongly doubt! Septimus is a Fourth Year man, my dear, at present working for a Fellowship. I don't see Harry, by the way, or Charis: is he still virtuously doing his duty by her?"

She smiled, but answered, with a touch of constraint: "Why, yes! I believe he has taken her out to do some shopping."

She did not believe it, nor would she have been surprised to have learnt that Charis was at the moment seated on a bench in a secluded part of Kensington Gardens, between her brother and her lover, agitatedly telling Endymion of her conviction that they were to be for ever parted.

"I wish you will stop talking such flummery!" said Harry. "I've told you a score of times that nobody can part you for ever!"

"Couldn't do it for ever," agreed Endymion.

"Once I am imprisoned at Alver—"

"Ay, that's the worst of it!" said Endymion, his brow darkening. "Devilish shabby trick, I call it! Shouldn't wonder if it was a plot: devilish clever fellow, Alverstoke, up to all the rigs! Y'know, I haven't been easy in my mind since he told me not to be quite so particular in my attentions. Amiable enough but giving me the office—that's what I thought! I was right, too. Well, what I mean is, might have seen you at Ramsgate, but not at Alver. Everyone knows me down there, and you may lay your life some snitcher would tell Alverstoke, if I was to show my nose within ten miles of the place!"

"And when we leave Alver, you will have been sent on a dreadful mission, and Frederica will drag me back to Graynard!"

"Not if he's been sent off on a mission," interposed her more practical brother. "Now I come to think of it, she couldn't do it in any event: she hired the place to Porth for a twelve-month."

"Harrogate, then—so that Felix may drink the waters!" said Charis bitterly.

"She might do that," Harry admitted.

"I shan't go on a mission," suddenly announced Endymion. "I shall sell out. Nothing my cousin can do to stop me. What's more, once I've done it, there's nothing *anyone* can do to stop me marrying Charis!"

"But I am under age," said Charis sadly.

"Ay, that's the devil of it! And when I think of having to wait for two whole years, and very likely not being given the chance even to *see* you—well, it's enough to drive one to the Border! Not that I would!" he added hastily, and with an apprehensive glance at Harry. "Too ramshackle by half!"

"Oh, no! I *couldn't* do such a shocking thing! Perhaps, if Frederica realizes that we are unalterably determined—But she won't give her consent! I know she won't!"

"Just a moment!" interrupted Harry, sitting up with a jerk. "Lord, why didn't I think of that before? By Jupiter, I have it!"

Two anxious faces were turned towards him; Charis said breathlessly: "You have what, dearest?"

"You don't need her consent: nothing to do with her!" Harry said, his eyes sparkling with mischief. *"She's* not your guardian: *I* am!"

XXVII

It was surprising, Frederica thought, how much benefit
was to be derived from two nights of unbroken sleep.
She felt very much better, far less depressed and irri-
table. Her affairs having been taken back into the Marquis's capable hands, she had very little to worry about:
none of the complicated arrangements attached to the
removal of a family from a house in London to another
a hundred miles distant, and no housekeeping cares to
contend with at the end of the journey. To one who,
from early girlhood, had never had a respite from these,
this was bliss indeed. It ought to have made her happy,
and she was obliged to take herself to task when she
found that she was looking forward to several months
spent in sylvan solitude with a slight sinking of the
heart. Not that it would be really solitude, of course:
there would be Charis, and the boys, and the unknown
Mrs Osmington, the widowed cousin whom Alverstoke
had decided, in his usual highhanded way, to instal at
Alver. There would be Septimus as well, and no doubt
his mama would drive over to visit them. It was bound
to seem a trifle flat at first, and she would certainly miss
her friends in London; but Alverstoke meant to come
down for a few days, which would make an agreeable
break. He had given her a carte blanche to invite any
of her friends she chose to stay with her, begging her to
consider the house her own. She had no intention of taking him at his word, but as she was unable to think of
any friend whom she particularly wanted to invite this
resolve cost her no regret.

Alverstoke was going to escort them to Alver, too:
that was another of his sudden and highhanded de-
cisions! She had protested, as in honour bound, but he
had merely said that he had business there, so she had
said no more, though she guessed that his business was

to introduce her to his cousin, and to make sure that his servants had provided every comfort for the party. How anyone could say that he was selfish and heartless was beyond comprehension! No one was ever less so; it made one quite hot with anger that people should dare to misjudge him so wickedly.

For the rest, everything was going on fairly well. Mr Peplow had invited Harry to accompany him on a visit to Brighton; Buddle and Mrs Hurley were thankful to be granted a long holiday after the exigencies of a London house; and Charis, though in unequal spirits, seemed to be growing more resigned to her fate. To be sure, she was subject to sudden attacks of woe, which made her run out of the room with her handkerchief pressed to her eyes, but Frederica, recalling the agonies attending the dismissal of her first very undesirable suitor, hoped that the present agonies would be of similarly short duration.

Septimus Trevor, a well-set-up young man, with easy manners, and a general air of cheerful competence, she liked on sight. So, which was more important, did her brothers. She made an excuse to leave him alone with them, to become acquainted. She felt a little doubtful about Felix, who, unlike Jessamy, was not at all eager to resume his studies; but when she came back into the room he greeted her with the information that *this* Mr Trevor knew much more than the *other* Mr Trevor: they had been talking about coal-gas, and the transmission of power by compressed air; so that doubt was laid to rest, leaving her with only one serious anxiety: Felix's health.

This was a very real anxiety, and would not be allayed until Sir William Knighton had seen Felix. He was better, certainly, but far from well yet. He flagged quickly, became too easily excited—even, she suspected, a little feverish—and his normally sunny disposition had given place to irritability, and occasional fretfulness.

"I expect it is just that he doesn't feel in high force yet, and that he will be better in the country, but I can't help feeling anxious," she told Alverstoke.

"No, and you can't think of anything else, can you, Frederica?"

"I suppose I can't," she confessed. "I do *try* to!"

"Do you feel that you may be able to—without trying—if Knighton gives you a comfortable report?" he enquired.

"Oh, what an unspeakable relief that would be! Yes, of course I shall!"

"I'm glad," he said cryptically. "I feel pretty confident that he will, and I trust it won't be long delayed!"

"He is coming to us on Thursday, before noon."

"Good! So, then, am I!" said his lordship. "*After* noon!"

"Of course!" she twinkled. "No need to tell me *that!* I only wish he may not arrive to find Felix at his very worst, but I'm much afraid that he will. Felix is already out of reason cross about it—declares he is in *prime twig,* and won't let any doctor *maul* him!—and he won't at all relish being made to stay in his bed until Sir William has examined him! Oh, well! If he becomes outrageous, I shall ask Harry to try if he can divert him!"

But when, on Thursday morning, Frederica, with a recalcitrant brother on her hands and various household duties left undischarged, desired Buddle to send Harry up to Felix's room, Buddle said that he rather thought Mr Harry must have gone out.

"Oh!" said Frederica, rather blankly. She hesitated, wondering whether to send for Charis. But as Charis had chosen this, out of all other mornings, for a display of affliction, weeping over the tea-cups, and refusing all sustenance at the breakfast table, she decided against it.

"I fancy he must have taken Miss Charis out for an airing, ma'am, for she is not in the drawing-room," volunteered Buddle.

Frederica's brow cleared. She had been nursing some uncharitable thoughts about Harry—so careless as to go off to amuse himself when his little brother was to be examined by one of the first physicians of the day!—but she realized at once that she had been doing him an injustice: he was clearly trying to be helpful, by taking

Charis off her hands! She said: "Ah, very likely! Never mind: I'll go up to Master Jessamy's room."

She found Jessamy immersed in his books, but he agreed at once to try what he could do to entertain Felix; and, when she apologized for disturbing him, said, with one of his darkling looks: "It is time *one* of us did something to help you!" He then stalked out of the room, with Lufra at his heels.

Touched by this outburst, Frederica called after him that it wouldn't be for long, since Sir William might be expected at any minute; and went downstairs, to discuss with her housekeeper the various things that must be done to set the house in order before they left it.

She had not far to go. Mrs Hurley, a stout woman, having toiled upstairs from the basement in search of her, had halted on the first floor, to recover her breath before attempting to mount the next flight.

"Oh, Hurley, you shouldn't have come up all those stairs!" Frederica said. "I was on my way down to you!"

"No, ma'am, I know I shouldn't, not with my palpitations," said Mrs Hurley. "But I thought it my duty to let you know at once!"

This time-worn phrase, which in general heralded the disclosure of a very minor household disaster, did not strike dismay into Frederica's bosom. She said: "Oh, dear! Is something amiss? Come into the drawing-room, and tell me about it!"

"Dear knows, Miss Frederica," said Mrs Hurley, following her into the room, "I wouldn't trouble you with it, with all the trouble you have to worrit you already, if I didn't feel in my bones that you'd wish to be told immediately."

Broken china! thought Frederica.

"But," pursued Mrs Hurley, "the instant Jemima brought it to me, her only being able to read print—and not much of that either—I said to myself: 'Doctor or no doctor, Miss Frederica must see this at once!' Which is what it's my belief you weren't meant to do, ma'am. And nor you would have if I hadn't sent Jemima up to Miss Charis's room to take down the curtains to be washed, for the room was swept and the bed made while Miss Charis was at her breakfast, so that there was no reason for her to think anyone would go into it again this morning."

"Miss Charis?" Frederica said sharply.

"Miss Charis," corroborated Mrs Hurley. "There was this, laying on the dressing-table, and Jemima, thinking it was a letter for the post, brought it down to me. It's for you, Miss Frederica."

"For me—!" Frederica almost snatched it out of the housekeeper's hand.

"And Miss Charis's brush and comb aren't on the table, nor the bottle of scent you gave her, ma'am, nor anything that *should* be on it," pronounced the voice of doom inexorably.

Frederica paid no heed, for the information was unnecessary. The letter in her hand had evidently been written under the stress of strong emotion. It was freely blotched with tears, and largely illegible, but its opening sentence stood out boldly.

Dearest, ever-dearest Frederica, Charis had written, with painstaking care, *By the time you read this I shall be married, and many miles away.*

After that, the writing deteriorated into a wild scrawl, as though Charis, having made this promising beginning, had not known how to continue, and had finally dashed off the rest in a hurry.

But the beginning was all that mattered to Frederica. She stood staring at the words until they danced before her eyes, unable, in the first moments of sickening shock, to believe their incredible message.

Mrs Hurley's hand on her arm recalled her to her senses. "Do you sit down, Miss Frederica, my dear!" Mrs Hurley said. "I'll fetch you up a glass of wine directly: no need to tell Buddle!"

"No, no, I don't want a glass of wine! I must think— I must think!"

She allowed herself to be pushed into a chair, and tried to decipher the rest of the letter. It seemed to consist entirely of pleas for forgiveness, mingled with assurances that only desperation could have driven the writer to take so dreadful a step. At first glance, Charis

appeared to have subscribed herself, *Your wicked
Charis;* but closer scrutiny revealed that the word was
not *wicked*, but *wretched*. Frederica thought bitterly
that *wicked* more exactly described her sister.

She raised her eyes to Mrs Hurley's face. "Hurley—I
don't know what can be done—if anything, but say
nothing of this, I beg of you!"

"Certainly not, ma'am! That you may depend on!"

"Thank you. You have guessed, of course."

"Oh, yes, I've guessed, ma'am!" said Mrs Hurley
grimly. "*And* I know whose door to lay it at! If *some*
people, naming no names, had attended to their rightful
duty, instead of picking quarrels, and flouncing out of
the house so highty-tighty, it would never have happened, because that great Jack-of-legs couldn't have
come here, like he used to, in spite of anything I said to
her, which I did, and Buddle too! So now she's eloped!
Oh, dear, dear, however could she do such a
thing? Not but what they say what's bred in the bone
will come out in the flesh, and it's what her poor, dear
mother did, after all!"

"Oh, if I could think what's to be done!" Frederica
said, unheeding. "There must be *something*—though I
feel almost inclined to let matters run their course! To
do such a thing, and at such a time—! No, no, what am
I saying? If I had been kinder, more sympathetic—!"
She started up. "Hurley, I must see Lord Alverstoke! If
anyone can help me, he will! Tell Owen to fetch a hack,
while I run up for my bonnet and gloves: there's no
time to waste in sending for the carriage!" She stopped,
halfway to the door. "No, I can't! I was forgetting. Sir
William Knighton!"

"Just what I was thinking myself, Miss Frederica,"
said Mrs Hurley. "There's a carriage coming up the
street at this very moment, which was what put me in
mind of the gentleman. Now, is it going to pull up at
our door, or—yes, it is!"

Frederica hurried over to her desk, and sat down at
it, dragging a sheet of writing-paper towards her, and
dipping the pen in the ink. "I'll write to him!" she said.
"Wait here, Hurley, and take it down to Owen! Tell him
to carry it to Alverstoke House immediately—in a

hack! It's not yet twelve o'clock: his lordship won't have left the house. Tell Owen it is to be given into his lordship's own hand—not left with the butler, or one of the footmen! *Is* it Sir William?"

"Well, he has a bag in his hand, as you'd expect, ma'am," reported Mrs Hurley, from the window, "but he doesn't *look* like a doctor, dressed as nattily as he is! Ah! Now Buddle has let him in, so it must be him, you having given orders you was not at home to visitors!"

"Oh, heavens, he will be upon me in a trice!" said Frederica distractedly. She signed her name quickly to the very brief note she had written, and had just sealed it with a wafer, set all askew, when Buddle announced Sir William.

She arose, handed the missive to Mrs Hurley, and, summoning to her aid every ounce of her self-command, moved forward to meet Sir William.

If he thought her civility forced, and her answers to his questions disjointed, he must have assumed her to be suffering from shyness, she supposed, or from dread of what his verdict might be, for he did not seem to be at all surprised at being confronted with a lady who said: "Yes—no—I can't remember—let me think!" He was not even impatient; and under his calming influence she very soon regained her composure, thrusting Charis to the back of her mind, concentrating her attention on what was being said to her.

He was quite as successful in his handling of Felix. Encountering a hostile scowl, he said, with his pleasant smile: "How do you do? Yes, I am another bacon-brained doctor—as though you hadn't been plagued enough already!"

The scowl vanished; Felix blushed, and shook hands. "How do you do, sir? But I'm *perfectly* well again, I promise you, and there was no *reason* for my sister to have sent for you!"

"Well, you certainly look to be going on in a capital way," agreed Sir William. "However, since I'm here I may as well take a look at you, don't you think?"

Felix submitted. At the end of the examination, he demanded to be told whether he might get up, to which Sir William replied: "Yes, of course you may.

It would do you a great deal of good to go out into the fresh air, so I suggest that your—brother, is it?—takes you out for a drive round the Park. Abominably stuffy, is it not? But I understand you are going down to Somerset: how much I envy you!"

Frederica, directing an enquiring look at Jessamy, received a nod in answer, and led Sir William back to the drawing-room.

He stayed for some twenty minutes, and relieved her mind of one at least of its cares. The possibility of repercussions could not be disregarded, but he considered it to be remote, provided his instructions were faithfully carried out. He paid a graceful compliment to Dr Elcot, and wrote out a prescription to replace Elcot's medicine, saying that, excellent though that was, he fancied that his own might perhaps be more beneficial now that Felix was convalescent; and went away, recommending her, with his understanding smile, not to fidget herself over the boy. "For that, you know, would fidget him!" he said. "I have written down the name and direction of a Bath practitioner in whom you may repose complete confidence. But I don't anticipate that you will require his services!"

Meanwhile, Owen had given Frederica's letter into the Marquis's hand. He had found him on the point of setting out with his sister for Somerset House, the Lady Elizabeth having recollected that she had not yet visited the Royal Academy Exhibition: a scandalous omission which, as she positively *must* bring her extended visit to an end on the following day, had instantly to be repaired. Having no respect for his lordship's matutinal habits, she swept them aside, telling him that after deserting her for the better part of her stay the least he could do to atone was to escort her to Somerset House.

The Marquis spread open the single sheet, read Frederica's note at a glance, and nodded dismissal to Owen. Lady Elizabeth, her eyes on his face, said: "What is it, Vernon? Not Felix?"

He handed her the note. "I don't know. You will have to excuse me from accompanying you to Somerset House, Eliza: pray accept my apologies!"

"Don't be such a gaby! I am coming with you! Ver-

non, I am dreadfully afraid that some accident must
have befallen one of them! *I beg you will come here
immediately. I have no time to write more, but will
explain when I see you. Pray do not delay!* Poor girl,
she is plainly distracted with worry!"

"Yes. Therefore, let us not delay!" he answered
curtly.

They reached Upper Wimpole Street just as Frederica, having, as one in a dream, seen her brothers set
off for their drive, had mounted the stairs again to the
drawing-room, and was once more trying to decipher
Charis's letter. When Alverstoke entered the room,
which he did unannounced, going up the stairs two at a
time, and leaving his sister to follow him, she looked up
eagerly, and sprang to her feet. "I knew you would
come!" she said thankfully. "I beg your pardon for
sending you such a hurried note—you see, Sir William
was at the door, and I had no time—"

"Never mind that!" he interrupted. "What is it, Frederica? Felix?"

"No, no! he's better—Sir William thinks he will soon
be quite stout again. It is far, far worse—no, not *that*,
but—"

"Gently, my child, gently!" he said, taking her hands,
and holding them in a strong clasp. "If I am to help
you, just tell me what has happened! And without flying
into a grand fuss!"

Lady Elizabeth, arriving on the threshold in time to
hear this blighting command, blinked, but Frederica, re-
gaining control over herself, conjured up the travesty
of a smile, and said: "Thank you! I am behaving very
badly. I don't think even you can do anything. I don't
know why I begged you to come, except that it was the
first thought that came into my head—before I had had
time to consider. . . . But I am afraid it is useless."

"And still I am in the dark," said Alverstoke.

"I'm sorry! I can scarcely bring myself to tell you
—Cousin Eliza! I beg your pardon! I didn't see—"

"That's of no consequence, my dear. I came to help
you, if I could, but I think you would prefer to talk to
Alverstoke alone, and if that is so, I'll go away," Eliza
said.

, "No. You are very kind! I had hoped to have kept it secret, but I see now how impossible that must be." She drew a painful breath. "You see,—Charis has—has eloped with Endymion!"

Eliza gasped; but Alverstoke said, with no perceptible loss of calm: "Have you proof of this? I should not have supposed that Charis would consent to any such exploit; and if Endymion persuaded her into it I can only say that I have been strangely mistaken in my reading of his character. A high stickler, my blockish cousin, Frederica!"

Mutely she held Charis's letter out to him. He took it, and, after one glance at it, groped for his quizzing-glass. Eliza, drawing Frederica to the sofa, said: "My dear, surely you must be mistaken? You can't mean that you believe them to have gone to Gretna Green?"

"I think it must be so," Frederica replied. "Where else could—"

"Then you may stop thinking it!" interposed Alverstoke, looking up from the letter. "Where have your wits gone begging, Frederica? *By the time you read this I shall be married, and many miles away.* My dear girl, even such a henwitted female as Charis could not suppose that she could be transported to the Border within an hour or two! How fortunate that she didn't bedew the start of this hubble-bubble effusion with her tears!"

"Then where *can* they have gone?" demanded Frederica.

"That I haven't yet discovered. I should doubt whether I ever shall, but one never knows: something may yet emerge."

"Nothing but what she might as well have spared herself the trouble of writing," said Frederica, sighing.

He said nothing, continuing to frown over the letter for several minutes, while Eliza, possessing herself of Frederica's hand, sat patting it soothingly. Silence reigned, until the Marquis broke it. "Ah!" he said. "Not *licorice,* but *licence!* The clue to the labyrinth is now in our hands, Frederica! It's a pity the pen spluttered at the preceding word, but no doubt it is *special.* Your sister, my love, has married my blockish cousin by special licence. Whether or not this constitutes an elopement I am not yet in a position to say, but it really doesn't signify. The case is not desperate, nor will it be incumbent upon me to pursue the couple to the Border—a prospect, I must acknowledge, which filled me with repugnance. All we have to do is to throw dust in the eyes of the quizzes and tittle-tattlers. It will afford me great pleasure to do so! I wonder who told Endymion that he could be married by special licence?"

Frederica sat up. "But he couldn't!" she said. "Charis is not of age!"

"Do you mean that you suspect Endymion obtained a licence by telling lies about Charis's age?" demanded Eliza. "I don't believe it! Why, that's a serious offence!"

"No, that is not what I suspect," he responded. "Endymion may be a cloth-head, but he is not a scoundrel, my dear Eliza! He would neither marry Charis by special licence, nor across the anvil, without her guardian's consent."

"Well, if you are not her guardian, who is?"

He did not reply. He was watching Frederica, a look of amusement in his face as he saw her stiffen.

"Harry!" she uttered. *"Harry!"*

"Well?"

She got up quickly, the incredulity in her eyes turning to wrath. "How *could* he? Oh, how *could* he? Helping Charis to a *disastrous* marriage—helping her to deceive me—knowing what my feelings were—! And she! No wonder she sat crying all through breakfast! With this on her conscience!"

"Did she?" said his lordship, interested. "She certainly wept all over this letter. What an inexhaustible flow! Do you suppose she was still weeping when she joined Endymion at the altar?"

"I neither know nor care!" snapped Frederica, who had begun to pace about the room, as though her rage had to find a physical outlet.

"No, nor anyone else!" agreed Eliza. "Really, Vernon, how can you be so flippant? This is not a farce!"

"It bears a strong resemblance to one!" he retorted.

"Would you think so if it concerned one of *your* sisters?" asked Frederica fiercely.

"My dear, I should be sure of it! Louisa, for instance? No, I think I prefer Augusta in the rôle."

She gave a gasp, and choked on an irrepressible gurgle of laughter.

"That's better!" he said encouragingly. "Shall we now consider the matter without quite so much heat?"

She did not answer; but after a moment or two she went back to the sofa, and sat down again. "If what you think is true, there is nothing to be done, is there? If I had had time to have read that letter more closely —to have considered it—I should have known it was useless to suppose that you could prevent a marriage which must already have taken place." She smiled rather wanly. "In fact, I sent for you to no purpose at all! I beg your pardon, cousin!"

"Oh, not to no purpose at all!" he said. "It is certainly quite out of my power to prevent the marriage, but I trust I can prevent *you,* Frederica, from making a mull of it! What we must do, you and I, is to make all tidy. I'm well aware of your sentiments: you wished Charis to contract what the world calls an eligible alliance, and you believed that you could bring this about."

"And why shouldn't she have done so?" intervened Eliza. "Charis is a most beautiful girl, with charming manners, and great sweetness of disposition. If her understanding is not extraordinary, pray, how many gentlemen care for clever women?"

"There was only one reason why she shouldn't have done so," he replied. "She lacked the ambition to contract such an alliance, or even to sport a figure in society." He smiled at Frederica, a little mockingly. "You never would believe that, would you? Yours was the ambition—oh, not for yourself! I don't think you have ever wasted a thought on yourself!—and it was you who delighted in the admiration she won. *She* didn't, you know. She told me once that she preferred the country to London, because in London *people stared so!* She prefers country parties to London ones, because she thinks it more comfortable to dance with her friends than with strangers. This, from a girl who had nearly every prize in the Marriage Mart dangling after her!

I've never concealed from you that I think her a lovely and excessively boring wet-goose, but I'll say this for her: she hasn't an ounce of conceit!"

"I didn't wish her to contract a *brilliant* marriage—only one which—But there's nothing now to be gained by repeating what I've told you before!"

"I haven't forgotten. You wanted her to be *comfortable*. But her notion of comfort isn't yours, Frederica. She's a persuadable girl, and I daresay she might have obliged you by marrying young Navenby, if she had not met and fallen in love with Endymion."

"And she would have been happy!"

"Very likely. Unfortunately, she *had* met Endymion, and it appears that from that moment her mind was made up."

"Fiddle! If you knew how many times she has fallen out of love as quickly as she fell into it—!"

"I'll take your word for it. But I would point out to you, my child, that with I don't know how many sprigs of fashion with far more address than Endymion paying court to her, she did *not* fall out of love with Endymion. So perhaps this marriage won't prove to be as disastrous as you imagine. The manner of it is—to put it mildly!—regrettable, and that is all that now concerns us. It must be wrapped up in clean linen."

"If it can be," said Eliza doubtfully.

"It can't. Only consider the circumstances!" said Frederica. "There has been no advertizement of an engagement; no guests were invited to the wedding; and it has taken place two days before we leave London! How could such a scandal be scotched?"

Alverstoke flicked open his snuff-box, and inhaled a delicate pinch. "Difficult, I admit, but not impossible. I don't immediately perceive how to get over the omission of the engagement-notice—unless we sacrifice Lucretia? What do you say, Eliza? *I* am perfectly willing to do it, if you think it would answer."

Frederica could not help smiling. "You are quite odious," she informed him. "Besides, *how?*"

"Oh, by making *her* the bar to the marriage! She became so alarmingly ill at the very mention of it—she would, too!—that it was thought the effect of seeing the announcement in print might carry her off."

"Whereas the news that Endymion was secretly married would have restored her to health!" said Eliza sarcastically.

"What a good thing it is that you came with me!" remarked his lordship affably. "You have your uses! Try if you can discover why the engagement was kept secret: I can tell you why only the immediate relations were present at the wedding." He flicked a few grains of snuff from his sleeve. "Owing to a bereavement in the bride's family, the ceremony was private. We'll put that in the notice."

Lady Elizabeth said reluctantly: "Yes, that could be done. But why wasn't Lucretia present?"

"She was."

"You will never induce her to say so!"

A derisive smile curled his lips. "Would you care to bet against the chance?"

"No!" said Frederica forcefully. "You mean you would try to—to *bribe* her, and I won't have it! Besides, it wouldn't answer: you know it wouldn't! You must forget I was so stupid as to have applied to you: I can't think what made me do so, for it is no concern of yours, and I had no business to embroil you in it!" She put up her chin. "I must make the best of it myself, for I know it was my fault. If only she doesn't regret it—and people don't—don't refuse to receive her—" She faltered, and stopped, dashing a hand across her eyes.

The door opened. In a voice of deep disapproval, Buddle said: "Mr Trevor, ma'am!"

XXVIII

Frederica said instinctively: "No, no! I'm not receiving visitors!"

But Mr Trevor was already over the threshold. He bowed slightly to Lady Elizabeth, and then, as Buddle withdrew, advanced towards Frederica, saying, with his pleasant smile: "You mustn't blame your butler, ma'am. He told me that you were not at home, but I overbore him."

The Marquis raised his quizzing-glass, the better to survey him. "It seems strangely unlike you, Charles. No doubt you had your reasons."

"Yes, sir, I had," responded Trevor, unabashed. He looked closely at Frederica, as he shook her hand. "I came—in case you should have found that letter, which I think you have—to tell you that you need not regard it: all's well, I promise you!"

She was so much astonished that she could only stare at him. He pressed her hand reassuringly before he released it, repeating: "I promise you!"

She found her voice. "Not married? *Not,* Mr Trevor?"

"No, no! It—er—came to nothing!"

"Oh, thank God!" she cried. "Where is she?"

"She's with Mrs Dauntry at present, but I trust she will be able to return her tomorrow. I thought, since she had a valise, that it would be best for her not to come home tonight. On account of the servants, you know."

"With Mrs Dauntry?" she said, quite bemused. "But how—why—?"

"Charles, how the devil do you come to be mixed up in the affair?" demanded Alverstoke.

"Well, it's rather a long story, sir!"

"Are you going to tell me that you knew of this deplorable scheme?"